I AM NOT BRAD PITT

And Other Stories

Ross Dreiblatt

Stone Tiger Books

First published by Stone Tiger Books in 2021.

Cover and Jacket design by Rob Carter

ISBN: 9781735667683
eISBN: 9781735667690

Stone Tiger Books
225 E. 35th Street, Ground Fl.
New York, NY 10016

For Lenny and Berniece

I AM NOT BRAD PITT
And Other Stories

Ross Dreiblatt

I AM NOT BRAD PITT

"As flies to wanton boys, are we to the gods;
they kill us for their sport."

William Shakespeare

1

Even though I was not actually guilty, I know many of you think that I got what I deserved. You probably think people like me get by on their looks and coast through life without breaking a sweat. Well, in my case, coast through someone else's life. I know for a fact, from the "fan mail" I get here, that there are lots of you out there who think I'm just a crazy man spinning a conspiracy theory. I'm used to that kind of judgment; it doesn't bother me. I don't need to defend myself from that. I will tell you all right now, I am not, nor have I ever been, a religious man, but I will confess my sins today. I am guilty of many, many sins.

But none of those sins is murder. That one belongs to my lookalike buddy, Brad Pitt.

To set the record straight, it took me a while to see my resemblance to Brad. I mean, I never thought I was that good-looking. I was a geeky kid—glasses, acne, bad haircuts, debate club, math nerd. And the fatal blow? I was a big kid. About eighty pounds overweight, just five pounds shy of being officially obese. I was ground zero for awkward. Deathblows for any teenager trying to make friends and learn social skills, so I retreated inward. Friends? I had a few loyal friends who were fellow dorks, but mostly TV and movies were my friends. I was also fascinated by data, by numbers.

I'm not telling you all this to get sympathy. Yes, I was a sad case growing up, but this is who I am. I am not a monster; I evolved into Brad. There was no plastic surgery involved, either. This is all me.

My point being that by the time I had left high school, the mirror had become my enemy. I hated the image I saw, so I avoided looking at one, and in college I even avoided owning one. Looking in the mirror would trigger all of my self-loathing. The longer I looked in a mirror, the uglier and fatter I became.

It wasn't until my last year of college that I put my foot down. I was going to lose weight if it killed me. I would not leave school and go out into the world as that near-obese, self-loathing kid anymore. I dieted, exercised, stopped eating fast foods, soda, desserts. By the time I graduated, the weight had come off. But that wasn't enough to make me Brad Pitt.

My relationship with my reflection began to change, but not entirely. I was no longer a big guy, I could see that. Sometimes. The image I saw in the mirror was still competing with the image that had been burned into my brain all of my life. If I went off my diet for one meal, the old me would show up in the mirror immediately. It was hard to trust what I was seeing.

That's why I didn't see the resemblance to Brad. Back then, it wasn't even a thought that I could look like a movie star; I just wanted to stop being afraid to see myself. In photos from that time you could clearly see I looked exactly like Brad Pitt. In fact, almost a dead ringer. But Brad Pitt wasn't Brad Pitt yet, either.

I was twenty-five years old and still thought of myself as the fat ugly duckling. The mirror had always been my opponent, so I still avoided it. It became instinct to cover up my looks with a hat that would overshadow my face, clothes that would hang loosely instead of formfitting, never looking at anyone eye to eye for too long. This ability, the ability to will myself ugly, would come in use later in life when I needed to "de-Brad."

Memorial Day weekend, 1991. That's the weekend Brad and I were born. Well, that's the weekend we both became Brad Pitt. *Thelma and Louise* came out. Until then, he was just a lucky guy who did okay in the gene pool. And I was a guy who had no idea that I was just as lucky. But that movie changed both our lives.

The fateful moment when Brad's destiny and mine would become entwined forever occurred about a month after the movie opened. I remember it very clearly because I did not want to see it. I was dying to see *Backdraft*. It was the closest thing to an action movie that was playing that weekend and I didn't want to waste my Saturday night at a "chick" movie. My friends outvoted me. I grudgingly went along. I mean, what else was a nerdy, lonely twenty-five-year-old with no self-confidence to do on a Saturday night in Madison, Wisconsin?

I had to admit, the movie was pretty good, but when Brad appeared on screen as the sexy hitchhiker, it didn't register with me. Like everyone else, I was struck by his charisma. I could never have that swagger, that charm! Never even entered my mind that I could be his twin brother.

However, it registered with a couple of the women who were with my friends that night. We went out for beers after the movie and they kept insisting that I looked like him. I thought that they were making fun of me. There was no way I would ever resemble this guy who oozed sex on screen like that. I never oozed anything—well, not anything good. One of the girls took out her brush and tried to give me his hair, but I just swatted her away. I ignored them that night.

But not the next day.

I woke up the next morning with this question creeping through all of my thoughts: What if I do look like him? I mean, what if I was really, actually that good-looking? Wouldn't that be something? But it couldn't be possible. People who looked like that knew they were good-looking. Didn't they?

I wet my brush and styled my hair the way Brad's character did in the movie. I had a cowboy hat in my closet from an old Halloween costume. I put it on and stared at myself. *Maybe*, I thought. *Maybe I might look like him.*

This was where it all began. I let my hair grow out and grew my sideburns a little bit. I went to the mall and bought the clothes that he wore in *Thelma and Louise*. Yes, the exact clothes. Being the nerd I was, I cut out pictures of him from a magazine that had his outfits and took those pictures shopping with me. When I looked in the mirror, the reflection was a very different image than I was used to seeing. But what if it was lying? Could mirrors lie?

I needed someone else to see this.

For Halloween that year, I broke off from my tradition of hiding behind a costume to cover up my perceived flaws.

My friends were floating the idea of the Simpsons or Pee-wee's Playhouse as group costumes. I declined. I had a surprise.

When I showed up to our annual Halloween party as J.D. from *Thelma and Louise*, complete with clothes and hair, there was silence. Long, excruciating silence. I had purposely come late to the party so that I could get everyone's attention. This was difficult enough, as it was not in my DNA to seek attention. Even having my friends take that much notice of me was going to require what little confidence I had. I stood in the doorway as a small group gathered in front of me. I remember two distinct things about that moment: One woman, who was dressed as Lisa Simpson, was staring at my crotch. No one had ever looked at my crotch, and now Lisa Simpson was staring at it. After another few seconds Marge Simpson yelled out, "Smile like him." I knew the "Brad grin" that Marge was looking for. It was in all the photos of him that I used to track down his outfit. It occurred to me that I was focusing on the clothes and not the attitude. I put my hands on my hips, leaned a little sideways and gave them the cocky Brad grin. That's when the screaming and squealing started.

I had a superpower. I *was* Clark Kent. I could run into a phone booth and become Brad Pitt at a moment's notice! This was like going to sleep an orphan and waking up as the secret Getty heir.

So maybe I might have taken Brad out for a test drive a few times. I may have gone to local bars on weekends, by myself, with my *Thelma and Louise* outfit on, and maybe I started to get laid a lot. Okay, no maybes, I did this. So sue me.

My new superpower gave me a little more confidence in life. I walked with a little more swagger, I smiled with a little more intent.

This newfound confidence wormed its way into my personal life. Now that I had gotten somewhat used to having this superpower, I used it at work to get ahead. I'm still at my core a nerd, so I found that by using these looks I did not have to have a dazzling personality to get ahead.

I was a bean counter at a large insurance firm in Madison, a worker bee in an anonymous cube farm. I'm not a charming guy, not particularly gifted with chitchat. I'd just as soon discuss statistics and probability as anything else. The internet was finally invented and this helped me to continue to avoid human contact. At a company Christmas party, one of my coworkers attempted to hit on me. She shocked me, but I was a little drunk, so what the heck! Of course, all I could talk about was Y2K and the impending doom. This was in 1994. She was not impressed.

I began to interact with management a little bit more. I just smiled his smile and brushed back his long hair and people assumed I had the charm that went along with the looks. I got promoted twice.

In 1995, *People* magazine announced that Brad Pitt was the sexiest man alive. *Really?* I thought. I still didn't feel like the sexiest man alive. By this time, I knew that I could look like him, and I had gone through two girlfriends I had picked up in bars because I looked like him, but that was all they cared about. I noticed a pattern with my girlfriends: they always wanted to go out, never wanted to stay in. They wanted to show Brad off. They wanted to be seen with him, get treated better when they were with him. What did we talk about? Parties they could take me to, what I would wear to those parties. I felt like Brad Pitt was a mask I could wear to hide me. Still, I could not stop being him. Being me didn't work as well as being him, so I went ahead and changed my hair to Brad's spiky new do.

I decided that I wanted to swim in a bigger pond, so I moved to Chicago and became a financial analyst for Goldman Sachs. I am convinced that they hired him, not me. The interview was all about using my superpowers. I had a decent enough grasp of finance for the job, but for this type of position, they usually required two degrees from the "right" schools. I remember talking on the phone to their recruiter who was trying to tell me politely that she couldn't even forward my résumé because it lacked the "proper" background. I told her, with complete Brad confidence, "Just get me into an interview. I will get the job." Well, maybe I was not quite as confident as I was cynical. By this time, I knew that looks trump everything. I had five interviews with them and learned how to easily win over the interviewer. Less talk, more smile. Me, my B.A. from U of W, and his looks got me hired.

I moved quickly up the ladder at work because my boss wisely saw that negotiating complex financial deals would be more successful if negotiated by Brad Pitt. I'd sit at the negotiating table and grab their eyes with Brad's smile. Even the men! Actually, especially the men! My upper legs were raw from all the hands placed on them during business meetings.

But then Brad finally challenged me. He threw down the gauntlet. I mean, really asked, "Are you with me? Willing to put your money where your mouth is?" That was the year *Fight Club* came out.

Fight Club is a brilliant film about an alter ego who looks like Brad Pitt. Let's just say this movie resonated with me. Maybe more than I'd like to admit.

Up until then, for me to keep my own Brad alter ego alive, it was just a matter of hair styles, but with *Fight Club* it was the body as well. My body wasn't bad at this point, but it wasn't even close to the shape he was in. Also he buzzed his head. And the facial hair. Goldman Sachs didn't allow facial hair.

I made a plan. I guess this was where the lines started getting crossed. Instead of casually going to my hairdresser and updating my haircut, I plotted to become him. Or more accurately, to remain him. I hired a trainer. Four days a week for three months. Turns out, I'm a little beefier than Brad when I pump iron, so we had to adjust the workout. I hired a dietician so I could get just the right combination of food to produce the sinewy muscle I needed.

I changed my job. This was during the heady days of dot-com madness, and I found a job at a start-up that not only welcomed facial hair but practically demanded it. And of course, I buzzed the hair off. I became not only Brad; I became *Fight Club*.

∞

Life was changing for the both of us. We were both getting older, maybe getting that nesting instinct. Brad got married for the first time. I started to tire of the sex. Well, maybe not the sex per se, but the women. They all became the same to me. They all wanted him, not me. I never had to put much effort into finding women, I just showed up somewhere and they would start talking to me. They really didn't care much what I had to say. They would laugh at my jokes, and I learned from their cues whether I was welcome to take them home.

But actual dating? I was afraid to admit it, but this was a skill I had never acquired. Talking to women about their lives was not necessary for me, since most women came on to me for his looks and cared little about what was underneath. The double-edged sword? I felt like there wasn't that much underneath.

All of that changed one fortunate weekend when I was bored enough to go on a blind date with some friends from work. I still remember that first encounter with Sophie Taylor. She was sitting at a table in the restaurant when I walked in and we were introduced by our mutual friend, who loudly proclaimed, "See! I told you he looks just like Brad Pitt!"

She calmly held out her hand and smiled. "Don't worry, I won't hold that against you."

Bam! She had my attention. She was a little bit older than my usual conquest, much more confident, sophisticated. For the first time since becoming Brad, I was a little bit intimidated by a woman.

"Why do you say that?"

"Well, I'm not going to assume that because you're so pretty you aren't intelligent or just relying on your looks to get by. So I think that's kind of nice of me, don't you?" Her smile spread across her entire face. Sophie was not classically pretty; she was not like my typical Jersey Shore type of woman. She was impressive. Her features were distinct, with big eyes that were always searching, a big nose that curved a little bit to the left.

I smiled back at her. She didn't say this maliciously; she said it with a wink, a dare. I was fascinated by her bravado and now totally intimidated. How could I tell her that she was right? She wanted honesty. Fuck, I'd give her honesty.

"I agree, it's really nice of you, but I'm afraid you're wrong. I'm totally empty inside. Not one original thought in my head. Nada. I was counting on looking like a movie star to win you over. Now I don't know what to do. It's all I got."

She scrutinized me a bit more. Was I pulling her leg? Her smile came back.

"Okay, then let's start with that. Not one original thought in your head, right? Let me hear about some of your unoriginal thoughts."

Sophie wanted to know who I was. She was paying attention. This was new to me. Before I knew it, I started blathering on and on to her about statistics and probability.

"What's the probability of you having a doppelgänger?" She was genuinely curious.

"One in a trillion." I knew this from research. I also appreciated that she asked about my doppelgänger, not me being his doppelgänger.

"You probably have differences in how your features are measured." She was staring at me like a science project. "Even identical twins have some huge differences in facial measurements."

"Measured? What does that mean?"

Sophie plucked an olive out of her martini before explaining. "Sorry, I have a bad habit of focusing on minute facial details. I restore artwork at the museum, and I'm restoring a bunch of eighteenth-century profiles, so the devil is in the details. How far your eyes are from your nose, how close your lips are to your nose. My guess is that there are some big differences there."

This was refreshing, I was talking to a grown-up. Someone who knew details about art and who talked about my face as something other than a ticket to get in a club.

For those few hours I totally forgot who I looked like. I didn't worry about hair, maintaining the movie star smile, or if there was someone hotter in the restaurant. I think she saw me in the same way she saw the paintings that had to be restored. She knew that if she scraped the paint and dirt off the surface a little bit, there was something better underneath, and she could bring out the beauty hiding within.

Since all of my relationships were based on who I looked like, it was a whole new experience to be with someone who wanted me, not him. She challenged me in ways no other woman would ever do. In relationships, I never had to do any heavy lifting. If I didn't like the way a woman spoke to me, I could easily move on to the next one. Sophie unmasked me. She demanded more, demanded I value her as she did me.

I finally had to learn to care about another person, figure out how she would feel about decisions I made, think about what she was feeling.

For a while I almost forgot about him. Almost.

Having Sophie in my life also challenged Brad. Why did I need him anymore? Had he outlived his usefulness? I finally had a normal relationship, it wasn't like I needed his looks to go out and get women anymore.

I definitely didn't need more attention from women. I was locked on to Sophie. We moved in together and I assumed we'd get to marriage sooner or later. So for the most part, I thought my obsession had passed.

Until *Ocean's Eleven* came out. Brad had a whole new look. He was now older, but still Mr. Cool. *I could become that*, I thought. In earlier days I would have run right out to my stylist and had my hair redone. I would have found the clothes he wore. But now, it suddenly felt wrong. After all, my primary use for him was to gain access to women, so it felt like putting on the Brad mask was getting on a runway to cheating.

This was when I began to realize that maybe I was addicted to being him. Once in a while when Sophie and I would go to a concert or a five-star restaurant, he would come out again. I took great pleasure in preparing to become him for a night so we could get to the head of a line or better treatment. It satisfied some need in me I couldn't identify.

That's when I thought it must be about the power, not about the women. Or maybe about the attention. Maybe it was something out of my past, when I was afraid of getting attention, and now the pendulum had swung where I hungered for it.

Do they have an AA for this kind of addiction? Celebrity Anonymous? Being Hooked On Looking Famous Anonymous? I don't think so. I wish they did, because as you will soon see, what happened in Las Vegas did not stay in Las Vegas.

2

My big mistake was being careless. You could call it arrogance, hubris . . . I was just plain sloppy.

I was working for a mid-level financial services firm in Chicago. I was the director of financial products, which was a fancy title for sales manager. I had a team of people working for me and we were doing pretty good. My team broke sales records and the company rewarded us with bonus money and a trip to a conference in Las Vegas.

On the last day of the conference, the company held a dinner for us at a high-end steakhouse. This was our big final blow-out, with lots of food, booze, and some gambling afterward. After three days of listening to detailed descriptions of financial products, interest calculations, and selling techniques, my team and I were more than ready to let off a little steam.

There were twenty of us, a big group to handle in a busy, high-end Las Vegas restaurant. Of course, there was the pre-drinking before setting out for dinner, and our group was ready to party. I was no exception.

Looking back, I could see that I was careless with my super-power. I mean, would Superman don the cape after a few drinks? What do you think would happen if Batman went out on a bender and decided to suit up?

A Brad superpower was not something to be played with.

The company had reservations at a steakhouse in the MGM

Grand. My boss ran ahead of our group to make sure our table was ready. We were just entering the lobby of the hotel when I got a text from my boss that it would be another ninety-minute wait because the restaurant was so backed up.

This was when I decided to answer the bat signal. With a few drinks in my system, I loudly announced to everyone: "Fuck that, we are getting seated now!"

My co-workers were whooping it up. They had no idea what I meant, but they loved my drunken, fuck-you attitude. I didn't know if I could pull this off, but the liquor in my system had absolutely convinced me that I could. It had been a while since I had brought Brad out, and I had an itchy trigger finger. *Ocean's Eleven* had just come out, and I was eager to become the new suave Brad.

Up until this point my biggest party tricks had been getting mistaken for Brad. Mostly small-time, like getting to the head of a line at local restaurants, getting a free drink here and there. Getting twenty people into a crowded Las Vegas restaurant was a magic trick I had not practiced.

I needed to put on the uniform. I saw a men's clothing shop in the hotel and ducked in. Since I was going for the *Ocean's Eleven* look, I grabbed a light straw fedora, a mauve silk shirt, a silk scarf, and a pair of well-fitted slacks. I stopped into a men's room and gave my hair the Brad Pitt comb-over.

I left the men's room in full Brad drag. I had my spidey senses on full alert. I saw a few people look, another person point. I was feeling good. I found a co-worker and grabbed him.

"Holy fuck, dude. You are him!"

As we made our way to the entrance of the restaurant, I grabbed a few more of my co-workers. I needed to have a small entourage around me, like any major movie star would have. We pushed ourselves past the line of people waiting and approached the hostess at the podium.

I leaned on the podium and took off my sunglasses. "Hi, how are you tonight?"

She looked up, and her glance lingered on me for a second too long. I knew that glance. I had her.

My co-workers nudged their way up front, waiting to see.

"Oh my god." The hostess's eyes went large.

"What's your name?" I asked her.

"Casey."

"Casey, I don't want to have a big scene here. Can my friends and I get a private room for dinner right now?"

She stared right at me and could barely talk. "How many in your party, Mr. Pitt?"

"Shhh. For tonight I'm Tobey, okay? I don't want to start a stampede. There's twenty of us."

She had a big smile. "Hold on a minute and let me see what I can do. Okay?"

She ran back toward the kitchen.

My boss was in shock. Like Perry White watching Clark Kent take off his tie and glasses.

Casey returned with a man in a suit who leaned close to me. "Mr. Pitt, I'm delighted to welcome you to our restaurant. I have a private room for you in the back, can you give us just a minute to prepare it?"

"Of course. What's your name?"

"Don. Don Abraham, front of house manager."

"Don, I want to thank you personally for this favor. I'll make sure your boss knows how well we were treated."

"Thank you, Mr. Pitt—I mean Tobey."

"Also, can you please make sure that no one knows I'm here? I really don't want a scene."

"You can trust me; I'll take care of it. Some of the biggest stars come in here for private dinners. Can you and your group follow me?"

Five minutes later we were sitting in their private room with four bottles of Krug on the house.

Mistake #1. This was a crucial point during the trial. My co-workers and most of the company knew that I resembled Brad Pitt, but now they had witnessed the "malice and forethought" part.

Of course, the dinner was a wild success. This would probably be *the* water cooler topic at the office for years to come. That is, if I hadn't been convicted of murder. While my co-workers were high-fiving each other and flirting with the waitresses, I was in a daze. I had just convinced, with very little effort, a total stranger that I was one of the most famous people in the world. Whatever Brad Pitt had, I could have. Doors could be unlocked.

What other doors were there?

At the end of the dinner, I went around to the wait staff and thanked them personally. I made my boss give everyone crazy tips as well.

We moved over to another hotel for some drinking and gambling, but I didn't care about drinking and gambling anymore. I was a freaking superhero and wanted to test my powers even further. I was in Las Vegas, and some of the world's best clubs were right here on the Las Vegas strip. I waited until my co-workers started to disperse and go to sleep or do whatever they wanted to do. I didn't want anyone to witness this one. Ha! I thought I was being smart.

I decided that in order to be Brad I needed a black SUV to ferry me to the club, so I went to the hotel concierge and asked her to order one. The concierge also did a double take, but since I was charging the SUV to Tobey Crawford's room, I didn't think

I could pull off a free SUV.

Mistake #2. I think this was how Brad Pitt eventually found me. The breadcrumbs tracking the SUV to me.

The hottest ticket at that time was CRAVE at Caesar's Palace. I made the SUV pull up right in front of the club entrance at the side of the hotel. I walked past the line for the club like I had a twelve-foot dick and a pocketful of Benjamins. I had a slow-motion moment as I approached the two huge, muscled bouncers guarding the door, and I didn't even stop my stride as I took off the sunglasses and smiled. The two doors opened right up. "Good evening, Mr. Pitt."

My heart was beating fast, and I was giddy with power. I had no idea it was this easy.

Leanne, my lounge hostess, popped up out of nowhere. Needless to say she was gorgeous. Tall, with a small black dress that clung to her Las Vegas stripper body, she put her arm around my arm and guided me into the club.

"Welcome back, Mr. Pitt. I have your private cabana lounge ready. Are you . . . alone tonight?"

Fuck. He had been here before? I didn't think of that. *Should I know people's names?* "Just me tonight." No entourage! What mega worldwide star comes in without an entourage?

Leanne walked me to a VIP cabana just above the side of the dance floor. Within a few minutes, champagne and food arrived. I didn't know who ordered them. Leanne sat next to me and poured me a glass of champagne. "We have your favorite, Mr. Pitt. I also have the Italian olives and the French cheese that you liked so much from your last visit. Is there anything else you need?"

"I think this will do."

"Is there anyone you'd like to invite to join you? Even though you just sat down, I already have like a million requests from everyone in the club, so just let me know."

"Not right now. I think I'll just have a few sips of champagne first. Would you care to join me?" I wondered if she would tell me what Brad usually did when he came in.

"I'd be delighted."

"I can't remember the last time I was here."

Leanne topped up my champagne. "Not that long, I think. You were promoting *Ocean's Eleven*. You gave us a free screening. Loved-loved-loved the movie."

I became aware of people trying to look into my cabana. There was a big side of beef dressed in black guarding the velvet rope at the entrance. I assumed he was security from the club. Fuck, I was a big worldwide celebrity without an entourage *and* no security guard! Amateur hour.

The side of beef approached Leanne and whispered in her ear.

"Mr. Pitt, I have a request from Britney Spears to join you. Would that be okay?"

All I wanted was a couple of free drinks and maybe something to eat. I wasn't quite sure how to deal with Britney Spears. "She's the one who went crazy and shaved her head a little while ago, right? Is she still . . . not right?"

Leanne laughed politely. "Yes, she had a little trouble last year, but I think she's good now. She's been in here a couple of times since without any incidents."

I stood up as the queen of pop music was escorted to my table by an entourage of dozens. She gave me a kiss on the cheek and then started going on and on about the time we met at the Teen Choice Awards. I was sure she would sniff me out. Tongue-tied and nervous, I reverted back to Tobey Crawford. I kept staring at her hair to see if it was real or if she was wearing a wig. She had shaved her head in some crazy video a little while ago, I thought.

"Brad? I'd love to dance with you."

We were still standing, and she was uncomfortably close. Her chest was grazing mine. This was not what I wanted, although at the same time I was a little fascinated to see how another famous person reacted to Brad. I wasn't going to dance. No way, no how. "How about a drink first?"

"Are you working on a movie here again? I really loved *Ocean's Eleven*."

"No, not filming, just doing some . . . business."

I had no idea what to say to Britney, other than, "You're not crazy anymore, right?" Her eyes never left mine for a second. She was asserting control over me. If she looked hard enough, I was sure she would find Tobey.

"You know I've been trying to do movies. What would it take to get into a Brad Pitt movie? Oh my god, I can't even imagine being on screen with *the* Brad Pitt." She giggled and placed her hand on my leg. Upper upper leg.

Now I was really freaked out. Did Britney want to fuck me to be in a movie? How could I get out of here? I had no exit plan. "I think that would be a great idea." I picked up my glass to seal the deal with a toast.

She leaned in and rubbed our noses together. Then she licked my face. My face had never been licked. This was getting out of control. Would I be forced to have sex with Britney in order to keep up my charade?

She leaned back and laughed. "Oh my god, I just licked Brad Pitt!"

I was not looking at her anymore. I was looking just past her, at the cell phones recording us. I glared at her muscle-head security guy; he noticed the gawkers and started chasing people away.

Britney turned around. "Clyde? Get them damn phones!"

"I better get going." This was my out.

Britney grabbed me and gave me a quick kiss on the mouth. I wasn't a superhero; I was Cinderella running from the fancy ball before my SUV turned back into a pumpkin.

3

"Nervous as a long-tailed cat on a porch full of rocking chairs." That was an old phrase my grandmother used to say. I kept hearing my grandma's voice saying it over and over on Monday when I went back to work.

The whole office had heard about the triumph at the MGM steakhouse. But I wondered if they had watched any of the gossip shows all weekend showing the cell phone video of Brad Pitt and Britney Spears playing kissing games at a club in Las Vegas.

I spent all of my free time on Monday checking gossip websites, and none of them had any comment from Brad Pitt. "Calls to Mr. Pitt's representatives have not been returned."

Britney issued a statement saying that "Mr. Pitt is an old friend and there was nothing unseemly about their interaction."

In a weekend, my whole life had become so . . . odd. How many guys had to spend Monday morning worrying that their girlfriend and everyone at the office would figure out that they had made out with Britney Spears?

I was tempted to confess to Sophie, as I thought she might get a kick out of it. That was my rational thinking. However, my rational thought was buried by my shame of my addiction to being Brad. I didn't want to risk exposing this part of me to her, so I never mentioned it.

By Tuesday it seemed to be blowing over. People at the office would make Brad Pitt jokes, but I could handle that. The gossip sites had moved on to other scandals. I started to breathe easier.

But Brad Pitt found me. I'm not sure how he did it, but I think it was the SUV that took me to CRAVE. That was the only link to my real name.

At 10:34 on Wednesday morning, I received a call at my office from Ted Caswell.

"Is this Tobey Crawford?"

"Yes."

"My name is Ted Caswell, I'm a lawyer for Brad Pitt."

It began.

During my murder trial, the prosecution made a big deal of how I actually thought I was Brad Pitt, how much trouble I took to become him. However, the truth was just the opposite. He went to a lot of trouble to become me. I was just trading on his looks. He was stalking me. With intent. At the time, I couldn't convince my lawyer to use that as a defense. But now I'll tell you what he refused to admit into trial evidence.

Ted Caswell, lawyer for Brad Pitt. Immediately I had sweat stains on my underarms. Like an animal sensing danger in the forest.

"What can I do for you?"

"Mr. Crawford, first I'd like to ask you to stop impersonating Mr. Pitt. This is bad for him and could be very bad for you. The consequences for issuing a restraining order would be pretty severe. We'd have to notify your employer, and this is not the kind of action that reflects well on an employee of a financial service firm such as yours." He stopped talking to let it sink in for a few seconds. "Not to mention how it would affect any of your personal relationships."

I heard my heart beating loudly in my ears. My shirt was

soaked with sweat. Not only had he found me, he knew all about me. I stuttered, "It was just this one time. You know, a little drunk in Las Vegas."

"I hope so, Mr. Crawford. However, Mr. Pitt is not an unreasonable person. I think he assumed it may have been a one-time thing, so for now, there won't be any formal legal actions."

I exhaled. "Please thank him for me."

"Actually," Caswell's tone changed, "you can thank him in person. Mr. Pitt would like to meet you. He's inviting you and your girlfriend to visit him at his Malibu house this weekend. All of this will be at his expense. Can I tell him that you'll meet him?"

I didn't have time to process the request. I was hit sideways. "Um, sure."

"Great, I'll send you the details later today. Thanks for your time."

4

Sophie was laughing at me. "Did you really think I would be worried that you were going to start dating Britney Spears? Puhleeze."

We were in a lounge at a small private airport in Chicago, waiting for Brad Pitt's jet to arrive and take us to Los Angeles. After the phone call with Pitt's lawyer, I confessed all to Sophie —well, an embellished version of what happened in Las Vegas. I told her my co-workers made me do it. Telling her that I did it purposely of my own accord was just too much truth. She just rolled her eyes at me. This is why Sophie was a keeper.

"She was freakin' crazy about me!" I protested.

"That doesn't bother me . . . that much. I know what I signed up for. Women are gonna crush on a guy who looks just like Brad Pitt. I get that. But I know who you are. Or maybe I don't? What's a little disturbing is how you went full metal Brad Pitt. The more I think about it, that's traveling close to crazy town."

"Too much liquor and testosterone on that trip. That's all," I snapped back, but maybe that wasn't all. She always chuckled at moving to the head of a line with me or getting a table at a sold-out restaurant because people assumed I was Brad, maybe with a little encouragement. But like any good addiction, the idea of being Brad Pitt still burned inside me. Our pilot entered the lounge, allowing me to stop reflecting on my secret life.

"Mr. Crawford and Ms. Taylor? Hi, I'm Captain Craig Feder, I'll be flying you to Los Angeles. Would you come with me to board the plane?"

The plane was small, but it screamed "rich entitled people fly this way." There was a cozy, plush living room inside. A hostess greeted us and served cocktails. We settled down on a double-wide chaise lounge to watch TV. As the plane reached cruising altitude, a chef greeted us and asked what we'd like to eat.

After a few hours of cocktails, bacon kobe cheeseburgers, French fries with truffles, and a movie, Sophie peered over her appletini at me. "Why is this big mega movie star buttering you up?"

"What do you mean?"

"Did you not ever read Hansel and Gretel . . . Hansel?" She took another sip.

"Do you think he wants to push us in an oven?" I was a little light-headed from the last mojito.

"Just think about it. That's all I'm saying."

I should have listened more carefully to Sophie. I miss her more than anything.

∞

When we landed, we were met by Ted Caswell, Pitt's lawyer. "Welcome to Los Angeles! Mr. Pitt and Ms. Jolie are very much looking forward to meeting with you. I'll be driving you to their house in Malibu."

In the car, Sophie immediately grilled Caswell about Brad Pitt's intentions, but Caswell was tightlipped and only told her that Brad would explain everything. She whispered to me, "Why is a freakin' lawyer acting like his personal chauffer?" I should have thought of that. It would have made me pause if I were level-headed. But I wasn't. I was going to spend a weekend with the biggest star on earth. The sexiest man of the year. My career as Brad Pitt had netted me some small perks here and there, but now I would get to see the big stuff. An hour later we were riding along Los Angeles's famous coastline and pulled into a walled-off enclave with mega mansions planted solidly in front of the Pacific Ocean.

We stepped out of the car into a courtyard, and the sun blinded me. Or was it Brad's aura? I cupped my hand over my eyes and tried to see through the bright rays. I saw the hair, the aviators, and the bright white smile. His mouth opened.

"Holy fuck! It's me!"

He stepped off the front porch into full view. He was a little scraggly, unkempt beard and hair a little long, but no doubt it was Brad fucking Pitt.

"Man, thanks so much for coming. You must be Sophie. I'm Brad." He leaned in to hug her, and she offered up her hand to shake instead. He adjusted like a pro to her warning shot. "The real Brad, of course." He clapped me on the back. "C'mon in, Angie's dying to meet you. She thinks you're a freakin' genius, buddy."

I think I can trace the war back to this moment. I remember it clearly. When I asked Sophie later about the handshake, all she could offer was, "It was just instinct. I'm not really a hugger." Just instinct. Survivor's instinct.

Sophie and I followed him up the long driveway to the house. I couldn't think of a single thing to say to a movie star. I knew intimate details of his life, but I didn't know him. *Do I start talking about his kids?* He had five, but about two months earlier they had announced another child was on the way.

The house was a true movie star house. A wall of glass two stories high was the only thing that separated me from the Pacific Ocean. As we entered the living space, a dark silhouette emerged from a chaise lounge on the deck behind the glass. Angie. Her nude body rose from a lounger on the outside deck, clearly showing the baby bump as she threw a wrap over herself and made her way to meet us.

Angie slowly walked toward me, nothing but those famous lips, cheekbones, and big eyes. Wordless. She stopped about six inches in front of me and ran her fingers along the edge of my face. "No scars, is this natural? No work done? Because this is excellent."

"This is all me. I'm just a freak of nature, I think. But my eye color is different."

Angie nodded. "Jesus freaking Christ."

"I know, huh?" Brad steered her over to Sophie. "Sweetheart, this is Sophie, his girlfriend."

"You and I have a lot to talk about. Come, let's get you a drink." She whisked Sophie out to the deck.

Brad continued to stare at me. "I cannot fucking believe this. This is better than I thought."

Better than you thought? "What were you thinking?"

"Your accent is a little off. Do you know how to do my voice when you're me? Ah, sorry, you're looking a little overwhelmed and probably jetlagged, and we have the whole weekend anyway. Kids are with my mom and about a thousand nannies so we can just hang out. I have a guesthouse out back, let's get your stuff up there. You like Jet Skis?"

∞

A few hours later, I had a beer in my hand in the guesthouse, staring at the ocean. I was a little tired from the flight, the liquor, the Jet Skis, and more liquor, but I was still exhilarated. Brad seemed like a fun guy. Not a lot of pretense except for the zillion-dollar house and all the fame. He seemed really happy just to let go today. He wanted to go into town with me and see who got more autograph hunters, but Angie had put the kibosh on that.

Sophie returned to the guesthouse a little while later. Her skin was glowing, her hair shiny and perfectly in place. But she wasn't smiling. "Wow, look who got a makeover. How was your afternoon?"

"We had Ricardo come over and give us massages, then Katie comes by and does the mani-pedis. And after that it's time for Miss Rachel's facials. You'll be pleased to know I drew the line at the Botox injections. I swear to god they are fattening us up for something."

A pleasant ringing emitted from an iPad on a night table. I looked down at a message on the screen. "Dinner in the main house in ten minutes. Totally cas'."

When we arrived for dinner, Brad was watching a basketball game on a huge TV, and Angie was overseeing a chef in the kitchen.

"C'mon in!" Brad beckoned us. "We'll have dinner on the deck tonight. You guys enjoying yourselves? I want to be the consummate host."

We moved to the deck just as the sun had set. Traces of stars appeared in the night sky. Brad lit torches around the table and popped open a bottle of wine.

I was about to open my mouth to thank him for all he had done when Sophie tugged on my hand.

"Brad . . ." Sophie had trouble spitting out the name. "I feel like we won a contest . . . This doesn't seem real. Like a dream we didn't know we had. You have to tell us, especially after my boyfriend practically fucked over your life, why this is happening. I mean, I'm enjoying all of this, but I can't really enjoy it all until I know what made you fly us here."

The elephant in the room. Sophie had always been so levelheaded. Even star power couldn't overwhelm her. It was Brad's kryptonite.

There was a long moment of silence as Brad summoned a smile to his face, like he had practiced for years on the red carpet. His eyes were pointed at Sophie. But her face remained unchanged.

Her head was tilted slightly, eyebrows raised.

"She's waiting for the other shoe to drop," Angie blurted out as she walked onto the deck, rescuing the moment. She gave Brad a long stare and held out a wine glass. "Just water for me please."

"You don't think I'm just a genuinely nice guy?" Brad asked Sophie.

I was caught off guard. He was challenging Sophie out in the open, and then he laughed. "Of course! I get it. I'll fill your wine glasses and drop the other shoe."

"Before you drop the shoe," Angie intervened again, "should I tell Ryan to go or stay? Do we want to drop by the thing at Streisand's house or not? I can't stay up late." She put her hand on her stomach. "So maybe a drive by?"

"If we go, I can drive, so let Ryan go." Brad finished pouring the wine.

"You're not driving liquored up. I'll tell him to stay on for tonight."

"We could always just cab it there," Brad yelled back to Angie.

"Excuse me, Brad," Sophie cut in. "Drop the fucking shoe already."

"Of course, of course. This is kind of cruel, holding it back, huh?" Brad took a deep breath and a gulp of wine. "I want you to work for me. I think you can guess what the job would be. You would be me for a living."

Become Brad Pitt for a living? His double? I knew from my research that actors had stand-ins for them on the set. People who looked like them for scenes where they were not required to do dialogue or were viewed off in the distance.

"My life is not my life. I feel like I don't even own it anymore because I'm constantly followed and hounded. You would be a diversion, especially in the next few months when the paparazzi will come down on us like the plague. Once the babies are born it will be out of control."

"Babies?" Sophie looked at Angie. "You're having twins?"

She nodded.

Brad held his drink up in the air. "So it will be twice the hell! But! If you show up in Venice, I can go to the hardware store just like a regular fucking person and buy stuff to fix the nursery up. If you go to Paris for a week, I can show up in St. Louis and visit with my folks if I want to. Honestly, I can make myself look homeless, but once word gets out that I'm somewhere, all the major gossip sites send cameras out. If they think I'm in Paris or Madrid, they won't think about looking anyplace else."

I was dumbfounded. My fantasy life. "How would that work?" This was a big upgrade from stand-in. My leg was shaking. He was speaking to my addiction. Setting it free.

"I'd give you a schedule, a wardrobe, and tell you where to go. I'd make all the reservations for dinner, hotels, airfare, whatever. For a few days you'd get hounded by the press, but mostly you eat at nice restaurants, sleep in fabulous hotels, and run away from people with cameras."

Angie nudged him. "The shoe hasn't finished dropping, honey."

Brad took another gulp of wine. "This would be a full-time job. You'd have to quit your day job. Although you will get paid a shitload of money. I wouldn't expect you to do all this for me and not pay you crazy money. Crazy, name-your-price kind of money. Also, live wherever in the world you want, although LA would make more sense, but your call. This is a shitload to think about, so let it sink in, think about it. Ask any questions. I don't expect an answer until you've processed it. For now, let's have dinner."

"You botched that up." Angie reached across to pour more wine into Sophie's glass. "What about Sophie? How does this affect her life? Does she just wait for him at home while he's being you in Paris? How does that work?"

This was an important point, I thought. But I could barely hear it. I could live like Brad. I could travel like Brad. I wouldn't ever have to work a real job in my life. Living large would be my job title. The demon inside of me was now unleashed. I could hardly hear what he was saying to Sophie.

"Fuck." Brad took another gulp and looked Sophie in the eye. "I'm sorry, but I have given this a lot of thought." He stared hard at her. I could see Sophie shift; she was uncomfortable. "Of course you don't put your life on hold for him. However, I'll take care of you, too. Wherever he goes, there's always an open ticket for you. If he decides to live in Amsterdam or Paris or Modesto, you can go with him at my expense. This is obviously something you guys need to talk about, but I'm open to suggestions and any questions." He gave Angie a shake of his head. "One caveat: when he's being me, you can't be seen with him on a regular basis, otherwise you'll start a chain reaction with the gossip sites."

Their chef walked out to the patio with our dinner right on cue. Sophie and I were still shell-shocked. But for different reasons. We shouldn't be eating dinner, we should have been huddled up and in deep discussion. I barely touched my food. What I should have done was stand up and declare that we were not doing anything until Sophie and I talked this out.

Sophie didn't even pick up her fork. "How long do you expect us to work for you?"

She said "us" louder than any of her other words. I put my fork down.

Brad stopped eating and built his red-carpet smile for her. "As long as we all agree to this or get tired of it, or if you hate it, we can stop it. But as long as you guys are happy, you're on the payroll."

"What kind of money are we talking about? You said, 'name your price,' but what is that—millions, tens of millions, hundreds of millions?"

"Damn!" Brad looked across to Angie. "Forget the traveling offer, I want her to be my business manager!" He turned back to Sophie, smile and all. "We can work that out, but I promise you this, whatever happens in the future, you won't ever have to work again."

"But what if I like working?" Sophie cradled her wine and tilted her head.

"Nothing to stop that from happening. You'll have a nice nest egg for the future kids and grandkids."

Sophie considered his answer for a minute before turning to Angie. "What do you think?"

Angie put her hand on Sophie's hand. "Honestly, it's a little screwy. I can only imagine what you're thinking: big, rich movie stars invite you out and try to buy your lives, right? I'm a little weirded out by it. On the other hand, I'm willing to see if this works for all of us. Movie star life sounds very sexy and glamourous, but in reality we spend a lot of our life trying to figure out how to live a normal life. We're constantly under siege from paparazzi. It scares the kids. And I'm frightened of the kids being targets for . . . for whatever is out there. So, if you're willing, I'm willing, too. If it doesn't work, it doesn't work."

Sophie nodded and looked at me. "Well?"

I was sure this was where Brad spotted the cracks between us. I wanted this more than anything. I wanted Sophie to forget all of her objections and just say yes. I wanted to live in this house forever. I wanted to get lawyers to drive me to private planes so I could fly all over the world and be greeted like a rock star. All of these thoughts were racing through my mind, delaying my response. A delay that Brad was probably timing. "I need some time to think."

Brad raised his fork. "Shall we eat?"

During dinner Angie mentioned the "Streisand Thing" again, and Brad agreed that they should go. "Wait a minute, what if Tobey goes instead of me? If he can pass for me in that room, we know this whole thing is foolproof! I can stay back here and catch up on some basketball."

"Don't even think it," Angie admonished him. "C'mon, everyone, we'll all go for like an hour. Why don't we change and meet back down here in fifteen?"

Back in the guesthouse, Sophie shut the door and pointedly said nothing. I looked at her, a little bit freaked. "Well, Gretel? Cat got your tongue?"

"I'm not going to say anything . . . yet. This is really your decision to make when it comes down to it."

"You hate it though, don't you?"

"This is really about you." She turned away from me, getting ready for the Streisand thing. "I'm willing to be influenced."

It dawned on me she had no idea of the breadth of my addiction. Being a huge worldwide mega star fucked with your head. Even if it was just for a few hours every once in a while. The feeling of power, the constant ass-kissing—she had no idea how it felt and no idea how I felt when I was Brad. There was no way I could have explained this without exposing myself as a complete psychopath. I even thought she would be pleased about Brad's proposal. But it was clearly a threat to our relationship.

Why didn't I think about that?

She saw that I was hesitant. She was probably annoyed that I was not on the same page as her. "Look, we'll do this Streisand thing and when we get back we'll discuss it all. We'll stay up all night talking or we'll wait 'til we're back at home and have some distance. But I don't think either of us has really absorbed this yet, okay?"

"Agreed." I needed some more time with my thoughts.

The iPad rang: *"Sophie, come on down and meet me in the main house. Brad wants to hang back with Tobey for a few minutes. Angie."*

"You're on your own for a while, Hansel. Good luck." She kissed me on the forehead and left.

I sat down on the balcony and stared at the real stars in the night sky, listened to the waves hitting the beach. This could actually be my life, but if it made Sophie miserable, how could I? Why did I just assume she would love the idea? This fantasy was not possible. I couldn't do this and risk losing Sophie. But I could taste the sweetness of having all that power and no responsibility. No accountability in my life. It was like the undertow I was staring at, drawing me under, and I wanted to be pulled in.

Lost in thought, I forgot about time, forgot about the Streisand thing.

The strong stench of pot knocked me out of my thoughts. I looked at the beach in front of me and couldn't see anyone, no lit joints in the darkness. The smell was getting stronger. I walked back into the darkness of the living room and saw the glowing end of a rolled joint, heard a long intake of breath, smelled the distinct, pungent smell. A cloud of smoke. My eyes adjusted to the dark and I saw him. It was Brad, but no beard and no long hair. He had cut it to look like me. Also no clothes. Maybe some underwear?

He stepped into the sliver of moonlight between us. He was *Fight Club* Brad. Tighty-whiteys and sinewy muscles. If I were a cat, my tail would be up in the air and I would be hissing. I felt very, very threatened.

He walked right up to me and turned me around in the dark. He held on to me a little too tightly. We were facing a mirror, and he turned the lights up with a remote control.

"We can become one," he whispered into my ear. "Is it you? Is it me? Look how hard it is to tell." He moved behind me, leaving no distance between us. He put his hands on my shoulders. "This is extraordinary; don't you think?"

"I . . . I am not sure what . . ." was all I could spit out. Why was he touching me like this?

"Just think about it. Everything, and I mean everything, can become yours."

I was distracted by the image in the mirror. The same mirror I had hated for so long was displaying a completely new reflection. His head was on my shoulder. Like a flaw in the mirror, emitting a double image. We were a two-headed monster.

He put his arm around my neck and brought the joint to my lips. "Just inhale."

He leaned into me. My brain was racing. *I shouldn't do this*. This was where Hansel got pushed into the oven.

He slipped the joint into my mouth.

The undertow pulled me under. I took a deep hit off the joint. I exhaled. "Holy fuck." Oh my god, I was worrying about Brad Pitt fucking me!

Brad smiled in the mirror. "Relax, buddy," he said, as if he had read my thoughts. "You have to practice my voice. I'll give you lessons."

He pushed the joint into my mouth again. I took another hit, exhaled, and started coughing. "Now?"

"Not now. We'll have plenty of time for that. Just let me leave you with this. You've only had a very small taste of what life can be like. It can be so much more." He handed me the joint and gave me a bear hug from behind. "You have no idea what this means to me."

I wanted to open my mouth and say words, but I couldn't think of them fast enough. Words like "What the fuck does this even mean?" and "Who the fuck are you anyway?" Instead, I inhaled another toke.

Brad backed away from me toward the door. "You need time. Stay here tonight. I'll go out to the party and leave you with your thoughts."

I went back out to the deck to see the ocean. My breath slowed, and I could feel my body become calm again. The pot was beginning its work. Strong fucking pot. One more hit. I felt calm and warm and powerful at the same time. The ocean in front of me was mine. Or it could be mine. Those stars could be mine. Every fucking thing could be mine.

I reached out my hand and, yes, I could feel the stars. Like warm butter dripping down my arms. I pointed at one bright star in the corner of the sky, and I could actually move it across the sky by pointing at it. Was this the power that Brad Pitt had? Had he transferred it to me now?

Or was it really fucking powerful pot? Either way, this was a sweet life. I smelled the ocean spray and let the night breeze cool my face.

I went back into the guesthouse and lay back on the bed. I was really the King of the World. The mattress swallowed me up. I let go and let it have me.

A few minutes—or was it a few hours?—maybe even days later, someone grabbed me and was pulling me back.

"Jesus Christ, it reeks in here. How much pot did you guys smoke?" It was Sophie.

I smiled the smile of a happy god and pulled her down onto the mattress and into the new world that we could share together and go sailing further and further.

∞

The next day was a chore. I was not the King of the World. My brain was foggy, and I couldn't think clearly. I knew this even before I got out of bed.

Sophie stood at the base of the bed with a tray of coffee and croissants. "Good morning, Hansel. Looks like you really filled up on the house made out of candy. Hopefully this coffee will bring you out of the oven."

I looked at her beautiful face through my haze. "I'm really fucked up."

"I know. Eat your breakfast. And then let's get the hell out of here."

An hour later Sophie was helping me into the main house with our luggage. She understood that I was in no shape to discuss the offer. This was a good thing, because I knew that she hated it all—the weekend, the offer, and probably Brad. But I still felt the warm embrace of Brad's world. I needed the drugs to wear off to see if the embrace disappeared with it.

Brad was behind the stove in the kitchen, making pancakes. He glanced at me and stared for an extra second. "Buddy! I bet you are really, really hungry about now. No worries, I have my grandmother's special chocolate chip pancakes coming to the rescue. Have a seat. You can't travel on an empty stomach."

Even though I had torn through a basket of croissants twenty minutes earlier, I was still really, really hungry. I wanted those pancakes like nobody's business.

"Where's Angie?" Sophie poured another cup of coffee.

"She had to run back to town this morning. Shiloh meltdown. Won't stop wailing until she sees her mom. She's really sorry she missed you, but she wanted to let you know what a great pleasure it was meeting both of you this weekend."

Without Angie as a buffer, there was palpable tension in the kitchen. As I wolfed down the pancakes, Brad tried to make small talk with Sophie, but she wasn't having it. He tried relaying some stories from the Streisand thing the night before and looked to Sophie to complete the story, but she just nodded back politely. Brad was trying his best charm offense on her, but all of his arrows were hitting a brick wall.

The war had begun.

Breakfast ended and it was clearly time to go. Sophie practically ran to the limo with our luggage. Brad grabbed my hand and rubbed my arm. "Hope to hear from you soon, buddy." He winked at me. "I'm off the grid for a couple of weeks, but you can call me anytime, no problem."

The flight back was filled with silence. Icy-cold silence.

"Do you want to talk about it?"

"He gives me the creeps." Sophie reached into her purse for her makeup mirror. "That's besides the fact that he totally ignored me and sent his girlfriend to keep me away from you the whole weekend. Although I do love the makeup she gave me."

"Okay, so to play devil's advocate," I was being coy, "I have had plenty of bosses and co-workers who give you the creeps and it never mattered that much."

"Plenty? God, that whole crew at your office is full of creeps, but they're not in charge of your life. They're not trying to make you become them. Or maybe if they are they're just not as good at it. But this is a whole other level. He made me feel like an accessory, like I'll just follow along with you because he's Brad fucking Pitt. That really bothers me."

I was silent. Now I really felt like shit. The real question she should ask me next was, why did I stand for it? But she didn't, and the question hung between us like a ghost.

She grabbed my hand. "I know this is an overwhelming choice. You've got stars in your eyes, anyone would. But let's take a look at reality. You'd be running all over the world having the time of your life. I'm here in Chicago. I can't give up my life to chase a fake Brad Pitt. I can see maybe being talked into going on an occasional trip, but I really like my life here. I like having you in my life here. Eventually, though, you would get tired of me, and I would resent not having a full-time partner. We'd lose touch with each other. I can't be in a relationship like that."

I nodded solemnly.

"Also," Sophie was not quite done, "I'm not convinced he really needs you to do this. He's willing to pay millions of dollars so he can go to the supermarket or whatever? Maybe I'm just a little paranoid, but I think he really enjoys controlling someone else's life."

∞

Monday morning, back at my desk at work, my head was still in the clouds, and I fought between living in Brad world and in the present. In hindsight, this was Brad's plan. Dazzle me, keep me off balance, assert his will into my life. Seduce me.

I was already seduced by the thought of being him. He knew that. He knew it would take some effort to push me over the edge, and he only had that weekend to do it. He came at me with everything he had.

Sophie saw it all very clearly: separate us as much as possible, and then let his life sink into me and take root before she could object to it.

She had become the enemy. His enemy.

She was trying to save my life.

It had come down to a simple choice: Sophie or Brad.

I had to go cold turkey. I had to let Brad go.

∞

Ted Caswell called later that week and asked if I had any more questions. He spoke to me like it was all a done deal and I was now part of Team Brad. He went on to tell me that he was ready to talk about money and living arrangements. If I needed more time, Brad was completely open to spending more time with me.

"Ted," I stared at the picture of Sophie on my desk, "Brad's offer is beyond generous, but I don't think I can do this." Some of the most painful medicine I would ever swallow.

Silence.

"Brad will not be happy about this."

His tone was not quite the happy-happy tone he had a few minutes earlier. The change in his voice threw me off. I felt threatened. Or maybe my addiction was threatened.

"Please thank him for me. Bye, Ted." I hung up. I couldn't talk to him any longer. He would try to talk me back in, and it would be easy to convince me. He would remind me of the life I could have had, and I would forget every single thing Sophie and I had talked about. All at once, I felt two distinct things: sadness that I would not have the life I secretly dreamed of, that I wouldn't ever be able to get my "fix" of being Brad again, and exhilaration that I had just escaped something very dark and very heavy that I couldn't identify.

But I hadn't escaped. It was just beginning.

5

A week later, I received a legal notice served to me at my office. Brad Pitt intended to sue me for damages for impersonating him with intent to defraud. He was suing me for ten million dollars.

I was served with great pomp and circumstance by a sheriff and an accompanying deputy. And a police dog. Seriously.

Or what looked like a sheriff and a deputy, I should have said. I know better now that with Brad, not everything you see is real.

My office wasn't that big, about sixty people, and everyone took note, including my boss and his boss, the CEO.

The CEO walked over to my office and leaned against my doorframe. "Everything okay? Anything you want to tell us about?"

"Some drama with an ex, I'll handle it." How could I explain to the CEO that Brad Pitt wanted to sue me for impersonating him? And I was guilty! He flew me out to his beach house to offer me a job, which I turned down, and now he had gone all psycho on me.

Sure, any boss would get that.

"He still thinks for some reason that he can force you to work for him." Sophie was helping me think this through at a happy hour after work—well, more of a not-so-happy hour.

I was freaked out and my first two drinks had not had any effect on me. "Do I need to hire a lawyer? Jesus fucking Christ, this guy is really crazy."

"Honestly?" Sophie was sitting back and took charge like a general in a war room. "I would ignore it. I think he's bluffing. He's trying to see if you'll come back to him."

"I'm either in jail because I ignored a court order, or I get fired because my CEO thinks I'm going to jail."

"Alright, maybe get in touch with some legal people to see if you have to respond, but I think he's trying to manipulate you . . . again."

Again. I noticed that Sophie was done with subtlety. "Okay, but I need to have a strategy on this. I can't just react."

Sophie finished munching on a nacho and took out the makeup bag that Angie had given her. "Remember, their kryptonite is bad publicity, so let's think on that."

"What do you mean?"

"I mean, why not go public, have a press conference and tell-all? Try to shame him. Just be honest; reporters will have a field day. Tell everyone that he tried to get you to work for him. I mean, we can pretty much document everything. Even though we signed a non-disclosure form, I still have photos of the whole weekend on my phone."

"That's an intriguing idea." I finished drink number three and finally felt the courage that only liquor could provide. "Fight fire with fire." I may have had a different idea for bad publicity. Did this psycho motherfucker movie star forget I had his superpowers?

Later that night, after Sophie slipped off to sleep, I began my research. Brad had told me he would be off the grid for a couple of weeks. That meant he could be anywhere.

Anywhere I decided to show up.

I looked up his filmography on a fan site. It showed two films in progress this year: one in production in New Orleans, *The Curious Case of Benjamin Button*, and one unnamed project in preproduction in England. So he might have been in New Orleans or England. Well, I couldn't get over to England.

A little more googling effort revealed that Brad was heavily involved in New Orleans' recovery from Hurricane Katrina. He had built a whole neighborhood of affordable housing and owned a home down there.

This looked promising.

A search of the local papers in New Orleans showed that Brad and Angie were down there about two months ago, but no recent mentions.

I was going to N'awlins!

This had to be carefully choreographed. I needed to send a clear message to Brad Pitt: *Do not fuck with me*.

6

I was him again, and it felt like home.

I should say I was not quite him yet, just a few hours to go, but he was in me, waiting, pushing to get out.

I took Interstate 55 and finally crossed the Mississippi border into Kenwood, Louisiana, after driving all night from Chicago. It was a fifteen-hour drive, but I made good time. I left Chicago at midnight and would pull into New Orleans by three p.m. Enough time to get some sleep and get ready for a night on the town as him. One phenomenal blow-out night.

Planning a Brad outing was half the joy. It was the foreplay to becoming him. Plotting out the logistics, figuring out every angle to get maximum exposure as Brad with the least amount of risk. As with any addiction, anticipation was a big part of the high.

My original instinct was to book a first-class flight and let Brad out right there in Chicago. At the airport I would wear a hoodie and sunglasses and make it very obvious that I was somebody incognito. I could anticipate the feeling of people straining out of the corners of their eyes to see if I was "somebody." I would stare at my cell phone while pretending not to notice the attention. At the ticket counter I would take off my glasses and watch what happened after the big reveal. I really wanted that walk through security while nervous guards told me to put my bag on the conveyer belt. I could almost taste it. But not this time.

I didn't want my fingerprints on this. I was walking a dangerous tightrope. If my name was traced back to this weekend, then I would lose the lawsuit, lose my job. Lose Sophie. Everything. If I flew, then my credit card could be traced to the flights.

I also had an alibi, just in case it came down to that. I found a benign business conference in Chicago, "The Future of Digital Technology in the Workplace," registered for it, and then checked into a hotel for the conference. I even went to the convention, had them scan my badge and, after a few hours, made a beeline for the interstate. Once I got back to town, I'd have to check out of the convention center hotel. I had every base covered.

Closer to New Orleans, I headed for the New Orleans Lakefront Airport, a small airport from the golden days of flying located just a few minutes outside the city. This was where private jets landed and would most likely be the airport that Brad's plane would land. I had a limo reserved under the name Mr. Smith that would pick me up and take me from the airport to the Ritz-Carlton.

As I pulled into the small airport parking lot, my pulse was already racing. I was about to commit a crime, but even more, I was about to let Brad out.

I had his clothes—not just what I thought he would wear, but copies of his actual outfits that I found from pictures on the internet.

For airports, Brad liked earth tones. Unconstructed jackets with loose linen pants, a silk tee, and usually a scarf around the neck. A straw fedora and aviators completed the outfit. I stepped out of the car and stood tall in the parking lot. At long last, I was him.

"Brad Juice" started flowing through my veins. I had his confidence. I was fearless as the most recognized man on earth.

I pulled out my Brad phone for the weekend and texted the limo: *"Arriving ahead of schedule, landing in a few minutes."*

This time was so different from previous Brad outings. The weekend with Brad gave me the chance to observe him carefully. The nuances in his behavior. The way he smiled. He didn't just smile, he built it, starting slowly and letting it widen until all the teeth were revealed. He squinted when he didn't understand something. His handshake was aggressive and heartfelt. I was fully transforming into him. I couldn't fuck this up. There were no fuck-ups. If I fucked up, it would be Brad's fuck-up.

The limo pulled up and the driver jumped out, surprised to see me.

"Mr. Pitt, so sorry to make you wait, let me get your bag."

"Hey, buddy, we were early, no worries. Also, I'm Mr. Smith this weekend, okay?"

"Of course, Mr. Smith."

I had also been working on his voice. Just like he told me to do.

From the back of the limo I called the Ritz-Carlton and asked to speak to the manager on duty.

"Of course, Mr. Pitt, we're delighted to welcome you back to the Ritz-Carlton. Just pull into the back garage and I'll meet you there." Perfect! I didn't want to make a reservation in advance. Too much risk in trying to hold a room in his name. It all got very complicated the more I thought about it. I even used a prepaid Visa card to reserve the limo. But if Brad fucking Pitt showed up at your hotel and said "Gimme a room"? You are going to give him your best room.

Fifteen minutes later, we pulled up into the back entrance to the Ritz-Carlton at the edge of the French Quarter.

The concierge opened my door. "Welcome back to the Ritz, Mr. Pitt. I'm Charles Placer and I'm here to make sure your stay here is perfect; would you mind following me to your suite?"

As he led me through a separate entrance for celebrities, I remained cool, but I wanted to high-five this dude and scream YES! The plan had fallen into place and was going better than expected.

As I was escorted into an elevator, Charles asked me if I wanted the usual arrangements.

I wasn't sure what that meant. Payment arrangements? Room arrangements? Normally this would have made me break a sweat. The jig was up, my Brad mask would be ripped off.

But I was the new and improved Brad. The Brad who could move stars across the sky. I looked at the concierge, tilted my head, and squinted.

"Charge your business account?"

This crossed into felony territory. I'd done the research. It was the same as stealing a credit card.

"I'd like this one off the books, if you don't mind, buddy. I'll just pay cash."

"Understood, Mr. Pitt. We can settle that at checkout. We have the Presidential Suite available." The elevator opened to a small hallway with just one door. Charles opened the door into a huge suite. More than huge. Enormous. Grand-piano-and-spiral-staircase enormous.

A bead of sweat formed on my forehead; this had to be thousands per night. I didn't have this kind of cash. I should have told Charles I wanted a small room for the night.

But I didn't. I wanted to spend the night here in this suite. I couldn't become Brad in a regular hotel room, even at the Ritz. It just wouldn't work. I had covered my tracks pretty well. There was no way my name could be traced back to this reservation. Just my face, which was also his face. Fuck it. This would go on Brad's business account. As far as I was concerned,

I was Brad fucking Pitt.

I had a couple of hours until I would begin my damage tour. I found the bedroom and laid out my next outfit. When Brad was out on the town, his outfit choices were all over the map. Sometimes he was chic and suave and sometimes he was jeans, T-shirt, and backwards baseball cap, or a tracksuit with a trucker hat. For tonight, he would be backwards baseball cap, with the revered New Orleans Saints emblem, of course. His T-shirts were usually high-end faux faded tees with a blue-collar reference. Tonight he would be wearing an old faux Esso Oil T-shirt with faded jeans and Nikes with double laces. And of course, aviators, slightly oversized with dark brown lenses.

I opened the balcony doors from the bedroom, and I could see the whole town from there, the Mississippi River, Jackson Square, and uptown as well, since it was a wraparound balcony. The sun had just set, and the stars were just starting to appear in the sky. Which one would I move tonight?

I walked back into the suite and up the spiral staircase and found another more intimate suite within the suite. There was a huge royal four-poster bed, a small but sleek kitchen—fully stocked—a pool table, and a white marble bathroom that looked directly out on the city from a glass wall. An ice bucket with Brad's favorite beer and chips sat next to the Jacuzzi tub.

Brad had told me during our weekend together that he loved to take baths. It was his me-time to sit and reflect or read scripts and just soak. Personally, I hadn't taken a bath since I was a kid. I was strictly a shower guy. But I was him now. I needed to forget what I preferred and feel what he felt from a bath. I turned on the water.

I stripped off my clothes, but even this was different. I would probably have thrown my clothes off and stepped in. But Brad? He would probably slip into the Ritz's posh bathrobe, grab a beer out of the bucket, and step out onto the small balcony first.

I stepped outside and felt the warm breeze. I took a sip of the beer and gazed again at the sky. I couldn't have more than a sip; I needed to have total control. I dropped the robe onto the floor of the balcony as the warm New Orleans breeze embraced my skin. I walked slowly back into the suite and slipped into the Jacuzzi. I was him.

One night only. By tomorrow I would have to put Brad back in his closet. Tomorrow, I would be Clark Kent again. His offer floated through my mind. I would have been excellent. Maybe even a better Brad than Brad himself. Could I convince Sophie to let me give it a shot on a trial basis? If I put my mind to it, maybe I could find ways of making Sophie like it. I could buy us a nice place in Chicago as a compromise. I mean, it was obviously a job I was meant for; she couldn't ignore that. I felt bad that I never made a sensible argument in favor of it before Sophie closed the door on it.

No, there was just no way she would accept it. I would have to break up with her. That would be the only way. *Too complicated. Focus on tonight.*

7

The Plan:

In my research before the trip I discovered that the Marsalis family would be performing at a small club on the edge of the quarter. This was a rare event and sold out a few minutes after the show was announced. If New Orleans was the Kingdom of Jazz in America, the Marsalis family was royalty. Their roots went way back here, and they were not only superb musicians, but local heroes for their devotion to the local music scene and rebuilding the city after Katrina. Brad had worked with them in the past year or so on his own rebuilding projects, so this would be a real test to see if I passed.

First on my list for tonight: go to the Marsalis concert and be photographed there. Get Wynton Marsalis's attention and acknowledgment that I was Brad Pitt. I decided I might stay for a song or two after that, but the general plan was to let Brad out and get some media attention. First some local news coverage from the concert to document that Brad Pitt was in New Orleans, and then some social media attention. I wanted to get on people's Facebook pages doing things that would kill off Brad's good-guy image.

In front of the mirror in my suite, I compared my image to a picture of him on my phone. Almost exactly the same outfit. It was freaky. Even my old nemesis, the mirror, had to admit we really were the two-headed monster.

I walked through the lobby of the hotel with my aviators in place. I could almost feel the stares and double takes. I felt intoxicated, high from the attention. For a few seconds, everyone's lives suddenly revolved around my presence.

Could I step boldly out in front of paparazzi? This would be my next test. Work out the kinks here. The Brad Juice was flowing. Aviators on, hat turned frontward, and brim lowered a half an inch. Scarf wrapped a little closer to my chin. The doorman ran to the doors, and as soon as they opened, the cameras started going.

From what I could see there were about three photographers and a handful of onlookers with cell phones. The limo was just a few feet out by the curb. People yelled at me.

"Hey, Brad, what you doin' at the Ritz?"

"Where's Angie?"

"Where you headed, Brad?"

"Can you look this way?"

I ignored everyone and calmly walked to the car, letting myself be photographed. As I ducked into the back seat, I threw a wave out to the crowd and we pulled away. Like a pro. The paparazzi accepted that I was him. Now I was paparazzi bait.

"Fuck, yeah!" I said in the back of the limo. I needed this under my belt. In a few minutes I would be around people who knew him. Time for a drink? Maybe a small shot of something to take the edge off. I didn't see the harm at this point. If I was a little tipsy, it would be Brad who was a little tipsy. I opened up the small bar in the back and grabbed a bottle of champagne.

My driver lowered the privacy glass. "Mr. Smith? Looks like the front of the club is pretty swamped. Lots of people and press out there. I know there's a back entrance if you want me to use that."

I downed the rest of my glass of champagne. "Let's go through the front tonight."

The driver glanced at me in the rear view. "You sure, Mr.

Smith?"

"Positive."

∞

A few minutes later, the car slid along the curb and stopped in front of the club. Through the tinted glass, I saw the crowd. They stepped back off the curb and stared into the dark windows to see who might be inside. I counted at least six professional photographers in the crowd. The driver jumped out and ran around to my door.

I felt wetness underneath my faux retro T-shirt and underneath my baseball cap. I needed to take control. A deep breath. The balcony at Brad's guesthouse. I raised my finger and moved a star. I could do that. He showed me how. No matter what I did after I left this car, it would be him doing it, not me.

The door opened and the driver reached in to help me step out. I grabbed his hand.

The crowd pressed in and bulbs from cameras started flashing. Hands reached out and grabbed at my jacket. For the first time, I felt a little bit threatened. Being the center of attention was a great high, but the other side of the coin was that people wanted a piece of you, to grab, to touch. The driver did his best to keep people in front of me from rushing, but I was already overwhelmed. I realized I'd made a huge mistake. No security people. Fuck. In all the pictures I had studied I paid too much attention to his clothes and his mannerisms and didn't bother to look at his security setup. I pushed the driver through the crowd, inching my way toward the entrance. Fucking amateur hour. What kind of worldwide superstar would show up in a crowd without security? Would this blow my cover?

A few seconds later, some bouncers from the club surrounded me. I assumed they were from the club. One in front of me and one on each side, they pushed me inside.

The bouncer in front of me pulled my driver aside and started yelling, "You shoulda come in the back! What the fuck were you thinking? He ain't got nobody with him! Is this your first night on the job or what?"

I put my hand on the bouncer's shoulder. "Hey." He stopped talking immediately. The power of Brad was still there. "This is my fault. I told him to go to the front. Can I get a beer?"

"Of course, Mr. Pitt." He ordered someone to fetch me a beer.

I was ushered into the music hall in the middle of a raucous number. Wynton was on stage, blowing into his sax, sweating and stomping. The crowd was on their feet, jumping, dancing, and shouting. The bouncer grabbed me around the arm. "Let's get you up front."

He guided me around the edge of the crowd to the very front of the small stage. He waved to someone on the side of the stage and pointed at my head.

I was him. If I fell down drunk, Brad was falling down drunk. If I threw up all over the floor, Brad was throwing up all over the floor. I let the music in me, bounced up and down with the crowd around me, who started to notice that I was there. I clinked beers with a couple of people around me and danced. Some cell phones that were pointed at the stage turned my way. I felt a hand rubbing my back, but it was too crowded to figure out who was doing it, so I just let it go.

The music was building to a crescendo and the audience was going crazy. The hand on my back returned and became a little touchier. I turned my head and a guy in a cowboy hat gave me a big wink and a smile. I was thrown off for a second by Brad's universal appeal.

The song ended, and the hand dropped off of my back. Wynton took his proper bows and acknowledged the musicians on stage.

"Thank you! Nothin' like New Orleans, right? Right? We cannot ever lose this city. Since Katrina I been working with many friends who also don't want to see our city disappear. Some of them are well-meaning, but others are giving from the heart. From their soul. And I just noticed that one of those buddies who is giving from the soul is here tonight. So I'm going to ask him to come up here and show us his chops. Let's see some of that soul tonight. Brad Pitt, get yo ass up here."

I was lifted out of the audience and pushed onto the stage. Fuck. Not part of the plan. The crowd was clapping and screaming. I hugged Wynton and managed to wave to the audience. Beyond that I had no idea what to do or say.

"Shall we have Brad join us for a song?" Wynton asked the audience, and the crowd screamed and then chanted, "Make him sing!"

I was having my first dual ID crisis. The mask was slipping. On the outside I was clearly him. Even Wynton thought so. The audience was reacting to Brad, but inside I was becoming Tobey again. I wouldn't ever do karaoke, because I was so piss-poor at singing. Really bad. At this point I needed to erase Tobey. He didn't exist. Only Brad could exist. The plan would still work, and maybe work better, if Brad fucked up. It was not my fuck-up; I didn't exist here, only he did.

I took a good long swig of my beer. "Listen, y'all. I appreciate the sentiment, but trust me, you did not pay your hard-earned money to hear me sing. You really have to trust me on that."

"You ain't getting outta here that easy, brother." Wynton started up the band.

I didn't recognize the song, but then again, who gave a flying fuck? Brad would sing whatever he wanted to.

Wynton carried his mic over to me and put his arm around my shoulders. The band was doing a bouncy jazz tempo. He started singing, "I'm walkin' to N'awlins . . ."

I just repeated whatever he sang. He sang another line and I copied him again. As the lines kept coming, I started screeching as loud as I could. People laughed and cheered at first, but after a few minutes of my screeching, I could tell that Wynton had had enough. He had read the room and could tell the crowd's enthusiasm for Brad Pitt was waning.

Perfect.

"Okay, Brad, nothing personal, but stick to your day job, okay? I'll promise not to try and become a worldwide sex symbol. Everyone, Mr. Brad Pitt!"

I bowed and walked off backstage. Total fucking victory! In fact, if I wasn't such a pussy, I could have done even more damage. What if I wandered back up there uninvited? I could do that. Brad Pitt could wander on any stage he fucking wanted to. But first, I found a restroom backstage.

I locked the door and pulled a little packet of baby powder out of my pocket. I applied a few dabs on the tip of my nose and around my nostrils. Not too obvious? Yes, it should be obvious. I dabbed a little more.

Then I just waited.

Almost ten minutes later, there was a knock on the door. "Mr. Pitt, are you okay?"

I knew it! They were following my every move.

"I'm fine, just be a sec." I dabbed a spot of powder on a couple of fingers, put on the aviators, and I was good to go.

I burst out of the bathroom into the backstage area as a few of the club staff followed me. I watched their eyes carefully and a couple of them noticed the powder.

"I want to sing again, y'all!" I headed for the stage.

"Mr. Pitt, can you wait a second!"

I walked up behind the brass section and began swaying with the music. The percussionist gave a quick glance back at me, and his eyes opened wide as he noticed my "condition."

I started dancing a little more wildly and the audience plucked out their cell phones again. Wynton noticed the attention in the audience shift. He stopped playing his sax. I pointed at him and smiled. In the middle of the song, I ran up and gave him a big bear hug. "Let's dance!"

He was really perplexed. I could see it in his worried eyes. He couldn't just take Mr. Brad fucking Pitt off the stage, but the song had been ruined.

I started doing the bump with him. "Sexy time!"

Wynton gave the band a nod and they segued into "The Bump," a hideous disco song from the seventies. The audience went along and started clapping.

Wynton grabbed both of my hands with a big smile and danced me off to waiting bouncers. They held my arms as Wynton pulled the mic from me. "Mr. Brad Pitt, ladies and gentlemen, big supporter of New Orleans, liquor, and seventies disco!"

As the crowd applauded, the bouncer announced to me, "Mr. Pitt, I have your car coming around to the back entrance."

"But I don't want to go yet." Was he really going to throw Brad out of a club?

"Mr. Pitt, I can speak for everyone in this club, we are all grateful for your work down here, but I don't know what's with you tonight. You ain't behaving right, like I see you normally behave."

A lightning bolt of panic. Had I been outed? Had they figured it out? The Brad Juice stopped flowing. I mustered up a crinkled eye and tilted my head.

"Maybe you're just not feeling well." He reached up to my nose and wiped the powder onto his finger and showed it to me. "You know what I'm saying?"

I nodded at him while my heartbeat went back to normal.

Everything was still on course.

I followed him through a set of hallways packed full of people with VIP passes around their necks, all reaching out to shake my hand. I shook them all, some I slapped on the shoulder, a couple I rubbed their stomachs just for the fuck of it. We finally exited the back entrance in an alley with a couple of security guards but no car.

The bouncer yelled into a walkie-talkie for my car as the security guards walked over to meet Brad Pitt.

"Hey, Mr. Pitt, welcome to the Swamp Club! I'm Riley and this here is Otis. Can we get a picture with you?"

"Of course, fellas, be my pleasure." Riley was a big friendly side of beef. Otis was a little guy, and not as friendly as Riley. I could use a security guard like Riley tonight. Two birds, one stone? I grabbed his cell phone, put my arms around their necks, and took aim. I put my mouth close to Riley's ear. "Buddy, where can I get some really good pot? Anywhere close by?"

"Don't have any on me right now, but if you go about three blocks south toward the French Market, by the Dragon Club, there's a brother out front name of Clarence and he has some of the best shit, I promise. Tell him I sent you, okay?"

"Good shit?"

"The best, I promise."

I grabbed his hand. "You come with me then?"

"I'm at work right now, Mr. Pitt, I can't just take off."

"Call me Brad, buddy." I walked back to the bouncer at the door. "Hey, buddy, my friend Riley is gonna take a break, okay? Just a few minutes to help me out."

The bouncer pressed the talk button on the walkie-talkie. I wrapped my hand around his and stopped him. "It'll just be a minute." I pulled a hundred out of my pocket and stuffed it in his shirt pocket. "Thanks, buddy!"

I grabbed Riley around the shoulders and began walking down the alley.

"Umm, thanks . . . Brad, but don't you wanna wait for your car?"

"Too goddamned slow. Let's just walk it."

Riley began talking about how cool it was to meet me and how cool I was and how he was going to get the best pot, but I'd tuned out. I felt a strong surge of Brad back in my veins. I couldn't believe what I had just done. I performed on a stage as him. I made his friends believe I was him. I made those friends now believe he had a drug problem. I commandeered a security team with my face. I was walking around New Orleans and directing a drug buy just because I could. I had broken through to the other side. I could do any fucking thing I wanted to.

A few minutes later we were standing in front of the Dragon Club, and Riley ushered me around to the side of the building.

"Just hang here for a minute, Brad. I'm gonna fetch Clarence and in the meantime, I don't want no big crowds of women hollering around you until we finish the deal, okay?"

I gave him a thumbs-up, and Riley disappeared.

I stared at the New Orleans crescent moon above me. I never wanted this night to end. What a fucking life. Everybody did what I told them to do. Everyone wanted to be with me, everyone wanted to touch me, wanted part of me. I could disrupt a rare jazz concert, I could break the law, and they still wanted me. This was not real life.

But it could be.

Riley snuck around the building with a big grin on his face. He looked around and then beckoned someone. Out of the shadows, Clarence emerged.

"Ta-da!" Riley announced.

"Holy fuck! You were not shitting me!" Clarence, a small, compact young man, grabbed my hand and gave me a tribal handshake but didn't let go. "I am truly now the dealer to the stars. I am putting that on my business card!"

"I told you! And my friend Brad is ready to party."

"How do you do, Clarence." I built a Brad smile and clasped the top of his hand. "What do you have for me tonight?"

"Of course, Mr. Pitt, let's get to it." He pulled a slim leather fold from the back of his pants and opened it up. "Whatever you like in here, I can get you tonight. All these varieties are in stock. You tell me what you like and how much and you're good to go. This is all my top-shelf stuff, not the horse shit they sell over by Armstrong Park for tourists and college kids."

The case had about a dozen joints strapped in and rolled to perfection. Clarence pulled out the first one and ran it under my nose.

"Of course we have Hawaiian, this one is called Moon Beam. Very pungent and will keep you in euphoria for the night. Would you like to sample?"

I hesitated. This was off-plan. I didn't want to actually smoke just yet. I wanted to reek of it, get it on my clothes and my skin, but not smoke because I needed to remain in control of my senses to pull this off. I thought that maybe, when I was back in the hotel, I would smoke in the room and leave the stench in the suite before I checked out.

Clarence pulled out a lighter and put the joint in his mouth.

I should have just told him no. I would take it for later.

But what harm could one toke do?

I took the joint from Clarence and inhaled a deep, satisfying breath.

I exhaled and handed it off to Riley.

"That's the one," I announced.

"Good choice, Mr. Pitt, good choice. How much would you like?"

"I'd like ten joints rolled."

"That's it?" Clarence was taken aback. Clearly, he thought I would have been a bigger customer.

"All I need right now." I rolled off three hundreds. "That should more than cover it, no?" I was bluffing here. I had no idea how much pot cost. But who cared? I was Brad fucking Pitt.

Clarence pocketed the money. "I think that'll do it."

I shook Clarence's hand and took the ten joints. I gave five to Riley and grabbed his arm. "Let's get started."

"Brad, I got to get back to work," Riley explained as he tucked his joints away.

"Just a little bit longer." I gave him another couple hundreds. "Where's the strip clubs?"

"Hmm, you want the nice swanky kind, or you want the dark sleazy kind? The swanky kind are on Bourbon, which is probably packed to the gills right now, and we'll get mobbed before we even get near one, or there is a sleazy one a few blocks from here on the back end of some alley by Jackson Square."

Bourbon Street on a Friday night would be all the publicity I needed. But that kind of crowd could get out of hand. Maybe all I needed was someone's cell phone video of me in a sleazy strip club. This was a tough one. "What do you think, Riley?"

"Well, not that I would know, but I have heard from friends that the ladies are much nicer-looking on Bourbon Street, and most of what you get off-Bourbon are drugged-out hookers."

Riley obviously wanted the Bourbon Street club. But what better way to say fuck you to Brad Pitt than have him fool around with an ugly hooker. "Let's try the sleazy one first."

I texted my driver to come get us. "You hungry, Riley?"

"Could go for a po' boy about now. Best ones at Central Grocers. Friday night line out the door, but maybe not for Mr. Brad Pitt."

I winked at him. "Po' boys it is."

The limo found us and we hopped in the back. "Central Grocers, please." I slid the panel closed between the front and the back seat and pulled out a joint. This seemed like the ideal enclosed space to make myself reek. The one toke I had really hadn't done anything for me, so I felt pretty safe for another toke. I could get Riley to smoke the rest.

"You are hardcore, brother," Riley noted as he inhaled and handed it back.

"Finish it off, probably takes a lot more of it to fill you than me."

"I don't know about that, Brad. This stuff takes a while, but it packs a punch."

I registered a little blip of fear that I might lose control sooner rather than later. But it was too late to think about that, I was all in.

We pulled in front of Central Grocers and I saw a line winding around the corner to get in the place. "Ready to do your thing, Riley?"

"Ready. And hungry, too." He climbed out of the car and held the door for me. Some of the trapped smoke from the car escaped and voilà! We reeked!

People in line were staring back at me, some were waving and pointing. It was time to bring out Asshole Brad. I put on my aviators and ignored everyone. I leaned in to Riley. "Get me to the front of the line."

Riley grabbed my wrist and we cut to the entrance as he made space for me to pass through. I could see people were annoyed but not quite fighting annoyed. There was a family that we had to push past. The parents pulled the kids toward them with looks to kill on their faces. The mom sniffed at me very loudly.

But still, they moved. I ignored them.

Riley walked us to the end of the counter and approached the cashier. "Hi, I have Brad Pitt here and we'd like to get two classic po' boys and some Zapp's barbeque chips? The faster the better so we don't tie up your line with everyone trying to get a look at him."

The cashier looked up at me and I nodded at her. She covered her mouth in shock. I handed her a one-hundred-dollar bill. "Quickly, please?" I winked.

She headed back to a deli worker and gave him the order and then all of the workers looked up. Cell phones were now recording me, and it was about time for a nice show of Asshole Brad.

"Hey, y'all," I addressed the line inside the store. "Sorry to interrupt your meal, but I need one of these fuckers right now. I think you know what I'm saying, right?"

There was some polite laughter and then there was a "Fuck, yeah! Tell it, Brad!" from four college dudes down the line.

I was about to say something when it hit. It hit big time. Holy fuck, that was some powerful pot. I couldn't remember what I was going to say, but I wanted to move some stars in the sky something bad.

The cashier came over with our food and I reached out and kissed her hand. "You now have Brad Juice flowing through you."

The college boys in line laughed and high-fived each other. "Hey, I think my buddy here wants some of your Brad Juice, too!"

That was kind of funny. I opened the wrapping and took a big bite. Lots of meat, cheese, and bread and tons of olive oil. "Damn, you guys, this is some greasy shit, huh?"

Riley leaned in. "Maybe we should move on?"

Did I say that too loud? Was he noticing something bad happening? But that was good. Right?

"The oil is what makes it good, Brad!"

I looked up. I didn't know who said that. "It may make it good for you, but in about twenty minutes I'm gonna start farting like Hurricane Katrina and I *will* blow the top off of that damn superdome again!"

Dead silence. Were they going to hit me? Riley ushered me to the door, and the four college boys high-fived me on the way out.

Back in the limo, Riley warned me, "I think people are still touchy about Katrina."

"Well, whatever." I wasn't sure if I could steer this party anymore, but I knew we had to get to the ugly stripper joint. That was my plan. "Let's go see the skanky hooker strippers."

"You're the boss."

I leaned back and saw the sunroof above me. Time to move the stars. I stood up, opened the glass roof, and stuck my head out, but I couldn't see the sky. Cloudy night. Maybe I could move the clouds? I pointed at the clouds and tried my best to push them out of the way, but they wouldn't budge. I tried with my other hand, but that didn't work, either.

"Whatcha doing out there, Brad?"

I heard Riley's voice like an echo from a far-off valley. "Trying to move the fucking clouds. These fuckers are stubborn!"

We pulled up in front of the strip club, and Riley jumped out of the car.

I climbed out behind him. I looked up at the pink, red, and white neon sign in front of us: Al's Champagne Room.

"I love this."

Riley guided me through the entrance into a dark, padded, red-velvet vestibule. There was a weak yellow light over a booth with a half-naked woman behind a cash register. She was also dark, and I couldn't focus on her, but I saw two big pink nipples.

Riley explained who I was and that we needed a VIP section. But I could not take my eyes off the nipples. They were staring back at me.

"Mr. Pitt?" I looked up and saw a smile. "I'm up here, that's right. Come with me."

We followed her through a set of velvet curtains and into a huge room that was lit a little better. There was a central stage with a pole where a very skinny naked woman was sitting. Her legs were splayed open while a customer tried to fit some cash inside of her.

"Isn't that gonna hurt?"

All the heads scattered across the audience turned toward me. Oops, I was too loud again.

We were seated in a section behind a red velvet rope right next to the stage. The nipples woman wanted to know what we were drinking.

"Champagne," I declared for no reason I could think of other than I saw it on the neon sign outside.

Nipples told me "right away" and gave my crotch a nice long grab before she left.

That was kind of horrifying. But it felt really good. I wanted more of that.

Nipples was back with an ice bucket of champagne and some glasses. And some more strippers. They settled on each side of me. They were both wearing nothing but thongs and together they poured the champagne for me and Riley. All the eyes in the room had moved from the stage to me. I waited for the cell phones to appear.

I raised my glass. "To Brad motherfucking Pitt! That son of a bitch!"

The stripper on my left dug one hand into my waistband while the other hand caressed my crotch. Stripper number two, who was missing a tooth, which was freaking me out, massaged my chest.

The hands on my body felt good, but no one was recording it. WTF?

Missing-tooth stripper got up from our sofa and closed some velvet drapes around our section, and I felt a hand unzip my pants.

Shit. I needed everyone to see this. I pulled the hand off of my crotch, grabbed the bottle of champagne, and left the VIP section. I needed to be on that stage.

I climbed up on the stage with the top of my pants still undone and started gyrating next to the dancer. Damn, she was really skinny and had really tiny breasts. How did she get hired?

Finally, I saw a cell phone in the audience. I grabbed skinny hooker's hand and shoved it down my pants. "About time!"

A few seconds later a security guard jumped out of the shadows and snatched the phone out of the man's hand.

"Hey! What happened?" I yelled at him.

The security guard approached the stage. "Don't worry, Mr. Pitt, no cell phone recording allowed in here."

"No! Gimme his phone!"

The guard was taken aback. "What?"

"Give me his phone! You will give Brad Pitt his phone!"

Riley stumbled out of the VIP section without his shirt, zipping up his pants. "What's going on, Brad?"

The security guard started to sweat. "Some guy was trying to take a video of him on stage, so I grabbed the phone away and now he wants it."

Riley motioned the guard for the phone.

"Wait a minute!" A big guy approached in a T-shirt that probably fit him about fifty pounds ago and tattoos that covered most of his arms and neck. "I'll delete any footage, but please don't fuck with my phone."

Riley looked through the phone. "Ain't nothing there, Brad."

"Give it back to tattoo guy, Riley."

"You sure, Brad? Maybe when we leave?"

"Give it to him now."

Tattoo guy collected the phone from Riley. "Thanks, Mr. Pitt, I'm sorry about that—"

"Press the record button." I was going to get my footage out of this place.

Everyone was now staring at me. Tattoo guy looked baffled.

"Press it! I am Brad fucking Pitt and I order you to record this."

"Umm, okay."

I unzipped my pants and pushed the skinny stripper's hand in my underwear. I crossed my arms and leaned against the pole and stared at the camera.

The club was silent.

I hit Skinny's elbow and she moved her hand around in my underpants.

"You got that?"

Tattoo guy gave me a thumbs-up.

"Okay. Thanks. Riley, I think I need some more pot. Let's get going."

8

I was dancing. I was dancing in a small club. I was dancing in a big club. I was dancing with every woman in every club. I was dancing in the middle of Jackson Square with beggars and strange tourists. I was moving the clouds out of the dark sky so I could see the stars! I looked up at the imposing shadow of the church at the base of Jackson Square and I put one hand behind my back and bent my knees in a position so I was ready to duel. I pulled out my other hand and pointed it straight at the church bell and pushed! The bell was ringing and ringing. The ringing was so loud that it woke up the whole town.

The ringing woke me up. I opened my eyes, and I was drowning in Ritz-Carlton linen. The ringing didn't stop, and I was trying to adjust to the bright light coming in through the windows. The ringing was coming from my phone on the side table, and I grabbed it.

"What?"

"Mr. Smith? Sorry to bother you, but you asked me to be ready by two o'clock and it's two-thirty."

"What? Fuck." Two-thirty? I needed to go. Fast. "Okay, give me thirty minutes." I hung up and fumbled my way out of the bed and tried to remember what I had to do. I couldn't think from the combination of panic and pot hangover. I had to check out.

Had word gotten out yet? If it did, then Brad could still catch me in the room and shit would hit the fan. He could have the police there any second. Shit shit shit. I should have been out of there earlier, like four a.m. I left myself open. Fuck.

I dialed Charles while gathering my clothes.

"Mr. Pitt? How are you today?"

"I'd like to check out, and I'll put this one on my account after all, okay?"

I held my breath and waited to see if he'd scream, "Imposter!"

"Of course, I'll be right up for you to sign off. Also, a word of caution."

I was sweating again. A word of caution? Like, we have the police in the lobby?

"All of our entrances are covered with paparazzi, so if you want to avoid them, I can smuggle you out of the employee entrance of the building next door. Would you prefer that?"

Wow. Did all that footage get out already? "Yes, yes, let's do that." I was ready to hang up, but he kept talking.

"Also, Mr. Pitt, I might suggest that we arrange for a taxi instead of your limo? The photographers have the limo trapped."

I thought for a second. "Good. Let's do that." I hung up. Fuck, I was not in Brad voice.

I was a fucking mess. *Get your shit together and become him again.*

I walked slowly and deliberately around the bedroom and began folding my clothes to maintain control.

My hat, my shirt, my jacket, and my aviators from last night were missing. I started sweating again. The doorbell for the suite rang. I stuffed everything into my suitcase and threw a shirt on.

I ran to the door to see Charles with a clipboard. He sniffed and hesitated. I still reeked of pot. I didn't have time to shower or clean up. I didn't care, I just had to get the fuck out of Dodge.

"Mr. Pitt, I have everything ready for you to check out." He handed me a pen and his clipboard.

I looked at the bottom of the paper on the clipboard. Total $7,859.00. That was petty cash for Brad. I grabbed the pen; I knew what his signature looked like. I'd done an autograph here and there, but I had never signed a bill as him. I was crossing over into felony territory now. But there was no choice, I had to go now. I signed off and reached into my pocket for cash. I only had three hundred dollars left. And a big messy wad of singles? Fuck. I started off with three thousand dollars, so what the fuck did I do last night? I didn't have time to think. I handed Charles one hundred dollars. "Thanks, Charles, let's get me gone."

∞

At five a.m. the next day, I pulled into the parking structure for the Hilton at the Chicago convention center. I was beat and way behind schedule.

For the life of me, I could not remember anything that happened after the strip club. The fifteen-hour drive home did nothing to clear up my memory. I remembered smoking another joint in the limo with Riley and then it all went very vague. I was pretty sure I was dancing in a club and I was pretty sure I was in Jackson Square, but that was about it.

In my hotel room, I did a quick Google search on my phone. Nada. That would be fucked if none of this was reported. Very fucked.

Would I have to do this again? On the one hand, that was a lot of fucking work, and I wasn't sure I could pull it together again. On the other hand, I could plan better. My heart beat a little faster. Another night as him. I would be fucking awesome.

∞

On Monday morning I was back at work in my office and feeling pretty optimistic. I saw a review online for the Marsalis concert in the local New Orleans paper, and the first two paragraphs were all about Brad's interruption. *Yes!*

I couldn't stay focused on work. I kept checking the internet every so often for any mentions of my weekend.

About nine-thirty a.m. I hit the jackpot:

Hollywood Insider: Brad Pitt's wild weekend bender! Watch the footage of Brad Pitt's wild, drug-fueled weekend in New Orleans! Warning, some footage may not be safe for work.

Holy fuck, they had the footage from the concert, and it was him. I could not see any trace of me. There was no doubt, that was Brad fucking Pitt. I did it! I fucking did it. More footage from the sandwich shop. Me and Riley coming out of the limo with smoke pouring out of the door! Me—or I should say Brad—making a fart joke about Katrina. Yes! The voice was really good. They got the stripper footage! Damn, that skank was really going for it in my underwear.

Wait, I was at another strip club? There was some footage of me dancing between two strippers at another club. One of the strippers was wearing my shirt and hat and there were tons of people in this club cheering me on. I dropped my pants and mooned the audience? Fuck, what did I do? People stuffed dollar bills into my underwear. Ah, the singles in my pocket.

The final clip was me in Jackson Square in the middle of the night climbing up the statue of Andrew Jackson and riding his horse with him. Oh, shit, I humped Andrew Jackson! My hand was pointed toward the church bell. I knew what that meant. Genius. Fucking genius.

I did another search and now it was everywhere. I checked on CNN.com. Front and center. I scrolled down the article to the bottom: "Mr. Pitt has not responded to any of our calls yet."

Well, CNN, that's because he was shitting his pants. I figured he was rethinking that fucking lawsuit. *Should I contact him?* No. I would just let this stand as my message. If I didn't hear anything back from him, maybe I would strike again, just to make my point.

I had to tear myself away from reading all the coverage to go into some meetings. My head was spinning, and I was walking on air. The coverage was more than I could have hoped for. *Checkmate, asshole!*

About noon, I was back at my desk and trying to decide whether to ditch my brown bag lunch or celebrate by going for some deep-dish pizza around the corner. Reception buzzed my desk.

"Tobey? I have a delivery here for you."

"What is it?"

"A manila envelope from a Mr. Caswell."

"Can you send it back to me right away?"

"Will do."

Maybe a letter dropping the lawsuit? Or maybe a settlement of sorts? Who knew, but Brad sure reacted quickly, so I guessed I had his attention.

The office mail guy delivered the envelope, and it was definitely not a contract. There was an object inside. I ripped it open and found a cheap cell phone inside with a Post-it note on top that said "4 p.m."

Fuck. He wanted to talk?

The rest of the day until four p.m. was a blur. I was barely there, as my mind kept wandering to the call. Would it be him or Ted calling? I didn't want to talk to Ted. I had the upper hand. I was pretty sure they would cancel the lawsuit, but maybe they wanted something else? Should I ask for a settlement? Or at least some sort of guarantee that he wouldn't sue me again? Caswell probably wanted something from me, but I was the one with the leverage. He was in no position to make any demands.

At 3:55 p.m. I locked my office door and stared at the phone. At this point I couldn't even pretend to do any more work. At 4:01 p.m. the phone rang, and I picked it up on the third ring to pretend to be cool about it.

"Buddy! Whoa, you fucking nailed it!"

It was him. Now I was paranoid again. Maybe he was recording this? Trying to get me on record?

"And you got my voice! I have to give you credit, you really are paying attention. You fooled all of my friends. Seriously, they all think I went out on a bender and I'm getting all kinds of calls of concern. Even Angie was not quite sure, and I was with her all weekend!"

I was still silent. If he was recording this, I couldn't say anything. But he sounded so enthused, almost happy.

"You there? Ah, listen, I am not recording this. Seriously, without me warning you of me recording this and you agreeing, this could never be evidence, so no worries. I'll even say something that I don't want recorded for evidence: you were brilliant, absolutely fucking brilliant."

I exhaled. "Why did you sue me?"

"Because, buddy, I needed some pull with you. I was never serious about that, but I wanted to keep your attention."

Sophie was right on the money. "So you had a fucking deputy with a fucking dog serve me papers in my office? Do you know what kind of shit you put me through?"

"I guess I do now. I mean, most of the world thinks I'm a drug-addled asshole now, so I guess we're even."

"Even?"

"Tobey, it felt good, didn't it? I mean, from what I can see you were having the time of your life. That's a thrill ride you won't be able to ride again."

He waited for me to respond, but I couldn't. If I nailed him this weekend, he had me nailed now. An overwhelming sadness enveloped me. A truth staring at me that I wouldn't stare back at. He was right. This was the most thrilling weekend of my life and it would never happen again. I would never live like this again.

"You want it, don't you? I know you. Because you *are* me. I *am* you. This is not a coincidence. The chromosomes, the genes, the science that wound up putting two people on earth in the exact same mold at the same time? Why would it just be on the outside? You can't ignore this, Tobey. I want to celebrate you, celebrate us."

"Celebrate? What do you mean?"

"Join me. After seeing you in action, I'm more convinced than ever that this is where you and I need to be. I really think that you want this, too. I'm not talking about a simple body double; we will be partners. You and I together will be this one big thing that the world sees as Brad Pitt. But you have to want it bad enough."

I felt a fear whip through me that uprooted my entire being. I was afraid of him being right. "What do you want me to do?"

"I think you know what you need to do. I think if you think about this, you will not have a problem knowing what you need to do."

"Sophie."

"You need to convince her or . . ."

Or leave her. "This is a lot . . ."

"It is. But this is where I can't help you anymore. Look, I'm willing to take it on the chin for this weekend. I'm willing to call and make apologies and pay the bills you ran up. No problem. You know why? Because it showed me how really powerful you are, and how great we could be. But I have some limits."

"What limits?"

"If you can't . . . close the deal, I have to move on. It's going to be painful for both of us, am I right? I think you feel that. On a practical note, if you do this again, without me, it will harm us both. We have to be on the same page. Look, I could have shut you down pretty easily this weekend, but I didn't, because I wanted to let you see what we could be.

"When did you know? I was really careful."

"Probably by the time you were getting that handjob from the skinny stripper. Wynton called Angie between sets and asked if I was okay, told her everything he saw you do. Saw me do. So from that moment on, I was following your antics on Facebook and Twitter. Also, the business office at the Ritz put a hold on my business card for about ten thousand dollars, probably when you checked in. So you see, if we do this separately it won't work anymore."

He was right. I couldn't be him anymore. Not without him.

"I'll give you a few days. I know it's not an easy thing. I hope you can do this, buddy."

The phone line went dead.

I hung up, made excuses at work, and headed for home. Sophie wasn't there. I sat in the living room and tried to think clearly. Since Brad had hung up, my brain was in overdrive to work out a strategy. I had come to a couple of conclusions.

I wanted this. I wanted this really bad, but it also scared me. Moth and flame. Somewhere in the back of my mind I knew I was going to be burned, but that didn't bother me enough to put the brakes on it.

All of my former girlfriends had become infatuated with Brad. None of them really saw me behind his face. I now saw that as part of my addiction. A way of extending my Brad moments by having my partner think I was him.

Sophie had taken me by surprise. She saw me. She got me, despite the looks. Even though I had had relationships with plenty of women, I considered Sophie my first real relationship. She didn't give a fuck what I looked like.

I couldn't give her up.

The fucked part? Did she really know me? I had hidden this piece of me from her so carefully because I knew it would scare her away.

The more I ran toward Brad, the less I existed.

I didn't want to lose Sophie; she was the only way I had of hanging on to me. But I didn't really have the guts to tell her I was not who she thought I was. At least, not now.

∞

Sophie arrived home from work with some groceries and a defiant smile across her face.

"I think I figured it out." She sat next to me, pulled the *National Enquirer* out of a grocery bag, and slapped it on my lap.

I glanced at the front page: a picture of me with two strippers.

BRAD HITS THE PITTS!!! DRUGS!! PROSTITUTES!!!! SEX!!! ALL HERE!!!

Sweat beaded on my forehead. She had figured out it was me.

"I saw this in line at the checkout counter. I felt like such a housewife grabbing it and putting it with my stuff, but look at it!" Sophie opened it up to the centerfold story.

Pictures of me mooning a crowd, me getting felt up by strippers. Sheesh, could she see me that clearly?

"Do you get it?" She looked at me very pointedly.

Was this the end of us?

"He wants you to cover for him so he can do drugs and fuck hookers!"

Exhale. I picked up the paper and pretended to read it. Wow, even Sophie couldn't tell it was me.

"What a fucking scumbag. All that absolute bullshit about him being able to spend more time with the kids and the family and go to the fucking grocery store or whatever. Asshole. I knew he was a creep. And his wife is in on it! She doesn't give a fuck, either!"

"Unbelievable" was all I could manage.

"This," Sophie pointedly slapped the centerfold with the back of her hand, knocking it out of my grip. "Being able to act like this is worth how much money? I can't imagine what it's like to . . . have that mindset. To control two human lives so he can go out and fuck around? I can't even. We can't let this creep bully us. We just can't."

"Wow." The wow was very real. I realized that it was me who had produced the pictures that provoked the outrage that Sophie was displaying, that had trapped me between two worlds. Brad's phone call faded way back in my brain, locked in the space where my addiction hid.

9

In the ensuing days, I did nothing. I couldn't bring myself to tell Sophie, the love of my life, that Brad Pitt wasn't the only creep. It wasn't him, it was me. I had thought about reaching out to Brad, but what would be the point? He would only urge me to make the move now. But I couldn't.

I made a decision by not making one. I had figured that Brad would contact me and I would hash it out with him. Or maybe not. I would be in the same place again, feeling the undertow of being Brad and figuring a way to undercut my life with Sophie.

I began the process of putting my inner Brad away, squeezing it back into a coffin and hoping that it would just die.

The Brad phone rang Thursday afternoon. I reached for it, but I couldn't make myself pick up. I had nothing to say. I couldn't reconcile the two worlds I lived in.

In retrospect, it was a big mistake not to take that call.

A big fucking mistake.

On Friday morning I walked into the office, and Zoey, our receptionist, looked up at me and immediately became angry.

"How the fuck could you even show up?"

"What?" I was blindsided.

"I can't even look at you." She quickly unplugged her headset and ran into the break room.

As I walked into the office all eyes were on me. Something was really wrong. Really, really wrong. Instinct told me it was Bradrelated.

My boss, the CEO, and a security guard were standing in front of my office.

"Tobey," the CEO addressed me in a low formal tone, "can you come with us to HR, please."

I followed them down the hall into the HR office. There was a table laid out with papers. The director of HR and our legal counsel were seated on one side. I was sweating like a pig.

"Tobey, would you please have a seat." The director pointed to a chair with a folder laid out in front of it.

I slowly sat down.

The company's lawyer, a woman whom I had always thought of as smart, as a good co-worker, started the conversation. "Tobey, this morning I received four complaints from women in the office about being sexually harassed by you. As legal counsel for the firm, I have to address this immediately as dictated by our company bylaws and by the State of Illinois."

"What?" I could barely cough out any words. But I knew he had done something.

"The women who have come forward shared with me pornographic text messages and images that they received from you last night. Under our bylaws and state laws, because of the evidence presented to me, I have advised the company to terminate your employment, effective immediately, and I would advise you to seek immediate legal counsel."

"But I didn't send anything."

The director opened the folder in front of me. Inside were nude pictures of him. Pictures of him waving his dick, with texts that said, *"I know you have wanted this for a while."* More dick pics with texts:

"We can meet late tonight."

"I want this inside of you."

I felt lightheaded. All of the photos were taken here in the office. He was wearing my clothes. He was jerking off on office furniture, on the desks and chairs of the women who got the photos.

"This isn't me. These are not my pictures. That's not even my . . ."

The legal counsel interrupted me. "Tobey. This is now a legal matter, a very serious legal matter. We cannot have contact with you other than through counsel."

How did he do this? "This is *not* me."

"We also have to escort you off the premises."

My boss and the security guard walked me through the hallway as the whole office stopped what they were doing to watch. When we approached the exit, I looked at my boss. "You know me. I swear to God this is not me. I did not do this."

"Tobey." My boss glanced around to see if anyone was watching us. "I'm not supposed to talk to you, but I like you, so let me just give you some advice. Get your shit together. You've been kind of phoning it in the last couple of weeks, so something is going on. And maybe it's with that ex who served you papers or maybe you have some kind of substance problem, but get it together. You need to get some help. Be a shame to see your life turn to shit, that's all I can say."

"Please," I was pleading, "did you check the security cameras for who actually entered the building and did this? It could not have been me."

"We did. The cameras show you entering the building last night, with your company ID, and then going into the office and doing . . . Look, that's all I can say. Goodbye, Tobey."

I exited the office building and walked around downtown Chicago for hours in a daze as it settled on me what he had done. It must have been the weekend with him. Somehow he got a copy of all of my IDs in my wallet. All of my phone contacts. Did he do that after I passed out from the pot? There was no other way this could have happened. He was even wearing the suit I wore on the plane down there. Had he been planning on doing this since we first met?

I went home and pulled out the Brad phone. No answer.

I sat in the apartment, staring at the walls. How did my life turn to shit so quickly?

Sophie came home and found me sitting on the couch in complete darkness.

“Tobey? What’s wrong?”

She was all that I had left in my life. Would she go, too? I pulled out the folder and put it on the coffee table. “I got fired this morning.”

She glanced at the folder. “What happened?”

“It’s all in the folder.”

She picked up the folder and slowly leafed through the pictures. “Oh my god. Oh my god. He did this, didn’t he?”

I nodded.

“Holy shit, he’s a fucking psychopath! Tobey, you have to call the police. You have to call them right now!”

I shook my head.

“Why not?” She sat down next to me and touched my arm.

I lost it. Her touch, the simple and beautiful act of concern from someone who loved me. Who believed in me. I didn’t deserve it. A tear popped out and then another and I couldn’t stop crying. I was crying because someone like her loved me and because I was not an innocent victim. If he was a psychopath, then I was, too. The same genes, the same chromosomes.

She cradled me like a baby. “We’ll figure this out, don’t worry.”

“It’s no good. Do I call the police and say Brad Pitt is stalking me? That it was the movie star Brad Pitt who walked into the office wearing my clothes and jacked off on the furniture to get back at me? Then I tell them this story about him trying to get me to work for him for millions of dollars? Yeah, the police will be all over it, I'm sure."

"I don't care if they believe it or not. Something has to be done. I'm sure somewhere there is a record of him coming to Chicago. We will push this until the truth comes out. We have no choice."

We hugged for a good, long time.

But I had already figured it out. We had a choice. And I made that choice.

10

The choice. Sitting in prison for the past couple of years has given me time to reflect on my choices. Wasn't that the purpose of prison? Of all the choices I had, the one I should have made was the one I was never going to make. I should have broken up with Sophie and surrendered to Brad. I should have done it immediately after the weekend with Brad. Or I should have done it after the phone call with Brad. Or after getting fired. There would have been pain, but in the end everyone would have been happier.

During my trial, my lawyer got really upset at me for something, I can't remember what, but I remember him staring at me and saying, "I don't understand you. You look like a movie star, you're smart, you had a good career, you had all these choices that people don't have!" I walked out of his office immediately. Addicts don't have those choices.

And how to explain the need to be Brad Pitt? How to explain that I was one head of a two-headed monster?

I couldn't explain it when I began planning his destruction. I thought of it as a kamikaze mission to end my need to be him by destroying him.

The planning of this one was bittersweet. I knew it would be the last time I would ever do this, so it had to be worth it.

Then I struck gold. I had found it. The perfect place to commit the crime. On live TV.

The annual Met Gala in New York. The biggest stars in the

universe turned out for this one, and the red carpet event was broadcast live. Brad was not on the list of stars attending, but who would turn him down if he showed up on the red carpet? Anna Wintour, the editor of Vogue, held the annual event to raise money for charity. Stars contributed ungodly sums of money to get on the guest list. Supposedly she was a major control freak about who showed up and how they dressed. What would happen if Brad pissed her off? On live TV? Without even donating any money?

I became a heat-seeking missile aimed squarely at this red carpet. The Brad Juice was flowing.

I told Sophie I was going to Milwaukee to see my folks and try to explain to them what was going on.

"That's probably a good idea," Sophie replied. "Do you want me to come? They may have an easier time accepting this if the both of us are there."

"Thanks, but I think I'll be okay."

I still haven't explained it to my folks.

This trip was different from the New Orleans trip. I was not trying to pass as him. I was already him. No more tests. Just get it done.

Since I spent most of my savings on the New Orleans trip, I had to put this trip on my credit cards and not try to fake my way into a hotel room. I didn't know how I was going to pay for it when the bills came due, but as the kids say, I no longer had any fucks to give. In New York, Brad could stay anywhere. The only concession I would make was a limo. He needed to show up at that red carpet in a limo.

And what to wear? I didn't think I would be wearing a tux. A tux wouldn't grab enough attention. Even with Brad Pitt in it.

I flew into New York the day before the gala. I was staying at a nice anonymous Marriott on the Upper East Side in my own name. After the New Orleans experience, I had learned a lesson: do not associate with anyone or anything that has easy access to him. I would be Tobey until the last minute.

As soon as I was unpacked, I grabbed a cab and headed for The Nasty Pig, "Where America Shops for Fetish Wear!"

Time to get something to wear for the gala.

I expected to walk into a store that looked like a combination Halloween superstore and a dungeon, but instead it looked more like The Gap with slings instead of jeans. I was greeted by a young man with the requisite piercings, earrings, and mohawk. He was wearing a full black leather apron and not much else.

"Welcome to The Nasty Pig, I'm Colin. Any fetish in particular today?"

Hmm, not sure what fetish I was looking for. "I'm looking for something that's . . . bold. Something that may raise eyebrows at a formal party."

He looked at me carefully. "You know, you look just like—"

"I know, I know. I hear that a lot."

"It's really uncanny."

"What would you suggest?" I drove the conversation away from Brad.

"Okay, then, if you're really not Brad Pitt, I would suggest some of the newest in our classic line of leather wear. Let me show you what we've got. What kind of formal party? Like a wedding? I had one the other week and we had all of the groomsmen in a whole white leather gladiator thing, so that may not be as shocking as you'd think."

"A big formal charity event."

He looked at me slyly. "The Met Gala, perhaps?"

He caught me off guard. How would he know?

"I'm kidding. This week every queen in the city is trying to get into that thing. I think we'll take a look at some basic black, but for shocking, maybe we go with chaps and perhaps a nice pull-off pouch for the package. Would you like to follow me?"

I spent a couple of hours trying on the latest in leather wear, and Colin helped me decide on what to buy. A good part of that time was spent keeping him out of my dressing room. The total came to nearly twelve hundred dollars. I maxed out yet another credit card.

Colin finished the transaction and handed me a receipt and an invitation. "After you're finished at the Met Gala or whatever, Mr. Not Brad Pitt, you should saunter over to the Spunk Factory in Brooklyn. It's an invitation-only event and you will already be dressed perfectly. Although, even without an invite, I'm pretty sure they'd let you in."

∞

Red carpets were big complicated productions, but I had done my homework. Even Brad Pitt couldn't just get out of his car and land on the carpet. There are a host of checkpoints and check-ins, publicists, not to mention security, before you get in front of the cameras. Everything is timed to get celebrities the most exposure. A-List stars like Brad usually get the best timing and the most exposure, but it all had to be scheduled. My challenge was to do an end run around all the procedures and get in front of the cameras as soon as possible. If I showed up and had to wait or get stopped for any reason, that left me open to getting busted. A million things could go wrong. Someone could alert Brad or Angie at any time while I was there. I had to get in there quick and get out. If Brad heard that I was there, there would be a million ways he could shut me down. I had seen how much damage Brad could do in just a few minutes.

Saturday evening, close to launch time. I had my outfit on and a big flowing black cape to cover it all until the big reveal for the master of the red carpet, Ryan Seacrest. The problem? I was not feeling the Brad Juice in my veins. I was still nervous Tobey, thinking about all the fuck-ups that could happen. He knew so many people on that red carpet, he could easily call someone and say, "That's not me, stop him." I was also feeling sheepish about my fashion reveal. This was not something I would ever wear. In order for me to do this I had to become him. I needed to loosen up, forget about boundaries. I called room service and ordered a bottle of vodka and some mixers.

I turned on the TV and the coverage had started on *E!* Ryan Seacrest was already on the carpet interviewing the D-list crowd who had to show up early to make way for the bigger fish. I think he was talking to one of those crazy women from his housewives show, namedropping designers left and right. Tonight was all about how to outshine the rest. The gowns were so expensive that there were only a few people on the carpet who could actually afford them, the rest were all loaners.

The men typically showed up in the latest tuxes, or some of the rock stars made a statement and showed up in something funky. I was pretty sure my outfit would be a first for this red carpet. If I could do this.

Fuck that. No more doubts. This had to be my best Brad ever.

I finished off my drink and took the bottle down to the limo with me. In the lobby of the hotel I got some stares, but I didn't think that it was Brad getting the looks, I thought it was the cape.

The closer I got to the Met, the more nervous I became, so I downed another drink. When I was close enough, I asked my driver to just idle by the line of limos. I watched the operation carefully, trying to figure out a way to get past all the red tape. There was a red carpet laid out in front of the Met one hundred feet long where the stars posed against a backdrop to show off their clothes. After the posing, a handler guided them to press booths, like *Entertainment Tonight* and *Access Hollywood*, and kept them moving in succession. After the press booths, the carpet took a sharp right up the stairs to the building where all of the paparazzi and Ryan Seacrest waited.

A pregnant Kardashian climbed out of the limo in front of me. She had a few handlers, and it looked like they summoned someone from the carpet who darted over with a walkie-talkie and a clipboard. I watched as she stopped and talked to the press.

The vodka was settling in, but I was still not ready. I could not be Tobey. I must become him. A very fucked-up him. One more drink should do the trick.

The limo in back of us was blaring their horn. My driver stuck his hand out to get them to pass, but the driver kept blasting the horn.

A minute later someone was knocking frantically on my window.

A woman with crazy-colored hair. I knew the face; I thought she was a singer. I lowered my window.

"I just needed to see who's making me walk extra-long around your car in these heels because you won't move your ass! But since it's you, I guess it's okay."

"Miley Cyrus! Right? I'm Brad Pitt."

"I know you're Brad Pitt, everyone knows you're Brad Pitt. Now can you move your fucking car?"

In a split second I saw an opportunity. She was my ticket. Time to move. "Let me help you get down there, sweetheart."

I climbed out of the car and grabbed her arm. "I can also carry you, if your feet hurt."

"Oh, shit, do I want Brad Pitt to carry me onto the carpet? In that big fucking cape? You better believe I do."

For a second, I wondered if I could actually do it, since I was a little schnockered, but when I picked her up, she was so light, I could have probably tossed her over the Met.

As soon as we emerged from the limos and headed toward the gala, the feeding frenzy began.

Ready or not, show time.

At the entrance to the carpet, a handler rushed over with her clipboard and her walkie-talkie. A security guard stood next to her, looking us both over. "Hi, guys, you both look absolutely stunning! I'll get you going in a few seconds. Miley, when you get to the top of the stairs, a gentleman in black with your name card will escort you to your table. And Brad, I must have a bad list, because I don't have your name on it, so I'll get someone to update me if you wait a minute."

Miley kicked her legs up and leaned in for a smooch on the cheek for the cameras. Ah, the distinct aroma of Hawaiian pot on her breath. "You don't have Brad Pitt's name on your list? Oh my god, well he can come sit with me."

I pushed past the photographers and the security guard, carrying Miley onto the carpet as the handler spoke loudly and quickly into her walkie-talkie.

"Let's get this party started!" I set Miley down on the ground so she could display her gown to the press. The world had tilted a little bit. All of the press were leaving their booths and scrambled down to this end of the carpet. They screamed questions at me about what happened in New Orleans.

"Just letting off a little steam is all," I yelled back in his voice. Brad was here.

"Brad, do you have a few minutes for *Entertainment Tonight*?"

"Brad, how about some time for *TMZ*?"

I waved them all off. I was breaking protocol. I skipped the press and went around the handler, cutting ahead to the stairs. I saw handlers along the carpet whispering into their walkie-talkies. I needed to get to Ryan Seacrest. That was all I cared about.

"Wait up, big boy." Miley jogged after me. "I don't know what you're doing, but as long as you're doing it, you need to carry me up those stairs."

I thought about it for a second. Why not? I grabbed her again, but this time I threw her over my shoulder as she screamed.

I saw Ryan interviewing someone at the top of the stairs. He noticed the commotion below, grabbed his earpiece, and gave his guest the wait signal.

I slowly climbed up with Miley screaming on my shoulder and more cameras than I had ever seen in my Brad career. I stopped every few steps and gave Miley a pat on the butt for the press. When I made it to the top, Ryan had gotten rid of his previous guest and was waiting for me.

"Ladies and gentlemen, Mr. Brad Pitt and Miley Cyrus have just made a rather grand entrance. Brad and Miley, can we chat for a few minutes?"

I put Miley down in front of Ryan as she squealed, "Be careful with the dress!"

"Wow, what a surprise! I wasn't expecting you today, Brad, and least of all with Miley Cyrus."

"Well, honestly, I just picked her up in the parking lot."

"Miley, you look stunning in that gown; can you tell us who you are wearing?"

"Well, it's a Valentino, from his couture line, and you can tell how good this stuff is because it just survived that walk with him."

Ryan turned his gaze to me, and I heard chatter coming from his earpiece.

"I really dig the cape, Brad, can you tell us what you're wearing underneath?"

"Well, not much." Brad's voice was firmly in place. I really needed to pee. Shit. Ryan suddenly looked more nervous than

I did a few hours ago. His eyes were darting between my body, his off-camera director, and Miley.

"Well, what does that mean?"

"It means, not too much." I untied the string at my collar and let the cape go. It slid off of my shoulders effortlessly and settled on the stairs. I literally heard the crowd gasp and became aware of some commotion behind me. I picked my arms up and did a 360 for the camera. A leather harness showed my chest off with a shiny nipple clamp in place, but the real kicker was the assless leather chaps that Colin had picked out. "From the couture line of The Nasty Pig."

Miley put her hands to her mouth and stifled a scream. Ryan was staring at my body, speechless.

Miley gave my bare ass a little spank.

I turned around and presented my bare ass to Ryan. "Wanna take a slap?"

I was giving a big Brad smile for the cameras. But I also expected my ass to be sunburned from all of the flashbulbs currently pointed at it. None of that mattered. I felt like I had become the center of the universe. Every eyeball was on me, everyone wanted to be me. I got Brad. I felt like I had finally cracked him and understood why he became a star. He wanted this attention, he loved it as much as I did. This was what he wanted to share with me. I soaked it all in like the last few rays of sunshine before an Arctic winter.

Ryan finally caught his composure. "So what inspired this look tonight?"

"Actually, it was because I didn't think a gown would work." As I was talking, I noticed that Anna Wintour was now visible. She was with a couple of security guards in black about sixty feet away at the entrance to the gala. It looked to me like she wanted to have some words. I had to start thinking about an escape plan. And also, I really had to pee badly now.

I waved Ryan off as the crowd catcalled me. I was approaching the entrance to the Met, surrounded by people and velvet ropes on either side of me. Would they even let me in to pee? Should I just tell her I wasn't here for the gala?

I saw a line of potted bamboo against a wall. Yep. This would do. I gave Anna Wintour a "wait a minute" sign and unsnapped the leather pouch that held my "package."

I peed the pee of kings and relieved myself in the bamboo.

The men in black didn't know whether to rush me or watch Brad Pitt urinate. Even though I was no longer in direct eyesight of the cameras, I could see they were trying to get past the velvet ropes and security to get a picture.

Anna Wintour turned around and left.

While I was peeing, I pulled out my cell phone and called my driver. "I need you to be out front in a few minutes."

I gave it a good shake when I was done and smiled for the shocked people around me. "Just a little Brad Juice!"

The only way out was back down the stairs. I turned around and headed toward Ryan, who stopped talking to Tom Cruise and his wife and announced that Brad Pitt was now walking the wrong way.

The photographers were going crazy again. One of the red carpet handlers tried to point me back up the stairs, so I put my arm around his shoulders and took him with me. "Left my ticket in the car, buddy."

I got a text from my driver that he was ready to go, main entrance. At the bottom of the stairs was a wall of people, and I couldn't see a way through. I had to get out any way I could. By now, Brad could have had enough time to call the police.

I turned to my kidnapped handler. "You have a walkie-talkie?"

He held it up.

"Can you ask for security to clear a path to my car?"

"I'm not sure I'm allowed . . ."

Poor kid was really confused. Clearly, celebrity fuckery was not something they had briefed him on. I grabbed his walkie-talkie. "Hey, whoever is in charge of security, this is Mr. Brad fucking Pitt, and I need someone to clear a way for me to get to my car out front right now. Otherwise there might be more peeing going on, okay?"

A few seconds later: "Okay, Mr. Pitt."

I handed the kid back his walkie-talkie. "How it's done."

Within a few minutes, four security guards arrived and helped me navigate through the crowd of people and what seemed like hundreds of hands playing grab-ass on my butt.

When I finally arrived safely in the comfort of my back seat, the driver took off and asked if I wanted to go back to the hotel.

"Are we being chased?"

"Well, there are several cars following us from the gala. Do you want me to drive around a little?"

Maybe I wasn't done yet. Maybe there was another nail I could drive into the Brad coffin. This was my last chance as Brad, and I didn't want to let go. The night was still young. I fished around in the bag I brought from the hotel. *Found it!* I handed the invitation for the Spunk Factory to my driver. "This is where we're going next."

∞

We pulled up to a warehouse space and I saw some doormen dressed in leather at the entrance. In back of us, two cars pulled in across the street. The back doors of the cars were barely opened before photographers began falling out of them. I jumped out of the limo and headed to the doormen.

Through my research I knew that Brad had a huge gay fan base. More like voracious. Of course, I had actually seen it before; I have had men hit on me from time to time, and in New Orleans there was that guy who was getting touchy-feely with me at the concert. I knew that Brad was supportive of gay people, but now I could show he wasn't only supportive, but was secretly one of them.

The three burly guys at the door were really confused. They had no idea why a limo and photographers were showing up at their party. They didn't recognize me yet. This was what I called the "Out of Place Brad Phenomenon." This was why I didn't get "recognized" in a local Walmart or at a carwash or Starbucks. No one expected Brad to be there. I might get a double take, but it is more of a "No, that couldn't be him buying toilet paper at Kroger" kind of look. If you saw me in the lobby of a fancy hotel, eating at a fancy restaurant, then it made sense to people. This was a situation that didn't make sense, so people would not recognize me. They will go against everything they see to deny recognizing Brad, because the logic just isn't there. Brad Pitt would not be showing his bare ass up on a Saturday night at some gay leather party in Brooklyn.

The bigger burley guy gave me a once-over and double-checked my invite. The two others were arguing with the photographers.

"Private event, can't let you in."

"What kind of event?" The flash bulbs started up again, pointed at my ass entering the club.

"This is The Nasty Pig's annual spunk party."

"Do you have any idea who's going in there right now?"

I stalled at the door long enough to hear.

The doorman had had it with these guys. "What the fuck are you talking about?"

"That's Brad Pitt right there, genius. I'm here to cover him, not your spunky party or whatever. What the hell is a spunky party anyway? And what's a nasty pig?"

Big Burly dropped my invitation and looked at my face again. I winked and put my finger to my lips. "Our secret, buddy."

I heard pounding dance music coming from somewhere in the warehouse and made my way down a shadowy hallway. I saw shadows here and there, but my eyes weren't acclimated to the darkness yet, and I kept bumping into people. By people, I should say men who wanted to touch each other in the dark. I kept walking toward the music and finally arrived at a large dance space where the music was ear-shattering and the room was filled with sweaty, half-naked men dancing.

"Well, well, well, Mr. Not Brad Pitt!"

My couturier had found me. He was wearing even less clothing than yesterday. "Colin! Wow, what a party you got here."

"A-list all the way. How did your event go?" He smiled at me.

"Perfect. Everyone loved my outfit, so I gave a shoutout to The Nasty Pig."

"Nice to know, what event was that?"

"You'll probably find out soon enough. Listen, Colin, is there a back door or something where I can sneak out of here?"

Colin rolled his eyes. "If there's a hotter party than this in the city and that's where you're headed, you better bring me along!"

"No other party, I'm just tired."

"Hmm, why would Mr. Not Brad Pitt need to sneak away? Well, I do know a back way that has this great little dark alley, so follow me."

I followed Colin out of the dance space through a maze of dark hallways, bumping into more clusters of men along the way and getting randomly felt up. Finally, I saw the glow of a red exit sign.

"Hopefully the alarm doesn't work on this." Colin pushed open the door and found himself face to face with a handful of photographers. "What the fuck?"

One of them pushed past Colin and saw my face. "Got him!" He immediately started snapping, and soon, like a bad zombie movie, the paparazzi pushed their way in and invaded. The clusters of men in the shadows ran for the hills.

I put my hands over my face like I was trying to hide, but I was also slow-walking it away from there. I was glad they were getting the pictures, but how the fuck would I get out?

I headed closer to the dance space, and my entourage reached critical mass. I had a layer of paparazzi following, and behind them the crowd of curious leather onlookers grew deeper. Finally, the burly security guys came to my rescue and started pushing out the photographers.

In the commotion I ducked into the men's room. All eyes on me. Great. I saw a guy in regular street clothes and grabbed him. "How would you like this leather outfit I'm wearing? For free! It's worth a fortune."

"Umm, sure." He was bewildered, but he slowly realized that someone who looked like Brad Pitt was about to make him a proposition.

"I'll trade these for what you're wearing, right now."

He looked me over and his face lit up. "If we can change right here. You first."

About twenty minutes later, I was able to walk out casually past the paparazzi. They were all over my limo, so I grabbed a cab waiting out front and hauled ass back to the Marriott.

11

I woke up in the Marriott the next day, relieved it was over. I didn't have to think about Brad logistics this morning. I could just climb out of bed and be on my way in my own sweet time. It was a big fucking hassle to be him—no wonder he wanted to hire me. But at the same time, from now on, I would have to be happy with the old perks of being him, like getting to the front of lines and receiving better treatment with a wink—"We know who you are." Meh. Didn't hold a thrill for me like it used to. For now, the beast inside of me had been fed. I was hoping that it would just lie dormant and I wouldn't feel the hunger again soon.

I did a quick Google search and found that Mission: Destroy Brad was a huge success. It was all over the internet. Both New York dailies' online additions had front-page stories about Brad Pitt's "public meltdown."

There was plenty of coverage of the red carpet and the Spunk Party.

But then I noticed a sub headline: "Outrage in the Gay Community." Fuck, this was even worse than I thought. Apparently, the Spunk Party is for proponents of gay bareback sex? They didn't believe in condoms? Holy fuck. I had no idea! Brad, you are in a shitload of trouble!

Victory was definitely mine. He destroyed my life, and I just destroyed his career. It still didn't make me feel better about my life. But I had to let him know that he could not fuck around with me.

I packed up and headed to the airport, ready to fly back home, when I saw an odd text from Sophie.

"Where are you now???"

Did she find out I wasn't in Wisconsin with my folks? Or was she just asking where I was? She usually didn't do multiple questions marks, so something was up.

I texted her back. *"Heading back be home soon, why?"*

A few seconds later:

"But where are you NOW??"

This was odd. Maybe she wanted to know how long I would be? I would play it safe.

"Getting on the I-294"

Then nothing from her. I became a little frantic and called her. No answer.

Something was wrong. Did he contact her? It was not a possibility I had even thought about. Fuck.

By the time I reached home, I had tried texts and calls, but there was still no reply from Sophie. When I entered the apartment, it was my turn to find Sophie sitting in the dark, crying to herself.

I turned on the lights. She sat in front of her laptop and a box of Kleenex.

"What's going on?" I tried to sound earnest.

"That's my question."

"What do you mean?" My stomach churned, and my sweat glands worked overtime.

"Were you with your parents this weekend?"

Her eyes were pointed at me. She knew I wasn't there. But I couldn't bring myself to tell her where I was.

"No . . . but what happened here? What's got you so upset?"

"I got a call this morning from someone claiming to be your travel agent. They said that your flight from New York was cancelled and they couldn't get ahold of you, so they called the emergency number you listed on your reservation."

Him.

I mumbled some nonsense about not having a travel agent.

"At first, I thought it was just some kind of scam trying to get credit card numbers or something, but they said they already had your info and just needed to confirm your new flight. I asked her when you flew into New York and she gave me the date and flight numbers. I was dumbfounded, so I said this must be a mistake." She reached for a tissue and dabbed at her eyes. Sophie wouldn't look me in the face anymore as she continued, "You don't use travel agents as far as I know, and then she talked about your previous . . . New Orleans travel arrangements. So now I'm scared, thinking someone is making some horrible prank call, but she said she could send over all of the invoices if I like, since I'm on the account."

I couldn't think of anything to tell her. It was all coming out now.

"So I hung up, a little in shock. New York, why New York? I called your folks, and they haven't seen you or heard from you in months. So I searched online for . . . Brad Pitt in New York, and I saw all these headlines. And then I knew you were at a convention during the whole New Orleans thing with Brad Pitt."

"I . . . I . . . I—"

"Tobey. I don't want to ask this, I really, really don't. I want to be so wrong. I would rather just be a crazy, paranoid girlfriend, but I can't get around this. Was . . . that you?"

What to say when exposed? When you are caught in so many lies you can't count them anymore? When the one person on earth who you claim to love is staring at you like a stranger?

"Yes. It was me." My stomach dropped. In the same second I knew that I had lost her. But I couldn't let go of her. "It was the only way I could stop him. He was destroying me, so I—"

"Stop." She put her hand up. "I can't even digest this. You did all this stuff, all this planning. Then you went about your life here without even saying anything. You went out and did these . . . things."

"I don't know why I couldn't tell you. It's just something . . ." *Something I was addicted to doing.* I couldn't say those words. Being on top of the world for a few hours, being the one person who everyone paid attention to was more important than anything.

Sophie went into the bedroom. I followed her. She reached for a suitcase.

"I don't even know who you are anymore. I can't stay here. I can't live with a . . . person I don't know or don't . . ."

Trust. That word hung between us.

As she packed, I tried to think of something to say to her. But it was all so obvious to me now. Brad was more important than her. She knew it and now I knew it. I didn't know what to say to undo that. I didn't really know it until this moment. "Can I at least explain why I did this?"

Sophie stopped packing and sighed. "I don't know if I want to hear it right now. Tobey, you have to understand how deeply . . . violated I feel. I need to get away from you right now."

The impact of her words hit me like a tornado. I backed out of the room. Regrets were flying at me from every part of my brain. Him. He hit me one last time. I couldn't let him have this.

Sophie left the bedroom with her suitcase and stopped in the living room to pick up her jacket.

She headed to the door and I followed. "Please. I don't want you to leave."

"Not now, Tobey." She opened the door and walked out to the car.

I followed her out, shouting, "It was him. You understand that, right? He called! He's trying to break us up."

"Please stop!" she shouted back at me through her tears. "I don't give a goddamned who called, do you not understand that?" Her voice was getting louder and louder. "You lied and lied and lied to me! You didn't just lie to me—I don't even recognize you, do you not get that? You have to understand all of that, okay?"

I tried to help her load her suitcase, but she grabbed it away from me. She fumbled with the car door and then sped away.

I walked back into my apartment and sat. I was empty. Literally empty. Nothing inside. The worst thing about all of this was that now I had a craving to say, "Fuck this," and go out and be him. Make the world do what I wanted for a few hours. I curled up on the sofa and just lay there, trying not to think about how much damage I had done and the reasons why I had done it. It made no sense to me now.

I found a bottle of wine in the kitchen and began drinking to stop my mind from racing, to soothe my brain into sleep.

I woke up the next day and tried to figure out what to do. If there was anything to be done at all. Maybe with time I could talk to Sophie. Maybe I could figure out this Brad thing. Maybe explain this to her. I checked my phone. Unsurprisingly, no message from her. She just needed time, I hoped.

There was also the immediate problem of everyday life. I had no job, no savings, and with pending sexual harassment charges, no chance of getting another job. I thought this must be the bottom. The bottom that addicts hit when they lose everything because of their addiction. My life truly could not get any worse.

But then it did.

I had vastly underestimated him. He had everything figured out. I was amateur hour compared to him.

It was true, I wrecked his career, or at least put a big crimp in it. His people put out a statement about him going into rehab and stopping production for some movies, but when you're Brad Pitt you find a way to come back.

I was naïve. Really naïve. I thought this game of chess we were playing would be over. But I came to a gunfight with a butter knife. He wanted to make sure I would never do this again.

He said we were the same person. It wasn't possible. I could not be him. Would never be him.

I know that now. I didn't know it when the police knocked on my door later that evening.

There were about a dozen of them. They had my apartment surrounded and had guns drawn.

"Tobey Crawford?"

I nodded in shock. Him again. Now what?

"I have a warrant for your arrest, can you please put your hands on your head?"

Could I be arrested for impersonating him? Why were they using guns? Did he get Sophie to corroborate his evidence? Oh my god, how did this happen so quickly? I put my hands on my head. "Arrest for what?" There were a million things now I could be arrested for. But which one merited this show of force?

Another police officer walked around behind me to put me in handcuffs while the first police officer read me my rights.

"But for what?" I was shouting now, just to be heard above my own thoughts.

"For the murder of Sophie Taylor."

12

The trial didn't last very long. My attorney begged me to take a plea deal before it went to jury, and at that point I agreed. The evidence was there. The longer the trial went on, the crazier and guiltier I looked. Second-degree murder with a minimum fifteen-year sentence and a chance for parole. If I was found guilty by a jury, there was a good chance it would be first-degree murder—twenty-five years to life with no parole.

The papers dubbed me the Brad Pitt Killer, because . . . duh. Also because I kept insisting that he murdered her. He did, of course, but who was going to believe that? No one.

Sophie was stabbed multiple times in the chest and abdomen in a Hyatt on Michigan Avenue. She had checked in the night before, alone, and had a reservation for a week. Other customers heard some loud noises coming from her room that night, but no one called the hotel or police. A video tape showed me, or someone who looked exactly like me, coming into the hotel around ten p.m., going to her room, and exiting about thirty minutes later. That was the night I was drinking myself to sleep.

Forensics on the video showed blood stains on my clothes as I left. It also showed me grinning directly into the camera for a few seconds before I left the hotel lobby.

She was found by the hotel maid the next day.

The police contacted her next of kin and asked them why

anyone would want to kill Sophie. There was no evidence of a break-in, everything showed that she knew the killer. They showed her parents the picture from the security camera. The police were at my apartment an hour later.

My case was looking to be a high-profile case, because everything about Brad Pitt is high-profile. Some ambitious attorney could make his name defending the crazy guy who claimed Brad Pitt murdered his girlfriend. Larry Osterhouse was my first attorney. A fat, sweaty guy who desperately wanted his name in the papers. When he couldn't get me to take an insanity plea, he started looking for reasons to get off the case. My explanation didn't fit his narrative. Also, I'm convinced he hated me because I looked like Brad Pitt.

I explained everything. Every single fucking thing. He insisted on a psych exam. The results of the exam disappointed him. I was not crazy, but the shrink said that I have this delusional fantasy that Brad Pitt and I are the same person and I didn't know where to draw the line. In every other measure of sanity, I came up clean, so they wouldn't be able to put me away on an insanity plea. I probably should have taken his advice and acted more insane. Insanity pleas were much more lenient for murder cases.

I asked him to find Ted Caswell, Brad's lawyer. How would I even know that if I didn't know Brad Pitt? At first he humored me. This is what I found out: There is no lawyer named Ted Caswell. Sophie had pics of our weekend with him on her phone. Her phone could not be found. I gave him the burner phone Brad sent me. My attorney looked at me and then just tossed it in the trash.

Finally, in a last bid to convince him I was telling the truth, I showed him the legal papers served to me by Brad for impersonating him. I didn't want to use those, but there was nothing in my story that could be proven, and I wanted to show him anything that proved Brad knew about me. That we had contact. Even if it made me look even more like a lunatic.

I pushed the papers across his desk.

He raised his eyebrow at me. "When did you get these?"

"Maybe two months ago."

"Did you respond? Talk to a lawyer?"

"No. I told you what I did. I went to New Orleans and—"

"Okay, not that story again. Let me check these out, okay?"

A week later when we met, he took my legal papers out of his briefcase, crumpled them into a ball, and threw them at me.

"You have to stop bullshitting me. You're wasting my time with this crap."

"What?"

"Don't give me that horse shit. These papers are all part of your shtick. Look, this is very, very serious. The courts don't think you're crazy, so now we go to trial for first- or second-degree murder. That's very fucking serious."

"I don't understand. The papers—"

"These are completely fake. All of the names of the judges and the officers of the court are made up. No such people. This is something you faked, you copied it off the internet, even the notary seal here is fake. Now tell me, what made you fake this bullshit and then make me chase this down?"

Jesus Christ. Brad was a fucking mastermind. "But they had police come to my office and serve me. They even had a dog!"

"Well, the police show no records of that, so maybe you can be honest and tell me that you hired some actors? Look, Tobey. Tell me you faked this, then at least I can demand another shrink look at you, okay? Just tell me you staged all of this."

At that point I was still insisting that they investigate Brad. Shortly before the trial began, Larry quit.

Meanwhile, evidence against me began mounting. Prosecutors were digging into my background. They found out about my erratic work performance culminating with my being terminated for sexual harassment. I had two neighbors who saw Sophie and I fighting loudly in front of our apartment the night before she was murdered. My co-workers who saw me "become Brad" for a night in Las Vegas were ready to testify that I thought I was him.

They also found a pair of pants with Sophie's blood in the dumpster behind my apartment. They were my size.

Right before we went to trial, I begged my new attorney to take me seriously. She was a small woman and all business. She had no time or patience for human emotions. "Please, can't you just take a look at some records that will show that Brad Pitt flew here the night of the murder? There has to be something on record."

"Mr. Crawford." She stopped taking notes and looked at me with her no-nonsense face. "In order to get any records pertaining to Brad Pitt's whereabouts or his personal information, I will need to obtain a warrant from the State of Illinois. The state will only issue that warrant if I present compelling evidence that Brad Pitt murdered your girlfriend. The only evidence I have is that you look like him. No judge will take this request seriously. Not one. This is not an avenue we can pursue. Is that clear?"

That was now clear.

As the trial began, it became obvious to me that this was going to be a slam dunk. The state had established a motive. They knew from evidence that Sophie and I had a fight and she moved out into a hotel. They knew that based on my work history I was having personal problems and that I was sexually harassing women. They had video of me at the scene of the crime. They had Sophie's blood on my clothes. The only thing they were missing was the murder weapon.

I told Miss No Nonsense to make a deal.

Even though I did not kill Sophie, I felt guilty. I felt like I needed to be punished for not loving Sophie enough. For not realizing what I had and who she was. For not realizing who I really was. I miss her every day.

It took me years in prison to come to terms with this. I may have been a lousy boyfriend, and I may have been blinded by my need for attention, but I did not kill her. He did that.

I have also heard that Angie finally left him. Maybe she found out who he really is. I don't know for sure. I do know that in the middle of their ongoing wrangling over custody and payments that I was contacted by someone who had "mutual interests" and asked if I would be willing to provide her with more specific details of my relationship with Brad. I agreed and even signed a contract to do so. Shortly after that, Brad agreed to her demands.

Brad, you were wrong. You and I are not alike. I think I know you better than anyone right now. Really. I and I alone know how far you'll go to win, to preserve your own skin, to get what you want. No one else knows that but me.

I cannot be you. I cannot play with a human life like that.

At least, not yet.

I'm warning you, Brad. I will get out of here in six years.

And I will still look like you.

PLEASE ALLOW ME TO INTRODUCE MYSELF

"The gods too are fond of a joke."

Aristotle

1

"The most important thing is not your G-spot or whatever. Don't forget that." Alby pointed his drumstick at Darla. "The most important thing is the band."

"Okay, so it's like, if he fucks my G-spot . . . or whatever, he fucks us all, right?" Darla passed the joint along to Lee and rolled her eyes at her bandmates. "And which one of you will be swallowing his sperm?"

"Tell him we'd all be happy to," Lee deadpanned, trying to put his guitar away and taking the joint from Darla. "How fucking insane is this, huh?"

Darla nodded in silent agreement. This was fucking insane. Tonight, the high priest of rock, Keith Richards from The Rolling Stones, had checked out their show and gave them a thumbs-up. Even though the show had ended over an hour ago, they were all still sitting in mild shock on the makeshift stage of the Smokehouse in Astoria. Odder still, something was different about their gig tonight. She felt more harmonized with the band than usual. She could anticipate their moves, or at least they followed every one of hers. Not usually the case.

And why tonight? One of the biggest rock stars on the whole freakin' planet had wandered into their Wednesday-night gig at some shithole in Astoria. It wasn't like they were some up-and-coming band, either. Spunk and Funk had been around for about five years and had a nice consistent following but no buzz. Darla remembered the days when she started with the band and they had some buzz, but that had settled down as fans moved on to the next flavor of the month. She hated to admit it, but the band was exiting the dream stage and entering the hobby stage. Harry, the leader of the band, seemed content to let them coast on the fumes of their initial limited success. Lee was his co-captain and never challenged Harry. They were all good musicians, but there seemed to be a tacit agreement between them: they were real musicians, and they didn't need to be famous, they just needed to play.

Keith Richards was enthusiastic about their sound and let them know he thought they had something special, but he kept looking at Darla while he spoke. She wasn't the leader of the band, even though as the vocalist, everyone assumed it was her band.

Keith had pulled her aside and asked if she would meet him for drinks later at the Carlyle Hotel in Manhattan.

Of course, when Keith Richards asks you to meet for drinks, you meet for drinks. "Sympathy for the Devil" had been running through her head for weeks, though. Precognition?

Darla stared at her three bandmates, Disco Harry, Lee, and Alby, and smiled at them. "Maybe we change our name from Spunk and Funk to No Funk Just Spunk?"

"Up to you and your actions, missy," Disco Harry weighed in.

She picked up her faux rabbit and pleather jacket and gave them all the finger. "Jealous bitches." She took off for the Carlyle.

Darla settled in on the N Train into Manhattan, sitting opposite a couple of kids headed into the city. They were talking very loudly about which club they should hit. They had probably done their drinking in Queens where drinks were cheaper and were now looking to find a "really cool scene." Classic bridge and tunnel trash, so goddamned full of themselves, the kind of posers that just annoyed her, but not tonight. She was still buzzed from the band working so well together and, of course, because she was going to visit Keith fucking Richards.

Funk and Spunk was a cool little band, and they had a good sound. Most of their reviewers called their music blues-infused dance music, but they really thought of themselves as a blues band. It was Harry who liked to inject disco into their songs. He was a self-proclaimed "Disco Diva," but that was the hook that kept people coming to their shows.

Still, why would Keith be interested in them, and the big question: Did he want to sleep with her? It didn't make sense. He could probably fuck anybody he wanted. She wasn't model-pretty and didn't have a centerfold body. Most guys called her looks "interesting" or "exotic." She just figured it was the big nose and wide-set eyes. Her body was okay, maybe she could lose a few pounds, but she was also hitting thirty-four this year. Not exactly bimbo material. Her voice was good, though. Years ago, a reviewer for *The Village Voice* proclaimed that she had a "powerful set of pipes."

She was a good singer, and her voice gave the band its identity. *Though I'm not without my charms*, she deadpanned to herself. Who knows what turns on rock stars?

The subway train slowed and then stopped in the middle of a tunnel. A muddled voice said something about a delay. Fucking MTA.

She didn't really want to sleep with him. Maybe as a bucket list item for a good cocktail party story. "Oh, yeah, I remember that time I fucked one of the Rolling Stones, I almost forgot!" And even if she did, would he actually give them a record deal? Something didn't add up. None of the bandmembers were looking for fame and fortune. It seemed like if any big labels or management companies were looking to sign them, they would have done it by now. They just got used to being a decent band that got regular small gigs. Well, except for the drummers. Alby was drummer number four. They couldn't seem to hang on to a drummer for long. They were always ambitious. And young. Which was why she never thought twice about sleeping with any of the drummers. She figured they'd be gone soon enough.

The muddled MTA voice announced that they were moving. Or was it saying they were soothing? She couldn't hear above the stupid club kids across from her. The train did not move, so maybe it was saying something about soothing.

Still, Keith's surprise appearance had reignited an old dusty hope. Could she make a living from singing? It would be nice to give up her day job. How long could she go on waiting tables? Maybe she should go back and finish her degree and work in an office. So much stuff she wanted to do but would probably never get the chance. She also wanted kids, a husband, a big house, a farm, a penthouse apartment, to write a book! Her clock was ticking fast. *Fuck, I just want to sing. That's all I can handle right now*, Darla thought. Maybe sleep with the occasional drummer. That's not a bad life. For now. The train began moving.

She got to the hotel at about two a.m. and walked through the hotel lobby to the entrance to the bar, but there was a velvet rope blocking the doorway. Did she get here too late? She peeked her head in and saw a group of people sitting in a cloud of smoke in the back near a grand piano. A guy in a dark suit got up and walked over to her.

"Private event, bar's closed."

"I'm here to see Keith Richards. Tell him Darla is here." *And fuck you, asshole*. She really hated doormen and gatekeepers. Sanctimonious motherfuckers, every last one of them.

The guy in the suit walked back to the group. Keith stood and waved her in. "C'mon back!"

He seemed quite animated from behind his sunglasses, talking loudly to a teenage boy across from him. There was a table in front laid out with a few bottles of champagne, whiskey, vodka, and plates of sushi and sliders. The bar looked like an old-school sophisticated club from the fifties, which she loved.

When she approached the table, Keith stood and raised a glass. "Ah, here she is. Hello, love, this is the one I been telling you about. I'm sorry, darling, forgot your name."

"Darla."

"Darla, darling? Perfect. Come over and meet me grandson, Olson, and some of his mates here."

She found a seat behind his crew as Keith finished up a story about meeting Saddam Hussein back when the Stones were touring the Middle East in the seventies. "We had no idea, I actually thought he was our driver. He was backstage with a pass and all. He kind of expected us to know who he was. God rest his bloody soul."

Darla was fascinated by his face. It was full of age, creases, and wrinkles, but the voice and the energy that came out of him defied the visage. In fact, there was an energy in the room, kind of like being at a pep rally. His aura? Some people must have that effect on people. She was not one of those people. Which, again, led her to wonder why he wanted to meet with her at a closed bar in a hotel. Would he really try to sleep with her?

At that moment he stopped talking, looked at her, and cocked his head.

Did she say that out loud? No, it was a thought, but he had reacted to it.

"Okay, kids, off you go. I need to spend some time with Darling Darla." As the kids got up to leave, he patted the chair next to him. "Have a drink?"

Darla looked at the liquor on the table and decided she'd make herself a vodka cranberry. If she was going to fuck him, she'd need a little liquid courage.

"Don't worry, darling, I'm not going to fook ya."

Darla spilled the cranberry juice onto the thick patterned carpet. How was he reading her thoughts? "I wasn't—"

"Yes, you were. I can just tell by now. It's what all the birds think when we first meet, even the blokes now, too, so relax, have your drink, and let's talk a bit about you."

Darla sat down across from him, not because she was scared of him, but because she wanted to watch his face behind his trademark bandanna and sunglasses. It was like an old black-and-white photo from the Civil War, showing the scars of years of battle.

"Dug your show tonight." He took a quick swig from his glass. "You been together a while, I guess. I like the way you take sad songs and make them dance songs. Like your voice, too. You guys are good."

"Wow. That's . . . amazing hearing that from you." She couldn't shake the thought that he wanted something from her and not the band.

"How long you been a band?"

"Just about five years."

He leaned over toward her. "Tonight you was playing like you was all magnets and just got pulled together."

Darla couldn't argue. That's exactly how it felt. "Is that how it is for you and the Stones?"

"Mostly, some other outside forces as well. Tell me how you came to be singing? Seems a fluke to me."

Darla took a sip of her drink. How did he know so much? Was it something in her singing? Was this a critique? "Kind of a fluke, yeah."

"Oh, I don't mean nothing bad by that, your singing is beautiful, really fab, don't be put off. You're not a trained singer; it's instinct, which, to me, is preferable. Tell me how you found singing."

"In church. I was raised by . . . very religious parents."

"Church? Oy, really? You into all that business?"

"Nah, I never took the church real serious, but singing in church was . . . religion for me." Growing up, God was the tooth fairy, God was Santa Claus, God was always a Disney movie to her, but she loved the singing, loved the old church building, the sacredness of the space where she could let loose what was hiding in her heart when she sang.

"Good to hear that." He settled back into his chair. "Your voice *could* take you places; I mean past your bandmates. I get the impression that as good as they was tonight, maybe it ain't always that way, that they also seemed kind of . . . tired. Kind of like they was clockin' in for a factory shift."

"What do you mean?" Did he want her to quit the band?

"It don't mean quit the band, in case you was wondering." He smiled slyly and lit up a cigarette. "I mean you and the band do okay, am I right? But the band maybe ain't enough for you—maybe for now, but not later. Still, you got the stuff, you should probably take some more control of yourself."

Darla wasn't exactly sure what he was trying to tell her, but it kind of thrilled her that he thought more of her than he thought of the band. It was like sitting with an old fortune teller. Maybe he had that gift also?

He nodded at her and smiled.

"Wait, how are you doing that?"

"What?"

Reading my mind. How are you doing that?

"It's complicated. I'll get to it."

Darla felt her arms tingle, and her legs also felt as if her blood was rushing through her veins, faster than usual. Panic set in. She had not let go of her drink since she sat down, so he couldn't have put something in it. Was the vodka already spiked?

"Relax, darling, no drugs in your drink. Best way I can explain it, it's kind of a tribal thing; we share some blood from the past."

Darla had no frame of reference for someone invading her mind. She felt her heart rate shoot up, perspiration started dripping from her face, her energy level surged. "What's going on here? Is this why you wanted to see me tonight?"

"Somewhat. I knew you when I seen you."

"Knew me? Like from the past?"

"No, none of that kind of business. You could be . . . immortal, if you like. I mean, you got enough in you to go for a few lifetimes, do some good, not get silly or bored with it all. It's in you. When I see one, which is getting rarer and rarer, by the way, I need to meet 'em."

Why the fuck is he talking about being immortal? What the fuck does that mean?

"It means live forever. No expiration date. Just go on and on."

Not die?

"Yeah, like me."

"You're immortal?"

He nodded.

He's a crazy drugged rock star with ESP or . . .

"I think most people call them vampires." He pulled his sunglasses off. His eyes were blood red. No whites whatsoever. "That's what you did to me, by the way! Kind of like a vampire boner. Finding another does this kind of shite."

Darla leaned forward and searched his eyes. Was there some kind of drug that could do that? It was really, really freaky.

Keith put his sunglasses back on. "Kind of cool, though, huh?"

"So where are the pointy teeth?" *So he's on some drugs and he can read my mind. The vampire thing, is it some kind of goth trip?*

"The fangs show up when it's time is all I know. Can't force 'em."

"When it's time?"

"Okay, so put away all that shite that you been seeing on TV and the movies about vampires, all just Hollywood bull. Truth is, when it's time, meaning when a person in my vicinity wants to become immortal and has the tribal blood like you, the fangs just pop out."

"So if I wanted to become immortal, the fangs would pop out of your mouth?"

"Probably."

"And then you just bite me and take my blood?"

"Well, technically, but you know, you can still say no. It's not like I need the blood at this point. Or if you feel kind of sluggish about the whole deal it don't work."

"The fangs go back in?" Maybe she should just leave now. He was really into this vampire thing and she wasn't sure she wanted to play this game with him. But she had never been around people this famous, this rich. Maybe this was how they had fun?

"Eventually, but if I bite you and you're not totally sure about it, then I just get really sick, vomit, the runs, just like eatin' bad fish or something, and then it doesn't really take for you. You just get two off-lookin' holes in your neck. Eventually, just scars over."

She took a deep breath. *Just stay and see where this goes.* "Is the whole band . . ."

"Naw, just me and Mick. The other blokes don't have the blood thing going."

"Do they know?"

"We told 'em. Not sure if they ever believed it."

Darla leaned over to grab his box of Marlboros. She rarely smoked, but now she craved a cigarette. Maybe it was his "tribal" blood in her. Why would he go to all the trouble to have her come out here to hear this bullshit story? Nothing was making sense, except she did feel different. Like she had been chugging energy drinks all day. And he could really read her mind.

He lit her cigarette and smiled at her. "Fucking unbelievable, I know. For now, just pretend what I'm telling you is true and see where that goes."

"When did you become a vampire?"

"About four hundred years ago. Mick and me was working for some bloke making musical instruments for the king of Austria. Mick asked me, I said why not, and his fangs popped out."

"Musicians in the seventeenth century?" She tried to smile. *I'm just having a pleasant conversation with a rock star vampire.*

"You know, funny thing is Mick was writing the same songs back then. He was trying to invent rock and roll, I think—push history forward. When we met, he was trying to make something that sounded like an electric piano. You know he tells me he invented the harpsichord! Don't know if I buy that."

"Are there more vampire rock stars? I mean, if I become . . . immortal, do I automatically become a rock star?"

Keith dropped his cigarette in a barely finished cocktail next to him and waved his finger at her. "Not yet. You need to think. Takes a lot of energy and drive to do what me and Mick done. Being immortal not only gives you the time, also gives you the energy. Like you been feelin' when I'm around, right?"

Darla nodded. This was what she felt.

"Honestly, right now, you don't have the energy to become who I think you could be, or even who you think you want to be. You become immortal? You could do it. I'd sign you and your band if that's what you wanted. That way I know you guys could be better than you are, be something special."

"Wait, let me get this straight. So you're telling me that if I want to become a famous singer, you have to bite me, and I become a vampire?" Sleeping with him would have been much simpler than whatever this was.

"Look, what I'm saying is only a select few people can become immortal. You're one of them. If you decide to become one, I can help you with your music ambition. You don't want to do it, no problem. But without the spark you get from being bitten, I don't think you'd get very far. For instance, you guys made a CD?"

Darla hesitated. She felt defensive now. "We made a CD about two years ago. It got good reviews in the local press."

"How many you sell?"

"About four hundred, but people don't buy CDs anymore, they download."

"Is your music online?"

Darla took a swig of her drink. She could see where he was going. "Umm, Spotify."

"Can I download it?"

She sighed. "Well, maybe not right this minute." They'd been dropped for low sales.

"I heard that! Who's your agent? Your manager?"

"The guitarist's uncle. He's a lawyer. He knows some people."

"So why ain't you pushin' this uncle? Why ain't you trying to get more sales? See what I mean? This is the result after five years? You don't just sing a pretty song and the magic happens. Takes a lot of balls to make it happen. Lots of know-how. I could sign you guys tomorrow, but I get the feeling that you'd just wait for me to do all the work for you."

"Okay, okay, I see your point. And by the way, our CD is great even if no one bought it. But how does having this tribal blood make me do stuff? What difference would it make?"

Keith lit another cigarette and poured himself a drink. "I ain't no scientist, mind you, but from what I seen, your blood is everything. It tells everything in your body what to do. Something about getting bit, purifying this kind of tribal blood, activates it, makes it move faster. Sometimes it stops you from aging, sometimes it makes you younger. Don't know all the rules and such. Never been no Harvard study on us."

Darla didn't know what to think about this. She was receiving a proposition to become a vampire. Or was it a proposition to become a famous singer if she was willing to be bitten? Her mind was racing, and she couldn't process it. Would she turn into a bat? Hang out in a coffin? Burn in sunlight?

"No, no, and no. All of that's a bunch of tripe from movies. Listen, I'm in town for a couple more days. Think on it. Anyways, four-hundred-year-old vampires need rest. In the meantime, if you need me, all you got to do is call me. Don't even need a phone." He winked at her, gave her a peck on the forehead, and left the bar.

Darla remained in the bar and pulled out her phone. She had half a dozen texts from the band asking if the sex was good and where their contract was.

She texted them back: *"No sex and no record deal. Sorry. Think he just wanted to chat."*

A few seconds later:

"Chat? Really? C'mon! Tell us!"

She replied: *"He has some . . . drugs in him I think. Talk to you guys later."*

She didn't know how to explain this yet. She privately texted Alby: *"You around?"*

Alby replied quickly: *"Up for a BC???????"*

She smiled to herself. Booty call. With all of this energy still bouncing around inside of her, no matter the origin, she wanted to fuck his brains out.

"See you at my place in 30."

∞

Darla sat up in bed and leaned against Alby. She loved this moment with him. Post-sex, sun coming up in her cozy Lower East Side studio apartment. It was like an old worn photo of a dream she had long ago.

He was only twenty-three, but he was a really good twenty-three. He had terrific instincts in bed and knew how to cuddle. If she was a few years younger, he might be a keeper. *I'm a cougar! Fuck.* She tried to keep the attachment to him light, but he made it really difficult. She absolutely knew this was a no-win situation. He'd meet some hot young thing, if he hadn't already, or he'd move on to some other band and they'd just drift apart.

"You good?" Alby wrapped his arms around her and nuzzled her neck. His long hair fell out in front of her, providing cover and tickling her nose.

She pushed his hair out of her face and reached for her stash box next to the bed. "One joint? I can make us some breakfast."

Alby reached over to look at her clock. "Gotta get going soon."

"Where you going?" The words came out before she could stop them. Why not just handcuff him to the bed?

"Things to do, people to see."

She lit up a joint and handed it to him. He took a deep toke and made his way out of the bed. *Who are you going to see, huh? Is it someone younger and prettier?* Christ, she was so needy. Ugh. She hated that. Getting worse as she got older. She wanted to pull him back into bed. She laughed to herself. Maybe if I become a vampire this will stop!

"Alby? If I tell you some crazy shit that happened last night with Keith Richards, will you promise not to tell the other guys?"

"Sure. I love hearing crazy shit." He started putting his clothes on.

"He told me he was a vampire. He told me he wants to bite me and make me a vampire. He also told me that I could become a famous singer if I'm a vampire but only if I become a vampire. The thing about it was, he was so deadly serious."

"Really?" Alby finished buttoning his shorts and stared at her. "What kind of drugs was he on?"

"I wish I knew. He could also read my mind. I mean word for word, no shit."

"What kind of drugs were *you* on?" Alby giggled and sat down on the edge of the bed. "That's really . . . odd."

"Also Mick Jagger. Vampire. I don't know what to do about this. I mean, on one hand I have Keith Richards telling me he likes my singing and I could be famous, and then he goes to crazy town and wants to bite me."

"Tell him yes!" Alby slapped her leg. "Just to see what he does! Fuck, at the very least you'd be friends with crazy Keith Richards, right?"

"So you'd do it?" She was hoping he'd leave his hand on her leg. Needy needy needy. Fuck.

"Fuck yeah. What's the downside?" He started putting his shoes on. "He nibbles on your neck or something like that, you get to know a cool rock star, and you become famous."

Damn, he moved his hand off of her leg. "Okay, but this whole . . . famous . . . thing. I mean, I'm not sure about it. I just want to sing. And make some money doing it. But now, just to get . . . fame, I have to have a rock star nibble on me. Doesn't sit right. I always thought that stuff didn't matter to you. I mean, why'd you join our band?"

Alby pushed the hair out of his face and grabbed the joint from her. "Drummers don't get famous! But it seems like a cool thing. You know, always having people like you and want you and doing whatever you feel like doing."

She was hoping he would agree with her on the fame thing. This was where the age difference came into play. It seemed to her that everyone under thirty wanted their fifteen minutes. They wanted their own channels on YouTube, they wanted thousands of people to follow them on Twitter, they wanted to influence people, they wanted attention. It annoyed her. Reminded her of her own weakness. They all seemed so needy, all of them begging to be loved and admired. This was what fame seemed to be, a kind of bottomless hole of neediness. A whole generation of people who could never get enough attention. They needed a cure, not an audience. "Hmm. So why did you join the band?"

"I like your music. It's very cool what you guys are doing. Also getting laid on a regular basis is very cool." He leaned over and kissed her nose.

She closed her eyes and inhaled him. "But it's not forever, is it? You know, the band."

"Nothing is forever, right? I mean, unless you're a vampire!" Alby stood. "When's the next gig?"

"Friday night. Zinc Bar in the Village."

Alby put on his jacket and left her apartment.

Darla hugged her pillow. Nothing was forever.

Or was it?

2

Darla extended her hand out to acknowledge the band as the audience at The Zinc Bar in the Village clapped at the end of their set. The room was full, some sitting at tables, some standing in the back. Probably no more than two hundred people, tops. The crowd was enthusiastic, but this was a Friday-night audience in a good mood from the house drink specials. Some of them were starting to yell for an encore, which was nice, but she figured that was the liquor talking. She didn't think they had played all that great.

Disco Harry had come in late on most of her leads, like he wasn't even paying attention. Lee missed a bunch of cues. For most of their set, they had just left her hanging, and she had to hold notes longer, improvise until the music showed up. It was bad enough when they did this at the start of the songs, but when they missed cues in the middle, it really threw her timing off. This was so different from their amazing night in Astoria just two days before. What had happened? Maybe it was the chat with Keith and she was just noticing what had been there all along. They could be better, but the boys did not give a fuck any longer.

She huddled with the band as the demand for an encore grew louder. Harry wanted to do a version of Thelma Houston's disco hit from the seventies, "Don't Leave Me This Way." It was always a crowd pleaser, and Darla could belt it out like nobody's business. But she was still pissed off that she had to carry them and smooth over all of their mistakes tonight. Maybe it was time for them to work a little harder. She shook her head at him.

"What?" He looked at her and opened his hands.

She stared back at him. Maybe she'd sing something he'd have to figure out. Keith's critique was really affecting her. Had she been delusional about the band? A shiny, silvery glint behind Harry caught her eye: a tambourine sitting on a speaker. Lee must have brought it; he was into sound effects. It called out to her. She walked past him, picked it up, and began to shake it. The audience started to quiet down.

Harry was staring daggers at her now. "Talk to us."

Lee was sitting behind the synthesizer, checking something on his phone.

Alby was twirling a drumstick in his hand, ready to do . . . something.

She turned to face the audience. They stared back at her and, liquored up or not, she would have them, she knew she could do it. Bunch of drunks? She would grab each and every one of their hearts. This old Bob Dylan folk song was something she had played years and years ago at an open mic night in some crappy coffee shop somewhere.

She started singing, "Hey Mr. Tambourine Man, play a song for me . . ." She poured her whole being into it, she could feel the audience's surprise and then delight. It was her voice and her heart that captured them. These moments made her life worthwhile. She was communicating with people she had never met, absolute strangers, people whom she may not have typically given the time of day, but she could embrace them, make them forget everything except her voice. The band had never rehearsed this. Alby followed her with a light timpani, but Lee and Harry didn't even try—nothing, not a note.

When Darla finished the song, the audience stood and applauded. The song turned out even more powerful a capella.

She heard some hollering for more, some whistling. The song, the lyrics, and her voice had made them vulnerable, their hearts were open. That's how music should work. She took a deep bow and marched off the stage to the dressing room.

Disco Harry followed right behind her. "What the fuck was that about?"

"What?" Darla played it cool. She could see he was pissed. Let him erupt, she would be ready.

Lee and Alby filed into the dressing room, and Harry slammed the door closed. "You totally ignored us. And that fucking song, where did that come from?"

"Ignored you? You mean like you ignored me all night?" Darla would not have it. "You know, when I start to sing, the band is supposed to play? I think that's how bands work, right?"

"What's this about?" Lee stood next to Harry. "C'mon, we need to get our shit off the stage."

Harry kept staring at her. "For some reason, Darla's got her panties in a twist."

"Yes, my panties are twisted. Do you know how sloppy you two were tonight? You were just phoning it in." Darla didn't realize how much anger she had, but she couldn't stop it. "We're headed toward airport lounge and bar mitzvah territory here, guys."

Harry kept eye contact with her. "Where the fuck is this coming from? Did we play the best-ever set tonight? Maybe not, but they still loved us. We gave the audience some really good music. Not sure what your beef is."

"Audience? No, that wasn't an audience, that was a Friday-night crowd, happy to be in any fucking place. Where's our fans? What are we doing to keep these people coming back? Why aren't we trying to sell some of those ancient CDs sitting in the trunk of your car? We haven't updated our Facebook page in months. Do we not give a fuck anymore?" She looked at

Lee. "Well?"

Alby leaned against the door and crossed his arms.

"What's gotten into you?" Harry went on the defensive. "Is it the visit with Keith Richards? Did he say something about the band? Look, the fact that we get to do this, play our music and play it for people who pay to listen, is a fucking blessing, you know that? I don't give a fuck what your buddy Keith thinks. I mean, when we started out, no one, not one person, would give us the time of day. Now? We're doing what we want to do. We play the music we want to play. How many musicians get to do that?"

Lee slid his phone into his back pocket, put his hands on hips, and looked up at Darla. "I'm not sure what your point is here."

She took a deep breath and looked at Alby. He buried his chin in his chest, like a little kid afraid to watch his parents argue. "My point is: Do we want to get better? Do we want to play more? For more people? I just feel like we'll be stuck in garage band status for . . . forever. I mean, how much did we promote tonight? Did we just assume our fans would show up? Should we try to make a new CD? These are the things a band thinks about. And maybe if we did, we could hang on to a drummer for more than a month." She looked at Lee. "That's my point."

Harry crossed his arms. "So you want us to be more popular, you want us to play more, okay, but couldn't you just say that? I'm not sure what got you all set off. I mean, I'm working a full-time job, I got a kid that's still in day care . . ."

Darla took a deep breath. Suddenly she felt bad for Harry. He looked totally defeated. This was all he wanted. This was good enough for him. That wasn't a big secret, it had been pretty obvious all along. She shouldn't push him any further.

"Look," Harry took a deep breath, "I can ask Uncle Lenny to try and book us some more or something, but this is not his full-time job either, so I have to get all over him just to get him to do anything. If one of you wants to try talking to him, be my guest. If you're not happy . . ."

She felt like shit now. Like a bully. Harry just wasn't cut out to be the leader of the band or a promoter, he just wanted to play his music and have some fun. He was hoping it would all work out, all fall into place, but that's not how this business worked. And at the same time, maybe she was just as guilty. Why wasn't she willing to do all the things that Harry was supposed to do? What was she willing to do for the band's success? "Look, I'm okay, let's just drop it."

"Are you sure?"

There was a light knock on the door. Darla looked up at Alby, who nodded and went out to respond.

"I . . ." Darla hesitated. Why did she attack him? He is what he is. This was her life. Singing once or twice a week in between waitress jobs and fucking drummers. Her sad life wasn't his fault, it was hers. "I'm sorry. PMSing."

"Guys?" Alby stuck his head inside the room. "Some old guy with a funny hat wants to come in and meet us."

Harry turned around to face him. "What?"

The old man in the funny hat pushed past Alby and entered the room. "Hi, guys."

"Fuck, Alby, that's Bob Dylan!" Lee rushed to help him into the dressing room.

"Wow, he's still alive?" Alby blurted out.

Bob Dylan reached out to shake Harry's hand. "Yeah, pretty much. Still alive. How do you do?"

"My honor, Mr. Dylan. I'm Harry."

Bob turned to face Darla and held out his hand. Underneath the brim of his Mountie hat, his eyes were small slits covered by wrinkled lids, his smile was tight, just barely showing any teeth. She stood still in front of him, trying to understand why he was here in this room with them after she had just sung his signature song. More precognition?

"I'm Bob Dylan, and you?"

"Of course you are. I'm Darla." She snapped out of her thoughts and shook his hand.

"You guys were great." He didn't let go of her hand. He took his other hand and covered her hand with it. "I don't think I've heard a version of tambourine like you did tonight. Fantastic."

"Thanks . . . we didn't even know you would be here. Honest." Darla felt a tingle in her hand that started to travel up her arm. "This is Lee, and the guy who thinks you're dead is Alby, our drummer."

"Of course not. How could you know I would be here? I was just having dinner next door. This is kind of my old stomping grounds."

Bob nodded at them but still held on to her hand. His grip creeped her out. The coincidence of singing his song when he happened to be in the audience freaked her out as well. He wanted something from her.

"This is insane!" Lee took out his phone. "We're like catnip for rock stars or something. Can we get a pic?"

"Of course, a picture. Catnip?"

"On Wednesday night, Keith Richards dropped in on our show!" Lee swiped his phone to show the picture of Keith and the band.

The tingle in Darla's arm traveled to her shoulders and then her neck and head, giving her a jolt of pain. She pulled her hand out of Bob's grip. Something was . . . wrong.

He turned around to look at her. "Wow, Keith was here, that's so interesting."

"Yeah, funny, we were just arguing about our popularity." Harry gave Darla some side eye. "But it seems like maybe we're more popular than we think, huh?"

Bob cocked his head. "Popular? Why would you care about that? You just have to make good music. People will always want to hear good music."

Harry's face lit up. "That was exactly my point. I mean, when you were starting out, all you had to do was play good music, right? There was no internet, no YouTube bullshit, and people still found you. I mean like, *everybody* found you."

Darla followed Harry's words. Why did he keep fucking that chicken? She'd surrendered already. But he was absolutely intent on keeping the band where it was. Ambition was a dirty word now. "Mr. Dylan, after listening to us, are there any tips you could offer or anything you saw that we could do better?" She kept staring at Harry.
Bob searched his pockets, brought out a stub of a cigarette, and lit it up. "Just do your best and you'll be fine. Don't be concerned about having fame."

Darla was a little bit offended. He just assumed she wanted fame. That wasn't what she was looking for. She just wanted to sing. As much as possible, to make a good living at it. She didn't need to be famous.

"Guys, you know, I'd like to have a word with Darla here for a second. Can you excuse us?" Bob Dylan took one puff of the cigarette butt and stamped it out on the floor.

Alby looked up at Darla. Harry and Lee looked at each other and then at Darla.

Was this really happening again? Darla could not fathom why she was getting all of this attention, first from Keith and now from Bob Dylan. She knew her voice was good, sometimes really powerful, but maybe it was better than she had thought.

"Well, I guess we know whose milkshake brings all the boys to the yard." Harry smirked. "Sure thing, Mr. Dylan. Let's get our shit off the stage."

The guys left the dressing room, leaving Darla alone with Bob Dylan. *Why are all these old rock stars stalking me all of a sudden?* She rubbed her temple, trying to subdue the last remnant of pain from the jolt she had felt. "Umm, so, thanks for coming."

"What did Keith Richards want from you?"

"What? I don't understand—"

"Did you make any agreements with him?"

"What are you asking?" He came off like a humorless little prick. Even if Keith was looney tunes, at least he had some charisma, some flair. "Why are you here?"

"To save your soul." He blinked at her.

"From what?"

"From evil itself. Keith is not good for you. You have to stay from away from him."

Darla's childhood in the church flashed through her mind. All of the condemnation, all of the good versus evil, all of the us against them. All the parts she hated, without the singing. "How did you find me? This whole thing is—"

"Wrong. This is whole thing is very, very wrong. No one is immortal. No one can promise you that. You must never compromise yourself. Besides, he's a terrible musician. Just really awful. His stuff is so derivative. "

"Okay, can we stop with the church stuff? This is like a bad episode of something on the Syfy Channel. So you're saying that you know that Keith thinks he's a vampire, right? A real-life fang-toothed vampire who bites necks and stuff. And for some reason you know he met with me. Tell me what the fuck is going on here. Are you like the rock star vampire slayer?"

"That's very funny." Bob took off his hat. His wiry gray hair was uncombed, unruly. "Has he already offered you immortality?"

Darla nodded. She wasn't sure what freaked her out more, his monotonous tone and dim, lifeless eyes, or this weird mindfuck that two old rock stars were playing with her.

“Does it seem attractive to you?”

She took a deep breath. “I don’t know what to think. Keith Richards drops in out of the fucking blue and tells me he’s a vampire and two days later you pop into my life and tell me my soul is in trouble. Just tell me what the hell is going on. This can’t be real.”

“Good, I’ve caught you in time. Don’t give in to your base instincts. He’s offering you fame, money, power, but that’s all an illusion. No one lives forever. No one. Only God can do that. And if God is not offering you that, then—”

“He must be the devil?” Darla wanted to leave. She didn’t want to stand here and get a religious beatdown from him. So he thought she would actually make a deal with the devil for fame? This little fuckwad thought she was that shallow. He didn’t even know her. Hadn’t bothered to get to know her. At least Keith had asked about her life.

“No, he’s not that important of a figure.”

At this point Darla was exasperated. He was not being straight with her. He was going to keep droning on about her soul and fame like a bad movie. At least he couldn’t read her mind, could he? *Can you hear my thoughts? Nod if you can.*

He stared blankly at her.

Good. “Do you really believe there is such a thing as a vampire? I mean, have you seen Keith bite someone with actual fangs?”

“I have seen it. They exist.”

She got a chill up her spine.

“He’s ruined and killed a lot of good people. Very talented people are dead because of him. This is the truth. Do you have a cigarette?”

“I don’t really smoke. How does he kill people?”

"Shit, I want a cigarette." He started rifling through his coat pockets and pulled out another stub. "Ah, this will do. Look, once you get bit, and you don't like it, your soul becomes tormented by this thought of living forever, meaning you'll see everyone you ever loved die eventually, not to mention that once you make that choice, you start to realize you can't unmake it, so it makes you a little crazy, a little ruthless, and all of the worst possible traits start to surface. The face of evil." He lit his cigarette stub. "Ah, much better. So a lot of the lost souls kill themselves."

"But if you're immortal . . ." she countered, but then she felt kind of stupid for introducing logic.

"There is one cure for immortality. It's a drug that was invented centuries ago for this purpose."

Just then, Alby popped into the room. "We're taking off now, going over to Minetta Tavern for a beer, you ready?"

Darla looked at Bob Dylan and then to Alby. "A few minutes, okay?"

Alby raised an eyebrow.

"Promise." She nodded at him.

Alby reached out to shake Bob's hand. "Pleasure to meet you, Mr. Dylan, glad to see you're alive and all."

As soon as the door closed, Bob continued, "Minetta Tavern? Wow, that old place, used to play there way back." He shook his head. "Since the sixties, Keith has been on a binge, biting people right and left. Not sure why, but he didn't think twice. Tried to get me, but I was never a fan of his music, so I just didn't pay him any attention. Lots of my friends were bragging about being bit, though. Most of them are dead now. Ask him about that."

"How could they die, what's the cure for immortality?" She was thrown off by how serious he was about this, just like Keith had been. Just no fucking way. *Jesus, I'm turning into a crazy person.*

Bob took a last pull on his cigarette butt. "Heroin. Only heroin will kill off a vampire."

Darla took this in. Heroin overdoses in music were legendary.

"If you ever see him again, ask him about Janis Joplin or Jim Morrison. Ask about Sid Vicious or Amy Winehouse."

She was done with this. Music legend or not, it was time to tell him what she thought. "Mr. Dylan—"

"Bob."

"Bob. I don't think Keith is a vampire. He's a person on some very powerful drugs with a lot of crazy ideas. I don't know what kind of drugs you may be on, but no one is going to turn me into a vampire. This is not normal. I am *not* looking for fame and fortune by becoming a vampire, is that clear? In fact, I'm not looking for fame and fortune at all. I just want to sing."

"He can read your mind, right? You can talk to him without opening your mouth. Do you think that is normal? Can you explain that? These things exist in this world. We have to stop them."

She didn't know how to reply. She didn't want him to make sense.

"Be very careful." He reached into his coat pocket again and pulled out a business card. "Promise you'll call me before you get tempted." He put on his Mountie hat and left the room.

Darla stuffed his card into her back pocket. She needed a drink. She needed to be with normal people and talk about normal things.

∞

Darla left The Zinc Bar and walked over to Minetta Tavern to meet the band for beers, one of the traditions they'd kept for years.

She was still disturbed by creepy old Bob Dylan. He knew about her visit with Keith, he knew that he could read her mind. He said he had seen a real vampire. Why the fuck were these big stars so goddamned crazy? Just fuck all of this. They both liked the band's music, but all the rest of that bullshit immortal stuff was too much to swallow. For now, she would just ignore it; it would be a story she could tell her kids. If she ever got around to having kids.

She got to the door of the tavern and took a deep breath. Where did all that great energy go from Wednesday night in Astoria? She didn't want to walk in here with her fists in the air. Maybe she wouldn't mind the band's stasis so much if they played like they did for Keith all the time. That felt to her like the joy of making music, why she loved it so much. But now their energy was disjointed, uneven. They were coming from different places, and the music reflected that. She had to face the truth, though. Harry and Lee were not going to up their game. This was as good as it would get. The question came down to what she was willing to do.

Keith Richards had put a bug in her. He had given her hope that her life could be better. He had said the F word: famous. But that was not her thing. She had to be real, she just wanted to sing. Maybe if she were ten years younger, but as a thirty-four-year-old woman singing in New York City, she didn't have a long shelf life. Fame was something little kids wished for. And housewives of various cities.

When she opened the door to the tavern, the hostess recognized her and gave her a big hug. Darla had waited tables there a couple of years ago and the staff still felt like old friends. Harry, Lee, and Alby were at their usual table in the back. Alby waved and her heart melted a little. For better or for worse, this was her family. At the end of the day they should be able to come together and have a beer. And maybe later she could have some quiet time with Alby. She smiled to herself as she walked over to their table. This wasn't a bad life.

She sat down and ordered a beer, and she could see from the empty shot glasses that the guys were probably already liquored up. When she pulled her phone out of her back pocket to snap some photos of them, Bob Dylan's card fell out of her pocket. Harry picked it up off the floor and stared at it for a minute.

"Damn, you work quick, girl!" Harry held up his beer to her. "So tell us, is Bob cut or uncut? Inquiring minds . . ."

"Dude, he's Jewish!" Lee laughed.

Darla let it go. Sometimes when Harry drank, he liked to pick on her.

Lee's glasses were crooked when he looked up from his drink. "Was he bigger than Keith?"

Darla gulped her beer down. Could she handle the two of them tonight? They were being more assholish than usual. Something had changed. There was a resentment, a nastiness in their joking. Or was she just being too sensitive? "Damn, you cocksuckers are some bitter, jealous bitches tonight."

"What did he want to talk to you about?" Alby tried to change the subject.

Darla sighed. How to explain it to them? "Some crazy shit. I don't know, the bible, dead rock stars, heroin. These guys live in another world, I think."

Harry put his beer down and leaned in close to her. "You don't want to tell us what he said, do you? C'mon, did he promise you something? And what about Keith Richards, what exactly did he want? Why can't you be straight with us?"

Darla took another gulp of her beer. Was this a thing now? "I'm telling you guys, they both said they liked the band but then they both started talking about crazy stuff."

"Crazy stuff, like they'd like you to sing for them or whatever. Should we start looking for a new singer?" Harry picked up his glass. "Why can't you just be honest? You're tired of the band, right? You want more. You want to be some big, famous singer, and our shithole little band isn't enough for you."

Was it the drink? Or was this resentment always bubbling underneath the surface and she never saw it? "I'm not leaving the band, guys, just calm down."

Lee adjusted his glasses. "Did you call these guys? Tell us the truth, did you get them to come and see us? Or rather, see you?"

Alby finally piped up, "Guys, she's telling the truth. She told me that Keith Richards really believes he's a vampire. A real fucking vampire! And he was, like, telling her all about what life was like hundreds of years ago."

Lee straightened his glasses. "Oh, I see, you tell him what Keith Richard says, but not us. I guess that's just pillow talk though, huh?"

"Hey, wait a minute." Alby was getting flustered.

Darla held her hand up. "It's okay, Alby." She didn't understand what was happening right now, but apparently her rant after the show had opened up Pandora's Box. Harry and Lee were tag-teaming her. They had had plenty of disagreements in the past, but this felt different. Did they talk to each other about her? They must have. They were friends long before she had come along. "What is this all about?"

"The facts." Harry sat up. "All of a sudden, two rock stars in a row show up to our shows. They *only* want to talk with you —not the leader of the band, but you. Then you have these . . . conversations with them and won't tell us what's going on. Oh, sorry, it's about vampires. Righhhht. Put it all together. Hey, that's fine, you want to be some big, famous singer, you want to be the star, not just a singer in a band? I got no problem with that, just be honest."

"I have been honest." Darla pushed her chair back. "Do you guys think I have a bunch of rock stars on speed dial, and I can just call them up and say, 'check us out'? What is this?"

"That's my question." Harry took a swig of his beer. "From what I see, you feel like you're wasting your time in this band. You're bored or feel like we're beneath you. Then tonight, you totally give us a big 'fuck you' and do your own thing on the encore. Sounds like you don't even need us."

"Not only do you fuck us with the encore song," Lee continued Harry's rant, "but it just happens to be a song we never rehearsed, and the famous author of that song just happens to be in the audience. What a coincidence!"

"It was a coincidence." Darla could now see their beef about the encore, but they were really pushing this too far. "I never said you guys were beneath me or that I was bored, where did you get that?"

"Look, I got no problem with your . . . ambitions." Harry drained his glass and ignored her protestations. "Whatever you think you need to do to get there, that's your business. You need to fuck Keith, no problem, fuck Bob Dylan, no problem." He pointed his glare at Alby. "Hell, you fuck all of our drummers, why would it bother me who you fuck. Not judging."

She took a deep breath and stared at Harry. "Are you seriously calling me a whore? I mean, seriously?"

"Well technically, I don't think money has changed hands, so it would be more like a slut." Lee downed a shot. "Opportunist slut, maybe?"

"Yeah, not just your garden-variety slut for sure." Harry clinked his glass with Lee.

Darla stood up from her chair. She couldn't sit with them and drink any longer. "Listen to me carefully, shit-for-brains, I did not contact either of them. I don't know how they found out about the band." Her anger was building, moving her. She grabbed her beer glass off the table and emptied it on Harry's head. Then she grabbed her coat off the back of her chair and marched out.

She walked a few blocks to calm herself down. So this was what they thought of her. Was it all because she dared to ask them to be better? It felt like the end of the band. The schism that opened tonight was too wide to come back together. Fuck. She stopped at a bus stop and sat on the bench.

There wasn't any trust left. She couldn't go back to them. All of that hatred simmering—for how long? She'd have to face the prospect of starting over, singing on her own or starting up a new band. *I'm alone. I'm thirty-four, a waitress alone in New York. I just want to sing.* She closed her eyes and breathed in. She wasn't a kid anymore. She needed to seriously think about what chances she had.

But maybe there was another option.

Why the fuck not?

"Keith Richards, can you hear me? Is this really the way to contact you?"

She felt stupid. *What am I doing? I'll just go home and cry. Figure it out later.*

"Hello, love! Yeah, this is how it works. What's up?"

She ran her hand through her hair and took deep breaths. *"Can we meet up again?"*

"Right on. Tomorrow, Carlyle again, ten p.m."

3

On Saturday night, Darla sat in a Starbucks across the street from the Carlyle. She got there early to collect her thoughts before she met with Keith. She was sipping a macchiato and making a checklist in her notebook. She wanted to be clear with him about what to expect. She had to be smart and logical about her life now. No more emotional decisions, no more vague wishes and dreams, just facts and plans.

She wrote down: *Vampire/bite?*

Now that she was going to take this nonsense seriously, she figured that the bite was probably some technical process. She had been googling vampire bites and found all kinds of crazy cults and bad dental surgery photos. There was also some kind of medical procedure that was the latest trend among the filthy rich: blood transfusions from healthier younger people. Was that what he meant? He would have to make it clear to her what he was talking about. She would need time to examine whatever he thought this vampire or immortal business was.

Crazy Bob Dylan?

She also wanted to ask Keith why Bob Dylan was so against whatever it was that he was doing.

Singing career/What does he offer?

She had to put together a whole new band. She couldn't go back to Funk and Spunk. She hadn't heard a word from them all day, except for Alby. He had texted her late the previous night that he had quit the band. He made her smile. She wanted to ask him to come over, to crawl in bed with her and just hold her until she could fall asleep, but she was in such a bad, needy place that she was afraid she'd scare him away forever.

The band was an open wound. Lee and Harry had obviously been harboring all this resentment for a while. All of that gentle ribbing from them over the years had not been as gentle as she thought. She felt betrayed. All that time with them, she thought that they were just a happy little band with a cool sound, but really, they hated her. How did she miss that? Fuck 'em.

She was starting from scratch again, essentially. She dreaded the idea of going back to begging for gigs, looking for talent nights at crappy little clubs, trying to explain why she was no longer part of the band that most people knew her for. Ugh. But she had to be smart and make sure she was taking the right action. The world had changed so much since she had started out. The biggest change was her age. She was no longer a cute young thing who could spend nights in clubs hanging out with bands and asking about auditions.

All of the advice online for singers was about branding. What did she want her brand to be? What kind of commodity was she? Who were her demographics? Also, she would have to figure out how to build a social media presence. She hated all of that bullshit, but this was the reality she had to deal with. All the stuff that Harry was supposed to do for their band but never bothered. In their last meeting, Keith had hinted that he expected her to take this kind of stuff on, but how could she explain to Keith that she just wanted to sing?

The Starbucks barista interrupted her thoughts by loudly stacking the chairs on the tables. Subtle. Ten p.m., time to go. She packed up her notepad and made her way across the street to the Carlyle Hotel.

∞

Once again, the bar was closed to the general public. This time there was a sign that said PRIVATE EVENT. Rock star power, closing a bar down on a Saturday night. She poked her head in and saw that the whole bar was empty except for Keith in the back. The same bouncer from the other night, this time in a dark suit, popped up out of nowhere and moved to stop her.

"Your name, please? I'll need to see an ID."

Darla did not have the patience for this. "Eat me." She moved past him toward Keith.

"Hello, love! It's okay, Rodney, I got it." Keith waved at her to come in.

The closer she got to him, the more she could feel her energy rise. It was happening again, like the other night. She felt more . . . powerful. It was a giddy feeling, like she could run a marathon and still not be tired. She made a mental note to add this to her checklist: How does this tribal blood theory really work? It sounded like bullshit, but damn, she felt good.

"Welcome back. Have a drink? Can I order you a bite? I mean food!"

She sat down next to him and took out her notebook. "A glass of rosé would hit the spot."

"Rodney? Bring a bottle of rosé, would ya?" He turned toward her. "I'm sensing some drama going on, no?"

She was a little put off by the sunglasses tonight. "I had a major falling out with the band last night. I brought up some . . . points with them after a gig on Friday night—you know, like we had talked about—but they didn't really agree."

He smiled wide at her. "You want more, don't ya? Good for you. More is always good. Some are scared of more."

Rodney brought over the bottle of rosé and poured Darla a glass, avoiding looking at her, and left them alone again.

Darla picked up her glass. "I don't know if it's more or better or just . . . different."

"More, better, it's all good. You want what you want. You can get it."

Darla took a sip of her rosé. This was the good stuff. "Bob Dylan might not agree."

Keith tilted his head and lit up a cigarette.

"Bob Dylan caught our set last night. He came backstage after the show."

"Well that's something. He like your music?"

"Yeah, he liked it, but he was . . . downright creepy. And he's dead set against the whole vampire thing, which he seems to know a lot about."

"I never got Dylan's music," Keith explained. "Nice sentiment and all, but no drama. Just spitting out the words. You gotta sit up real close and pay attention. I mean, not really singing, is it? Like some cat been stepped on. I mean, that's all fine for sittin' in ya flat with a bottle of sherry, but you go out for some music, you want to move, right? You want something to hit you blind-side." He reached for some nuts in a dish. "You know what I'm saying?"

"Tell me about heroin. He said I should ask you about Janis Joplin, Jim Morrison, Sid Vicious, and Amy Winehouse." Darla reached for the nuts. "He said you . . . bit all those people."

He cocked his head and lowered his glasses, revealing the blood-red irises. "Vampire eyes is the worst." He flipped his glasses back up. "That time was pretty wild, back in the sixties. All the drugs and such. Really nothing like it. I mean, me and Mick would sometimes go for decades without bumping into someone with the blood, like you. All of a sudden, everyone we saw had some kind of tribal connection. So it was kind of wild for us. Some people was beggin' us to bite 'em. Fangs poppin' out all the time. So yeah, we got carried away."

"Did you try to bite Bob Dylan? Is that why he's so . . . adamant about it?"

"Don't rightly recall. I'm sure me or someone prolly tried. Maybe that's what got him all churchy. Heard he was born again or some such nonsense a few years back."

"Decades without biting? Don't vampires have to have fresh blood on a regular basis?"

"I told you, clear your head out of all the Hollywood B.S." Keith stubbed his cigarette out on an empty dish and lit another one. "You know, back then there weren't no instruction manual, like if you get bit, do this and go here and eat this. All just by word of mouth. So drinking the blood, as far as I can tell, stops the aging process. You drink a lot, you don't age, even get younger; you stop, you age. I don't get no random pangs for blood, otherwise I'd just bite any old bloke on the street. Like I said, fangs have to pop out, can't force 'em."

She marveled at his ability to spin these vampire stories. She didn't know how to take them, but he didn't miss a beat. She glanced down at her notebook. "What about this heroin thing?"

"Right, so me and Mick was back in Austria, probably sometime in the mid-1800s, when we hears about some drug made to kill off vampires. Some guy in London. We decide to make our way over there and see what the fuss is about. We been talking about going to London for a time anyways, so that's when we first came over. We fell in love with London, by the way. Been there ever since."

Rodney stopped by and leaned toward Keith. "The hotel is complaining about the cigarette smoke drifting out into the lobby."

"What's that? I rented the bloody room, just tell them to charge me a fine or whatever, alright? If it scares off their customers, tell 'em to come see me." He flicked his ashes onto the carpet.

Rodney left the room.

"I'm bloody Keith Richards fer chrissake! Anyways, so we get to London and turns out some wanker bit the wife of some scientist guy and she run off with the guy who bit her, so's this scientist guy spends years studying vampires and drugs. He manages to convince one of 'em to let him experiment on him and voilà, he finds out that a specific strain of heroin can pretty much kill off a vampire. Takes quite a bit but eventually does the trick. So unknown to me, Mick actually pinches some of the stuff and keeps it to himself."

"Why?"

"Turns out he was a wee depressed, missing some of his old family and all, so he was thinking of maybe offing himself that way."

Darla just knew this must be bullshit. "Weren't you, like, a major heroin addict? I mean, that's kind of what you're known for."

"Oh, that rot. First, if you get to live forever, the two things you think about are how to make a lot of fookin' money, cuz eternity is a long time if you don't have money, the second thing is keepin' yourself entertained. I mean, nowadays it's a lot easier to keep yourself busy, but over the course of a couple hundred years maybe I tried a few substances, you know? Weren't much else to keep me busy sometimes. No drug can kill me, right? So why not see what all the fuss is about? So, yes, heroin kills a vampire, but only a very specific mixture of the stuff. Very, very pure, really difficult to make these days. Not something you can just buy on the street. I mean, you'd probably have to fly to some other part of the world and pick the poppy plants yourself to make vampire killer heroin. The kind of heroin that I was using was a whole different brew, more crap synthetic stuff in it. That stuff don't kill you, saps your brain a wee bit."

Darla stared at him in disbelief. "I don't get this. So all these people who died, how did they get the killer heroin?"

Keith took a long sigh. "Don't rightly know. After getting bit, everyone kind of took off on their own, didn't much keep in touch. Actually, not even sure how they found out about that mixture. Me and Mick never told no one about it. Wondered if someone who stayed at Mick's house may have nicked some of his original stash. You're the first one who ever asked about it."

"How does Bob Dylan figure in all of this?" Darla was still disturbed by his visit. "He gave me a headache when he touched me."

"Not sure what his deal is. He was always a bit of a damper, though. You know the type, just no fun at parties. Funny he gave you a headache when he touched you. I mean, not funny-funny, but just shows you," he reached over and touched Darla's hand, "differences in people."

Darla felt a surge go through her body, like the best sex she'd ever had, like she had just run a mile and all her endorphins were exploding, like she had been studying for a test and she knew all the answers. Whatever this was, she wanted . . .

"More." Keith lowered his glasses and showed her his red eyes. "Everything is so clear now, ain't it?"

Darla couldn't help herself. She smiled at him. "What is this?"

"It's you, love. It's who you could truly be. You're feeling your true self is all. Your best self. Now, tell me what's true about you now that you didn't know before."

Darla closed her eyes. She could clearly see her options, what was wrong and what was right. She was a great singer, she had so much talent. There were all kinds of talents she had that she had never even explored. She could be a great songwriter, too, she could see a way to singing for a living—it wasn't a matter of whether it was possible, it was a matter of doing it. She could do it. She thought, *Yes, I want this life!* She knew that money would come from this, she could have everything, anything! She'd never felt this way, and now she wondered why.

She could have it all. She opened her eyes and looked at Keith's. "Whatever the fuck this is, I want it. I do want more. I want . . . everything."

Keith took his glasses off and opened his mouth. She watched as two shiny white incisors began slowly descending from his mouth.

"Holy fuck!" She pushed her chair away.

Keith looked at her and cocked an eyebrow, pointing to his mouth. "Fangth." Talking through them was a challenge.

"Jesus Christ, they're real! I didn't think . . . you had real . . . fangs."

"Well, I been telling you."

"Oh my god, that means . . . it's all true. The immortality, the heroin, the dead rock stars."

"Did you think I juth made it all up?"

"Well, kind of." Darla had to rethink everything now. Life itself was no longer what she thought it was. But immortality? Holy fuck.

Keith's fangs began to recede back into his mouth. "Second thoughts now, huh? See how this works? I would never lie to ya, darlin'. I know it sounds a bit . . . fantastical, but you get used to it. It ain't a bad way at all. Another glass of rosé?"

Darla grabbed the bottle and poured another glass. "I'm a little scared of this whole thing now. I didn't think I was going to become like a real . . . ghoul."

Keith lit up another cigarette. "Wouldn't call it a ghoul, more like Superman. Wish we had the power to fly, though, but that whole bat thing is a myth, too. Ah, well. Look, I'm still a person, none of this dramatic undead business, really. You just lives longer, and you get a lot of shit done."

"But you can't die, right? I mean, what about getting cancer? Or jumping off a building?"

"Ah, the life or death stuff. Now, your blood becomes much stronger so you don't get sick so easy, but it don't make you immune to some stuff. Mick and me had some really bad stuff over the years, but eventually you just heal. Still, don't feel great when it happens. Now, I imagine if you was to jump off a building it would hurt like shit. The blood don't protect you against pain, but you would just heal eventually. I met a bloke in London way back, cut off his hand to see if it would grow back."

"Well?"

"No, poor sod stuck for eternity with one hand."

Darla swallowed her wine. "I just don't know. Maybe I need more time. I mean, really all I wanted was to be a singer. Just a good singer." Did she want to trade her humanity for a career? Was that what it came down to? Become some kind of freak, just so she could make a living? It felt like a deal with the devil. Like Bob Dylan had said.

Keith smiled at her. "There it goes, the devil business. Oh, sorry, didn't mean to overhear you in there. But listen, you really think that if there were a God he wouldn't be on my side? Being superhuman? Healing from disease? You'd think he might like that, now. No, instead this God gives you cancer, poverty—all kinds of shit I seen. And this is the way we was born, mind you. If he's doing all this meddling, he's the one that did this, too."

He was making sense. But still, was this worth it? She couldn't answer that question.

Keith leaned toward her and pulled his sunglasses off again. "Try to think about it this way." He grabbed her hand again.

Darla felt the energy surge inside her once more. It was like a drug that made her think clearly, without any petty fears or doubts clogging up her mind. Doors opened up in her brain, with even more desires, and more ideas, and no mental roadblocks. Her life could be . . . everything. She could live without fear, and sing and sing and sing. And finally, she thought, *I could be really fucking famous if I want.*

She looked into Keith's deep red eyes. "Let's do this."

Keith's fangs slowly descended again.

Darla pulled her hair away from her neck.

Keith pulled her wrist up to his face. "Don't need the neck, thith ith juth ath good. Leth . . . pervy, you know?" He pulled out an alcohol wipe from his jacket pocket and wiped her wrist down. "You may feel a pinch, like you wath getting a thot."

"A what?"

"Thot!" Keith made a motion like an injection.

Darla nodded. She took a deep breath and braced herself. The notebook in her lap slid to the floor. *Here it comes, a whole brand-new life . . .*

She watched Keith slowly sink his fangs into her wrist. She winced as they pierced her skin. The process was a lot neater than she imagined. He wasn't actually sucking her blood in, it looked like the incisors were vacuuming up the blood into Keith's mouth. It took about two minutes, and when he pulled his fangs out they withdrew back into his head.

He let go of her wrist and the fresh wave of boundless energy that she had experienced with his touch was now hers. She giggled. "I'm a fucking vampire!"

Keith pulled a backpack up to his lap, pulled out a Band-Aid, and stuck it onto her wrist. "Now, I got some stuff for you, gotta give you your training wheels."

Darla stretched her arms. She felt fantastic, rejuvenated. "Wow. This feels amazing. Who knew?"

Keith was still rifling through his backpack for something. "Listen, I want you to take it easy for a day or two. You're probably feeling like you could party forever, but you need to get used to this. You got a long time to do things, no need to do them all tonight, although you might feel that way, right?"

A smile burst out of her face. She did feel that way! It was like getting her first bicycle when she was little and wanting to ride all over the city. The endless places she could go, the new experiences she could have. She wanted to do something, do everything. "I love this!"

"Bugger." Keith pulled out his phone and began texting. "Just give me a minute, darling, I got a vampire starter kit for you."

"Starter kit?"

"Yeah, vamps in the twenty-first century is a whole new thing. Used to be just bite and go, but now it's kind of a bit more organized. Much better experience getting started."

Rodney entered the bar with a small shopping bag and handed it to Keith.

Darla looked at Rodney. Maybe she shouldn't have been such a bitch to him. He was kind of a good-looking hunk of beef. For a second, she thought about giving him a nice slap on the ass.

"Whoa, girl! Let's pull it back a bit. Thanks, Rodney, better get outside before you get yourself raped!"

"Sorry." Darla started to feel a little self-conscious. "It's just so . . . new."

"You have to be careful. You're hungry now, in every sense of the word, and you don't want to fill up on junk at the buffet. You could get into some trouble chasing after Rodneys and such all night." Keith pulled out a small box with a new phone in it. "This here phone is your new best friend. Don't ever go nowhere without it. When you get home, do the whole sign-on thing and you see this app here?" He pulled up an app with a red icon displaying the letter F. "This here's called ForeverBook. It's like an app for vampires. Tells you everything you need to know. Specially when I'm not around. Got a red eye to London tonight. Wish I'd had this little gadget four hundred years ago, so this will answer a lot of questions, okay?"

She took the phone and noticed she could see Keith's irises for the first time. "What happened?"

"Now we got the same blood, so no more vamp boner." He reached into the small shopping bag and pulled out a pill bottle. "Tonight, go home, play around with your new phone, and take two of these. Will help you get to sleep. Trust me, darlin', you need to get some rest before you run around with your new superpower. These pills will help. I'll have my car take you home. I'll probably be in London when you wake up, but just get ahold of me with your mind anytime. Clear?"

Darla took the bag from Keith and nodded. "Thank you so much." She felt like she could fly home, but she would take his car.

Keith walked her to a town car waiting in front of the hotel. "Nice and slow, for now. Not advice I usually give. We'll talk tomorrow."

He knocked on the window and the driver lowered the glass. "Take her straight home, now. No stops, understand?" The driver nodded, and Keith kissed Darla on the forehead and opened the car door for her.

Darla took a deep breath before getting in. New York City was new again. The energy of the city that everyone talks about was something she could feel now. There were a million things going on in Manhattan at midnight, and she wanted to be a part of each and every one of those things. She got into the back seat and took out her new phone. There was no way she could go to sleep, no matter how many sleeping pills she took.

She pulled out her phone and texted Alby.

"You around tonight?"

"Who is this?"

"Darla. New phone number."

"Hey! You okay? I'm at Cow Bar in Hell's Kitchen"

"On my way"

Darla opened the glass partition. "Can we make one stop?"

"Sorry, I can't. Keith's strict orders to . . ."

Darla wouldn't have it. She wondered if she could do that same thing to the driver that Keith had done to her. She reached her hand over, touched him on the shoulder, and concentrated on sending a shot of vampire energy into him.

"Of course, ma'am, no problem! One stop will be fine, I think!"

She smiled to herself. Superpowers working. *I am fucking Wonder Woman!*

They pulled in front of The Cow Bar and Darla stepped out of the town car, regarding the line for the club. Yes, these were the hideous bridge and tunnel people that she always avoided, but not tonight. She could feel their energy, their hope, their needs. They were just people like her. She laughed to herself. *Or how I used to be.* How could that be? What a difference having this strong blood made. She absolutely hated trendy scene bars or lounges like this one, but tonight she felt an absence of hate, an absence of judgment. She felt . . . free.

She walked up to the bouncer at the door.

"Evening, are you on the guest list?"

"I'm on everyone's guest list tonight."

The bouncer cocked his head and smiled.

She could tell her energy was infectious. She placed her hand on his leg near his crotch and wondered if she could focus her new energy on another person with a specific intent. "I don't think they've invented a hashtag for this yet."

The bouncer's eyeballs moved up toward his eyelids as he started to breathe heavily. "Oh my god, oh my god!"

Looks like it worked! I bet you Wonder Woman could never do that.

"It's good, isn't it?"

He opened the door for her.

∞

She walked into the packed club and absorbed the energy from the crowd. A smile spread across her face. People were here looking for connection, basic human touch, and she felt connected to all of them, like she knew them, understood them. This was the same high she got from singing. They wanted love, they wanted attention, they wanted to forget bad things.

The place was so crowded that she could not see the bar. Normally this would really piss her off—nothing worse than coming to a bar and not being able to get a drink—but that was PB! Pre-Bite! A crowded room was no longer an obstacle to her. She started to navigate her way into the space, and a drunk young woman with big hair and a tiny dress knocked into her. Darla's old instinct would have been to push back harder, but that was PB. She looked at the woman and touched her shoulder; the poor woman was desperate to find her friends, to find something tonight that would make her life a little happier.

The woman broke into a smile. "Did I bump into you? I'm so sorry, are you okay? That was so . . . careless of me."

"I'm fine, enjoy your night!" Darla rubbed the woman's shoulder and moved on. *Goddamn,* she thought, *I'm in total control. Not only control of myself but control of my environment. This stuff is fucking amazing.*

Now, how to find Alby. She couldn't see him above all the people in the club, but she knew that wouldn't be a problem. She knew he was there; she could feel his presence. In fact, she thought she could smell him. It was the scent of his body after a night of cuddling, that was what she was following. She moved toward the corner of the club where his scent was coming from. She knew she was getting closer, like he was pulling her toward him.

People in front of her parted as she got closer, revealing Alby leaning against a wall in the back, talking to some of his friends. She held her head up and thought, *I'm here, Alby*.

He immediately looked up and saw her. She could tell he was happy to see her. In fact, she thought she heard him think, "*She made it!*"

She hugged him and felt an intense arousal spread from her chest throughout her body and into his. She felt the energy surge back into her from his body. Their chemistry was more than just hormones; this went deep.

"Damn, quitting a band agrees with you, huh?" Alby rubbed her back. "You look great!" He looked over to his buddies. "Guys, this is Darla, the singer from Spunk and Funk that I was telling you about."

They all shook her hand and she seemed to be able to speak to them through touch: *Leave the two of us alone here.*

They immediately left the area. *Fucking A.*

"What did you do? You're . . . different." Alby looked into her eyes.

"I became a vampire." She showed him her bandaged wrist. "Keith Richards bit me just a little while ago."

"He actually bit you? On the wrist? Well, whatever he did, it must have worked."

She could hear some more thoughts, not hers. He was happy that she was doing so well, but he wondered if she was on some kind of drug. She could hear his heartbeat.

"It wasn't a drug at all, just his fangs." Her vision started to become clouded. Did they just lower the lights?

"Okay then."

She could hear him again. He was thinking about Keith trying to use his teeth to gnaw on her wrist, not actual fangs. She had had the same problem picturing it PB.

"But I gotta say, man, I feel really good, too."

"Just like the night he came to the club and saw the band, right?" She was thirsty now, incredibly thirsty. She grabbed the beer out of his hand and took a sip, but that didn't help. She wanted something else to drink.

"You okay?" Alby was leaning in to look at her eyes.

She could see more of his thoughts. He still thought she was on drugs. She could understand that—she had to explain this new energy, this new power in her blood, but more importantly, she needed to drink something . . .

"Your eyes, something is in your eyes, I think."

It hit her. Alby had the tribal blood. She wanted to drink him. Vampire boner. This was so fucking primal, she needed to have his blood in her body. She pulled him closer and hugged him. "Do you want to become a vampire, too? You would love it. Live forever, no more obstacles. It's like fucking heaven."

Alby held her tight and rocked her. "Sure! Sounds excellent."

His body wanted this, his blood was reacting to her blood, words weren't that important now. Darla felt a slight ache in her upper gum. Her fangs had come out. She was just seconds away from the ultimate bond with Alby for all eternity. She opened her mouth and plunged her fangs into his neck. She felt his blood enter her body and jump right into her entire nervous system. Her thirst was being quenched, but at the same time she wanted more. His blood was bringing something new and different to her life, something exciting that she couldn't define yet.

"Ouch!" Alby backed away from her with a jolt and grabbed his neck. He felt his skin and saw blood on his hand. His eyes widened as he looked at Darla and saw her fangs out. "Shit. You have fangs."

"Of courth. I told you I wath a vampire now." Keith had been right, talking through fangs was not easy.

A woman near them turned around and saw the blood dripping from Alby's neck and then Darla's fangs. "Oh my god!" She dropped her drink glass to the floor and screamed loud enough to be heard over the crowd around them. More people turned to stare.

Her fangs retracted, leaving a small trail of blood from her lip to her blouse. "You changed your mind?"

Alby seemed dazed. "I wasn't thinking that you would . . . bite me."

Darla didn't know what to do or say. She still needed, wanted, his blood, but he had rejected her. How could he do that? She felt her stomach cramp up. Something was wrong. "I'm sorry. Something . . . fucked up . . ." The cramp shot up into her sternum and before she knew it, she was vomiting on herself.

The people around them backed away in panic and disgust. Darla ran to the back of the bar, looking for a bathroom. She found a line of women waiting in front of a door. She pushed them aside and forced her way into the bathroom, then pulled open a stall door and grabbed a woman off the toilet. "Move!" She shoved the woman out of the stall and began retching uncontrollably.

Sudden pain spread all over her body, like a thousand pinpricks inside of her veins. She tried to breathe, to gain some sense of normalcy, but her stomach kept roiling and she started throwing up again.

Amid all of the women yelling in the restroom, she thought she heard Alby's voice in the background. "Give her some room."

Darla finally stopped heaving and took deep breaths. She knew Alby was behind her somewhere, but she could not look at him, could not face him. She needed to get out. She wouldn't even bother to clean up. She stood up and quickly pushed her way out of the bathroom. A security guard was waiting for her just outside the women's room. He leaned over to say something but she kept moving. It was difficult to walk, as every step increased the tiny pricks of pain already shooting all over her body, and she didn't know if her stomach would seize up again. It felt like her body was rebelling against her. Against the decision to become a vampire.

The crowd in the club parted as she made her way forward. Darla kept her eyes on the exit and tried not to notice their looks of revulsion and loathing at her vomit-laden body.

She finally made it outside and ignored the stares of the crowd in line. Where was her car? She pulled her phone out of her pocket and texted the driver. *"Pick me up now!"*

She wanted to go home and forget everything. Forget she ever met Keith Richards, forget she ever wanted to be a singer. *What the fuck have I done to my life?*

4

Darla did not get out of bed the next morning. She didn't see the point. Her stomach still felt like shit and she wanted to hide from her life and all of the bad decisions she'd made the last couple of days.

She ran her fingers along the bite marks on her wrist. All of this nightmare because she wanted to sing. She felt like she had made a deal with the devil, given her life away as a career move. The echoes of her old Sunday school classes tortured her. She had been tricked. Creepy old Bob Dylan had been right. Her soul was no longer hers. She was a slave to this . . . thirst.

I should never have done this, she thought. *Now this will be my life forever, whatever forever means.* She could not stretch her mind that far. She knew that she didn't want to have to live like a freak. And the worst part, Alby had rejected her, watched her get sick all over herself, in a club full of people. There had to be some way to fix this, to click the undo button and become a normal person again.

In desperation, she reached over to her nightstand and grabbed her purse. She looked through her wallet and found Bob Dylan's card. Maybe he had some kind of solution, hopefully something besides heroin. She briefly thought about swallowing the whole bottle of sleeping pills that Keith had given her. What would it matter? She couldn't die, right?

She sat up and grabbed her vampire phone. There were a few texts from Alby.

"Where are you?"

"Is everything okay?"

"Do you need me?"

Her eyes watered up. All this time she thought he considered her a fuck buddy, but he really did care. And how did she respond? By trying to turn him into a monster. Biting into him like a hungry fucking needy animal. Like a bitch in heat. How could she ever face him again?

She dialed Bob Dylan's number, feeling like she was back in church again. She'd have to tell him that he was right, that she didn't listen to him, like confessing to a priest. A dark, heavy atmosphere of judgment, sin, and guilt hung over her. She hit the send icon and felt a tingle crawl from her hand, up her arm, and then jolt her head again, just like the night Bob had shaken her hand. She dropped the phone to the floor.

"Hello?" Bob's voice rang out.

She stared at the phone while she rubbed her head. "What the fuck is happening to me?" she whispered.

"Hello, is anyone there?"

She still got a dangerous vibe from him, like he wanted to harm her.

"Darla, is that you?"

She hit the end call icon and crawled back under the covers. The phone rang. She peeked out and saw BOB DYLAN on the screen.

Fuck you, fuck everybody, and fuck every fucking thing.

After a fitful hour of trying to go back to sleep, she heard Keith's voice in her head.

"Darlin', it's me. You okay?"

Should she talk to him? She was stuck in vampire hell. Her eyes started to tear up again. She was stuck for the rest of her endless life.

"You there? I sense something is wrong."

"This whole thing is fucked! Fucked beyond belief. You lied to me, you tricked me!"

"Whoa, sweetheart! Something tells me you didn't go straight home and get some rest last night."

Darla remained silent for a few seconds. *"What does that matter? I had the worst night of my life. I feel like . . . like a goddamned monster. I hate this!"*

"Tell me what happened."

She took a deep breath. *"Alby, the drummer, I met him for a drink last night and my fangs came out. I felt like . . . a lowlife whore. I just bit him."* Darla started to cry. *"I couldn't stop myself and then I got sick, I got sick everywhere. And the pain, all over. My body still hurts. This is really bad."*

She heard Keith laugh, like Satan's chuckle, she thought. Laughing at her pain. *"Fuck you!"*

"Hey, there, I told you to go home and rest! I told you to set up your damn phone, you didn't do any of that. I was telling you to do that for a reason! Of course you got sick, I told you right off that if the bite don't take you get sick as a dog."

She felt guilt again. She didn't follow instructions. It didn't matter, this was still fucked. *I'm not a human being anymore,* she thought. This blood didn't make her stronger, it made her weaker, needier than she'd ever been. When Alby rejected her, it was more than just a rejection of her blood, it was her very soul he was rejecting. She felt so unloved, so repugnant. Alby saw all of her weakness and then rejected her.

"Come on, now. Just calm down. The sickness will pass. Promise. I been there, too."

She wouldn't answer him. Maybe she didn't follow instructions, maybe the sickness would pass, but she was still a freakshow, an unlovable, needy freakshow.

"Look, love, I just landed in London, so I'll have a vamp friend in town come over to help you soon as possible. In the meantime, open up the F app, that will help also, alright? If you don't do anything else, go take a look at the F app."

Darla pictured her phone in her mind and pressed the end call button.

Her real phone buzzed again. More texts from Alby.

"You still alive?"

He sent a photo of his bite marks.

"How cool is this? #Thisaintnohickey"

He made her smile. He felt sorry for her, a pity text. That was the best she could expect from him. She couldn't bring herself to respond.

She closed the texts and saw the bright red F app staring back at her. Was there something in the stupid app that could help her? Something for self-loathing vampires? She tapped on the icon.

WELCOME TO FOREVERBOOK

Soft pastel-colored graphics floated pleasantly across her screen. She swiped her finger across the logo:

MENU

WELCOME

SET UP

FAQ

CONTACT US

The **WELCOME** option was highlighted, so she opened it up. A video popped up and began to play. A young man sitting in a lounge with the ForeverBook logo behind him began to talk. She thought she recognized him from somewhere.

"Hi, welcome to ForeverBook! I'm Mark Zuckerberg, CEO and Super User! I'm here to help guide you through your super cool new eternal life. One of the really excellent things about becoming immortal in this age is that we have all these really cutting-edge tools at our disposal to help manage our eternal experience and connect with others in the Forever community. I'll go over some basics with you on how to utilize the app. When this video ends, you'll see a bunch of options appear under the Welcome banner. These are instructions on how to set up your account, how to provide updates to your Forever Family, how to invite others into your Forever Family, how to connect with others on ForeverBook, and our privacy policy. And remember, your data is always safe with us. You control how much of your data can be seen by others. Also, we promise never to sell your Forever Family data to any company without your permission. Welcome to Forever!"

The video disappeared into the background. Darla went to the **FAQs.** She saw:

`Bite and run?`

`My sponsor did a bite and run on me, and I haven't heard from him since. He just tossed me the phone and left. How do I connect with the vampires? (See More)`

She swiped to see the answer.

`Sorry to hear that your sponsor did not fully attend to his aftercare commitment that we here at ForeverBook always stress. However, you should always be grateful to your sponsor for giving you the gift of eternity! First of all, we don't like to use the V word to describe ourselves or our` family. The V word is an inaccurate slang term that many find offensive and divisive. We always like to refer to ourselves as members of an eternal community. After all, we're just people who live longer!

Secondly, while it's preferable to have your sponsor guide you through your first experiences as a new member of the eternal community, your growth and enjoyment do not depend on it. The F app is packed with resources drawing on the experience of thousands of people who have centuries of information available to you with just a swipe.

In some cases, if your sponsor is not available as your guide, they may have made arrangements for another member of the community to help you. Check your profile to see if this has been set up for you, or contact your sponsor to find out if he can authorize a local guide. A local guide is usually someone who is connected within your immediate eternal family. (See Becoming a Local Guide)

Darla exited the FAQ section and found the **My Profile** option. Her profile popped up. It had a template for basic info. Name and location, photo, and a section about her eternal family, which already had some information that Keith must have put in:

Eternal Sponsor: Keith Richards

Date of bite: 8/5/17

Eternal Age: 34

Local Guide: Yes

Hmm. Keith assigned her a local guide. Maybe that's the friend who was coming over to help her, but she couldn't find any more information about how that would work.

She spent some time setting up her profile and went back to the main page. A red warning bar appeared that she didn't see before. She opened it up.

WARNING: This warning is based on your location, specific family and members. This warning is based on reporting from local members:

AVOID ALL CONTACT WITH BOB DYLAN.

She closed the app. Now she was just a little scared. How come the app didn't tell her why to avoid Bob Dylan? Fuck, somehow, she was doing the whole vampire thing wrong.

Her intercom buzzer rang. She was instantly on guard. Was it Alby? *I can't see him now, I just can't,* she thought. The buzzer rang again. He would never just drop by, so maybe it wasn't him. She took a deep breath and pressed the talk button.

"Who is this?"

"This is Keith's friend? I come over to help y'all!"

She was taken aback by the woman's sunny southern accent.

"Third floor, top of the stairs, #3A." She pressed the button to let her in. A few minutes later, there was a polite knock on the door.

"Howdy, Darla, I'm here."

Even before opening the door, she felt a shift in her energy. The same shift that she felt when she met Keith for the first time. She started to feel better. Darla opened the door and gasped.

Dolly Parton stood in front of her. The blonde hair piled high, the insanely huge breasts, and the smile that ended with signature dimples.

"Howdy! I'm Dolly Parton. Keith asked me to come over?"

"Of course, come in." Darla could not take her eyes off of Dolly. "You're really Keith's vamp friend? Do you live here in New York?"

Dolly moved right past her into the apartment. She had a shopping bag with her and dropped it on her small dining table. "I got a place here in the city. I just happened to be in town when Keith called."

"This is . . . crazy."

"Well, crazy as it may be, I think you could probably use a nice big hug about now? No?" She opened her arms wide for Darla.

Darla's heart melted. She couldn't resist and hugged Dolly Parton. She laid her head on Dolly's famous chest and let out all her tears as Dolly petted her hair and rocked her like a baby. Was this all she needed? The anger, the resentment, and the humiliation she had felt all began to drain out of her system. Dolly's touch was healing. There was no other way she could describe it. It must have been that tribal blood thing.

"I know, sweetie, I know," Dolly soothed her. "I'm sorry, baby. Keith did a terrible job of settin' you up. But that's men for you."

Darla stopped crying and stared at Dolly. "I cannot believe that you're really one of them—I mean, of us."

She smiled back and nodded. "Yep. In fact, one of the oldest ones around these parts. I met Keith about a century ago. I could tell he weren't always a reliable sort, but I still love him like the dickens. Here, let's sit on the bed here. Keith told me what you been through, and I know just the thing that'll cure you, so I brought some of my homemade chicken soup. Just the thing for what you got." Dolly pulled a covered dish out of her shopping bag. "You got any spoons?"

Darla could smell the soup and opened the dish. Her eyes

began to tear up again. How could anyone be this thoughtful? To know that what she needed at this moment was a hug and homemade soup? She reached into a drawer and pulled out a spoon.

“I’m guessing you’re probably oozing with regrets? Wish you never met Keith? Am I right?”

Darla gulped the soup down. She could not believe how good it tasted. “Oozing is a good description.”

“My recipe is fabulous, isn’t it? Handed down for like seven generations! Listen, when I got bit it was by my husband, on our wedding night! Can you imagine? This was way back, barely after Jesus was born. Anyhow, back then they didn’t tell us girls much about wedding nights, if you know what I mean. I just thought that his crazy red eyes were some kind of sign that he was really in love! So he asked me, ‘Y’all wanna live with me forever?’ and I just said ‘Okeydokey.’ Out come the fangs and *bam*! I was a vampire! Oops, not supposed to use the V word anymore. So he just bit into me and said, ‘Okay now, y’all ain’t gonna never die. And don’t never talk to no one about it.’ That was it. He didn’t explain nothing, so there was a lot of trial and error with me.”

“God, that’s awful. Were you angry?”

Dolly pulled another dish out of her bag. “If you can handle it, I also made some fresh biscuits and gravy, but you can always freeze these for later. I wasn’t angry, just a little bit confused. I never expected him to bite me, but I’ll tell you one thing, that honeymoon night was quite memorable. Damn, I can still remember it to this day! Back then there were no movies or TV shows or even books about Dracula or that kind of nonsense, so I didn’t have that kind of frame of reference. But a few years go by and a plague hits. Everyone I knew died, and that’s when I started feeling a little strange, like maybe it was true that I was never gonna die. My hubby still wouldn’t talk to me about it, until a couple of years later when we was in some market and my eyes went all crazy red. Then he kinda explained about how it works. That's when I started to feel angry, like my old man had turned me into some kind of monster."

Darla put down her soup and stared at Dolly. "That's *exactly* how I felt."

Dolly rubbed her back. "Oh, I know, baby. Trust me, you may feel like a sack of poop now, but it'll pass. The good has more than outweighed the bad for me in the last couple of thousand years."

"What's it like to be alive for so long? Are you tired of it?"

"Those are some excellent questions." Dolly began to portion out biscuits and gravy for Darla. "In a way, I was lucky that I got bit so young, so I was able to keep my curiosity about the world intact. That and no matter what I look like on the outside, I feel like a teenage girl on the inside, so I'm not sure what it feels like to get tired of life like you supposed to when you grow old. I have been all over the world many, many times, I have watched so much history change, I have met and loved so many, many people. I consider this a special blessing."

Darla exhaled. Dolly made it all sound so simple. "Is your original husband still around?"

"Oh, yes, he is. We went our separate ways after a while. We waited 'til the children was grown. He's living in Dubai now and I go see him every once in a while."

"Children? Oh my god, how many kids do you have? How does that work?"

Dolly scooped up a dollop of gravy for Darla's biscuit and laughed. "Lordy, I have had hundreds! Can you believe that? In fact, folklore says I can still have more! But no, I'm done with all that. Well, for now."

Darla put down her soup. Hundreds of kids? She could not imagine. But she felt better now about being bit. Her energy levels were getting back to vampire normal, her stomach was calm.

"Now, that's enough about me, let's talk about you. Keith tells me you're a really great singer and you're from the south, so we got a lot in common. You learn to sing in church?"

Darla nodded. "It was so much a part of my childhood, of who I am. But aside from singing, I never much liked the church."

"I know what you mean. Especially with your current condition, you might feel a bit conflicted, but pay no matter to the stuff from your childhood in the church that might rise up and scare you. Look, I was around when they wrote the damn bible, and it was a work of fiction back then. The odd thing is I also just love being in churches. Way back when I was a girl, churches were like malls or coffee houses, that's where people gathered to chat and such."

"It is kind of a mindfuck, though. I keep thinking that this is, like, evil, against God."

"Of course you do. But you want to know what evil is? Evil is not being able to love or be loved. Nothing much else matters than that. Speaking of which, Keith tells me you had a run-in with a gentleman last night that sparked this whole crisis. So tell me about your young man."

"He's not really my man. I mean, he's kind of my man, but we don't have like a formal thing." Darla took another bite of her biscuit. She realized she had never spoken to anyone about Alby before. She didn't have a close girlfriend to confide in. But she felt so comfortable talking with Dolly. "We're more like . . . really familiar with each other. Like we have always known each other, comfortable. But he's a good-looking young guy, and I don't expect him to be all about me. Okay, well, the thing is, I'm a dozen years older than him. And I feel so desperate around him all the time. Like a lecherous old lady, grasping for youth." Yes, that was the problem. She'd been afraid to say it to herself, but she wasn't afraid to say it to Dolly.

"A dozen years?" Dolly was giggling. "I'm sorry, sweetie, I don't mean to make light of you, but in my timeline that's about two minutes' age difference. You'll see, it don't matter a hoot now. And you know what else? You want love, we all want love, no shame in it at all. You shouldn't feel bad about that; you should feel proud that you have such a heart."

Darla took this in. She had never thought about her thing with Alby as love. She had never really been in love before. Did it take becoming a vampire to feel love?

"If this young man means something to you, you'll need to give more consideration to bringing him into the family." Dolly took Darla's empty soup bowl and began to rinse it out in the sink. "I think you can benefit from my experience. You're creating a special eternal bond with him, goes deeper than a marriage. A marriage is nice, but it's temporary. Says right there in the oath, 'til death do us part, right? If he still wants to be bitten, you should do it right. I can help y'all out with that."

"Was I not done right?" Darla now wondered if Keith fucked her bite up.

"Don't blame Keith. Men are just bad at this kind of thing. And a flashy phone don't substitute for human touch in my book. Ideally, you need someone to spend your first few days with you, kind of like a sitter, 'cause you never know what will come up, like your fangs popping out first thing. By the way, that is pretty amazing. I really don't know many people who had that happen so soon. It's a sign of a good life to come."

Darla immediately thought about texting Alby back. Maybe there was some hope for him, for them. She looked at Dolly's face, and her smile was infectious. She just wanted to giggle with her. Jeez, this tribal blood stuff was powerful.

"What is it, sweetie?"

"It's just that . . . I'm still amazed at the past few days of my life. You, Keith Richards. Are there a lot of famous vampires? Is this like a big . . . thing?"

"Well, yes, there are quite a few of us, I will say that, but think about it. I truly believe that celebrity is just a byproduct of being a vam—immortal. I mean, all those famous people you see all cocky and fearless, right? That's cuz we aren't afraid of anything. I mean, there ain't no death, so what in life can stop me? And if I don't make my dream come true right now, I still got plenty of time. Ain't no clock ticking for us."

"But not all really famous people are immortal, right?"

"No, of course not. Lots of posers out there. I mean, when people see how confident we are, how energetic we are, they naturally will try to copy it, but only so much copying you can do. You'll know who is really immortal and who isn't. You'll be able to feel the presence of someone who's family. Now, don't you worry about getting crazy red eyes all the time. There's quite a few different tribal bloodlines, and you'll only get bothered by those in our own bloodline."

Bloodline. Alby was in her bloodline. "If Alby wants to become immortal, after all that mess from last night, how should I handle it?"

Dolly started putting the leftover biscuits and gravy in the freezer. "You need to talk with him and see how he really feels. Touch him, let him discover his own true self. Now, you should definitely not do this in a crowded bar! Probably right here in your own apartment is just fine, make it nice and comfy for the both of y'all."

Darla would do it, just like Dolly had told her. "Would you help me?"

"Of course, sweetie. As long as I got some free time, I'll be glad to help. I'll go ahead and send you a friend request on the F app so we can be in touch. In the meantime, you best start thinking about getting your singing career on track. I think you'll see if you put your mind to it, y'all can make things happen now." Dolly held her hand and smiled, revealing the trademark dimples again. "I think you'll find people to be more receptive now."

5

Darla waited for Harry and Lee in the back of Café Reggio in the Village. She loved this little place. It had been here for years, a rarity in New York's cutthroat rent environment, where old, trusted establishments folded and gave way to CVS and Starbucks. She loved the worn, dark wood floors, the stained and scratched marble tables, and the old waiters with their "fuck you" New York attitude.

After a day of rest, just like Keith and Dolly had assured her, her energy had returned, and she felt back in top vampire form. "Follow instructions" was her new mantra.

Since Dolly had told her to start thinking about her singing career, she weighed putting together a new band, or even auditioning for another band. There were all kinds of possibilities now, but her thinking had changed. Thanks to her new blood flow, her mind was no longer ruled by petty annoyances or fear. She could see things clearly and objectively. Without the emotional baggage weighing down her vision, she could see that the best and quickest option was to continue with Spunk and Funk.

Spunk and Funk was a good band. When they played in harmony, they were a great band. She loved the music, loved Harry's disco spin on blues. The key here was harmony. The night they played for Keith seemed so effortless, so joyful. What if she could make that happen with every gig?

What could be done about Harry and Lee's resentment? The more she thought about them, the more she could see where they were coming from. All of the time the band had been slipping into mediocrity, she had been complicit. She'd never said a word, implying she was okay with the band's direction. Naturally, they would get uncomfortable when she pointed out their shortcomings, when she was just as guilty as they were. She was also getting attention from famous people, and they weren't. These were things she could fix. She would take care of all of the band's social media. She would even take care of getting the gigs and promotions. What they needed from her was trust. She needed to earn their trust back.

She invited them to meet her to make her case. This reunion would be a test of her new vampire powers to see if she could make this right.

She saw Harry and Lee get out of a cab in front of the café. She felt herself tense up, blood moved into her shoulders, her gut tightened. She struggled to gain control of herself and began to lose confidence. She started to perspire.

Harry and Lee spotted her and made their way to the table. They sat down without a word.

Her blood seemed to react to them, just like during her first night out in the club with Alby when she could feel the crowd's mood and get a sense of what they wanted, a sense of what made them happy or unhappy. Her body was telling her that there was hostility mixed with anger roiling through their systems. Could her vampire touch change their mood? She still wasn't sure how it worked, only that she could make people feel good by touching them, giving them more energy.

Harry flipped his sunglasses off his face to the top of his head. "Well?"

"First, thanks for coming. I really appreciate this." She could sense a wall; he was determined not to be persuaded by anything she said. "I think it's important that we clear the air. And I think we can do that." She reached over and patted Harry's leg and tried to focus on sending him a surge of energy, but instead she felt anger coming back from him. No change at all. Was she doing it right?

A waiter approached Harry and Lee. "Whadda you guys want?"

Lee waved him off. "Nothing for me."

Harry agreed. "Me, neither."

They didn't even want to stick around long enough for a coffee. This was going to be more of an uphill battle than she had thought. But they had agreed to meet her, so there must be something they wanted from her. Darla decided to use her lifeline. *"Keith, you around?"*

"Sorry, guys, you can't sit in here without ordering something." The waiter, an older man, held his pencil to his pad and waited.

Harry sighed and looked at Darla; he seemed ready to leave.

"Just put a minimum charge on the bill, I'll take care of it." Darla touched the crusty old waiter's hand to see if her power was working. Maybe he'd forgo the charge.

"Ten-buck minimum per person."

Maybe she should have rested a few more days. "Fine."

"Need some advice here, Keith, if you can hear me!"

Lee crossed his arms and looked at her. "Go on. Talk."

Darla took a deep breath. "First off, I want to apologize to both of you. I really respect both of you as musicians and I think I took that for granted. I think I let my ego get in the way of performing. I never meant to ever suggest that you guys aren't good at what you do."

Harry shifted in his seat. "Yeah, so?"

She could feel a big "fuck you" coming from his blood. Why wasn't her energy having any effect here? *"Keith!"*

"Despite what happened this past weekend, I think we can move on and make this work."

Lee laughed. "I think she's begging to come back because she can't find anyone who wants to play with her."

Darla looked at Lee and smiled. "No, I'm not begging." Her anger was creeping back. She was losing her immortal perspective and instead was thinking about abandoning the whole idea.

Keith's groggy voice shot into her mind, and she felt a small surge in energy.

"Hello, love, you okay? You know it's three in the a.m. in London? Interrupting some prime beauty sleep."

"Sorry about that! But I need a little coaching. I'm trying to get the band back together and it's like my vampire energy is stalled. Not sure what I'm doing wrong here. I mean, even my touch didn't make much difference to this crusty old fart waiting on us."

"Maybe she's realizing how good she had it, now that it's gone, huh?" Harry put his hands behind his head and slid down on his chair. "Maybe her big rock star friends don't want her anymore, either?"

"Sheesh, I can feel these guys from here. You sure you want this?" Keith chimed in.

"Yeah. I like our sound. But they're really pushing my buttons right now. I'm trying to take the high road here and be nice—"

"Ah, that must be it. Why you tryin' to be nice?"

"Well, to get things done. I thought I would just—"

"Don't think, darling. How to put this delicately . . . You ain't nice. You're kind of a ball buster. You ain't polite and you ain't a demure typa gal. Everything works better when you are your truly nasty, ambitious self. That's who you are. Nothing wrong with that. All them possibilities you seen when I touched you? They ain't gonna come from a personality change. Best way to say it I think is your blood don't flow right if you ain't being who you are."

"Anything else here?" Lee pulled out his phone and started fiddling with it.

Darla took a sip of her drink and thought for a minute.

"Darlin', this ain't so tough. What do you want? Just get to it. You got a need, a hunger, go and take what you want. Like my grandkid says, let your freak flag fly!"

"But I don't want them to hate me, right?"

"Bloody hell, all bands hate each other. Here's a big secret: can't stand Mick! Fookin' wanker. Somehow we still can make great music together, sometimes even better that way."

She looked into Harry's eyes. "No, I'm not begging. Here's the deal. You guys are good, we're good together. But let's be honest, you *are* lazy. You know it and I know it. I can deal with that. If you want, and I mean if you're willing to give up a little control of the band to me, I can take us places. Places you can't even dream of. I can even make you play better."

Lee put his phone down and sat up in his chair. "What?"

"I can walk away from you guys right now and find a new band. It'll be a pain in the ass for me, but I'll do it. I'll make a new band happen, you can bank on that. You guys? You need a singer, a really good singer. Without me in front of the band, you guys will lose bookings. Face it, my vocals are a draw. And you are both too tired to chase down new gigs. That's the truth here. It'll take you a while to replace me and there's no guarantee that it'll work. I'm committed." Darla felt her blood moving, felt her power returning.

Harry started to say something, but Darla held her finger up.

"Think about what I'm saying and you'll see I'm making sense. I'll take care of all of the promotion, all of the bookings . . . and I'll make sure to invite all my rock star friends. All you guys have to do is continue to make great music." Darla reached across to put her hand on Harry's arm and sent a jolt of energy to him. She felt his wall going down. He wanted to surrender to her.

Lee looked at Harry and then at Darla. “Are we supposed to just forget the way you treated us, like we were your backup band, monkeys performing on cue?”

She looked over to Lee. She had always thought of him as an extension of Harry, but he had his own inner turmoil going on. She could feel his fear now. He was afraid of the future. He was kind of like she had been PB. He needed reassurance.

“You don’t have to forget anything, Lee.” She touched him and gave him a jolt of vamp energy. “All we have to do is play really great music together.”

Harry looked at her and nodded.

She had them, she could feel it in her blood, in her bones. The same way she knew when an audience was in the palm of her hands.

“What about Alby?”

Darla took another sip of her drink. “Don’t worry. I’ll take care of him.”

“Okay, love? Now that you got your inner ball buster going, okay to go back to sleep?”

6

When Darla got home from her meeting with Harry and Lee, she was feeling unstoppable. She had gotten the band back together on her terms.

She called Alby.

It turned out, he wasn't disgusted with her and he didn't feel sorry for her, he was genuinely concerned. At first he thought she had taken some bad drugs, but he couldn't figure out the fangs. He was a little freaked out by them but also intrigued. In fact, he couldn't stop thinking about them. She then explained as much as she knew about being a vampire and how the fangs worked.

Then she asked him, "Do you want to become a vampire?"

While she awaited his response, her stomach cramped up, perhaps out of instinct. If he rejected her again, would she be able to see that objectively? He had rejected fangs, not her. She remembered Dolly's words: "You want love, we all want love, nothing to be ashamed of." Even a ball buster needed love. Would he take an eternal journey with her?

"I totally want to live forever! I want superpowers, fuck yeah!"

She exhaled. "Are you sure, now, because I can't go through that whole throwing up thing again."

"Positive. Do I get to meet Dolly Parton?"

Dolly had agreed to supervise, but she also said that once the bite was done, she would take off so they could "enjoy their new energy" alone.

Darla had spent the morning cleaning and was putting the finishing touches on her place to set the right mood. But what was the right mood for biting someone? Dolly would be over in a little while with Alby's new vampire phone; she could ask her for advice.

She looked over her small studio apartment and wondered if she needed anything else. Maybe some candles? Yes, of course, candles.

The door buzzer rang. Darla looked at her phone—Dolly was a little early. *Great, more Dolly time for me*, she thought, and buzzed her in.

A few minutes later there was a knock on her door.

"It's open!"

She turned around, expecting to see Dolly's famous dimples, but instead Bob Dylan stood in her entryway with his requisite Mountie hat, wrinkled trench coat, and an old boxy briefcase. "What the fuck?"

He slowly eased the door closed and slid the deadbolt into place. "Nice to see you again."

Her vision dimmed. Vampire boner? Now? *Holy fuck*, she thought, *he has my tribal blood. Why is he locking my door?*

"Ah, your eyes. I can see I'm too late. I know you tried to call me. I wish you would have spoken to me before you did this."

She remembered the warning on the F app about Bob Dylan. "I made my decision and I'm happy with it, now would you mind leaving?" She never imagined in a million years that she would be asking a rock legend to leave her apartment, but this was her new crazy life. She tried to walk past him to unlock the door and let him out.

He blocked her. "I'm afraid I can't leave yet." He reached out and grabbed her wrist, sending a shooting pain straight to her head. She tried to pull her hand away, but he wound back his other arm and smacked her in the head with the sharp square edge of his briefcase.

Dazed by the hit, Darla stumbled and slid to the ground. She had a pounding pain on the side of her head and could not see clearly. Escape was her only thought as she tried to scramble to her feet, but he hit her again with the briefcase and she slid back down to the floor. She lay on the floor breathing heavily and could feel blood trickle down the side of her face.

Bob put his briefcase on her table and opened it.

He took out some handcuffs and came at her again. Darla tried to push herself away, but the pounding pain from her headache made it difficult to move.

He crouched down and slipped the handcuffs onto her wrists. He took a rag from his pocket and stuffed it into her mouth.

Darla tried to kick him, but he grabbed the handcuffs and dragged her over to the bed. He left her on the floor, propped against the bed.

She spit the rag out of her mouth. "What's going on? What are you doing?" He bent over to push the rag back in and she scratched him on the face and began screaming.

Bob took a deep breath and smacked her hard across the face, sending another shooting pain through her head. He put his hand on top of her head, magnifying the pain from the smack, like being pounded on the skull with a rubber mallet. He fastened the rag back in her mouth to make sure it would not come out.

A few minutes later she felt handcuffs being fastened around her ankles.

"Keith! Dolly! Help me! Bob Dylan is trying to kill me! Please, help!"

Bob stood in front of her. "What you have done is a grave sin against God. Only God can grant life."

"Help me!"

Dolly's voice entered her head. *"I hear you Darla, is he in your apartment now?"*

"Yes, he has me handcuffed and he's hitting me, can you call the police?"

"That son of a bitch, just hold on."

"I have to take action now. This is for your own good. For your immortal soul."

He held up a hypodermic needle. "This is the only way now."

Darla's eyes widened and she broke into a sweat. *"He's got a needle! All those rock stars dead, it's him! He's a killer!"*

Bob smiled at her. "You will thank God for this when you meet him. It works so much quicker when you're in this condition, too, when your blood is in its heightened state." He pulled a rubber hose out of his briefcase. "Did you know that each strain of heroin has a specific name? It's usually named by the chemist for a specific purpose."

Darla tried to push herself under her bed, but he crouched down in front of her and pulled her out. She kicked at him and managed to land a blow to his face, knocking the needle out of his hand.

Bob grabbed her handcuffed feet with both hands and pulled her out again, then gave a hard smack to her face.

Tears poured down her cheeks. She was losing this battle. *"Dolly, I think this is it."*

Bob picked up the needle. "As I was saying, this strain is called Wooden Spike." He crouched beside her. "This will be the greatest day of your life, because you will return to your Savior, and He will forgive you. You will be loved again by Him."

The door buzzer rang.

Bob shook his head. "Is that Keith? Do you think he can help you now? He can't. You should have never looked to him for salvation. Through me, God will give you the salvation that you seek."

Bob picked up the rubber tubing and kneeled on her legs to keep her from moving. He rolled up her sleeve and began tying the tubing around her arm to look for a vein.

"Dolly, if you're out there, I only have a few seconds left."

"Hang on, hang on, I'm coming." Dolly's voice was out of breath.

"Please, Lord, receive this soul back into Your bosom, back into Your Heaven." He jabbed the needle into her arm and pressed the plunger down.

Darla tried to wiggle away from him, but her energy was fading, the drug was entering her bloodstream, slowing her thoughts and also dulling the pain. She heard some noise outside. Something was happening . . . the fire escape. She looked up at the window across the room and saw Dolly's legs come crashing through the window, shards of glass showering across the floor.

Bob let go of the needle and looked back at Dolly standing over him in a blue-and-gold-sequined conquistador pantsuit with a baseball bat in her hand, brushing broken glass off her chest.

"You have fucked with the wrong woman, asshole." She swung the bat and brought it down on his neck, sending him crashing across the floor. He lay there moaning and holding his neck.

"The needle, pull it out of my arm!"

Dolly looked at Darla and plucked the needle from her arm. "Sweetie, stay with me, we're gonna get you some help right away." She crouched over to untie her gag.

Darla saw Bob move. He raised himself up. *"Behind you!"*

He pulled on Dolly's famous blonde hair and momentarily threw her off balance. A small patch of hair came off in his hand.

"Now you done it!" Dolly kicked him in the gut, sending him back to the ground. Dolly picked up her bat again. "Where are the keys to the cuffs?"

Bob lay on the floor, moaning. "Pocket."

"Which pocket?"

"Right jacket." He was breathing heavily.

As Dolly reached down to grab the keys, Darla saw Bob's hand move. He grabbed a knife from his pocket and stabbed Dolly in the gut.

Dolly stumbled back, the knife sticking out of her midsection, and blood started trickling down her gold-sequined pants. "You did not just do that?!" She staggered across the room, staring at her wound.

Bob grabbed at a dresser and pulled himself up. "You will both know the warmth of our Lord's forgiveness. Soon, very soon . . ."

Dolly pulled the knife out of her stomach and picked up the bat. She swung it at his neck, and he went down. "You can't kill me with a knife, asshole." She swung the bat again and brought it down on his crotch. He gasped and passed out.

Darla's adrenaline started to drain, and she felt her life force weaken. She wanted to hug Dolly, to thank her for saving her life, but she didn't have the strength to move. She felt a warmth envelope her, like a comforting old blanket. There was no more pain, there wasn't anything she had to think about except being happy. *This is what I want*, she thought, *just this feeling*. Her eyelids were heavy; it was so much easier just to close them. *I just wanted to sing*. That's what she was trying to say to Dolly, who was shaking her and yelling, but she couldn't hear the words anymore.

7

Darla's world was now pink. It felt soft, and sometimes this new world changed to yellow or blue, but always a really pleasant pastel color. The colors themselves brought feelings. Pink was soft like fur, yellow was warmer, the blue smelled sweet like chocolate. This was Candyland! Now all three colors blended together, and Darla felt that all was perfect.

She knew that she should probably not stay in this safe, cartoonish painting. She had a distant memory, a reminder from somewhere or something that this was a dangerous place to be, but at the same time, it was just so . . . nice. She wanted to stay here forever. She found something to lean against—maybe it was a tree? From here she could see the whole landscaped silhouette of hills and waterfalls changing colors and . . . a new color, something quite bright. White! Beautiful cool white light.

She moved away from her tree toward the light. Was this the mythic white light that appeared at the end of your life? She felt sure it was.

Holy shit! Bob Dylan was right. She was overwhelmed by the feeling that this was . . . God. She was being summoned, pulled to the mythic white light. Did Bob Dylan succeed in killing her? Was this the end of it all? She should be pissed at him, but she couldn't summon any anger. There was no need or room for it in this pastel world. *Just truth,* she thought, *that's all I want.*

As she walked closer to the beckoning light, she no longer felt fear either, just a desire to find out what could be in there.

But there was something hazy in there, something dark—a shape, the shape of a person. *Dolly? Is that you?*

Dolly stood in front of her, arms wide open for a big hug. Darla ran to her with her arms open as Dolly brought her hand around and slapped Darla hard across the face.

Darla opened her mouth and sucked in a deep breath. She needed more air, her lungs working overtime trying to breathe. She opened her eyes and Dolly was staring back at her, yelling.

"Stay with me, Darla! Stay awake, baby!"

Darla saw a bright fluorescent white light. Different from her other white light. This one was harsh, unforgiving. She sensed movement. She was inside something moving. An ambulance. The physical pain flooded back into her body. Her face ached. Was it from Dolly's slap or Bob Dylan's beating? There was more yelling and confusion inside this tiny space, more body aches. She closed her eyes.

She was back by her tree, but now she was cold, shivering. She hoped the world would turn yellow again and warm her back up. This was the end, wasn't it? The ambulance was reality; this world was not. But she liked it much better here.

Bob Dylan's words bounced around her head: *"This will be the greatest day of your life, because you will return to your Savior, and He will forgive you. You will be loved again by Him."*

It looked like he had told her the truth. Would God now forgive her? What was her sin? Greed? Stupidity? That seemed kind of lame. She took a breath and let the chocolate-perfumed air into her lungs. *I guess this is it*, she thought. *All of this drama because I just wanted to sing. Why would God, if that's him up there, not like that?*

She saw the white light off in the distance. She knew she would have to go there sooner or later.

Did she really lose her life just to be famous? Fuck, she didn't even get the fame part, either.

She got up from her tree again and started walking toward the marvelous, brilliant white light. Her heart felt heavy, but at the same time she was glad she didn't have to deal with any more pain or confusion. Uh-oh, a hazy figure in the light again. Keith? She didn't want to get slapped anymore, but it wasn't Keith.

Oh my god, it's Alby!

She ran to him but couldn't get close enough to touch him. He was beckoning and moving his mouth, but she couldn't hear his words. She looked closely; his mouth was saying "Come to me" over and over again. He was backing away from her and still mouthing the words. She followed him. He still wanted her, even after all this? She had to reach him, just to say good-bye. Finally, she caught up with him and reached out to touch him.

She opened her eyes and saw Alby's face staring down at her, a white ceiling behind him.

"I think it worked! She's awake!" Alby's sweet voice danced in her ears.

"I knew it!" Dolly's voice in the background.

Darla heard the beeping sounds of hospital equipment, saw Dolly's blonde curls dangling over Alby's shoulder. Darla's hand felt the metal rail guard of a hospital bed.

"But her eyes are still clear, not red." Alby looked over toward Dolly.

"Put both of your hands on her arm!"

Darla saw Dolly's face above her.

"C'mon, Darla, c'mon back to us."

Darla closed her eyes and was back at her pink tree. Keith was now sitting next to her.

"You're bloody hard to get ahold of."

"Yeah, well I've never overdosed on heroin before, sorry about that."

"Yeah, it's a little odd, give you that. Nice high, though, ain't it?"

"Really nice, but you're not going to hit me, are you?"

"Gotta get you to wake up."

"I'm awake, okay? I like it here better. I swear I'll hang up on you. I just think this is where I should be. Okay?"

"Your call."

"Well, now that you're here." She shifted so her back was against the tree, keeping her eyes on the white light in the distance. "I have some questions I need answered."

"Fire away." He lit a cigarette.

"This," Darla pointed toward the white light, "seems real, right?"

"It does, don't it? I seen it a few times me self."

"So there is a God, and that means—"

"Whoa, I wouldn't drag it that far. Could be the Cookie Monster up there, or even Elvis for all anyone knows."

Darla took this in. "C'mon, walk with me. I feel like I don't have much time left."

They got up from the tree and started toward the light.

"Small thing that's been bothering me. If being a vampire makes you young, why are you so . . ."

"Okay, love, I get it. I look like hell, I know. I been prettier, that's for sure. That's the internet did to me."

Darla stopped walking. "The internet ages vampires? What the —"

"Hold on, just hear me out."

"Okay, go on." She resumed walking.

"First rule of Vampire Club, you don't talk about Vampire Club, ha! Anyhow, what I'm saying is that we try to keep all this vampire stuff on the down-low. I mean, I don't care who knows, but generally people want to kill you or something weird when they find out it's true." He put his arm around her. "Case in point right here. But right now I'm in the public a lot, so if I look twenty years old all my life, that would invite some unwanted attention. So someone smarter than me figured out that if you doesn't partake for a certain amount of time, you age like a regular person. So when the time comes and I'm tired of being famous Keith Richards, I just fake my death and hide out somewhere. When I start to partake again, I can reverse the aging process. They even got instructions on the F app now."

"Ah, pretty smart. So the internet?"

"Yeah, before the internet it weren't nobody's business. Now my business is all over the place. Before this technology . . . you know, I been through a few lifetimes already. It was always pretty easy to duck out of one life and start up another. Now, it's all complicated."

"Were you always Keith Richards?"

He put his finger to his lips. "Shhh, original name was Emre, can't bloody remember the last name. Got it written down somewhere."

They stopped walking at the base of the white light.

Darla looked at Keith. "Why me? Especially since you're trying to age?"

"Your blood was . . . begging for it. Loud and clear. Never had no one wanted it that bad, so it may have set me back a few years."

"But I just wanted to sing."

"Right." Keith threw his cigarette butt into the white light.

"It's true."

"If you just wanted to sing, sing in the bloody shower, sing in the subway, but stop with this 'I just want to sing' bollocks."

"What do you mean?"

"You want the whole enchilada. You want fame, you want fans, thousands and thousands of fans, you want recognition, you want money, lots of it—just admit it."

"Fuck you, I never cared about any of that. I don't need any of that. I don't think you understand how real people think."

"No, fuck you, missy. You don't understand how you think. The fact that you got the blood in you means you want more than most people. That blood don't run in people who just want to sing."

"Are you telling me that all vampires are greedy, fame-seeking assholes, is that it?"

"And you is one of them. Maybe you should be straight with yourself before you walk off into your virginal white light."

Darla tried to walk past him, but he stopped her.

"And what's so bad about that? You know what's sad? That you didn't get to enjoy none of that stuff."

Darla could feel tears rolling down her face. "I can't—"

Keith held his finger up. "Hold on a minute, darlin', juggling another conversation . . . Yes, got her. A few minutes, I imagine . . . Okay now, what was you sayin'?"

"I can't . . ." she started to protest, but the landscape was changing. The colors were draining, everything was becoming white. "I can't . . ."

Keith smiled at her. "Yes, you can." He wound up and hit her across the face so hard she spun around. Alby was in front of her now, arms outstretched.

"You," Darla mouthed.

"Me," he whispered back.

Darla opened her eyes and stared directly into Alby's face. He was lying next to her in a hospital bed. "She's back!"

"Go on, tell her!" Dolly yelled from the foot of the bed.

"I want you to make me a vampire now!"

Darla's vision became cloudy, and she felt the slight pain in her gums again. The thirst overcame her. She wanted him, his blood, she wanted to sing, she wanted every fucking thing.

Keith was right. This is who she was. She plunged her fangs into Alby's skin and felt her life return to her body.

8

The Self Realization Fellowship Lake Shrine – Pacific Palisades, California

November 15, 2024

"Help! I'm trapped. I don't think I'm getting out of here alive!"

Darla smiled. *"Sorry, you're on your own, Alby."*

"Forgetting who you owe your life to again?"

"You're gonna pull that card for eternity, aren't you? Didn't you check your F app this morning? There were warnings everywhere about her."

"Umm, forgot. C'mon, she's on me like a bad case of herpes. I can't shake her. I need your firepower."

"Okay, just hold on. Where are you?"

"In a room in the windmill thing."

Darla was sitting in a line of limos waiting to get into the entrance of the Self-Realization Fellowship Lake Shrine. *"Should be a few more minutes."*

Her limo pulled up in front of the entrance and she stepped out into the Los Angeles sun. Seventy-two perfect degrees in November. Maybe it was time to get a place here.

Photographers behind the red carpet immediately started snapping photos and yelling questions.

"Darla! Over here!"

"Darla, can you tell us if the band is playing at the memorial?"

"Hey, Darla, Alby arrived separately. You guys still together?"

She waved them off as an usher approached her and directed her toward the entrance to the facility. She saw a small sign with an arrow: KEITH RICHARDS MEMORIAL.

Darla looked around at the gathering crowd and asked the usher, "Which way to the windmill?"

"Just follow the path along the lake to the left, can't miss it."

She was amazed and amused by the park. It was like a non-denominational religious theme park. But very, very peaceful. She looked around the lake and saw a white mosque, an English chapel, a houseboat? It was almost like her heroin dream. Crazy. And then she saw the windmill and made her way over there.

She walked through the entrance and could smell Alby's scent coming from a room in the back of the building. She walked down a hallway and opened the door to the room where Alby was trapped.

Madonna was standing over Alby in a corner of the room. She turned around to face Darla. "Love! You're looking delicious." She ran over to her and kissed her cheeks. "Of course, I know your beauty secret."

Darla smiled and sighed. She truly felt bad for her. Madonna was making a last grab for life. Her body was patched together by surgeons trying to keep the aging process from happening, but there was only so much good that could do before you looked like Silly Putty. She could feel Madonna's will to live, her drive, her bottomless ambition. She'd had a good life, accomplished more than most people, but there was a limit imposed by her blood.

"You know, I was just talking to Alby about this party idea I had . . ." Madonna looked back at Alby, who shot Darla a big fake smile.

Darla held Madonna's hand. "I'm sorry, really, but we can't do that."

Madonna pulled her hand away. "Why not? You could use your magic phone to just send a mass invite—it would be the party of the century. I mean, we could do it for a charity or—"

"Madge, enough. You have to face facts. You don't have the—"

"You don't know that! I'm sure that I have the blood. I'm positive, all it takes is finding the right bloodline. If enough of you are there, I'm totally sure that someone will be my blood . . . mate."

"That's not how this works. The bloodlines are like magnets. If you were part of a bloodline, you couldn't hide from them if you wanted to. You have to let go."

Madonna started to cry. "I won't ever accept that. Listen, what if—"

"No. Enough, okay? Just, enough already."

"Then I'll out you and the whole fucking bunch! I'll tell everything I know who's a vampire, how the whole thing works, and that Keith Richards is not really dead."

Darla sighed. "Listen, I'm sorry you're frustrated, really I am. But let's think about this. Once you go to the press and start screaming about vampires, it only makes you look really . . . sad. Maybe the *Enquirer* or something like that would go with it and you'd wind up as a bad joke on late-night TV. You don't want to throw away everything you have to become an international punchline."

"Why are you being such a cunt?"

Oooh, she brought out the C word. Darla thought it would just get worse from here. Time to shut this down. "I'm not being a cunt. If I were a cunt, I'd remind you that the blood transfusion idea you had almost killed you off and you still didn't learn from that. Yes, I know all about it. Word gets out in vampire circles, so it would be wise to stop being such a pain in our collective asses."

"I can't believe this. I'm not done. I'm just not done." Madonna glared at her and stormed out of the room.

"Alby, let's get going." She took him by the arm and they started walking along the trail to the chapel where Keith's memorial would be held.

She gave Alby's hand a squeeze. "So are we even now?"

"Ha, not even close!"

"Lucky for you she just wanted your blood and not your dick. Not sure if I could have stopped her in that case."

Alby sent an energy surge into her hand. "How do you know she didn't?"

They approached the chapel and she heard Keith in her head.

"Darlin', you got a minute?"

She let go of Alby's arm. "Getting a message from the corpse, I'll be a minute. Save me a seat." Darla walked over to a tiled bench overlooking the lake and sat down.

"What's up, dead guy?"

"Need a favor."

"Sure, what?"

"Need you to set up a back channel to get me funds. The one ex who knows I ain't dead is arguing about money now."

"Some of your kids know, right? None of them will do it? Or Mick?"

"Rather not ask the kids, too complicated. Mick? Fook him. I think this last lifetime is it for us. By the way, did he ask you to sing at the tribute concert next month?"

"Haven't heard a word from him."

"Bloody wanker! My last dyin' request!"

"So where to send the money to?"

"I'll send you the instructions on the app. Argentinian bank, so I think you need to send it with Spanish instructions."

"How long you staying down there?"

"Who knows, maybe 'til I look twenty again. I know, don't say it, could be awhile."

"I don't want to be late for your funeral, so I gotta get going. By the way, I'm afraid to ask, what's in the urn? Marlboro ashes?"

"Nah, too easy. Actually, it's a pig. Thought it would be fitting."

"What a waste of good bacon!"

"All right, make sure there's plenty of tears at the service, maybe some wailing, too."

"Tell me, what are you gonna do with your next life? More rock and roll?"

"Ah, blimey. An innocent flower, like me self? I just want to sing, that's all."

"Fookin' asshole." Darla hung up on him and went in to get her seat.

KEEPING COMPLIANT WITH THE KARDASHIANS

"To live without evil belongs only to the gods."

Sophocles

1

What in God's name was I doing?

That was the question weighing on my conscience as I sat in the bright pink waiting room at ME Communications on the top floor of a sleek office building on Sunset Boulevard.

Maybe it was a midlife crisis? I had thought that only happened to men. Maybe I was wrong. What else had I been wrong about?

It was 2019 and I was done with my job. The world was spinning faster and faster and I thought to myself, it can't get any worse than this. When 2020 rolls around I will make sure that my life is better. It couldn't get any worse.

I was forty. So, yeah, mid-life. Men bought expensive sports cars. They traded in wives for younger models, right? But I didn't care about cars, and I was single. All I had was my career, so it made sense that this was what I would change.

The wall behind the glass reception desk was lined with Warholian portraits of a cutesy little dog. Did I want to work for a company that had such hideous taste in art? And the bright pink paint? Not to mention the chandelier adorned with pink feathered boas. A teenage girl's idea of piss elegant.

The young, pretty receptionist sitting at the glass desk texted and giggled out loud.

Maybe I should just leave.

Stop it. I had to stop thinking about escape. Stay focused. Did I want this job? Did I want to change my life? I thought I did.

The receptionist's phone buzzed. She finished up her texting and answered the phone. "Guest Reception . . . Okay, I'll tell her!" She hung up, picked up her cell phone, texted for a few seconds, and then addressed me. "Trina is just getting off of a call and she'll be just a few more minutes."

I nodded. "Thanks."

Trina was the CEO of ME Communications. She had hunted me down. I was impressed by that. Flattered, actually. I was not easy to find. Well, not easy for anyone outside of the DC beltway. But she had found me at the right time in my life. Normally, I would never have even answered her call.

According to the background check I pulled on Trina, she was fifty-four years old. She had been a socialite and married a real estate tycoon when she was young. Had a minor role in one of the first housewife shows in Orange County. Divorced her husband shortly after that first season and started this company with the divorce money, doing public relations for the various housewives, turning each one of them into a media star. She branched out to other reality stars and over the years went from a boutique PR company to a media company worth almost a billion dollars. ME Communications was consistently at the top of every influencer list of Hollywood players.

I didn't know a lot about building a business, but aside from the tacky reception office, I had to give the woman some respect. To go from socialite to media empire CEO took some skills. That's why I decided to take her call a few weeks ago.

But the Hollywood definition of public relations was a whole different animal from what I had done.

My official title was Public Relations Specialist, but I was really a fixer. For the last fifteen years, I cleaned up messes for politicians, judges, lobbyists—just about anyone who had power and influence in DC. To be able to do what I did, you needed to be morally neutral. No judgments. I was good, too. Maybe too good.

After fifteen years of cleaning up other people's outhouses, I was so used to the stench that it had almost become an aphrodisiac. My pulse quickened when the phone rang in the middle of the night and some federal judge was stuck in a cheap hotel on a heroin-induced nightmare, or it could be a four-star general caught on his knees in a bath house. It was like getting a quick hit of endorphins. The most powerful people in the country were vulnerable to me. Only I could make things right.

I had moved past the moralizing long ago, so I could be clear-eyed and find the right solution to each "personal issue" the cleanest and quickest way. People in power were just people. They had their . . . peccadillos. You didn't stop having desires or fetishes just because you worked for the government. This was how I justified my work.

Little by little, without realizing it, my blood had become ice.

In 2016, when this latest regime blew into DC, I thought I'd be okay, but the calls were off the charts in terms of the "personal issues" they had. My crisis of conscience came when a campaign chairman had called me at three a.m. I was half asleep, but I heard the words "hotel" and "dead teen." A full minute went by. My drowsy mind was already automatically calculating what to do with a dead body, who to call to cart it away. It didn't hit me for one full minute that I might be helping someone cover up a murder. I hung up.

I lay awake in bed for hours rehashing that call. Why hadn't I hung up right away? Why didn't I call the police? In that moment, hiding a dead woman in a hotel at three a.m. was no different than covering up a lawmaker's DUI or rescuing a judge from a meth lab. I had lost the ability to tell right from wrong.

I wanted to call someone and talk it out. But there was no one to call. I didn't have friends, I had contacts. Who wanted to be friends with someone who considered covering up a death to be just part of their everyday to-do list?

What kind of monster had I become? Alone and a monster. This was my life.

I closed up shop that day. I needed time to think about who I was, who I was becoming. By any metric, I would be considered successful. But at what price? I needed a change.

A few days later I got a call from Trina. She wouldn't tell me how she found me, but powerful people have a way of finding me. She told me that she'd heard I was the best at crisis management and securing positive results from the worst circumstances for very famous politicians, and she only wanted the best. Her client wanted someone with top DC access, and she assured me the work would not be as "dirty" as I was used to dealing with.

At first, I pushed her away. "Just hire a lobbyist, I can recommend a dozen right now who would jump at the chance to work for you."

Trina's answer made me pay attention.

"I could do that, but people in DC don't owe a lobbyist anything. You? My guess is that everyone in that town owes you a favor. I want that kind of firepower on my side."

This was a woman who knew her shit.

Over the course of a few weeks, we talked back and forth some more about the scope of work while I mulled it over. She finally invited me in to talk about an offer.

But I was still hesitant. In my world, I was the boss. People hired me to take charge. My word was always the last word if they wanted their problems solved. In entertainment, there was a different dynamic. Trina had told me that in her world, the client was king. I would have to be subordinate to the client. I wasn't sure if I could do that. That just wasn't me. But maybe I needed to change that. Become vulnerable to other people. Thaw out the ice in my veins.

"Trina will see you now."

I grabbed my purse and followed the receptionist. Row after row of glassed-in offices, all looking out onto the vast Los Angeles vista. So much glass. Desks, chairs, windows. More like display cases than offices. I was used to oak. Oak offices, oak floors, oak desks, and heavy oak doors that make a noise when closing. My work was usually discussed behind a thick oak door in the heavily carpeted office of some politician or judge who was in deep trouble. Nothing I did was supposed to see the light of day. How could you hide secrets in a transparent office?

Trina was housed in the largest of the display cases at the back of the office.

When I entered the room, Trina stood to welcome me. She was shorter than I had expected. I didn't know why I thought she'd be taller, maybe just expectations of someone in power. She looked good for her age, but I was sure she'd had some work done. Her chest was way too high and perky for a fifty-four-year-old. Requisite blonde hair.

Tie-dyed yoga pants? Are you kidding me? And thong sandals. *Jesus H. Christ.* Granted, they were Tory Burch, but they were just very expensive flip-flops. I wouldn't dress that casual for a yoga class, let alone the first meeting with a potential new employee.

I unbuttoned the jacket of my power suit and wondered if I should take it off. Was I overdressed? I didn't know this world. But my power suit was my armor. My suit was a statement. I was a force to be reckoned with. Yoga pants also made a statement: don't take me seriously. I kept the jacket on.

She held her hand out to me. A woman's hands gave away her age. There were no procedures or fillers that could fix that. Hers were a little rough, leathery, kind of claw-like. "So fabulous to finally meet you."

I sat down and tried not to be distracted, but the views from her office were stunning. Downtown LA on one side and the Hollywood Hills on the other. And behind her, a cement block wall with the same extra-huge Warholian portrait of that cutesy dog from the lobby. The company logo was in raised white letters across the bottom of the portrait: When Our Client Says It's All About ME, We Agree!

"Would you like something to drink? Water, coffee, tea? We have a smoothie bar in our café if you like."

"No, thanks, I'm fine. Let's just get started." I wanted to cut to the chase. Show me the money. At this point, I was still on the fence, and for me to sign up, the money had to be good. Really, really good. I averaged about twenty thousand per month last year. An offer of double that would get my undivided attention. That would put me at more than half a million a year. Anything less than that and I figured I would just walk away.

Trina pulled a manila folder from the side of her desk and opened it. "I think you know I really want you on my team. You'd be a perfect fit here and for the client." She put on her reading glasses and picked a paper out of the folder. "I have put together an offer that I think you'll find very attractive."

A dog started barking, a small, yappy kind of bark. In the corner of the office a Pekingese raised its head out of a basket.

"That's Miss Elsa."

The dog jumped out of its basket and started sniffing my feet and then yapped at me. *Do not touch my Ferragamos, bitch.* Dogs got on my nerves. I just never had the patience for them. Little bundles of fur and germs.

"She likes you!"

I smiled and looked down at the dog, gritting my teeth. "Well, I like her, too." Miss Elsa cocked her head and stared straight up at me. Miss Elsa knew I was lying. Dogs had that sense.

Miss Elsa walked over to the door and scratched at the glass.

Trina held up a well-manicured finger. "One second." She picked up her office phone. "Jay? Miss Elsa wants to go out."

As I looked up at the Warholian picture behind Trina, it finally dawned on me. ME Communication. Miss Elsa was ME. Coincidentally, my own initials: Maddy Ellis. Maybe I should have petted her?

A minute later, Jay appeared with a leash. "C'mon, Miss Elsa! Let's get some fresh air."

"Make sure she poops!" Trina ordered as Jay left.

"Now, as I was saying, I put together an offer, but first I want to know if you have any more questions about the job or if there's anything that concerns you."

I had a lot of concerns. Yoga pants, yappy dogs, feathered boas on chandeliers. Not to mention this "client is king" crap. It all gave me pause. Made me wonder if this was a place I would feel comfortable. Maybe I'd just push her a little, see how much tolerance she had for me. "In DC, my work was pretty intensive. We're talking on-call twenty-four-seven intensive, so I have to tell you I never watch TV. I'm not familiar with any of the shows that you rep. I mean, I'm aware of some of the names of the people, just by pop culture osmosis."

Entertainment was such a vapid world. I just didn't get a lot of it. I rarely had time for TV that wasn't a news program. Someone once told me I simply *had* to watch a show called *Scandal* about a DC fixer. I spent an hour yelling at my TV. So much bullshit. I'd be so out of my element here. But at the same time, no more swamp. No life-or-death decisions that may affect the well-being of a democracy increasingly held tenuously together by duct tape and Elmer's glue.

Trina smiled and waved her hand. "I'm not hiring you because of your expertise on reality shows. Don't worry about that. Honestly," she leaned in, "just watch a couple of shows in your spare time and you'll get it. They're all pretty much the same. I have confidence that you can get up to speed with what you need to know. Now," she put her reading glasses back on, "The offer I'd like to make you is a one-year contract, renewable and open for renegotiation at the end of a year. We've gone over the scope. Contract can be terminated at any time if both parties agree. Contract is at will and can only be canceled by ME Communications for cause, otherwise you will be guaranteed the full salary. Cause would be non-performance."

She looked up from the contract. "Pretty standard. Also, this is inclusive of client only, and per your request, your services would not extend to anyone else other than the client unless agreed upon by all parties."

I nodded.

She finished reading and slid it over to me. "I'm offering fifty thousand per month. I think that's a pretty fair offer."

I took the contract. Fifty thousand was more than pretty fair, it was a little crazy. What was so bad about this work that she needed to make a crazy offer? But even with that bump in salary, I still didn't feel eager to make the leap. I wasn't ready to let go of my old life yet. I needed to have some time with my thoughts, feel comfortable with this whole new change. "Can I have a few days to think about this?"

"What's the hesitation?" She leaned her elbows on her desk. "I assumed, from our prior conversations, that you were on board. Is it the money?"

It wasn't the money. Maybe I just wasn't ready to commit. I could tell that she wasn't going to let me out of here without a fight.

"Tell me what it will take. Name your figure."

I decided to scare her off. I'd give her a figure so ridiculous, she would ask me to leave. Or at least come back with her final offer. At that point I would have an excuse to walk out and tell her I needed to think about it. "Seventy-five thousand a month plus expenses." I wanted to push her, see how serious Miss Yoga Pants really was. That would make me a millionaire. I couldn't imagine it. "And a twenty-five thousand signing bonus."

Trina leaned back in her chair and stared at me. She took a deep breath and squinted. "Are you telling me that if I offered you seventy-five thousand dollars a month plus expenses plus a signing bonus of twenty-five thousand, you would accept that offer right now?"

I nodded. She couldn't be that crazy. Could she?

She stood up and extended her claw across the desk. "Welcome to ME!"

I was in shock. I hesitated for a second, knowing that after I shook her hand, I was committed. No backing out.

It wasn't a handshake. It was a bear trap. She gave me a solid grip and the trap was sprung.

I was now Kim Kardashian's domestic and international issues publicist and advisor.

∞

A few minutes later I signed the contract, still shell shocked. Did I just trade my serious career, all of my hard work, all of my connections to the most powerful people in the country to be a reality show star's babysitter?

Trina got out of her seat. "Let me show you your office."

Office? Not in one of these display cases. "I usually just work from home or on the road. Don't think I'll need an office." I would never leave my work in an office that I couldn't guard twenty-four-seven.

But then again, what kind of information would I be guarding here? Kim's plastic surgery secrets?

"No worries." Trina waved a hand full of gold bangles and

bracelets in the air. "You'll probably need a couple of weeks to get settled in LA. In the meantime, you can use Spencer's old office."

We stopped in front of a smaller glassed-in office with a glass desk and views of the famous Hollywood Hills. She opened the door for me and sat in the seat in front of the desk. "We haven't had a chance to clean it out yet, so some of Spencer's stuff is still here."

"Spencer?"

"Kim's former publicist." She pointed a finger at the seat behind the desk. "Sit."

Normally, I would not have responded to someone ordering me like I was their Pekingese, but I was still dazed. On the desk, there were a few pictures of what must have been Spencer and Kim Kardashian. What kind of gig had I signed up for? I didn't do selfies, let alone selfies with clients. Ever.

"I know you need some time to get settled here and everything, but since you're in town now, I thought it would be nice to have a kind of meet and greet with Kim. She's usually really busy, but I think she'll want to push her schedule around to meet with you. I'll set up a little brunch for you at the house tomorrow. Just a general getting to know you, go over expectations, deliverables, that kind of thing, okay?"

I nodded. This was happening too fast for me. I hadn't expected to take the job today. I needed time to let this change sink in. My old life was gone. I wasn't even sure how I felt about this new life.

"Also, keep me in the loop on the big issues, but other than that, I trust you know how to handle your business."

Miss Elsa ran into the office and climbed onto Trina's lap, Jay following behind.

"Did she poop?"

"Like a pro!" Jay replied.

"Good girl!" Trina brought the dog up to her face. "That's my baby, my good poopy baby."

My good poopy baby? I tried to remember I would become a millionaire.

"Jay, this is Maddy Ellis. She's your new boss." Trina put the dog down and looked up at me. "Jay can handle all of your admin. Expenses, travel, invoices, and whatnot. He can also help with finding a place to live or giving you any history on the client. He worked for Spencer, so he can get you up to speed on anything."

I stood up and shook Jay's hand. A pleasant-looking twenty-something kid. Clean-cut, very well groomed. First job out of college? Would he be able to handle me?

"But!" Trina added as she stood up. "I still need Jay now and then. Miss Elsa loves him and only him, so when it's time for Miss Elsa to poop, I need to borrow Jay."

Trina left, and Jay stood at attention at the door. "Can I get you anything?"

I felt kind of sorry for Jay. He reminded me of all the Capitol Hill interns I'd bumped into over the years. Bright and shiny, willing to do slave tasks to get ahead and make connections. The same interns that I had to pay off to keep quiet about the corruption they witnessed or experienced. "No, thanks, but can you tell me if Spencer left any files on the client?"

Even though I had been in an entertainment blackout for the last fifteen years, I knew about the Kardashians. Kim Kardashian's reality had managed to penetrate my myopic world. I had done some research on her as well, but I still needed to watch her godawful show.

Jay went to an armoire in the office, pulled out a laptop, and put it in front of me. "Spencer's laptop."

"Is there a contact for him, in case I have any questions?"

Jay shook his head. "Actually, we don't know where he is. He kind of disappeared. He stopped showing up for appointments and didn't return texts or calls. After a few days, we had his landlord bust in his apartment. We kind of half expected to find him . . . you know, overdosed or something, but the apartment was fine. His clothes were gone. It's like he took off in the middle of the night."

"Well, that's odd. Isn't it?" Maybe I should have asked for more money. What did this Spencer know that I didn't?

"Not really," Jay explained. "I don't know if you have ever worked in entertainment before, but people sometimes just . . . go off. There's a lot of drugs, a lot of money, and people are kind of flakey, so sometimes they do flakey things. He'll probably turn up on Lindsay Lohan's Instagram next month."

"Was Spencer flakey?"

Jay hesitated. "You know, when you work so close to some of the biggest stars in the biz, it affects you. If you don't have your head screwed on straight, sometimes you start to think you're one of them because you're hanging out with them so much. It messes with your mind a little bit. I think Spencer bought into that whole trip."

I was a little bit amazed by Jay's perspective. How did he get this kind of understanding so early in life? "Wise beyond your years, Jay."

Jay smiled and leaned in. "Thanks! I know I look like a kid. I'm actually forty-two years old. Working for the Kardashians has some really great perks, like access to the best fillers and surgeons in the world."

For a split second I thought about breast augmentation. I hadn't been in LA for more than twenty-four hours and it had already seeped into my brain. "One more question, I've never seen her show—"

Jay immediately jumped up and closed the office door. "Not a good idea to say that out loud in this office. Also, never, ever say a negative word about any of the Kardashians in the office."

God, this poor guy was really nervous about this. He was looking over his shoulder at Trina's office. Maybe I should explain to him that I did not give a fuck. "I was going to binge watch their show at my hotel later and wanted to see which episodes you might recommend. You know, as a kind of primer on Kim."

"I can do that. I'll set you up an email account and send you some links to watch. In the meantime, if you want to go through Spencer's files, his password is 'luckybastard1,' all lowercase."

Once Jay left, I opened Spencer's laptop and his screensaver popped up. A photo of him, Kim, and her husband at some red carpet event. I was a little bit wary of the husband, Kanye. I hadn't kept up with pop music at all, but I knew he was some type of crazy rapper. What little I'd heard about him was how unstable he was. He was not part of my scope—I had that in writing now. My job wasn't to run defense for him, i.e. hide and clean up the crazy.

After an hour of reading emails between Spencer, Kim, Kris Jenner, and other assorted Kardashians, I had to say that his password was appropriate. Most of the correspondence was about attending parties, going to clubs, arranging shopping trips, and making personal appearances. Easy work, if you could get it. Most of the emails were not more than a paragraph and started with "Sup?" Jesus, how did I miss this easy money all these years?

I scrolled down and found a file labeled "*!!!!!*," and a new box popped up for a password. "luckybastard1" didn't work. Hmmm. Interesting.

Jay couldn't figure out the other password, either. "My guess is that's probably his personal stuff. I have full access to his files, so it's probably something he didn't want me to see."

I looked at him. "Does that mean you'll have access to my files as well?"

Jay nodded. "Well, sure. Since you're my boss. It's part of the admin function. I can take care of all your low-level requests when you're out of the office."

I was about to tell him there was no way he could have access to my files, but I took a deep breath and remembered I wasn't dealing with government secrets anymore. I was dealing with a woman who was famous for her fake tits, her fake ass, and her selfies. I put my guard down. See, maybe I could change.

"Thanks." I grabbed the laptop and headed for my hotel. Time to binge on this nonsense before I met with her tomorrow. It would all be fine, I told myself. How bad could it be? Nothing a new millionaire like myself couldn't handle, I was sure.

2

"You have arrived at your destination," Siri announced as I pulled up to the guard gate at Kim's home in Hidden Hills. Ahead of me was a long drive leading to massive iron gates and a glimpse of the faux royal palace beyond.

Maybe I should have asked for more money.

A guard with huge headphones stepped out of a guard house and walked over to my window. "Good morning, can I help you?"

"You landing airplanes today with those things?" I smiled.

He didn't answer. *Okay*. "I have an eleven-thirty with Kim. Maddy Ellis from ME." God, that sounded awful. "ME Communications."

He spoke into his walkie-talkie, "Ellis here for an eleven-thirty with KK, driving a white Hyundai Santa Fe." He leaned in my window. "Follow the driveway, through the gates, and to the left. Another guard will direct you from there."

I drove ahead as the iron gates opened onto a motor court in front of a fieldstone mansion. Stately Wayne Manor. Another guard with bulky headphones jogged out and directed me where to park. He opened my door and walked me to the house.

There were my oak doors. All twelve feet of them.

He led me in. "Can you please remove your shoes?" He handed me some white fabric booties.

Booties. A true sign of new money. Like feathered boas on chandeliers in pink waiting rooms. I had been around rich people and their oversized houses in DC. Houses that had real history in their bones and other houses that were made to look like they had history in their bones. In those places I wasn't greeted by guards, but by housekeeping staff.

The guards were probably the result of Kardashian paranoia and an overestimated sense of self. At least, according to the research I'd done.

The house seemed to go on forever in every direction from the grand entryway. I had read about the house the previous night. They shelled out twenty million dollars for it a few years ago and then spent a couple of years remodeling. I couldn't imagine. Private sector money, I reminded myself. I was so used to clients who had to deal with taxpayer dollars. Every penny had to be accounted for. It was usually when my clients got a little too creative with their accounting that I'd get a call from them to figure out how to spin it. Probably a good portion of my fees had secretly come at taxpayer expense. I wasn't used to a world where spending was not accountable.

I followed the guard down a flagstone-lined hallway to a cozy room with a fireplace, a sofa, some chairs, and a huge portrait of Kim and Kanye in matching leopard skin outfits over the fireplace.

"Wait here and I'll let Kim know you're waiting." He left.

I heard a high-frequency mechanical humming noise, which struck me as odd. An HVAC system? Kitchen appliance? I would have thought that people as picky as the Kardashians would not put up with noise from appliances.

I looked around the room and noticed that most flat surfaces were loaded with picture frames of Kim's famous selfies with movie stars. What was it like to be so fascinated by your own face that you wanted to see your image everywhere you looked?

Framed photos of Kim's magazine covers lined the walls. In the corner, a magazine cover of Kanye and some models on a runway. Kanye the designer. Even though his designs were not my thing, I had some begrudging respect for him. The man never seemed to stop. Music, fashion, a wife with a TV empire. Another photo from a fashion show on a side table. His clothes were lifeless, like rags. Nice for covering up flaws, but I could not imagine an instance where I would wear it. Did he design for movie stars? Or anybody?

I just needed a good power suit. Something well-crafted and tailored right. I had a dozen in my closet. A good power suit would intimidate a man in my former career.

But I wasn't sure if power suits would work in my new world. I had the worst time this morning picking out my outfit. I even tried on jeans. I had never worn jeans in front of a client. To me, they were just barely a step up from yoga pants. I stood at the mirror for a few minutes this morning in my jeans, but I just couldn't take that image seriously. Today was not the day to mess with my uniform. I changed my mind and put on my suit. My armor.

The guard came back. "Can you follow me?"

I followed him back down the stone hallway to the center entrance of the house into a great room lined with sleek furniture that looked like it had all been bought last night from a magazine ad. We walked through a dream chef's kitchen, gorgeous white marble everywhere with professional grade appliances, when I got my first glimpse of a Kardashian. Kris Jenner, Kim's mom, the power behind the throne, sat at the kitchen's overgrown marble island, talking on the phone. The high-pitched humming got louder, and I shook my head to try and clear it out of my brain.

She glanced up at me and glared for a full five seconds.

Instinctively I felt like she was an adversary. Maybe it was just a remnant of my past work, but that glare reminded me of all the wives, the girlfriends, the boyfriends I'd had to pay off or lie to on behalf of clients in the past. That misplaced anger in their eyes that said, "Get the hell out of my life."

Her face was . . . uneven. Lumpy on one side. I thought they had access to the best fillers?

The guard led me outside to a patio where Kim sat with her small daughter.

Her daughter jumped off of her lap, stood, and pointed at me. "That lady is here!"

That lady? Did she already know about me?

Kim stood to greet me. She was impressive.

When I watched her show, I could see that she was pretty, that her body was an exaggerated version of a fifties pin-up model. I knew that, but in person, she was even prettier. Her skin was flawless to the point of looking like a painting. Her makeup was picture-perfect, accentuating every angle on her face to its best advantage. She wore a black lace cover-up over a white bikini. Her Amazonian breasts poked through the sheer cover.

I held my hand out and she moved right in for a hug. "Maddy, right? Welcome!"

"That's me."

"I'm North!" her daughter yelled out. She eyed me, giggled, and ran off into the yard. Well, not a yard. This house didn't have a yard; this house had grounds.

I felt the same way about children as I did about dogs. Noisy and full of germs.

"Stay away from the koi pond! I'm watching you!" Kim yelled after her daughter, and then turned to address me. "I'm so happy you could come today. I have so much I want to talk to you about, and Trina tells me that you are a political expert."

I smiled and nodded. "I know how things get done in Washington."

She brushed her hand against my blazer sleeve. "This is gorgeous. Where did you get this?"

"Nordstrom's."

She smiled. "I love Nordstrom's, they carry some of my lines. This blazer is perfection; can I try it on?"

I hesitated, as if I hadn't heard her correctly. Maybe it was because I had been a lone wolf for so long. Maybe I didn't know what women talked about when they got together, but none of the women I knew had ever asked me for an article of my clothing.

She tilted her head and raised her eyebrows.

I slowly removed my blazer. In one short minute this woman had disarmed me. Took my armor. Was this a power move? Or was she really just that simple? I sensed it was the latter. My internal alarm would have sounded, like it had when I spotted Kris Jenner in the kitchen.

She slid into my blazer pretty easily, which surprised me. Of course, it couldn't close over her famous chest. "I love this." She took it off and took a photo of the label. "You know, it's so warm out here, you should just keep it off anyway." Kim tossed my armor onto a chaise lounge behind her.

"I have some lunch for us." She pulled a grocery bag off of a nearby table. "I got sandwiches from Conrad's Deli. They are the best! I wasn't sure what you like, so I just got, like, a bunch of them." She pulled wrapped sandwiches out of the bag and laid them out on a table. "I'm not supposed to eat this, but this is like a special occasion, you know? C'mon, sit down."

I sat down and grabbed the first sandwich I saw. Cuban Deli Style.

"I love their Cubans. Oops, I forgot the drinks. What do you want? I have anything you want." Kim picked up her phone.

"Water is fine."

She texted and put the phone back down. "My mom will bring some drinks out." She poked through a couple of sandwiches until she found one. "Pastrami Reuben. Do not tell my trainer."

I unwrapped the sandwich. I needed to get control of this meeting. That was just my nature. I couldn't sit here without my armor, chewing on a sandwich and ceding all control to Kim. "Just to get things started, can you tell me what you had in mind for me? What is it that you want to accomplish that you think I can help you with?"

She held a finger up as she chewed her way through her first bite of her Reuben.

Kris Jenner walked out onto the patio with our drinks. "Hi, I'm Kris." She set the waters down and held her hand out.

The humming noise got louder. Her face was no longer lumpy.

I felt vulnerable without my blazer. I didn't feel like a take-no-prisoners warrior, I was only a woman in a skirt and a blouse. "A pleasure. Maddy Ellis from ME. Communications."

"Well, Trina thinks very highly of you," Kris said without smiling. "I'm very excited that you can help us. We have big expectations."

"Whatever I can do, I will do." *Why won't that goddamned humming stop?*

"Great. I have some ideas about Kim's new venture as well, and I can't wait to share them with you, but right now I have some business I have to get back to. Hopefully we can talk in the future."

I kept a tight-lipped smile and thought, *Sorry, bitch, outside of my scope of work. Kim's is the only opinion I'm paid to hear*. I didn't want to alienate my actual client, so I didn't say anything. I was proud of myself for having that much constraint. But I knew that sooner or later I would have to set her straight.

Kim finished chewing her food. "Okay, let's talk."

The humming died down slightly. "What is that humming noise?"

Kim rolled her eyes. "I'm so used to it that I hardly even hear it anymore. Technology. My husband is a tech freak. He's always having some weird security thing installed around the house and it makes that noise. It gets better the farther away you are from the house."

That made sense to me. Fame and money would make them a big target. No wonder her husband was so paranoid. "Why don't you tell me what it is you see me doing for you?"

"Well, this is the thing." Kim put her sandwich down. "I have so many followers on Twitter, on IG, Facebook. Like millions and millions. And Kanye and I were talking about, like, being able to influence people. It's so easy for me to get people to buy something or look at a show, you know? But what about serious things? There's all these problems going on in the world, and maybe I could influence these people for real serious things."

"What kinds of things?" Was she thinking of running for office? I didn't want to be part of that kind of chaos. I thought the world had had enough of reality star presidents.

"Like, what are some serious things that you think I could help with?" she asked me, and took a nibble of her sandwich.

I glanced over her shoulder at my blazer sitting in the sun on the chaise lounge. Would it be rude to grab my jacket and tell her that I'd be back when she was serious? "Well, can you tell me if there is anything that you feel passionate about? Something that might affect your children's future or something that you think needs to be fixed now?"

"Like what?"

Pulling teeth. "What about climate change?"

Kim nodded to me as she wiped some mustard from her lip. "Yes! Let's do that one. And you know another one? Kanye is always talking about inequality, like how poor people and Black people need help."

"Good. I think those are great. By the way, will Kanye be involved with this?" I needed to clear this up. I would not chase after crazy people. Would not do it.

"No. You work for me. But he may be involved a little bit. Depends."

"I have to ask, are either of you thinking of running for office? Is this a way to get your feet wet?"

Kim shook her head adamantly. "Not me, anyway. My husband is always talking about being the president, though. But don't worry about that."

"Okay, that's good to know." I could exhale. "What do you want to do about these problems?"

Kim looked out toward a pool beyond the patio. Her daughter was climbing to the top of a slide and waved. "I know everyone thinks I'm just this dumb, big-titted bimbo. But I'm not dumb. I'm one of the highest-earning businesswomen in the world. You don't get that by being dumb. I run all kinds of businesses, and all of them are really successful. I have a knack for it." She turned to look at me. "But there has to be more. I want more than that. It's just that . . . I don't even know how to begin. I don't know how to start being . . . serious. I need your help."

I sensed sincerity. I could work with that. I found myself becoming charmed. She was actually kind of sweet. "There's a lot we can do. Just for starters, you could start a foundation. You could hold events that would highlight the problems or the solutions. You could market products that would specifically benefit the issues that you believe in."

Kim smiled and nodded her head. "All that sounds great. This really makes me feel hopeful. I think this is going to be fantastic. Would I get to meet politicians? I mean, those are the guys I really need to influence, too, right?"

"Sure, that could be part of it." I felt a little calmer. This was something I could handle easily. My mission: make Kim Kardashian a serious person. "I have to go back to DC for a little bit. What I'll do while I'm there is work on some proposals for you. I have plenty of resources available as well, and I'll list out options for educating you. I'll make sure that you have the best information and the best team to make this happen. When I get back to LA, we can go over it and work on a timeline, okay?"

"This is so exciting!" Kim's phone buzzed. "Sorry, I have to take this. I'll be a few minutes. Would you mind? You could walk around the yard, that might be nice. I have a small vineyard over that way, and you should see the koi pond, too."

I grabbed my blazer and put it back on. Whole again.

I walked toward the pool and saw her daughter climb out and run into the gardens further on. My mind was racing, thinking about the contacts who could help me out. I could probably get in touch with some of the top scientists on climate change. Any one of them would probably beg to have Kim Kardashian's massive following on their side. I needed to make sure she was well educated, too. I could probably find a local professor or activist who would be willing to meet with her. The inequality thing would be a little tougher. I needed to get in touch with the activists in that world. I wasn't sure my usual contacts would know the right people. My clients and contacts tended to be on the other side of the inequality argument.

I walked through an arbor and sat down on a pretty stone bench. This world was so . . . nice. Did I trust this yet? Maybe not, but maybe it was time to let my new life begin. I didn't think it would be difficult to work with Kim. This job wasn't bad at all.

I saw North running just beyond the arbor. I stood and thought I might as well look like I cared about her kid. In the distance, she was leaning over the koi pond. *Hope she doesn't fall in.* I walked and let the sun beat down on my face. *How do I learn to trust all of this?*

North pulled a koi out of the pond and held it over her head. *Maybe I should tell her not to do that.* I was within shouting distance. The humming returned.

Well, probably better not to mess with the client's kid.

She leaned her head back toward the sky, opened her mouth, and stuck her tongue out. I stopped in my tracks. Her tongue kept coming out. Longer and longer until it wrapped around the fish, like a lizard catching its prey.

I should have just walked away from whatever this was.

But I couldn't take my eyes off of her. Was I really seeing this? The small koi's tail was still moving.

While her long, thick red tongue wrapped around the fish, she dropped her hands to her sides and lowered the fish whole into her mouth.

I stood there, frozen, staring at her as the humming got louder.

North wiped her mouth with her hands and then returned my stare. She pointed her finger at me, smiled, and ran away.

3

I was back in DC two days later to tie up some loose ends, comforted by the familiar surroundings of a world I understood, like sleazy and corrupt politicians who had normal-sized tongues.

Macroglossia. Every time I was haunted by the image of the freakshow I had seen at the Kardashians' koi pond, I reminded myself of this word.

I had googled "lizard tongue" and it turned out that lizard tongue happens. It wasn't common, but common enough to have a Wikipedia page and an official diagnosis. It was called macroglossia.

I had seen a lot of crazy in my career, but I wished I had never seen that. I wanted to run straight to my car after North's performance, but instead I managed to hold it together for the next twenty minutes with Kim. I don't even remember what she said to me. The whole time she was talking, I wanted to scream, "DO YOU KNOW YOUR DAUGHTER SWALLOWS FISH WHOLE WITH A FREAKING LIZARD TONGUE?"

But the client is king. And how do you tell your brand-new client that her daughter is a freak of nature?

After I got settled back in DC, I contacted Lloyd, my legwork guy, and set up a meeting with him at Denny's, just outside of DC. No one in the beltway would ever come to Denny's. Even though this meeting didn't call for a clandestine destination, coming here for business was just a habit. I also had a thing for their Grand Slams.

I sat down at my favorite booth and signed in to their Wi-Fi network on Spencer's laptop. The browser showed my bookmark for macroglossia was still open. I quickly deleted it. I didn't want to see those pictures of people with freakishly long tongues anymore. North must have been born with this . . . deformity, but it could have been fixed with surgery. Why hadn't they fixed it yet? After all, who had better access to plastic surgeons?

Spencer had three new emails. Two of them were about logistics for an upcoming personal appearance for Kim. That was not part of my scope. Trina had a small army of people who handled those kinds of details, so I forwarded those to Jay. The third email was in Spanish. I ran it through Google Translate:

Dear Mr. Golden,

Thank you for your inquiry. I am most sorry that we do not offer the measure of security that you have asked about. We are just a small hostel, and it would not make economic sense for us to offer this to our guests. If you change your mind, please con tact us again for a reservation.

Yours Truly,

Se ora Ramona Esteval

Casa Esteval

Chungungo, Chile

Chungungo, Chile, Google Maps . . . Holy moly. All the way at the bottom of the map. Very southern point of Chile. This place was literally at the end of the earth. There was nothing there except a small fishing village. What was he running away from? Maybe he saw lizard girl in action and got scared off.

"Wow! I don't think I have ever seen you in jeans before!" Lloyd slid onto the bench opposite me.

I closed the laptop and smiled at Lloyd. "Things change, huh?" One day I was working to hide the darkest secrets of the most powerful people in the country and the next day I was doing PR for a lizard girl's famous mommy. This move was not a mistake, I reminded myself. I needed a change.

"You going all casual now with this California bullshit? What's next, yoga pants?"

"Funny." Lloyd was a jack of all trades. He'd been around forever. I was lucky to find him, as he had saved me a lot of time hunting people down and doing background prep. I met him about ten years ago when he was working for a very corrupt lobbyist whom I was trying to help get out of a "situation," as usual. Lloyd and I hit it off, and after the "situation" blew over, he quit and started his own consulting business called GSD Consulting. Get Shit Done. He was sort of a fixer's fixer.

I could have probably done this meeting by email, but I wanted to see Lloyd. I was leaving my old life, and this was kind of my goodbye party. I would miss him. I wondered if he would miss me. Would anyone in DC actually miss me?

"So, the Kardashians, huh?" He raised an eyebrow and smirked.

"Yep." I nodded. "You should think about moving out west. Easy money out there. Movie stars, palm trees."

He waved his hand at me. "Aaah. You just traded one reality show for another one. Besides, I got no heat out there. Don't know anyone. I'm probably gonna retire soon anyways."

"Retire?" I knew he had some grown kids, maybe even some grandkids. We had never talked about our personal lives, just insider beltway gossip. A good professional relationship. A contact but not a friend. I wanted to confide in him, to ask him if he thought I was doing the right thing, but the parameters of our relationship didn't allow for that. I trusted Lloyd more than anyone in DC, even though I knew very little about his personal life. What did he know about me? What did he think of me? I never cared what anyone thought of me before, so why would I care now? Maybe because I was making this big life-changing move and there was no one except me who cared.

He shrugged. "Thinking about it. So, what's she like?"

"You watch the show?"

He leaned in toward me. "I'm only gonna tell you this because you're leaving and you won't be able to laugh in my face anymore. It's my guilty pleasure. My wife is a big fan. She watches that shit all the time. So one day, I sat down on the couch with her while she was watching, and I got hooked."

"No way." Lloyd was the last person I would peg as a Kardashian fan.

"I know, right? But you know what, after a day of chasing down all the bullshit that we see every day, it's kind of . . . calming. It's so far removed from my reality, maybe any reality, so it's kind of an escape, I guess. I'm sure I've lost a few brain cells watching, but isn't that the point? They live these fantasy lives that any idiot would like to live, so you kind of sit there watching like a moron. My wife calls it aspirational. It's just good dumb fun."

I was genuinely shocked. So much about Lloyd I didn't know. Why didn't we ever connect on a personal level before? "I'm so . . . surprised."

Lloyd pointed his finger at me. "Tell one soul and I will seek revenge. So what's she really like?"

"She's actually very sweet." I thought back to our meeting. She had a child's excitement about life. It was almost refreshing. My clients didn't normally have any kind of wonder. They were bitter, jaded, and trying to avoid responsibility.

"Sweet?" Lloyd took out a pair of reading glasses. "That's a word you don't hear every day in this town. Well, good luck.

I hope it works out for you. But I think you'll be back. You're like me, you need the circus. That's what makes us tick, huh? I think you'll get bored."

The circus. The nickname for DC. I let his words brush past me, even though I was afraid in my heart of hearts that he was right. I had thrived on the chaos here. But I needed more than that. I needed something. I needed to be . . . human. The problem with my life was that I had become a fortress, an impenetrable fortress. I needed to become vulnerable. The best way I could do that was to put myself in a situation where I didn't know the rules. "They're paying me a ton of money to be bored. If I get too bored, I can always go shopping."

Lloyd nodded. "So what would a Kardashian need my help for? Don't tell me she's thinking about running for office?"

I shook my head. "No, nothing like that, God willing. She does want to have some influence on issues, though. I need you to put together some info for me. I don't have anyone in my rolodex on equality issues. I need a list of the best and most legit equality activists. The ones who are taken seriously on the Hill. Who's got clout in that world? I'm looking at women's issues, race issues, gay issues, whatever you can find out for me. I'll need the contacts and background on those groups as well."

Lloyd wrote some notes on a pad. "That it?"

"Tell me who on the Hill is especially receptive to this issue and who's looking for a good photo op. And same as above with climate change."

"When do you need this?"

I opened the laptop and looked at the calendar. I was due back in LA this weekend to apartment hunt. I wanted to get back to Kim by the end of next week. "How long do you need?"

He scratched his head. "Probably two weeks for a complete list."

"Can you do it in a week?"

Lloyd frowned. "I don't know."

"I'll pay double the normal fee."

He smiled. "One week it is. Anything else?"

I looked at Spencer's files on his laptop.

!!!!!

"Do you know any hackers?"

Lloyd straightened up. "What kind of hacking?"

"I have a file on this laptop that I inherited, and I can't get into it."

He shook his head. "Hackers are some serious and crazy fucking people. I wouldn't use one for that. I know a couple, but they wouldn't do that kind of small stuff. Maybe just call Best Buy or something."

I saw his point. Maybe I could figure out the password on my own. Or maybe I could find Spencer. I pulled out my phone and searched for a contact. "Troy Anderson."

"The FBI guy? You think he'll help you get into a file?"

"No. This is something different. I need help with a missing person. I haven't talked to Troy in about a year. You know if he's still around?"

"I think so. Bumped into him a few months ago at Benny's Grill." Lloyd opened his Denny's menu.

"Great. I'll give him a call. Breakfast is on me."

∞

Back at my condo a couple of hours later, I was struggling to figure out what to bring back to LA. I hadn't really thought through the whole idea of relocating to Los Angeles. I assumed I would still need to spend a lot of time back in DC to take care of Kim's business. Maybe I just wasn't ready to commit one hundred percent to LA yet. Besides, I could now easily afford to rent a place in LA and still keep this place.

But what about clothes? All I had were power suits. I had some jeans and "downtime" clothes, but they wouldn't fit in with my new job. Looked like I needed to shop. Maybe I'd just pack a couple of suits; that would leave more room in the suitcases for shoes.

I loved shoes. Shoes were my therapy. I was a typical girly-girl that way. First Kardashian paycheck I get? It's shoe fantasy time.

I looked around my place. I bought it ten years ago and had relatively few personal effects. Nothing I really needed to bring with me. I had a few pictures of my family, Mom and Dad, my sister and her kids. I wasn't even that close to them. Christmas and birthday cards. Work. I was always enveloped in work. I fought back a sadness. I needed to change this. I needed to start forming connections with people. I couldn't be a lone wolf anymore.

My phone rang. Troy Anderson, my contact from the FBI.

"Troy, thanks for calling me back. I wasn't sure if you remembered me."

"Sure I remember you. It was with the Gaylord case, right? The senator's kid."

"Brianna." The senator's daughter.

"She okay?"

"As far as I know." I hadn't really followed up. Brianna, a southern debutante from Alabama in every sense of the word, had gone missing and the FBI tracked her down to find her working a pole in a Montreal strip club. I was sent up there to do my magic and keep it all quiet. That was a very long week.

"What can I do for you?"

"I have a friend who's gone missing, and I wondered if you could help me."

"Is the friend over eighteen?"

"Yes."

"Any reason to suggest foul play?"

"Not that I know of."

A few seconds of silence. "Well, usually FBI won't do anything unless there's something that suggests the missing person may be in some trouble. Is there an MPR?"

"What's that?"

"Missing persons report. Hold on, let me get to the computer. Okay, what's the name?"

"Spencer Golden." I opened Spencer's laptop. "Address is 3314 Hollyhock Drive, Los Angeles, 90068."

I heard him typing.

"Bingo. An MP report filed two weeks ago by DeSantis Property Management . . . Relationship to missing . . . landlord. Looks like they want their rent. Since that report was filed, looks like no movement on this case. Have you spoken with the landlord? Maybe they have some new info?"

The sadness invaded again. If I went missing, would the only person who noticed be my landlord? I didn't even have a landlord. My own family probably wouldn't notice until a birthday or a holiday. "Is he still in the country? Can you check and see if he's used his passport since he disappeared?" I knew FBI agents could look this up, all depends on how "by the book" he was.

"Well . . ."

I heard him typing.

"Looks like he left the US on the fourteenth and entered Ecuador on the fifteenth. Quito Airport. No other entries since then. Does that help you any?"

"I absolutely owe you one. Although, God forbid you should ever have to call me in for a favor."

"I heard that!"

"One more question." I knew I would be pushing my luck with this. "Can you see if he's used his credit cards down there? Like at an ATM or a hotel?"

"Can't access his banking records. Need some official paperwork to do that. You'd need a next of kin to talk to the police or get yourself a good private detective. However, Ecuador's currency is the US dollar. So if your friend is looking to go off the grid, he could have easily brought some US cash with him to avoid ATMs."

"Thanks again, Troy. Great info." I hung up and wondered why Spencer would disappear to Ecuador and also why I was becoming obsessed with finding him. The *!!!!!* file was most likely something innocuous like nude selfies. I closed the laptop. Enough. I had real work to do.

4

After I returned to LA from DC, I had spent a few days looking at some places to rent but wasn't in love with anything. I wasn't in love with the hotel either, so I had decided to go into the office early and work.

I had received Lloyd's list of contacts, and his work was pretty extensive. He had listed all of the top lobbying groups for each cause, their budgets, how influential they were, membership numbers, who they were influential with, and the lawmakers who were most open to those causes. As a bonus he also listed any celebrities associated with those lobbying groups. None of them had the following or the firepower of the Kardashian brand. One problem was that some of the groups were competing with each other for lawmakers' attention or for the general public's attention. I thought that some kind of Kardashian foundation would probably climb to the top of the heap pretty quickly and could become a pretty potent force if steered correctly.

I needed to finish up some policy papers for Kim, boiling all of the issues down to some easy sound bites for her so she could decide how she wanted to tackle the issues.

I unlocked my office door and immediately noticed a new piece of furniture. A doggy bed. What. The fuck.

First of all, why was someone entering my office when it was locked? Second of all, I didn't own a dog, so why was this crap in my office? I knew the answer to that one: Trina. Did she think that her little pet could sleep in my office?

I took the bed and put it outside in the hall. Done.

An hour later, Jay showed up for work and immediately knocked on my door with the bed in his hands. He looked a little freaked out.

"Sorry to disturb you." He sat down. "You can't leave Miss Elsa's bed in the hallway. We have to have it in here. Trina will have a fit."

"So let Trina have her fit." I stopped typing. "If she wants that thing in my office, she can ask me like any normal person would. Then I will tell her 'no fucking way' and we'll all move on."

Jay's face contorted. His normal cheerful smile tightened, his eyes wide with alarm. I saw he was struggling to mitigate this.

"It's a little more complicated than that."

I folded my hands on the desk and gave him my full attention. "Explain."

He took a deep breath. "Miss Elsa is not only our mascot, she's actually an owner of the company. She's a partial owner, forty-nine percent, along with Trina. So technically, this office is Miss Elsa's property. She can decorate it as she pleases. We've actually had legal look into this . . ."

"That's crazy! How can a dog own a business? The dog would have to sign contracts and be liable, no one in the world would agree to that."

Jay was nodding. "Miss Elsa has an appointed guardian who takes care of all her business decisions."

"And who is that?"

"Kris Jenner."

I sensed we were slipping down a deep rabbit hole. "Kim's mother?"

"Yeah. Kris and Trina go way back. Way, way back. Kris gave

Miss Elsa to Trina and helped her set up this business."

I held my hands up. "Fine." This was not worth the drama that I envisioned lay ahead if I fought this thing. I needed to learn new tricks. Become vulnerable. "Put the bed by the door."

Jay's face contorted again.

"What now?" Was Jay my admin or the office police?

"The bed has to go in the back by the window. Miss Elsa likes the views from there."

Great, her little dog sitting over my shoulder. "Miss Elsa likes —" I stopped myself from finishing the sentence. Perspective. If this was the biggest annoyance in my new work life, it would still be a cake walk. I thought about my first paycheck, about finding an apartment with a room dedicated to shoes: Manolos, Louboutins, Ferragamos. "Fine."

Jay stood up, his face finally freed from the stress of having to defend Miss Elsa. "I'll take care of everything, so don't worry about her disturbing you. If she comes to your door, I'll let her in and I'll let her out as well." He placed the bed by the window. "It won't matter much anyway, since you'll be working from home mostly, right? You find a place yet?"

"Not yet. I spent the last few days looking, but nothing has really grabbed me."

Jay stopped and folded his arms. "You know who had a great place? Spencer. A nice little cottage in the Hills. Great views, really private."

My attention was piqued. "Private?"

"Totally. It wasn't a big place, but it was perfect for one person. Really cozy, surrounded by all kinds of lush foliage. Almost hidden off the road. Very LA."

I wondered if Spencer's landlord had started eviction proceedings. I smiled to myself. Two birds, one stone. Maybe I could figure out a little bit more of the Spencer mystery. "Can you get me Spencer's landlord's number?"

∞

A few hours later, I had everything ready for Kim. Policy papers on climate change and inequality, proposals for a foundation, timelines and action plans. I thought about taking a lunch break and heard breathing in back of me. Miss Elsa sat in her basket with her eyes fixed on me. Jay was as good as his word; I never noticed her come in.

"Spying on me, Miss Elsa?" She wasn't a bad or annoying pet. She just sat there staring and panting in her silly pink collar. Poor thing probably had no idea she was worth hundreds of millions of dollars. "Want to sell me your half of the company for a nice chew toy?"

Miss Elsa barked at me.

"Okay! I was just kidding!" Touchy little bitch.

I called Kim to set up our next appointment. To my surprise, she answered her phone. I had expected to go through "people" or to get a voicemail.

"Hi, Maddy! So good to hear from you. What's up?"

"I have all the information we discussed, so I wanted to set up another meeting with you to go over it."

"Hold on." I heard some muffled talk, a car honking. "Okay, how about in an hour?"

"An hour?" I didn't think I could get out to her house that quickly.

"Yeah, I'm on my way into Beverly Hills. You want to go shopping with me?"

My instinct was to tell her no. A normal business meeting concerning political hot topics doesn't happen on a shopping trip. I turned around and looked at Miss Elsa. But things here were not really normal. This was just the way things worked in this new world. The client is king, right? "Sure."

"Fabulous, let's meet at Prada. About an hour?"

"See you then."

I hung up, and a quick Google search showed me that Prada was just a fifteen-minute drive, so I still had some time to do a once-over on the docs. I buzzed Jay and he was at my door in a few seconds. Damn, he was good.

"I'll be out of the office this afternoon. Shopping meeting with Kim."

His face contorted again. "Prada at one?"

Was he listening to my calls? "How did you know that?"

"She just tweeted it. You need to leave now."

I cocked my head. "It's pretty close by."

"No, that's not it." He sat down. "Shopping with Kim is . . . different. It's not like just meeting your girlfriend at a store. It's like meeting several thousand people at a store. If you don't leave now, you won't be able to get near the place."

"I don't understand."

"Well, first of all, Kim doesn't ever shop alone. There's her entourage, could be anywhere from five to twenty people. Then there's the paparazzi. Then there's just the regular fans who show up. If you get there at one o'clock, you won't even be able to get near the front door. You need to leave now and get in there."

This was not how I wanted to talk to her about serious issues. There was no way she would be able to focus on policy papers. "I still have fifty pages of documents to print out. Maybe I should just reschedule."

Elsa barked from her basket.

An opinionated little bitch, too.

Jay shook his head. "We never reschedule or cancel on a client. Also, we never print out anything for Kim—she won't read anything on paper. Send it to her phone." Jay took out his cell. "I'll have a car take you over there. I know that Prada store pretty well. They have a quiet VIP room in the back for celebrities; you can use that for your meeting. When you get there, ask for Pauline."

I was dropped off at Prada at twelve-thirty, and sure enough, there was already a crowd gathered outside. A dozen photographers and then another few dozen onlookers. One older woman stood apart from the crowd, dressed in a matted zebra coat with an old, ratty blonde wig that wasn't quite secured on her head. Her lined face was caked with white powder and bright pink lipstick. She held up a sign that read "KIM IS THE DEVIL!"

As I approached the front door, the old woman walked in front of me. Her eyes were open wide with fear and panic. She smelled like a bottle of cheap floral perfume. "She is a demon from Hell!" She pointed a bony finger into my arm. "You will need to beware!"

The guard at the front door pushed her aside. "Rita, I'm warning you. I'll call the cops if you don't stay the hell back."

I guessed Rita was a regular at these things. I flashed my ME ID and he let me into the store.

This was one of Prada's bigger stores, two stories. The atmosphere was calm and quiet inside. In fact, I was the only person in the store. I wasn't a fashionista, but I knew shoes and bags, and this place made me want to shop. I liked Prada purses, very clean lines, simple but elegant. Very high-quality leather. Those things would last for years, but of course, no one who buys Prada thinks about using a purse for years. They were always out of my league. Until now. Could I drop five thousand on a bag? Maybe.

Each purse was highlighted in a beautiful little sparkling frame. The shoes were spaced apart on a glowing white counter, highlighting each pair. I didn't care much for their shoes;

they were more trendy than their purses. Too much bling. I hated their outrageously thick heels.

A young man with a tray of San Pellegrino bottles approached me.

"Good afternoon, welcome to Prada. Would you like a Pellegrino?"

"Sure. Can you tell me where Pauline is?"

He poured the water into a glass of ice cubes. "I'll be happy to get her for you. You are?"

"Maddy Ellis from ME. Communications." I would never get used to that.

A few minutes later an older woman dressed in a suit with bold alternating patterns of black and gold, a trademark of Prada, approached me. I didn't care for the design, but the fit was absolutely perfect. She extended her hand. "Pauline Gray, Regional Manager."

"Maddy Ellis, ME Communications."

"What happened to Spencer?"

Wish I knew. "He's no longer with ME. Communications. But I'm not actually his replacement. I'm working with Kim on another project. At the office they mentioned a private room? I need to go over some documents with Kim."

She nodded. "Come."

I followed her through the store to a glossy black door behind the accessories.

"Just press this buzzer on the side to get in. I'll have someone set up some drinks and snacks. Is ME sending anyone over to handle her?"

"I don't know."

She sighed. "Can you call someone over at your office and see? I'm short-staffed today. No warning about this visit at all. My store manager called in sick. I pulled the short straw."

"I'll text my assistant right now." This woman was not happy about Kim's visit. "I guess this really disrupts your normal sales, but won't the Kardashians spend more here than most of your customers could in a single afternoon?"

She squinted her eyes and looked at me. "Honey, you are new, aren't you?"

"Well, yeah."

"Kim and her family don't buy anything here. They won't spend a penny this afternoon. Prada will pay for everything. Even if she walks out of the store empty-handed, Prada will still send her a nice fat check just for showing up. Every retailer in the world wants to be on Kim's Twitter. But that's a very expensive piece of real estate. That's how this works."

"Really?" My mind caught up. Endorsement deals. Genius. I thought about my proposal. She didn't expect to get an endorsement fee for supporting a cause, did she? I would have to clarify that with her. "But still, isn't this great PR for Prada?"

She shrugged her shoulders. "Maybe. But for my store? I've got a staff of people on commission who won't earn anything today. I have a store that bleeds red ink every day a Kardashian comes in. I have to argue with corporate for a week afterward about who pays for security, for food. This all affects my bottom line as a regional."

My phone buzzed. A text from Jay confirmed someone else from ME was on the way. "Someone from ME is on the way."

"Good." Pauline glanced in a nearby mirror and adjusted her collar. "I need you guys to do the handholding. I'm really not in the mood today, okay?" She looked over my shoulder. "Aaron? Where are the Ostrich clutches? I don't see them." She looked back at me. "Excuse me."

"Okay." Well that was one hardened bitch. Reminded me of me.

The swarm of people outside had grown and now overflowed into the street. Cars were honking at onlookers who were standing in the road, holding cell phones above their heads. Security guards were trying to keep people from blocking the entire sidewalk, but they were failing. Police were doing crowd control on the overflow on the sidewalk across the street. I didn't understand this need for people to watch Kim enter a store and shop.

I had seen plenty of crowds before in DC. Protests were just a part of life there, and I completely understood why people protested. People were angry, people wanted change, they felt solidarity in numbers. Anger was a powerful motivator. Why else would you interrupt your daily life? But this crowd? Just to get a quick selfie of Kim? It wasn't like she was the Beatles or the pope. But it made me think; if I could harness this kind of following for political change, Kim could become an even more powerful woman.

A woman with a small dog entered the store. The woman was stuffed into a skintight white sweater dress with boobs pouring out of a low-cut neck. The dog started barking at the empty store.

"Quiet, Binky!" She looked around. "Can I get a water? Somebody?"

Aaron rushed over to her with a San Pellegrino.

"Do you have any munchies today?"

Her dog yapped at Aaron.

Binky and her owner wandered over to me. Up close, I couldn't guess the woman's age; her face was like a puzzle that was put together wrong. Her cheeks were too big, her chin had an unnatural point at the tip, and her lips were bright pink and bloated.

She took a sip of her water and left it on a display case. "You part of the entourage or an FOS?"

"FOS?" I really wanted to walk away and use the time to review my proposal, but I couldn't take my eyes off of this entitled train wreck. However, her shoes were to die for. Jimmy Choo's pink platform sandals. That was probably one thousand dollars worth of shoe leather covering her feet. Was this an actual housewife of Beverly Hills?

She sighed. "Friend of the Store. You know, if you spend enough money, they invite you to these kinds of things. This is my first one with a Kardashian. Neiman Marcus has a Jennifer Aniston shopping thing this afternoon, but I've seen her before. She's kind of stuck up." Binky began yapping again. "Can I get some water for Binky? Hello?"

I saw some movement out of the front window. Two black escalades pulled up as police moved the crowd away from the entrance. One of the police officers was arguing with my friend Rita with the ratty wig. Kim stepped out of the first car and, without looking at the crowd, entered the store. Four more Kardashian women emptied out of the cars and followed her in. Thank God no lizard girl today. Uh-oh. I didn't know any of her sisters' names. Dancer? Prancer? Sleepy? Doc? Did I need to know their names? I knew there was a Kylie, but I didn't know which one she was.

Kim looked around the store, saw me, and waved. I started to walk over there, but she grabbed one of the sisters and walked into the shoe department.

Guess I'd have to wait. I hated that. More "client is king" nonsense.

The women picked up shoes and bags. A staffer followed close by. Kim took some selfies with a few of the purses and handed the purses she liked off to the staffer.

Binky's owner returned. "No DJ, either. They usually have a DJ and some food. Don't think I'll come back for another one of these here. Ferragamo had dog treats. I liked that, but I hate their shoes."

The high-pitched noise returned. The same one that had pervaded Kim's house. Did they travel with that noise? Was it some kind of embedded technology?

Binky yapped loudly. I was getting a grade A headache. I didn't want to wait around any longer. Coming here for a business meeting was a huge mistake. Lesson learned.

Kim approached with her shopper in tow. "Maddy! I'm so glad you could make it." She pulled a mauve clutch from her shopper. "Is this adorable, or is this adorable?"

I picked it up. $6,550. "Beautiful." I was no longer in the mood to appreciate a Prada purse. My head was pounding. I was losing my ability to concentrate.

Binky started yapping again like he was on meth.

"Binky!" Binky's owner admonished her dog.

Kim bent down and looked Binky in the eye. The dog stopped barking and lay down, hugging its head to the floor and whimpering.

Kim stood back up. "Cute dog. Maddy, have you been upstairs yet?"

"I'd like to get this done first." My inner Jay popped up again. "If that's okay."

Kim grabbed my hand, walked me back to the accessories, and found the door to the back room. She'd been here before, obviously.

"Hopefully they have some good munchies back here for us."

The room was like a small plush airport lounge. There was a small bar and some flat-screen TVs on the wall and fresh flowers set on a coffee table, but no munchies.

I sat down as Kim picked up a phone on a side table.

"Hi, it's Kim. There's no food or anything back here. Okay, thanks."

I pulled my laptop out of my bag and set it up on the coffee table as Kim settled down next to me. "I have a lot of info for you. I think you'll be happy with all of the options you have." I brought up a slide with a listing of all of the top organizations that dealt with injustice or inequality issues. "Right now, there are about a dozen really good organizations that are taken seriously in Washington lobbying for injustice across the spectrum."

She leaned over the laptop to take a look. "Wow."

I flipped to the next screen. "There are about two dozen climate change organizations. Right now, they have a wider following and deeper funding than inequality or injustice does. All of these organizations that you see on the screen have a very deep presence in DC."

"Uh-huh." She nodded.

My gut told me she was getting bored already. I should probably skip all the details I had spent hours working on and cut to the chase or I'd lose her. Besides, my headache was getting worse, and I really just wanted an aspirin and a nap. "My recommendation is that you form a non-profit foundation that could umbrella any number of causes."

She clapped her hands together. "Oh, I love that! What should I call it?"

The door buzzer sounded, and two of the Prada staff and Aaron, the San Pellegrino guy, came in with trays of snacks and drinks.

"Put them right here," Kim ordered, and pushed my laptop aside to make room. "Can you tell my sisters that there's food back here? Thanks."

The staff left and I resumed my spiel. "You'd need to file for a 501C, a non-profit organization. There are some rules and regs around payments that you should probably know about."

"Can you form this foundation for me?"

"Sure." I nodded. "I could walk you through it."

"Will I get to go to Washington and meet politicians?" she asked me while reaching for a mini taco.

She wasn't taking any of this seriously. This whole thing was wrong. Lloyd was right, I would be bored out of my mind here. She didn't want a real foundation, she wanted a toy to play with.

The door buzzer sounded, and the sisters filed into the room.

I closed my eyes and took a deep breath. The humming sound was louder, and I couldn't think straight any longer. The sisters were talking and laughing while reaching over me for the food.

Kim leaned over to me. "Are you okay?"

I shook my head. "I have a splitting headache, sorry." This had never happened to me. My head felt like it was on fire, and there was pounding against my forehead. I was giving up, letting this pain take control. In front of a client.

For the first time in a long time I felt vulnerable. Defenseless. I didn't know what to do except sit there and cradle my head.

Kim reached behind me and lightly began to rub the back of my head. "Sometimes just a little massage will fix those things."

The humming noise faded away. Kim's hand felt like water putting out the fire. Water mixed with sweet honey. I was in a dream. A happy, comfortable dream. I opened my eyes. My headache had shriveled and retreated. My entire body relaxed. The sisters were staring at me and I smiled back at them.

"Better?" Kim whispered.

I nodded and looked at the food on the table. I remembered I was hungry and dipped a celery stick into a bowl of hummus. I looked over at my laptop. I forgot where we were in the presentation.

"Everyone," Kim stood up and addressed the women. "This is Maddy, and she's the one who's going to set up my new foundation. I'm going to go to Washington and make them listen!"

The Kardashians' voices bounced around the room in praise of Kim's new venture.

"Oh my god! That is so cool!"

"When are you going?"

"I totally respect that."

Yes, I thought, *we're going to make them listen.* I would make them listen to Kim. That was my job, and this was my new life.

This was what I wanted, wasn't it? I was learning how to trust, let go of my defenses, my old ways, and be open to these people. Become human.

But somewhere in my brain, the same place that my headache had retreated to, a tiny voice was telling me to run.

5

I parked my car in front of Spencer's former home. I assumed there was a house there because I couldn't see it from the curb behind the palm trees and the bright red bougainvillea that draped over the white adobe wall. It took me a good fifteen minutes to find the place. Google Maps had trouble with all the small winding roads up in the hills.

I double-checked my wallet: five hundred and change in cash. The leasing agent for the landlord wanted Spencer's place cleaned up before showing it. I wasn't willing to wait. I told him he'd get a two-hundred-dollar "early access fee" to show me the place tonight.

I stepped out of the car and inhaled the sweet fragrance of the bougainvillea. The sun was just setting over the Hollywood Hills, and from this vantage I could see the lights from Hollywood proper below start to twinkle.

A few minutes later, a Toyota pulled up and parked behind me, and a middle-aged man stepped out. He had game show host good looks. The sort of generic and inoffensive handsome face that would be perfect for a campaign poster in DC.

"Maddy Ellis? I'm Lawton, we talked on the phone earlier?"

I shook his hand and then took out my wallet. "Thanks so much for your trouble." I pulled out two hundred-dollar bills and handed them off. "My colleague at work was raving about this place, so I just couldn't wait to see it."

"Sure." He tucked the cash into his messenger bag. He took out the keys from his pocket. "Shall we?"

I followed him past an iron gate down a small slate path to a small casita, with a huge arched window overlooking a small front lawn and a heavy oak door with cast iron trim and hardware, all topped by a traditional Spanish red clay tiled roof. A storybook cottage that practically smacked me in the face with its charm.

"We got official notice from Spencer just yesterday that he was terminating the lease. Otherwise we'd be shit out of luck. Would have been on lockdown until the eviction worked its way through the courts." He opened the door and turned on the lights.

I walked into the living room and instantly fell in love with the place. White stucco walls with rust-colored Mexican pavers on the floor. Wrought iron–clad windows and a small working fireplace lined with blue Mexican tiles. Spencer's books were still in the built-in shelves on either side of the fireplace. His furniture was still here: an L-shaped dark leather sofa with a red and yellow Persian rug, a large coffee table that looked like it was once a barn door. Expensive stuff to just leave behind.

"The kitchen." Lawton extended his hand toward a coved doorway in the far corner of the living room.

Black-and-white-tiled flooring, white paint with another cute Spanish window over the sink. The kitchen was a small galley style. The appliances looked like they originally came with the place when it was built. It reminded me of the *I Love Lucy* kitchen.

"It is the original kitchen. Very retro. All of it still works great. If you follow me, the bedroom is on the other side of the living room."

We walked through another coved doorway and down a narrow hall. He opened a door to the left. It was set up as a huge, oversized walk-in closet.

"This was actually the original bedroom. Only room without windows. The bedroom in the back was added later."

This was a room that could hold a nice shoe collection.

I followed Lawton into the bedroom. It was a good-sized room. Queen bed. Dresser. I noticed all of the drawers were pulled open in the dresser. Bare nails in the wall where artwork had probably hung. Spencer wanted out of there quickly.

A pair of French doors led out to a small backyard patio. I stepped on some broken glass and noticed that one of the panes at the bottom of the door was broken. "Did someone try to break in?"

Lawton looked over at the door and shrugged. "Nah, I don't think so. If it was a break-in, the pane by the doorknob would be broken. Probably Spencer just kicked it by accident or something."

"Is this neighborhood safe?"

He nodded. "Oh, yeah. The only dangers are the raccoons that try to get in the trash or the occasional coyote that comes down from the hills looking for a small pet to eat."

I decided that this could be my home. A home where I could become someone new. "What's the rent?"

"Management hasn't set the rental price yet."

"Are you positive Spencer is not coming back?"

Lawton nodded. "He called the office yesterday."

"Did he leave a number?"

"I don't know; I didn't take the call."

"You sure it was him?"

"The office must be okay with it. He also faxed over a formal notice after the call."

If I remembered correctly, faxes always had some ID of where they were sent from. Time to do business with Lawton. "Can I get a copy of that fax?"

I saw him hesitate. This was where I needed Kim's magic power to win over people. A giggle, a smile, and *bam*, done. But I didn't have that charm, or her huge chest. I reached for my wallet and pulled out another hundred dollars. "Spencer and I work for Kim Kardashian." A little name dropping never hurt either. "She really misses him. I think she wants to get in touch with him, say goodbye."

"Umm, okay. I think I can manage that." He shoved the bill in his messenger bag.

"I'll take the place." I kept my wallet out.

"We still have to clean it out first, repaint and do some maintenance." His eyes dropped to my wallet. "Then it officially goes on the market, and then there's the application process. Probably be another month before we get all that done."

"I'll take it as is. No need to clean or move his furniture. I'll keep it all. I want to sign the lease tonight." I handed him another hundred.

"Okay, but I have to check and make sure we don't have a waiting list."

I handed him another hundred. "Put me at the top of that list, but I want this done tonight, okay?"

He took the bill and nodded. "I think I can do that."

I turned around and looked at the small broken pane on the door. Maybe done by a small animal? "Just set the rent at whatever you think is fair and let's get this done."

"There is one more thing I think you could do for me that would clinch this deal."

I had my back to him. His tone was a little too creepy. I watched his reflection in the glass from the door. My hand slowly reached inside my purse for my pepper spray. I felt perspiration collecting under my arms. Did I have enough time to open the door and run? I didn't see anything I could grab to use as a weapon. I took a deep breath and waited for him to put his hand on me. "Like what?"

In the reflection on the glass, I saw him reach into his messenger bag. What did he have? I clutched the pepper spray and removed the cap. I was about to turn around and spray him, when he pulled a piece of paper out of his bag.

"My headshot."

I turned and faced him as he handed the headshot to me. I unclenched the pepper spray in my purse.

"I've done a lot of theater and been on a few soaps. I was in season seven of *Survivor*, too, so I know how to work a reality show. It's all there on the back. But man, it would be fantastic if you could give this to Kim."

I exhaled. "Of course. Consider it done."

∞

I moved into the apartment the next morning. This would be so much better than working out of a display case in the office with the royal little dog panting in back of me. I opened the French doors in the bedroom and let the sun in. I could smell juniper from the garden.

The rent was four thousand a month, but that didn't bother me at all. Lawton could have charged me double that and I would have signed the lease. This felt like home. Even more so than DC.

Why would Spencer ever want to leave this place? He was becoming a very enticing mystery.

Lawton had arranged for someone to replace the broken glass in the door later today. I grabbed an empty box to collect the few personal things that Spencer had left behind. Some photos of him with friends and various Kardashians. I found a clothes hamper in the closet. I figured I should throw that out, since he still had dirty laundry in there. On top of the pile, I saw a pair of bloodstained jeans. Right underneath were a pair of the aviation headphones that I had seen Kim's security staff wear. I grabbed some paper towels and pulled the jeans out. Not only were they bloody, but they were completely shredded at the bottom. Shredded by glass? Maybe he got locked out of the house and kicked through the window. That would explain the broken window pane and the jeans. But why the lower pane? That made no sense.

Or maybe the shredded edges were done to him. Like by a claw, an animal's claw. Lawton had mentioned that there were coyotes up here. Maybe one tried to attack Spencer.

None of that made sense. A guy living in paradise with a fantastic life goes AWOL and leaves a pair of bloody shredded jeans behind.

I needed to figure this out. I pulled out the fax that Lawton had given me—well, the fax that I purchased from him.

This is my official notice that I have terminated my lease with DeSantis Properties, effective imme diately. I relinquish my security deposit to cover any costs associated with removing my personal belongings.

Spencer Golden

There was a phone number across the bottom border of the fax: +593 3-274-3448.

I opened up my laptop and googled it: Arte Café & Te, Baños, Ecuador. A small town on the edge of a mountain range about three hours from Quito. I dialed the number and pulled my dusty high school Spanish out of my memory.

"Hola, Arte Café."

"Hola, puedo hablar con Señor Spencer Golden?"

"Lo siento, creo que tu tienes el numero equivicado."

Numero equivicado. Wrong number. I hung up.

I did a quick search on the laptop. Thirty-eight hotels in Baños. He had to be staying at one of those. There wasn't another town for miles.

I checked the time. I had a lot of work to get done today. Complete the paperwork for Kim's non-profit, send it off to the legal team at ME to peruse, and then set up another meeting with Kim.

However, Spencer's bloody jeans, his big hurry to leave for Ecuador, and the files I couldn't open on his laptop were all gnawing at me more than the deadline to finish my work.

I could call all thirty-eight hotels in Baños and ask for Señor Golden. At most, two minutes per call? Probably wouldn't take more than an hour.

I dialed the first hotel.

"Hola, necesito hablar con Señor Spencer Golden, un huésped Americano."

"Lo siento, no tenemos un huésped Señor Spencer Golden."

I hung up and dialed the next hotel. And the next. Finally, after forty-five minutes I hit pay dirt at hotel number twenty-one, Hotel Alisamay. They connected me to a room. The phone rang and rang while I wondered what I would say to him. My name is Maddy and I have your office, your laptop, and your house, and I was just a little curious why you gave up this cushy life? I felt like a deranged stalker. Would he even want to talk? I didn't care, I just needed to get him on the phone. I called back to the front desk.

"Hola, quiero dejo un mensaje para Señor Golden, por favor. Gracias. Mi nombre es Señora Maddy Ellis. Estoy una amiga vieja de

los Estados Unidos." The desk clerk seemed to understand what I was saying. I left my number and hung up.

6

I parked my car in the Kardashians' driveway and the security guard with the aviation headphones opened my door.

I was dreading this visit. I did not want to see lizard girl in action again, not to mention the humming from their security system that gave me such a huge headache.

I had the paperwork ready for Kim's new foundation, The Serious Foundation. It had taken a little back and forth between Kim and I through emails and texting to get the name right. At first, she wanted to call it Lumina Silk, because that is also the name of the foundation that she sells and uses on her famous face. Get it? I told her the name should probably be a little more serious-sounding, and that's when she came up with The Serious Foundation. I then suggested that she could come up with a whole new line of cosmetics that benefit the foundation. She got very excited after that, so SERIOUS by Kim, a new perfume, would launch at the same time the foundation did. Available at Sephora for $62 for four ounces.

I had to give her props, the girl knew how to market herself. Just one quick mention on Twitter and pre-sales for the perfume were already in the thousands.

I took a deep breath and prepared myself to enter the house. Maybe this was not the day to wear jeans. I felt a little naked without my power suit, but the jeans were comfortable. Custom-tailored, and I barely blinked at the $475 price tag. I had to admit, they looked good, especially with classic Jimmy Choo red pumps. I grabbed my purse and followed the guard inside to the kitchen. I sat down at the kitchen island and waited.

"Be right there!" I heard Kim's voice echo from a stairway in back of the kitchen.

I pulled out the foundation papers and set them on the counter.

Kris's voice echoed from the hallway. "I told you we are on schedule! Don't push me on this, okay? We'll do this my way, or it won't get done."

The humming started. My shoulders stiffened. I had a bottle of aspirin in my purse just in case.

Kris walked into the kitchen, yelling into the phone, "It has to be done right and—" She saw me and stopped talking.

I gave her a polite bitch smile.

"Just a minute," she told her caller before addressing me. "Are those the foundation papers?"

I nodded.

"Good. I need to see them. Come to my office when you're done with Kim." She turned around and left the kitchen.

Jay's voice again, with a finger wagging. "The client is king." Kris was not my client, I argued with my imaginary Jay.

Kim bounded down the stairway with her kids in tow. "Hi, Maddy!" She reached in for a hug. "Kids? This is Maddy, she's helping Mommy with some really important work."

North stared at me without smiling. I tried not to look at her.

"You met North, this is Saint and Chicago. Say hello to Maddy."

"Hi, Maddy," Chicago and Saint responded to their mom's directive.

North caught my glance, opened her mouth, and wiggled her tongue. I quickly looked away and mustered a smile. "Hi, kids."

"Alright, Mommy has work to do, so you guys go down to the

playroom, okay? North will turn on the TV for you guys. I'll be down there in a little bit."

Finally, the kids left, and Kim sat opposite me.

"I'm so excited to do this. Do you want something to drink?"

I shook my head and slid the papers over to her. "I have the papers here. I marked all of the places where you'll have to sign. This is a pretty standard legal form for forming a non-profit. I ran it by the legal team at ME, but I would strongly encourage you to run it by your own lawyer just to double-check."

Kim perused the contract for a few seconds. "Wow, this looks like you did a lot of work."

"It's my job. A couple of things I would recommend, you'll probably need to begin staffing the foundation. At minimum, you're going to need a finance person, some legal representation, and maybe a day-to-day person to run basic operations."

Kim nodded and looked up at me. "This gets really complicated, doesn't it? But you'll help me with all of this, right?"

Her eyes were clear, and her perfectly lined eyebrows were arched upward. There was an innocence in her request that hit me. Like a kid asking for help with homework. "Of course, I'll guide you through it. Initially I'll do all of the lobbying as well, setting up meetings with staff on the Hill."

"The Hill?"

"Lawmakers and their staff."

She sat up and clapped her hands. "I can't wait. You know what? This calls for an official selfie!" She pulled her phone out of her pocket. "Come right here next to me and we'll hold up the contract together."

I froze for an instant. "Selfie" was a dirty word to me. It symbolized everything I hated about modern culture. The self-worship, the simple, mindless vanity. Besides all of that, I'd never been able to take a good picture. I hated looking at my own image. In my previous life I avoided being in photos like a vampire avoided daylight. The less exposure I had, the better.

“C'mon, stand right here next to me.” Kim beckoned.

I hesitantly got off of my stool and stood next to her. She put her arm around my waist and with her free hand held the camera in front of us.

“Hold up the contract!”

The client was king. I did as I was told.

She snapped the picture and giggled. “I'll send you a copy. Here, take a look.”

I gasped out loud. I looked good. Damn good. How did she do that?

“It's good, huh? I have an eye for that kind of stuff.”

“It's really, really good.” I couldn't stop looking at it. Was that me? I always thought of my face as plain. Not ugly, but not pretty. Sometimes my face looked like a generic line drawing. Round head, two dots for eyes, and a line for a mouth. The right makeup could make a little bit of difference, but at the same time, my average looks had always helped me fade into the background. In my previous life, not being noticed was an advantage. The light in her photo captured angles on my face perfectly, giving me an alluring, sophisticated look I didn't know I had. I saw definition in my cheek. Cheekbones? Where had they been hiding?

“Thank you,” I blurted out like an idiot.

“Put it on your IG. We can start promoting The Serious Foundation that way.”

IG? Instagram? A new dilemma for me: social media presence. I made a mental note to ask Jay to do that.

“Oooh, I almost forgot.” Kim walked to a nearby closet and pulled out a Prada shopping bag. “For you. You have done a lot of really hard work on this, and this is my gift to you.”

In the bag was the beautiful mauve Prada purse she had shown me on our shopping trip. It still had the $6,550 price tag on it. "Oh, Kim, this is too much. I don't think I can accept this." I brushed my hand against the soft tufted leather and fingered the brass clasp. Was I being bought? To do what?

"Of course you can accept it. I insist. Besides, it doesn't go with the outfit I had in mind for it. So if you don't take it, I'll have to throw it out."

It was a perfect match with the jeans I was wearing. I could see it pop against a black power suit. "This is . . . fabulous. Thanks."

Kim's phone buzzed. She read from a text message and picked up the contract. "Can you take this over to my mom to look at? She's in the office at the end of the hallway." She stood up and gave me a hug. "Thanks again."

Kim left the kitchen before I could protest that her mother was not my client.

I picked up the contract and headed toward Kris's office. I sensed it was time to do battle. I knew that Kris was Kim's manager, but I specifically called out in my contract that I only had to deal with Kim. I had learned this lesson a long time ago in my world. Clients always had spouses, business partners, lawyers who all wanted to give their input. I wasn't getting paid to listen to them. My job was to pull the client out of his own ass.

I wished I had worn my power suit.

I found Kris at the end of the flagstone-lined hallway, past the selfie room, in a huge office space with picture windows overlooking the grounds. She was behind a glass desk, like the ones in the ME office. She was texting and indicated for me to sit down on the chair facing the desk. The humming pervaded the room.

Kris finished texting and looked up at me. "The contract?" She held her hand out.

There was a brief moment where I thought about tossing it on her desk and folding my arms. Jay's finger wagged at me. I handed it to her.

She put on a pair of glasses and flipped through it. "You'll be personally doing the lobbying?"

I nodded.

"Give me the list of lawmakers that you're targeting."

I picked up my bag and pulled out the Kardashian file. Kris had all the mannerisms of countless cutthroat lawyers I'd dealt with through the years. Curt, to the point. Dehumanize your opponent. Classic intimidation techniques. I had used them plenty of times myself. Establish yourself as the alpha in the room and take no shit. Where had she learned that? The lightbulb flashed in my head. She had been married to a lawyer. I had almost forgotten; her ex-husband was the guy who grabbed headlines years ago defending O. J. Simpson. She was probably mimicking him. I handed her the list of lawmakers.

She read through it, picked up a pen, crossed out some names, then wrote something on the paper before passing it back to me. "These are the politicians I want you to contact."

She had listed a few names of politicians who were absolutely not friendly to Kim's causes. At the bottom, she had written "President" and underlined it.

Time for me to take back control. Kim may be great at selling perfume and lipstick, but politics was a different ballgame. "Okay, a couple of things. None of the people you listed will give us the time of day if I tell them what we're lobbying for. They're on the other side of the coin on these issues. Secondly, the president is very famously anti-science and anti-justice."

Kris shook her head. "I don't care what they think. Get Kim in the same room with them, that's all you need to do. Kim will do the rest."

"I don't doubt that Kim can influence them." I remembered the neck rub she had given me that cured my headache, the way she handled the annoying woman in the Prada store. "But we need to build a little momentum. We need to have her foundation become a recognized force on the Hill . . ."

Kris was shaking her head again. "That's not how this is going to work. I take it that you're the expert on lobbying and influencing lawmakers and all that, but my daughter and I are the experts on fame. My daughter is the most famous woman on the planet. Her fame trumps any one of those lawmakers. Even the president. Fame is a commodity, and Kim's fame is a highly prized commodity. Companies pay millions to get mentioned on Kim's social media. I get requests all day long for Kim's endorsement. You need to use her name like a sledgehammer and open those doors with it. I want this to happen quickly, is that clear?"

Endorsements? Did this bitch want me to use my very valuable DC connections just to sell ad space on Kim's Twitter account to politicians? Is that what she was getting at? I wasn't hired to hawk beauty products for her daughter. I was about to get up and leave, to make a dramatic exit, tell her to fuck herself and the horse she rode in on, but the humming grew even louder, stopping my thoughts in their tracks. The pounding in my head started again. I rubbed my temples and leaned forward. The throbbing in my brain pushed out everything I was focused on. It felt like torture. Did she deliberately turn up the volume on the security devices so that the humming would annoy me?

"Hey, Maddy?" Kim entered the room with the Prada bag. "You left this in the kitchen." She rested her hand on the back of my neck and began massaging. "You guys done here?"

The cool, clear feeling of water putting out the fire in my head traveled instantly from Kim's hands into my head. My body felt relaxed, even refreshed. I took a deep breath. I sat up and looked at Kris. Her face was fuzzy, out of focus. I thought that only happened on TV. It made me giggle.

"Everything in the contract look okay?" Kim asked her mother as she rubbed my back.

Jesus, she had a magic touch. The more she rubbed, the lighter I felt. Stress completely drained from my muscles. The humming faded into background noise. I felt like I had nothing in the world to worry about.

I only wanted to help Kim.

Kris smiled. "Looks good to me. I think Maddy and I have agreed on a strategy as well. Right, Maddy?"

I nodded. "We are going to take DC by storm!" I didn't know what that meant exactly, but I really liked saying it. "Can we take another selfie?"

7

I woke up in my new home the next morning with a hangover, but I didn't remember drinking the night before. In fact, I rarely drank, precisely because I hated having hangovers. I tried to get out of bed and got the spins as soon as I tried to stand up.

Was this dizziness connected to the headaches? I seemed to be getting them pretty often. I remembered sitting with Kris, discussing strategy, and then getting hit by a migraine. I remembered Kim massaging my head. What else was I forgetting?

Maybe I should see a doctor.

I tried to stand again and braced myself against the furniture so I could walk straight. I made my way into the living room, sat down at the laptop, and googled headaches and dizziness.

Shoot. Could be anything from brain tumors to a stroke to cancer. I closed the laptop. I'd give it a couple of days and see if it didn't just go away.

I brewed a pot of coffee and made some toast, and that seemed to help somewhat. I was feeling more stable. I checked my phone for messages.

DC Parks had returned my call about reserving a venue for Kim's kickoff. I just needed to confirm an approximate number of people.

Jay had called early this morning. Damn, he was good.

"Hi, Maddy, Jay here. A reminder that we have a team meeting to-

morrow. Trina says it's mandatory and you should come prepared to discuss your projects, your progress toward milestones, and any victories that you'd like to celebrate with the team. Lunch will be served, so send me your preferences and restrictions for meals. Also, per your instructions, I set up an Instagram account for you. I sent you the link with some instructions. My tip? Connect as many of your posts to Kim as possible and you'll get tons of followers—trust me. See you in the office tomorrow!"

Where was my brain? I totally forgot about the meeting and I didn't remember asking Jay to set up an IG account. Kim had said something about it. I must have asked Jay to do that. I never forgot things. At least, not this many things. I thought about a doctor again while I searched my email chain with Jay. Yup, sure enough, I had asked him. Damn. I read his instructions and then remembered something else.

The selfies!

I went into my photo file and found them. How could I look so damn good yesterday and feel this sick the next day? The selfie with Kim and Kris was even better. My smile was ear to ear in that one. Maybe I should smile more? My whole face became alive, healthy. It must be the lighting, because there was depth in my cheeks. Cheekbones! Normally it took an ungodly amount of makeup to get those to show up. And there they were without any assist from me except for my smile. Even my squatty little round nose looked proportional to the rest of my face.

I turned on my camera and took a quick selfie. First thing in the morning? I wouldn't look at it. Well, maybe just a peek. Ugh, horrible. Selfies should come with a warning: don't try this at home.

I opened up Instagram and stared at the screen for a minute. *Should I really do this? This is so freaking shallow*. But this was what the client wanted, so why not? I posted the selfies with Kim and Kris. I captioned the pics: "SERIOUS work with the

Kardashians." I debated with myself for a full five minutes about using exclamation points and hit the send button.

I was about to put my phone away and start work on the press release announcing the Serious Foundation. I still needed to float all of this past Kris and Kim for their approval.

I closed the app and just finished my coffee when the phone rang. *Unknown.*

"Hello?"

"Maddy Ellis?"

"Yes."

"Who the fuck are you? And what the fuck do you want?"

I was jolted by the volume and tone of the man's voice. "Who is this?"

"What the fuck do you mean 'who is this,' you fucking tracked me down. What the fuck do you want?"

It hit me like a brick. Spencer Golden. Damn! I had even forgotten about calling him. What was wrong with me? "Spencer? I need some information from you. I work at ME and I inherited your laptop—"

"You have my laptop? Ha!"

He sounded drunk.

"Here's my advice, Maddy. Throw that laptop out the window and run. Run for your goddamned life."

"Is that what you did?" A memory appeared out of thin air. I was arguing with Kris Jenner yesterday. That was when I got the headache.

He laughed again and then the laugh turned into a sob. "How did you find me? Can they find me? Did you tell them? Shit, I thought I was safe."

"I haven't told anyone, honest." What was he so afraid of? The only thing I could possibly think was that he owed money to somebody dangerous. A drug deal gone bad? "You're safe."

"No! No one is safe." He was shouting into the phone.

If this was some drug deal gone bad, was I safe? The broken window, the bloody jeans, the empty dresser. Whoever did that, would they come back here looking for him? "Were you attacked by someone? Is that why you're afraid?"

Silence.

Maybe he thinks I'm with the bad people who broke in. "Look, Spencer, I just need your password for the file with the exclamation points. That's all."

More laughter. "That's all? No, that isn't all. Be careful what you wish for. Here's what you do, ask the bitch who runs the place. Yeah, that's it. Put on the magic headphones and ask that goddamned bitch." More laughter.

He was too drunk to make any sense. "I don't understand what you're saying. Maybe we could talk when you're not—"

"Shitfaced? Ha! Little chance of that."

The line went dead.

I felt perspiration breaking out on my forehead. Anxiety crept through my nervous system. I took a couple of deep breaths. I couldn't make any sense out of what he had said, but I felt a fear building inside of me. It was undefined; I wasn't sure what I should be afraid of. It could be the fear of a drug dealer breaking into my house in the middle of the night looking for him. It could be the fear of the memory of Kris Jenner's anger that just popped up out of nowhere.

Or was it the fear that I was losing control over my life?

"Put on the magic headphones and ask the goddamned bitch."

I remembered the aviation headphones I found in the hamper. I went back to the bedroom and put the headphones on. I turned the Bluetooth switch on my phone, found my music file, and turned on the headphones. Nothing but scratchy static. There was no magic in these headphones, so what the hell was he talking about? I thought I had heard some talking in the background, but it was too staticky to tell. My best guess was that these were tuned to a very specific frequency. A secret service agent told me years ago how the frequencies worked.

I needed to get control back. Work. Finish up the foundation work and make some notes for the meeting at work tomorrow. Work always cleared my head.

My phone pinged. A reminder from my brand-new IG account. I now had three thousand followers. How many non-profits in the world would give their right arm to get that many followers? Maybe I needed to take her more seriously than I had been.

8

I walked into the office the next day with a false feeling of confidence. My alligator Manolo Blahnik pumps clicked solidly against the terrazzo floor, signaling to anyone within earshot that I was there. I was wearing a cream suit to keep my appearance light, but at the same time I felt reassured by my armor. I looked like I meant business, but I still didn't quite feel that way.

I didn't sleep well. Every time the wind blew, or I heard an odd noise outside, I wondered if someone was coming for Spencer. At one point I thought I heard an animal on the patio, and I could have sworn I saw two little glowing eyes in the bushes.

I was still bothered by his warning as well. *No one is safe. Run. Put on the magic headphones and ask the bitch.*

More than that, I now remembered arguing with Kris Jenner, but I couldn't remember what we were arguing about. I tried placing myself back in her office, tracing all of my actions in Kim's house, but it was like time was missing or lost in that room. The last thing I could recall was Kris looking at the foundation papers and the feeling of anger, then a blinding headache. From there I remembered the selfie and the purse from Prada.

I fingered the Prada purse as I walked through the office. Well, whatever did or didn't happen, I loved this purse.

As I neared the center of the office, I saw Jay holding open a door to the large central glass display case, the company conference room.

"Hi, Maddy, meeting will start in a few. I ordered you the sweet kale salad and a sparkling water for lunch, like you requested. I'll be at my desk if you need me."

I went in and found an information packet with my name on it and sat down. There were about a dozen other people seated. I had been introduced to them last week, but I couldn't remember any of their names. But that seemed like normal forgetfulness to me.

I found an agenda and a bottle of water on the glass table in front of me:

Welcome and Overall Company Business Update – Trina

Real Housewives Movie Update – Lauren

Partnership with Disney Studios Update – Decklyn

Partnership with Apple Update – Shauna

Kardashian Update – Maddy

New York Office Update – Eddy

London Office Update – Trevor

Moscow Office Update – Kerwynn

Beijing Office Opening – Wae Lu

BREAK FOR LUNCH

New Initiatives Update – Trina

Open Discussion/Questions – All

I opened the laptop and did a quick review of my presentation. The Serious Foundation, launch date TBD. Coincides with new product launch to benefit The Serious Foundation. Kickoff at iconic DC location. Concert later that day to benefit the foundation, still securing guest speakers and partnering with another agency to find top talent to perform. Six senators and eight congressional reps already contacted for lobbying efforts, meetings pending. President yet to be contacted.

I felt a little squeamish about confirming some of these meetings with lawmakers. I had to twist some arms to get appointments. Kris was right about Kim Kardashian's name getting attention on the Hill, but they all invariably asked what cause she was promoting. It was at this point where I wasn't on solid footing. I had to give them vague promises of a foundation that would envelope many causes. If I managed to get Kim a face-to-face with these guys and they felt ambushed because I was hiding the reason, my credibility on the Hill would take a severe beating.

I was still wondering about contacting the president. I would have to pull in a lot of favors to make sure I could actually get Kim in there. What was it that Kris had told me? Use her name like a battering ram? Something like that. I made a note to contact Lloyd. If anyone would know the best way to get into that office, it would be him.

Trina entered the office, followed closely by Miss Elsa. Ugh, yoga pants again. This time they were pure white. Her shoe choice was once again piss-poor: wedges. Yoga pants and wedges only worked for . . . well, for no one.

"Hi, everyone, so glad to see you all. Everyone doing okay? Good, good. So let's get started with a business update. Since we had another smashing quarter, I wanted to go over the biggest wins we had and later on, during our open discussion, I think we have some room for opportunities as well . . ."

∞

Two hours later it was finally time for a bathroom break while Trina attended to some urgent phone call. We were only at the Apple update, and I was bored to tears. Housewife merchandise updates, apps that let you track your favorite reality personality's shopping trips, housewife movies, housewife cartoons. Who gave a rat's ass? Seemed like I was the only one on staff doing anything close to meaningful. Actually, it could become very meaningful. I was becoming convinced that Kim could actually pull this off, that she could become a very potent political force.

I opened up my laptop to check for emails and in the corner of the screen, the *!!!!!* file stared at me.

I recalled Spencer's rant: *"Put the magic headphones on and ask the bitch who runs the place."*

I clicked on the file. *Password:*

The bitch who runs the place.

I typed in *TrinaAltman.*

Nada.

I tried *KrisJenner*. Nope.

I leaned back in my seat and thought. The bitch who runs the place. I swiveled around in my chair and there, in the small basket in the corner of the room, in her pink collar, was the most obvious answer.

I typed in *MissElsa.*

File opened! Yes!

Inside the file were about a dozen videos. Sex tapes? Ha. I saw one labeled "KK" and clicked on it. I turned off the sound. A blond man was sitting at a table, talking. I fast-forwarded through the video, but no sign of Kim.

I clicked on another one labeled "It." The French doors in my bedroom at night. The curtains were pulled back. Two glowing eyes in the lower windowpane. They disappeared, and a small paw pressed against the glass. The paw disappeared and something else filled the pane. I couldn't tell what was at the window. Fur? Hair? It covered the pane, and it was knocking into the glass. The glass cracked, and the video shot became jerky, moving up and down. He was moving, maybe running.

"Okay, everyone, let's get back to the meeting." Trina entered the room, and I closed the file.

Throughout the rest of the meeting I was preoccupied by that video. I made my own presentation when the time came, but I couldn't wait to sit back down and try to sneak another peek. The day went on endlessly with more presentations and then a lunch where I was expected to socialize, so I didn't have another chance to look at the files until the meeting finally ended around six p.m. I had to wait until I got home to finish watching the videos.

I opened the laptop, went back to the "It" video, and turned on the sound. Spencer was clearly talking to the animal that was pushing against the glass pane in the video. Was he drunk then? *"Leave me alone! I won't tell anyone, I promise, just please leave me alone!"* It ended with the sound of glass breaking.

The other videos were just random shots at Kim's house, sitting in the kitchen or out on the patio with some of the family. Otherwise, nothing noteworthy at all.

I went back to the "KK" video and played it with the volume on.

The blond guy was talking now. *"Look, dude, I don't know if that's the best idea. She was just a little girl back then, so she won't even remember me. I mean, she obviously knows who I am, but I don't know. Yeah, I met her a couple of times, once at the courthouse with her parents and then another time before the killing at O .J.'s house with her mom."*

O. J.'s house? KK? Oh my god, that was Kato Kaelin in the video. I knew he was involved in the O. J. case, but I couldn't remember exactly why. The rest of the tape was more of his remembrances of meeting Kim and the rest of the Kardashians during the O. J. trial. Spencer was off camera, trying to goad him into coming onto her show.

I opened a video labeled "KK2." They were in someone's backyard at a picnic table. Kato was swigging down a beer, and it sounded like he'd been drinking for a while.

"Shit, yeah! I saw every fucking thing. He did not do it. I repeat, O. J. is innocent. But I wasn't allowed to say that . . . Who? His own fucking lawyer! I sat down with him and told him what I saw."

"What was that?"

Kato leaned in. *"Dude, it was freaky. This . . . fucking furry little thing just kind of flew out of the bushes and latched onto her, and I saw it all over her head and she was screaming. O. J. came running out of the house, and he was actually the one who tried to pull it off of her."*

"Dude, you are so fucking drunk!"

Kato shook his head. *"Why would I make this shit up? Fuck. So Bob, Kim's dad, tells me that if I tell that to a jury, they will lock us all up in a loony bin and he can't use that testimony, so I have to say this other bullshit."*

"Do you know what that thing was?"

"No fucking clue. It was kind of furry like a dog. That little fucker moved fast, and it had this nasty little sound."

"Like what?"

"Like this humming, this high-pitched humming that gave me the worst fucking headache . . ."

Another memory surfaced. The high-pitched humming at the Kardashian house. Could it be the same? I turned the video off. Was that little furry thing the same thing that broke through the bedroom window?

I was shaking and I wasn't sure why. I ran into the bedroom and looked at the French doors. If that thing got in here once, it could do it again. I looked around the room and saw the dresser. It would just about cover the doorway. I got behind it and pushed it until it was in front of the French doors.

I sat down on the bed and felt stupid. What was I doing? Was there some evil creature out there that wanted to hurt me? No. I was becoming paranoid.

But still, if it somehow did exist, and did try to come in the bedroom window, the dresser would buy me some time.

Jesus H. Christ. I was losing it.

All the same, I thought I would sleep on the couch in the living room tonight.

9

I woke up the next day a little stiff from sleeping on the couch. My shoulders and neck were sore, but at least I felt rested. I walked into my bedroom and stared at the dresser blocking the French doors. *I should just move it back.* There weren't any high-pitched monsters out there trying to get me. I was connecting dots that should not have been connected, and it was making me a little crazy.

Well, maybe I would move it back later, after lunch.

I needed to get busy on the Serious Foundation kickoff. I went over my checklist while I made coffee.

Venue – Work on today

Guest Speakers – Confirm by end of week

Press Release – Roll out by end of week

Concert. Kim had farmed out The Serious Concert to another firm, but I still had to coordinate dates and times with them.

Product Rollout. I had to coordinate with the cosmetics rep to make sure that the Serious product line would be available for purchase by the time we had the kickoff.

Jay. He needed to confirm a meeting at the ME office with Kim and the other firms to coordinate the rollout.

I was also waiting to hear back from Lloyd. I needed to brainstorm with him on the best contact to get me a face-to-face with the president. But I really wanted to hear the gossip on the beltway, hear him gripe about how petty and dirty everyone was. Maybe I was a little homesick for DC. I needed to get back there at some point to take care of some of this planning, but maybe sooner was better than later.

While I was drinking my first cup of coffee, Jay called.

"Maddy? I've got the planning meeting set up with all of the other PR firms, but Kim wants a change, like usual."

"What's that?"

"She wants it at her house, and she wants it to happen this afternoon. She's leaving town tomorrow and doesn't want to wait until she gets back to do this."

"This afternoon?" I wasn't ready. "Tell her that's impossible." I did not want to go back to the place where I might see lizard girl and have memory lapses.

Silence. I pictured Jay's nervous tics, his face tightening. "What is it, Jay?"

"You know we can't do that. We don't ever reschedule a client, especially Kim. If Kim wants the meeting at her house today, we have to—"

"Okay, okay, I get it, Jay." I seethed silently for a few seconds. I hated being told what to do. I took a long, deep breath and thought about being a millionaire with a room full of new shoes. "Fine. What time?"

"One p.m. Kim will be providing food, so no need to eat first."

"Got it."

"Oh, and Maddy?"

"Yeah?"

"Congratulations on your IG account, you have over eleven thousand followers!"

I hung up and opened my IG app. 11,456 people were following me. For posting two selfies? Jesus Christ, I really did not understand Kim's influence. I scanned through some of the comments, most of them were about Kim and her Serious Foundation, but there were more than a few that commented on how pretty I was.

I stopped at a comment from Randy B. in Long Beach: *"Damn! You 2 are hot and sexy!!!"*

No, I couldn't be hot. Could I? I had spent all of my life on the presumption that I was neither hot nor sexy, that I was ordinary, and ordinary was just fine. It worked for me.

I felt a little high, disoriented. Like the first time I got flowers from a boyfriend when I was younger. No one had ever called me hot or sexy before. Was I hot and sexy now? I stared at his comment. Maybe I had this power that I never knew I had.

I noticed that Randy's "hot and sexy" comment got 1,446 likes.

Holy shit! I was hot and sexy!

I put down the phone and wondered what to wear to Kim's house this afternoon.

∞

I arrived at Kim's house a little early to set up for the meeting. The security guard opened my car door in the driveway, and I smiled at him. I was a hot and sexy beast now, so why not flirt a little?

I held my hand out for assistance getting out of the car as I moved my legs onto the pavement and planted my Louboutin black patent leather slingbacks on the ground. I'd seen that move from a villainess in a Bond movie as she was exiting a little sports car once.

I was wearing a little black cocktail dress, totally inappropriate for a daytime business meeting, but this was how I felt today. And the dress looked good on me, so why not?

The guard took my hand and helped me to balance while I got out of the car. He didn't even smile. Not even a nod.

Well, maybe I wasn't quite up to the level of a Bond villainess yet.

I was led into a formal dining room, or "salon" as the security guard called it. It was a huge room with a long dining table that seated sixteen. Hanging above the table was a chandelier that looked like an odd mix of old plumbing, TV cables, and translucent lightbulbs. Artwork that looked like a giant inkblot covered a whole wall. All very stark and modern. The glass table and clear Lucite chairs made it look to me more like the ME conference room than a place where you share food with your family. Double doors led out to the patio. The food was already set up on a buffet against the wall. I guessed I was the first to arrive.

I went about distributing meeting agendas on the table. I had a couple of folders for Kris and Kim, with the Serious Mission Statement proposal, the press release announcing the foundation, and proposed artwork from ME for the logo design. All of this needed approval before it could be distributed, so I left that at the head of the table, where I presumed Kim or Kris would be sitting.

I heard kids' voices laughing and talking in the hallway. I also heard a man's voice.

The humming again. My body automatically reacted and tightened up, ready for an onslaught of pain from the headaches that always followed the humming noise.

I sat down in a chair and took a deep breath.

Kanye walked into the room.

He had on a pair of the aviation headphones and was moving his head up and down to some mysterious beat. He was wearing a white chiffon caftan with a purple sweater tied around his neck and a pair of sunglasses.

Kanye walked around the other side of the table and stopped to stare at me.

I stood up, smiled, and extended my hand. "I'm Maddy Ellis

with ME."

He didn't take my hand, just continued bopping his head and mouthing words to the music that must have been coming from the headphones. The humming got a little louder.

I took my hand back. *Should I just stare back at him?*

He pointed a finger at me. "You, huh? Sheeit." He turned around, grabbed a slider from the buffet, and walked out of the double doors to the patio.

Me? Sheeit? I felt a little bit thrilled that I had just witnessed the legendary craziness of Kanye West. A little more gossip for Lloyd to eat up when I saw him next week. He'd get a kick out of that.

I opened my laptop and brought up my meeting notes. I had to make sure I left today with date commitments from the other PR partners and a firm commitment from Kim on the kickoff date. With those dates, I could begin scheduling Kim's PR blitz on the Hill.

I had a few more emails from lawmakers' staffers asking for more detail about Kim's causes. I hated being so vague about the foundation. I'd dealt with a few of these guys before, and I could tell by the wording in their replies that they were expecting a much more straightforward answer from me. They knew I was usually a no-nonsense communicator. All meat, no potatoes, as Lloyd used to call me.

The humming continued. How did Kim get used to this? I wondered how I could hold a meeting with that buzzing. I closed my email. I'd wait until I got home, free of the noise in my ears, before responding to emails. The patio door was open. Maybe I could wait out there for a few minutes to clear my head.

I stood up to leave, and Kanye came back inside. This time he walked on my side of the table and sat down in the Lucite chair next to me. He was still bopping his head with his eyes closed.

He stopped and took off the headphones.

"Some shit is happening." He glanced around the room and left the headphones on the table. "Ain't no joke, Madaleeeen." He laughed and pushed them toward me. "Madaleeeen. Got no sheen. Wants my peen." He sung the words to no one in particular, stood up, walked past me, and left the room.

Madaleeeen? I hadn't heard anyone call me that since grade school. How did he know my formal name? Why would he think that I wanted his . . . peen? I bet it was this little black cocktail dress. Damn, I knew it was inappropriate. Maybe I had crossed over from sexy right to slutty. I looked down at the headphones. I didn't see or hear any Kardashians nearby. I grabbed them off the table and put them on.

Peace and quiet! No humming. Heaven. Spencer was right, these things really were magic. Maybe I could ask Kim if we could use them at the meeting?

I sat back down again and opened my email to tackle the replies to the lawmakers. I stopped when I heard an android voice in my ear.

"Attention, please confirm inhabitants."

Another android voice replied.

"Confirming. One known as Kim Kardashian in playroom with one known as Chicago West and one known as Saint West. One known as Kris Jenner in office. One known as Kanye West in upstairs bedroom ingesting marijuana substance. One known as North West . . . traveling on first floor. One known as Madeline Ellis in dining salon."

Madeline Ellis? The name on my driver's license. That was some pretty deep-state tech. Must be how Kanye knew my name.

North suddenly appeared in the doorway of the dining room and stared wide-eyed at me. She reminded me of Damien from *The Omen*.

She was gently twisting her body, like a child hearing a nursery rhyme. I quickly looked back at my laptop. At this point, I felt like I was in some kind of cat-and-mouse game where she would look for just the right moment to taunt me with a glimpse of the tongue. She had to know that it freaked people out. I remembered her unabashed glee from the first time she unraveled it for me at the koi pond. Was it long enough to reach me from where she was? What would I do if she came closer? "Attention." The android voice came back on. "One known as Madeline Ellis is in possession of device number 3458 in dining salon."

Device number 3458? The headphones!

North walked away.

I tossed them on the table as Kris Jenner walked into the room and stood over me. Her face was lopsided again. Lumpy on one side, like there were sponges tucked under her skin. The humming noise was louder now. I braced for a headache.

"Where's Kanye?" She eyed me suspiciously.

According to the headphones, he was smoking pot upstairs. I shook my head. "I don't know."

She grabbed the headphones and walked out of the room.

Maybe it was all this humming noise that had put her in a bad mood all the time. I noticed the noise was loudest when she was in the room.

I was about to leave the room and go out onto the patio when the guard escorted a couple of other people into the room.

A very cute young Black man extended his hand with a business card and gave me a not-so-subtle once-over. His eyelids were half closed as he started at my legs and slowly raised them to encompass my chest and then my face, before he slowly unleashed a smile. "Darin Anderson with the NB Group." The NB Group was the agency in charge of the concert to celebrate the kickoff of The Serious Foundation.

I was speechless for a few seconds, as I had never gotten a once-over like that before. A very different reaction from the tight-lipped smiles my power suits usually evoked from men. Against my will, I became flustered, not knowing how to react. All I could manage was to shake his hand and nod. Then I remembered to smile. Total amateur hour.

At least I felt better about my slutty little black cocktail dress.

The middle-aged bottle blonde who came in with him handed me her business card. "Lucinda Shakowsky with Esme Cosmetics."

I took her card and shook her hand. Nice shoes, but they were Jimmy Choo knock-offs. The framed buckle on the toe was a trapezoid instead of a square. Jimmy Choo never does trapezoids.

"I guess we'll get started when Kim and Kris come in," I told them. "By the way, does the humming bother you guys?"

Lucinda looked back at the doorway and then rolled her eyes. "I dread coming to this place because of that. I mean, I love the Kardashians and all, but that goddamned noise drives me up the wall."

The guard brought in another woman, very pretty and young, dressed in the dreaded yoga pants. She also had long dark hair like Kim.

"Hi, I'm Bailey. I work for Kim's accountant."

I introduced myself and asked her if she had brought any budgets with her.

She just stood there blinking at me, and after a few seconds, she pulled an earplug from her ear. "Sorry! I didn't hear you."

"Did you bring the budgets?" I asked again.

She held up her phone. "All in here." She put the plug back in her ear.

This noise had to be addressed. "I'll ask Kim if they can turn it down or something."

Darin shook his head. "Last time I was here, I asked Kris to turn it down, and man, I thought she was gonna spit fire at me. So proceed with caution."

Lucinda took an empanada from the buffet. "Yeah, you do not want to get on that woman's bad side. Trust me. Let's just get this done as quickly as we can."

I nodded and dug around my purse for the Tylenol as Kim entered the room.

"Hi, everyone! Thanks so much for coming out here on short notice. I have to go to New York tomorrow for a shoot, and I really wanted to get this done before I left. I don't want to have to think about this, otherwise I get all preoccupied and the shoot doesn't go as well, you know?"

The humming went up a level as Kris entered the room, like a tiny buzzsaw in my head. "Are we ready to go?" She sat down at the head of the table. Her face had lost its lumps on the one side. How did she do that?

Darin and Lucinda sat down across from me and I followed their lead and brought out my meeting notes. Bailey sat next to me and took out one earplug.

Kim did not sit down. She stood behind Darin and Lucinda, nibbling food from the buffet as Kris spoke: "Do we have a timetable?"

"It's in the packet marked 'Kris,'" I answered. "It still needs your approval."

She pulled it out and studied it. The pain was beginning to form. A very distant pounding, like the headache was making its way up from someplace deep inside of me. I saw Darin rub his forehead and look down at the table. I grabbed a water and popped two Tylenol into my mouth.

Kris addressed Lucinda. "When will the cosmetic line be ready to launch?"

Lucinda pulled a manila folder from her purse and thumbed through some papers. Her smile was strained. "Currently, the first samples off the line will be ready next week, and if those are approved, it will take a month to get them manufactured and shipped. That's if there are no hiccups and if Kim can approve the samples next week."

Kris put her glasses on and started pulling more papers out of the portfolio I left for her. "That's too long. Take at least a week off of that."

"I would love to," Lucinda replied, "but we've already scheduled double shifts for the manufacturing, and it's pushing our costs way up. We're doing this expedited schedule as a courtesy to the Kardashians, and I really don't know if there's any room . . ."

Kris looked up. "I didn't ask if there was any room. I told you to take a week off the schedule."

Another memory popped up. Kris in her office ordering me, *"This is how it's going to be done."* I remembered feeling anger, so much anger. I had wanted to tell her to go fuck herself, to walk out. But then the headache attacked me. A headache that declared war on my body, trying to shut it down. I popped another Tylenol.

Lucinda started rubbing her head. Kim walked up behind her and began massaging her neck gently.

Lucinda's shoulders relaxed, her fisted grip on her papers uncoiled, and I could see her shiny pink nail polish. Her eyes were no longer slits; she was smiling. "Don't worry, Kris, I'll find that week and get this done!"

Kim's touch seemed to change Lucinda's whole demeanor. Was that what had happened to me?

Kris nodded and looked to Darin. "Music?"

Darin opened up a laptop. He had one hand covering his ear. "We got tickets ready to print, T-shirts ready to go as soon as artwork is approved, but we need more time on confirming talent. There's a lot of conflicts on some of the bigger acts' schedules, so we're trying to work around that. Some of the people you asked for are not free, and some of them are already making demands."

Kris sighed. "Please remind your talent that this is for Kim Kardashian's foundation. That's all they need to know. You need to bring them on board and have it done by next week."

Darin sighed. "It's not a matter of—"

Kim was now rubbing Darin's neck. He stopped mid-sentence, took a deep breath, and moaned slightly. "No problem. I'll have it all done by next week!"

Kris turned her gaze toward me. "What's happening with the meetings with lawmakers?"

I stuttered for a few seconds while I tried to absorb what I had just seen. Kim's touch made people obey. Kim moved around the table toward me. Her touch would end this pain, I remembered that. But I didn't trust that touch anymore. That was when I started to lose time, memory. She reached her hand out to me and instinctively I held up a hand signal for her to stop.

She exchanged a glance with Kris.

I would have to grin and bear it. I would get through this meeting with the headache somehow and figure out what I just saw later.

I would not take Kris's bait. Whatever she asked, I would just agree with.

"All the lawmakers' meetings are on schedule. When I have them all confirmed I'll send you and Kim a schedule." The dentist office drilling sound got even more shrill. I saw the phone in her hand while I was talking and wondered if Kris just turned up the volume control to this security technology when she wanted to punish people.

I suddenly wanted to go back home to DC. Far away from the Kardashians and their freaky house and noises. I was due back there next week, but it was too long to wait. I would change my plans. "I'm going to DC tomorrow to oversee the arrangements from there. I just need your approval on all of the paperwork inside the folder I gave you, and we're good to go."

Kris exchanged looks with Kim again. "In DC tomorrow? Well, since Kim and I will be in New York, maybe we can get together in Washington in a few days and go over the details." She picked up the papers I had given her and tossed them across the table to me. "Approved. Get back to me in twenty-four hours with a status on the meetings."

I mustered up a smile. "You bet!"

10

I laid my head back against a pillow on my couch and kept a warm compress on my forehead. It had taken a few hours, but the headache finally started to subside.

I consoled myself with thoughts about going back home to DC tomorrow. Back to my usual hangouts, my creature comforts, and my charmless condo. Jay had booked a first-class ticket for tomorrow afternoon. On a six-hour flight, I could get a lot of work done, so for now I would relax and recover.

I still could not make sense of what had happened at the Kardashian house. Kim seemed to have a sort of supernatural power to make people do things. She also had a kid with a lizard tongue and a mom with a shapeshifting face. If these were pieces of a puzzle, I was definitely missing some pieces. Kim and Kris were like some weird Yin and Yang. Kris carried this angry aura with the dentist office drilling sound around with her, and Kim would administer some sort of healing touch to clean up the effects of Kris's anger.

But her touch didn't just make the headache go away, it made people . . . obedient.

I wondered if Spencer knew this. He told me to run. Was this what he was trying to warn me about? I had left a couple more messages for him over the past few days, but no word from him. Was he avoiding me? Afraid to talk to me?

What about crazy Kanye's warning? He said some shit was going down. Did that mean anything, or was he just high and crazy?

Maybe I should try calling Spencer one more time. I took a deep breath and relaxed. Sleep, recover, get some rest. Figure it out later. I closed my eyes and drifted off to sleep.

I woke up in the dark to a noise in the yard. Three-thirty a.m. I heard bushes rustling just outside the large window in the living room. There was a scratching sound at the door. I sat up and looked around for a weapon. I remembered my gun. But I had left it back in DC, sitting useless in my nightstand. Damn!

Fireplace poker behind me. I jumped off the couch and grabbed the poker. I walked slowly to the window to see if I could peek at whatever was at my front door. Too dark to see.

Call the police? I approached the door slowly. The scratching sounded like an animal, not a person. That thing in Spencer's video? Was it back? I turned on the switch for the front door light and the scratching stopped.

I banged the poker against the door to scare it off and heard some noise. Maybe it was moving? I took a deep breath and opened the door slightly with the poker in front of me.

I saw something small, like a raccoon, run toward the bushes. But it couldn't have been a raccoon.

Raccoons don't have pink collars.

There was a deep gash in the corner of the door where it had been scratching.

I couldn't help but remember that Miss Elsa wore a pink collar.

Plenty of dogs wore them.

That could have been any neighborhood dog.

I turned on all of the lights in the room. I would never get back to sleep now. I kept thinking about the broken glass and bloody jeans with shredded edges.

I went to my desk and opened my laptop. I opened the *!!!!!* file and played the video where Spencer was confronting the thing that was pushing against the glass.

I slowed down the video and looked at it frame by frame. It went by too quickly at regular speed, but when I slowed it down, I could clearly make it out. Something pink. A quick flash, but clearly pink.

I closed the video and opened up my email.

`Jay,`

`My plans have changed. Please cancel the flight to DC.  Will be there in a few days and will make my own flight arrangements.`

`Maddy`

I hit send and opened a travel website.

I searched for flights departing to Ecuador.

11

I exited customs and immigration at the Quito airport close to eight a.m. a day later. I still had to pick up a rental car for the hour-and-a-half drive through the mountains to Baños. I turned on my phone. Only two messages. One from Jay asking about my ETA into DC and one from Lloyd. He'd found a contact for me with access to the Oval Office.

I found a coffee shop in the airport and decided to get a quick bite and take care of business here since I wasn't sure if I would have a Wi-Fi signal where I was headed.

First, I called the Hotel Alisamay and asked for Señor Spencer Golden again. When they switched me to his room, I hung up before it could ring. I only wanted to confirm that he was still there. I didn't want to scare him off before I arrived.

I sent an email to Jay:

```
Will be in DC in a couple of days. Will update you
further as my plans become more solid.
```

It looked like I had received my first bite for The Serious Foundation. The chief of staff for the congressman who repped Kim's district, Anthony Royce, wanted to set up a meeting with Kim for next week. I was a little hesitant. Doubt about ME Communications and that mysterious little dog clouded my thinking. I was no longer sure what I had gotten myself into, let alone what I would be dragging a congressman into. I needed to speak to Spencer and find out what had freaked him out to the point of leaving the country.

But this meeting with Congressman Royce would keep Kim and Kris off my back for a little bit. He was probably just looking for a quick photo op. I went ahead and confirmed the meeting.

Kim,

Great news! Our first meeting is confirmed with your local rep, Anthony Royce. He's really looking forward to meeting with you and hearing about The Serious Foundation. Attached is the official invitation. Will forward you the security protocols and procedures for visiting the House of Representatives. See you soon.

Maddy

I called Lloyd.

"Fixer to the stars, how you doing?"

It was reassuring to hear his voice. He was like an anchor in the sea of crazy that I was now swimming in. "Tell me about this contact you have in the Oval Office."

"Remember Gordon Lasky? He says he knows you from some work you did for Senator Williams."

I remembered Williams—he and his wife were swingers. Well, mostly he was, his wife wasn't so crazy about the whole idea. At one of their swinging soirees, she became very drunk and very fed up and ran out into the street half naked, screaming at the top of her lungs. She ended up balled up in the fetal position at a 7-Eleven. I was called in to do some magic. I constructed a narrative about her having a drinking problem, then going into rehab, blah, blah, blah. I remembered spending a lot of time and money buying up the surveillance tapes from the 7-Eleven where she crashed, too. But I didn't remember Gordon Lasky. "I can't picture Lasky. Was he a Williams staffer?"

"No, he's Williams' son-in-law. Apparently he watched you do your thing from the sidelines and was pretty impressed. Also very grateful. Anyhow, he's working for the current administration."

"The apple doesn't fall very far . . ."

"Apparently not. He's open to introducing you into the West Wing. He's a Kardashian fan boy. I had to reassure him that he would get a selfie with Kim."

My own selfie with Kim flashed in my mind. I had completely forgotten that I was now sexy and hot. "Well, that would be the easiest payoff in my career."

"Great, should I go ahead and let him know you'll be calling him?"

"Send me his number." I wasn't ready to pull the trigger yet. I had to finish this crazy trip first. I hoped it would help me understand who I was dealing with. Or what I was dealing with.

"Oh, by the way, Lloyd, I'm in town next week, can I buy lunch?"

"No more freakin' Denny's!"

"Okay, I'll find a place without puzzles printed on the placemat, promise."

∞

Baños was a small dusty pueblo, an outpost established years ago on a farther journey into the mountains. The concrete and clay buildings that made up the town looked like they had once been painted bright pastel colors, but the dust from the mountains had stained the exteriors into a beige sameness.

The Hotel Alisamay was situated on the edge of town, wedged

against tall green mountains. Surrounded by spiked wrought iron fencing, the three-story red brick and concrete hotel was just off the main highway. Not especially pretty, but it looked like it was built to withstand a war. It reminded me of a fortress or a bomb shelter. However, it did have a pool, daily maid service, and a continental breakfast each morning, so, better than I expected.

I checked into my room and unpacked in my bricked asylum. I noticed the windows in every room had security grills. Was crime that bad in this small, out-of-the-way town?

I didn't want to knock on Spencer's door and say, "Hey, I'm here." I didn't trust him yet and certainly didn't want to be asked to come into his room if he was on a bender. I wanted to meet him somewhere public; I just felt safer that way. I went down to reception and asked the woman behind the counter if she had seen him.

"Señor Golden no esta aqui ahora."

One p.m. Was he out to lunch somewhere? He would have to pass through the lobby in order to get back to his room. I would wait there for him to come back. I had a slight advantage, as I knew what he looked like from all the selfies, but he didn't know what I looked like.

I sat in the lobby with my laptop and waited. And waited.

Finally, close to five p.m., he staggered in the front entrance. Clearly, he had been drinking. I threw my laptop in my bag and stepped in front of him.

"Spencer Golden? I'm Maddy Ellis, we spoke a couple of days ago."

He straightened up and eyed me. He looked just like his photos, although his chic stubble had become a scruffy beard. His hair was a little longer, and his eyes were bloodshot. From his picture, I'd guessed he was about thirty, but he looked a little more haggard in person. He had dark circles underneath his eyes, and the healthy, tanned glow that I had seen in his selfies was gone.

He shook his head and slowly backed away. *"No soy Spencer. Vete!"*

Vete. Go away. "I came a long way; I need some answers."

He shook his head again, turned around, and marched back out of the hotel. I followed.

"Just a few minutes, Spencer," I yelled from behind him.

He kept shaking his head. "Go away. *Vete*. Leave me the fuck alone. Coming here was a stupid thing. That was a really fucking stupid thing."

I jogged up beside him. "Why? What are you afraid of?"

"Do they know you're here? Stupid bitch. Stupid, stupid bitch." He spoke without looking at me.

I ran ahead of him and blocked the sidewalk. "I saw it."

He stopped. "What did you see?"

"The thing in your video. The thing that broke the glass."

He squinted his eyes at me. "Where did you see this thing?"

"At your house. I rented the house after you left. I found your bloody jeans, too."

"You rented my fucking house?" He started to say something else, but then he stopped, shook his head, and looked across the street. Rosalita's Tavern. "Shit." He ran his hand through his hair and then crossed the street and entered the tavern. I followed him in.

A few old men sat at the bar, arguing about a soccer game on an old tube TV above the bar. Another old man sat alone a few seats away, staring into his drink. The tiled blue-and-white floor featured what might have once been an interesting design that was now obscured by grime. A dirty Ecuadorian flag hung on the back wall. This place felt like the last chance bar at the end of the world.

He led me to a small table in the back. A plump woman came out from behind the bar. *"Hola, señor, como esta? Una cerveza?"*

"Si." He looked at me.

"Una botella de agua, por favor."

Spencer shook his head and told the woman, *"No agua, dos cervezas."* He turned back to me. "You're gonna need a drink."

"I don't drink."

He called back to the bartender. *"Rosalita, dos dragos de tequila tambien!"*

After Rosalita dropped the drinks at our table, he downed his shot of tequila and took a long sip of beer. I left my beer and my tequila shot standing on the table.

"Tell me what you saw." He covered his mouth and belched.

"It was about three-thirty in the morning, and I heard something scratching at the front door. I was a little bit freaked out, so I banged on the door to scare it off. When I opened the door, I saw something running into the bushes. I'm pretty sure it had a pink collar. Like the thing in your video."

He took another swig of beer. "Miss Elsa."

"How can that be? How would she find the house? Is Trina bringing her dog up to the house to scare me?"

He shook his head. "She doesn't need Trina."

"Then how does a little dog like that manage to—"

He put his hand up. "You're assuming Miss Elsa is a little dog. She's not."

"What is she?" I wasn't sure how seriously to take him now. There was still an argument to be made that he was too drunk to make sense.

He shrugged his shoulders. "Fuck if I know."

"Tell me what happened when she broke through the window," I asked.

He sighed, grabbed my tequila shot, and downed it. "I'm going to tell you, but remember, I don't need you to believe this shit. I don't. You can think I'm some crazy fucking drunk guy or not, I don't give a fuck. I just don't want to be anywhere near that fucking thing again." He took another swig of beer.

I nodded. "Go ahead."

"Those videos you found, that's kind of like a catalog I was making. I was trying to make sense of all the shit I'd seen working for Kim. That's it. But I didn't know Miss Elsa was watching me. Sitting in that goddamned basket, she was watching every fucking thing I did. That night, she comes over and she wants in the house. She wants to do something to me. I'm not sure what, but I knew it was not good."

I wasn't following his story. First Miss Elsa is watching him and now she wants to do something to him. Was he too drunk to do this? "How did you know she wanted to do something to you?"

"Because she said so! She kept saying she was coming in, whether I opened the door or not, and I needed to be fixed."

I took a deep breath. I suddenly felt so damned stupid. Letting my own paranoia drive me this far to hear some crazy drunk ramble on about a talking killer attack dog with a pink collar. "The dog talks?"

He smiled and finished his beer. He grabbed mine and took a sip. "Are you stupid? Dogs don't talk. Miss Elsa is not a dog. The headphones. If you wear the headphones, you can hear what she's saying."

"The magic headphones?"

He nodded. "I put them on when I saw her at the door."

I remembered the android voice from the headphones at Kim's

house. "Go on."

"She broke through the window and came at me. I was standing next to the dresser. She came at me and started chewing and clawing at my pants and then ripped them up. I thought for sure that she was just going to kill me. I tried to stomp on her with my other leg, but she backed away." He stopped and took another swig of beer.

"Well, obviously she didn't kill you, so you got away?"

He shook his head. "I was looking around for something to hit her with. But there's nothing. All of a sudden I feel this wet slime creeping over my leg. This disgusting, slimy feel. It's her tongue. It's creeping out of her fucking mouth like a snake from across the fucking room! It's winding around my leg, and my leg starts burning."

I froze. Lizard girl. I saw that tongue come out of North West's mouth with my own eyes.

He rolled up his pant leg. A red burn mark covered his lower leg.

"I started to feel . . . like there was nothing in the world to worry about. I didn't have to do anything or think about anything. It was really fucking weird. I got this message from the thing. It's hard to explain, but it was telling me that Kim was my friend. That I could be part of the family. But at the same time," he took a deep breath, "God, it felt like I was being pulled out of my body. I had the feeling that my soul was being taken."

He seemed sincere. His panic sounded real to me.

"I'm realizing that this fucking thing is doing something to me, but I don't know what. I had to do something right that second, or else I felt like I would no longer . . . exist. I started stomping on the tongue with my free foot. It started screaming this hideous noise and moved closer, so I pulled out a drawer from the dresser and trapped her underneath the drawer. I stomped hard on the drawer like a motherfucker so that I crushed its tongue until it finally let go of me. I changed, grabbed some stuff, and ran. I don't even remember leaving the house. The only thing I could think about was getting as far away as possible. That's the last I saw of it. Of my house, of LA. Of my life."

We sat in silence. How much of this was true? Was it the liquor talking? But liquor usually made you tell the truth. Was there some strange creature that owned the company I worked for? Maybe the Kardashian kid was also a strange creature. "I saw North's tongue. She swallowed a fish. Whole, from the pond in the backyard."

He nodded. "I think all the kids have it. You could see Saint's tongue in one of the videos."

"I didn't see that. Which video?" I would have remembered another tongue.

"It's really quick. You have to go frame by frame or you'll miss it. The one in the kitchen with Kris. Her tongue snatches some food off the table. That's the other thing, these tongues come out like a bolt of lightning. *Bam!*"

I believed him. I didn't want to, but I did. I couldn't think of a reason why he would make up something this crazy. I had seen North's tongue. But at the same time, it was hard to accept as a reality that existed in this world. "Is this the same creature that Kato was talking about in one of your videos?"

"I think so." He turned toward the bar. "Rosalita? *Dos mas cervezas!*"

"How did you find out about the humming noise and the creature from Kato?"

"Finding out about that thing from him was just dumb fucking luck. The Kardashian producers are always looking for drama, and I thought some of that old O. J. shit would bring the drama. I wanted to bring him on the show, so I tracked him down. I thought this would be, like, the perfect Kardashian episode.

Past meets present, you know? I could have promoted the fuck out of it. Probably would have been a major ratings boost."

As he talked, I saw what must have been a hint of the old Spencer surface, the Spencer who was probably passionate about his job, proud that he was part of the Kardashian machinery, the type of guy who would always brag about connections to the Kardashians. The photos I had seen showed a confident, brash kid. This thing, this alien dog, really did a number on him.

"I did a couple of interviews with him. He didn't want to go on the show. I think he was kind of afraid, because the dude would, like, show up for the opening of an envelope. The second interview, we're all liquored up, and I mention that high-pitched humming sound at Kim's house, and that's when he opens up to me."

"Do you think that what he heard was the same humming? I mean, could it be . . . the creature that attacked her was Miss Elsa?" I was going to need a tin hat soon.

Rosalita stopped by with the beers. Spencer finished mine and started another one.

"I really think it must have been. There's, like, some kind of connection through the Kardashians, but I don't know."

"So, what's your plan?" Was he just going to hide for the rest of his life?

"No plan. Just to stay alive and find someplace where I can be safe. Someplace where they never heard of the Kardashians. I need to feel safe. Then I can think about a plan."

There were a few moments of silence while he stared off to the side. He nodded his head and then spoke to me. "You know, it feels good to finally tell someone what happened. Even if you don't believe me." He smiled for the first time. It was a nice smile. He had dimples buried in his beard.

"It's not that I don't believe you. I've seen and heard so many of the crazy things on my own, but it's just so hard to wrap my mind around this whole thing. That there could be some kind of alien life on the planet. Aliens working with the Kardashians."

He held a finger up. "I know! Here's what you do. When you get back to LA, open those video files again. Look at the ones at the Kardashian house. Then, put on the magic headphones and watch the videos. That's all."

I had my laptop with me. I even had the magic headphones. I used them on the plane to keep the noise out while I worked. They were actually really good for that. "Why the headphones?"

He smirked now. "That fucking humming you hear in the videos? That's not technical bullshit or whatever. That's them."

"Them?"

"Talking. It's them talking."

I reached into my bag and put the laptop and the headphones on the table.

He pushed his chair away from the table and stared at the headphones. "What the fuck are you doing?"

"What?" His mood had completely changed in an instant. Maybe he was a little drunker than I thought.

"Where did you get them?" He stood up and staggered backward away from me.

"They were in the hamper, with the pants."

He began to breathe heavily. "Shit. Shit. Shit. Why didn't she take them? This is not good."

"They were in that closed-off room. With no windows. I guess she couldn't get in there, right? What's wrong?" He was so freaked out that I started to worry about his safety. Would he do something crazy in this bar?

He stumbled into a barstool, knocking it to the floor. "That's why she came back! She was looking for the headphones. They can track those things."

"They? Like Miss Elsa?"

He ran his hand through his hair and pointed at the headphones. "I can't be here."

Spencer ran out of the bar, bumping into one of the old men watching the TV on the way out. I should have gone after him, but maybe it was better to give him some space for now. He had been so calm and normal for a few minutes; I didn't want to get him agitated again. I figured I might as well watch the video with the magic headphones and then see if he showed up at the hotel later on.

12

I waved to Rosalita. "*Una botella de agua, por favor.*" I waited until I had my water and then opened up the first video. Kim's kitchen. I put on the headphones.

Kris sat at the kitchen island holding Saint on her lap.

Spencer was narrating off camera. "Here with my favorite peeps on a Saturday afternoon! Hey, Saint! Wave hello to Uncle Spencer!"

Kris held up Saint's arm and waved. "Say hi to Uncle Spencer, sweetie. Oh, she wants her blankie. Anyone see it?"

Spencer's voice off camera again. "I think it's in the yard. I'll grab it."

The camera angle shifted slightly, and I heard Spencer walk away.

Kris looked aside. "Kim's location?"

The android voice: "One known as Kim Kardashian in playroom."

Kris nodded. "Activity?"

"One known as North West is feeding one known as Kim Kardashian."

North was feeding Kim? Shouldn't that have been the other way around? Did this feeding have anything to do with the creepy tongue?

Kris nodded again, then, "Status of DC project?"

"Sixty percent completed."

She put the baby down on the floor. "ETA?"

"Estimated to be operational within three weeks."

Kris grabbed a box from a nearby cabinet and put it on the table. "Status of backup plan?"

"Backup plan non-operational at this time. Success of DC project currently estimated at ninety-five percent."

She took out something from the box and put it at the edge of the table. I slowed the video down here and went frame by frame. That must have been the food that Spencer mentioned, and then—yes, there it was. It was really quick, like a lightning bolt, but the tongue grabbed the food off the table. This was not good.

Did they all have lizard tongues? That was statistically improbable, unless Kim mated with a lizard. What was the DC project? Was I part of that?

I must be.

Kris could hear the android voices without the headphones on. What did that mean?

I took off the headphones and rewound the video. I hit play and now I could clearly hear the humming.

I opened up another video, this time without headphones. Saint and Chicago were sitting by the pool. I heard the humming, but I heard Spencer talking in the background.

"Hey, kids, look at Uncle Spencer! C'mon, let's surprise Mommy with a smiley video, huh?"

This went on for a few minutes as neither kid looked at Spencer, just at each other. Spencer finally convinced them to look into the camera and smile. Kris showed up and picked up one of the kids. "Time for her nap! Say goodbye to Uncle Spencer!"

I rewound and put the headphones on.

"Hey, kids, look at Uncle Spencer!"

The android voice: "One known as Kim Kardashian is low. Requesting feeding."

"Location."

"Master bedroom."

"Requesting one known as Kris Jenner for transport."

"Requested."

I took off the headphones. What was this feeding that Kim was constantly getting? And why was she getting fed by her kids? I tried to think of all the ways these videos could have been manipulated by Spencer. But it would come down to why he would do that. And the tongue. I saw that tongue again. I started to perspire. I took a sip of water. I didn't want to watch anymore, afraid of the next freakish thing I would see and the contortions my brain would have to go through to explain it.

There were five more of these videos to get through, and I needed liquid courage. Screw the hangover.

I summoned Rosalita. *"Tequila, por favor. Grande."*

I needed the liquor to do its thing. After she set it down, I sipped as much as I could stomach, feeling the hot liquid travel into my stomach. I waited until I felt my muscles loosen up and then put on the headphones.

Four of the five videos were pretty much similar to the one by the pool. The android voice spoke as the kids stared at each other or at someone off camera. There were more feeding requests for Kim and Kris as well, plus a few transport requests.

The last video was troubling. If none of these were doctored, it proved that Spencer was telling the truth.

Spencer was in the back seat of a car, narrating a shopping trip with Kim and her sisters. He was surrounded by the women, and the humming noise was really loud without the headphones, but with the headphones there were two android voices talking to each other:

"Report filed from one known as Security Agent Richard Lockhart. Report indicates device number 1387 missing."

"Location probability?"

"With one known as Spencer Golden."

"Request one known as Kim Kardashian to retrieve from one known as Spencer Golden."

"Negative. Abort request. Device is not present in that location. Will extract device number 1387 from home of one known as Spencer Golden."

There was one more video for me to watch with the headphones. The break-in video.

I took another long sip of the tequila and let it burn its way down my throat again. I put on the video and hit play.

The paws against the window.

"One known as Spencer Golden, you are in possession of device number 1387. Open the door for retrieval."

Spencer's voice pleaded, "Please, just leave me alone!"

"Door must be opened immediately or there will be alternate methods of entrance and retrieval."

"I promise I won't tell anyone!"

The video became jerky. The sound of glass breaking. A shot of the bedroom ceiling. He must have put his phone on the dresser.

"One known as Spencer Golden must be brought into compliance. Hold still for compliance."

Spencer screamed. I heard grunting and then a piercing cry. The sound you would imagine a dog would make if you hit it really hard. Then, the sound of the dresser drawer opening and more grunting. That must have been Spencer as he was stomping on the drawer.

I pulled the headphones off and swallowed the rest of my tequila. I should have been falling down drunk by now, but I still felt mostly sober. I looked around the bar and felt alone and scared. I remembered my gun. I had a gun in my house in DC. I could shoot Elsa.

I threw my laptop and the headphones into my bag and left the bar. Even though it was chilly outside, I was starting to sweat from the tequila. I stumbled over the uneven tile on the sidewalk outside. I'd tell Spencer that I had a gun, that we could kill it. Maybe that would give him hope. He could stop running. We could fight this thing together. I was sure I could dig up a contact in the government who dealt with alien sightings. Then we could come up with a plan of what to do about this nest of lizard people.

I ran back into the hotel and up to Spencer's room. The door was wide open. Spencer was gone.

13

I walked out of the terminal at Ronald Reagan Airport and smiled to myself. It felt good to be back in DC. There was a crowd of protesters just outside of the taxi stand. I felt comforted by the familiar sight of angry people with signs. Home.

I pushed my way through the crowd to get into the taxi line. I couldn't wait to get back to my own familiar bed. I wondered where Spencer was sleeping tonight. Poor guy, scared shitless by that lizard dog. The thought of him running forever, not having a home anymore. I wondered if there was anything I could do for him, but he had left without a trace. He didn't want to be found.

Really, the only thing I could do to help him out was to kill Miss Elsa. But the more I thought about killing her, the more ridiculous it sounded to me. I could not just march into the office and shoot a dog. The best way to deal with this was probably to walk away like Spencer did. Well, not exactly like he did. I could just quit. Give my notice effective immediately and be done with it. Let the lizard people do whatever it was they wanted to do and live happily ever after in the blissful knowledge that I would never have to see them again.

I could easily open my old business back up.

A police siren a few yards away disrupted my thoughts. Looked like the protestors were getting rowdy. A group of them had just toppled over a couple of traffic control barriers. I hopped into a cab.

"3100 Connecticut Northwest." Jeez, my street was named after lizard girl. "You know what this protest is about?" I was so wrapped up in my thoughts that I hadn't even bothered to read their signs.

The cabby sighed and adjusted his cap. "Immigration ban. I mean, I get it, but shit, they been holding up traffic for hours with this stuff. They don't seem to understand that people have to get places and have to make a living. Look at this!" He honked his horn and pointed ahead.

A group of protesters were in the street, blocking access as the police tried to shepherd them to the sidewalk. I took my phone out to check my messages when I heard someone banging on the hood of the car.

The cab driver honked. "C'mon, you crazy bitch, get away from the car!"

I did a double take. The old woman banging on the hood of the car looked familiar. The Prada store. She looked like the old lady that tried to block me there. The same crooked, ratty blonde wig, the same powdered, wrinkled face, same bright pink lipstick and matted zebra-skin coat. Maybe I was wrong. I thought I was being paranoid until I saw her sign.

"Kim is EVIL!"

This was not a coincidence. What was she doing here in front of my cab?

She walked toward my window and shouted through the glass, "She *is* the Hell spawn! You know what to do! Summon the courage! You must do it! Do it!"

A police officer grabbed her arm and took her away to the sidewalk.

"Damn nut jobs." The cabby was shaking his head.

I felt like I had fallen through the looking glass. The old lady was the white rabbit. My reality was broken, shattered into a million pieces.

I fingered the door handle. For a minute I thought about jumping out of the cab and going after her. Just like Alice chased the rabbit. I had a million questions for her. How did she find me? What did she know about the Kardashians? When I saw her at the Prada store, I had assumed she was a crazy old homeless woman, but maybe she wasn't.

I opened the door.

"Hey, miss?" the cabby yelled out to me.

"One second." I ran after the cop who had taken her away. He had pushed her into the crowd on the sidewalk. I elbowed my way into the protesters, but I couldn't find her or the cop. I had waited too long. I stepped back out on the street and stood on my toes, trying to find that ratty blonde wig. I heard my cab honking at me.

"Ma'am? I have to get moving!"

I returned to the taxi. "Sorry, thought I recognized someone."

"You know what to do. You must do it." Had she really said that, or was my mind playing tricks on me?

"Excuse me," I felt perspiration underneath my clothes, "did you see the old lady who was banging on the car?" Did she really exist?

"Yeah! Crazy, huh?"

Okay, she was real. "Did you hear what she said to me when she came to the window?"

The cabby shook his head. "Something about doing it, I think? Eh, who knows. I had one homeless guy last week screaming at me about how fried zucchini was going to bring about the end of the world . . ."

I tuned him out. The old lady said I must do it. Must do what? I thought about Spencer. I could easily picture him becoming just as batty as the old lady.

I needed to quit this crazy job, like, now.

The cab dropped me off in front of my condo. The dull little brick building with the security buzzer on the doors, the one with a guard on duty twenty-four-seven. Safe.

I exited the elevator on the fourth floor and headed down to the end of the hall toward my apartment. As I got closer, my heartbeat increased. My door. There were marks on the lower right corner. I knelt down and took a closer look. Claw marks. The paint had been scratched off. Like a dog had been clawing at the door, trying to get inside.

Any dog could have done that. Plenty of dog owners in the building. But I couldn't make myself put the key in the lock.

I started to shake, frightened of what I might find inside. For all I knew, the crazy old lady would be in there playing with Miss Elsa. In a short amount of time the rules governing life had all changed. If you see a crazy person at the airport, you could also see her inside your apartment. Or a lizard dog could be hiding inside, waiting to suck your soul out.

I needed a weapon, but there wasn't anything in the hallway that I could use to defend myself. I had some pepper spray in my purse. No, I needed my gun, but it was inside the apartment.

The guard in the lobby. I could ask him to come in with me. Would that be a crazy thing? I didn't care.

I went back downstairs and found him. I sounded like a helpless woman, something I am usually not, but for the first time, I really felt like one. I hated giving in to fear. I had made my way in this city because I was fearless. Normal stuff didn't scare me. But I was no longer in normal territory. I remembered Spencer's description of Elsa sucking the life out of him, and now I couldn't think rationally.

I explained to the security guard that it looked like someone had tried to break in my apartment and I was scared to go in alone. I felt like such a little girl. But at the same time, I needed to feel safe.

I handed over the keys and he took out his Taser. He opened the door and went in. A few minutes later, "All clear, Miss Ellis."

"Thanks, would you mind staying a few more minutes while I check the closets?" God, I was so damn paranoid. So goddamned helpless.

Everything was just as I had left it. I opened the drawer in my nightstand and unlocked the gun lockbox. I took out my gun and checked under my bed, in my closets, in every nook and cranny in my apartment until I was confident that I was alone.

I gave the guard a twenty and thanked him. After he left, I wondered if this paranoia would gradually go away by itself. I couldn't live like this, always looking over my shoulder, questioning my reality.

I vowed that if Miss Elsa showed up at my door again, I would blow her little brains right out of her head.

14

I stepped into the Peacock Café the next day to meet Lloyd for lunch. The hostess told me that Lloyd was not here yet and asked if I would like to be seated.

"Yes, please."

I followed her to a table in the rear. I knew Lloyd would like this place—the food was upscale diner fare. White tablecloths and wine lists.

I normally would have looked the place over and directed the hostess to a better table with a view of the elegant Georgetown architecture just outside the restaurant, but today I didn't care. Even better to be out of the line of sight for any little dogs looking around for me.

I hadn't slept well the previous night. I kept my gun on top of the nightstand, and I turned on a white noise app after a while, because every little sound morphed into a lizard dog trying to break into my apartment. I tried to reason with myself. I lived on the fourth floor in a security building. No one could just show up at my door. Miss Elsa could not scratch at my window unless she had wings. Then I wondered if the lizard people had wings, too. What if Miss Elsa scratched at the front door to the building and acted lost and cute? The guard would open the door and he'd get zapped by the lizard tongue. Luckily, jet lag kicked in after two a.m. and I drifted off.

My trusty power suit and a pair of classic beige Ferragamo pumps couldn't boost my confidence today. My armor was no longer a protective shield; it was just a nice suit. But I had the gun in my purse.

There was no reason I could think of to continue trying to make sense out of any of this. I would send a note to Trina, telling her that effective immediately I would tender my resignation. Reason: just not working out.

There was a chance that she could take me to court for the twenty-five-thousand-dollar bonus, but I would gladly hand that back. No wonder she had made me such a crazy offer. No amount of money was worth this kind of insanity.

Would quitting make me feel safer? Maybe not. I would still know that Miss Elsa was out there, and consequently, Miss Elsa would know I was still out there. Seeing her claw marks on my door made it clear that distance wasn't an obstacle for her. She could hunt me down if she wanted to. I wasn't sure if quitting would stop her from chasing me.

"Finally! A normal restaurant." Lloyd sat down opposite me. "Sorry I'm late, got stuck behind an animal rights protest. Those people have the dullest signs, no wonder they never get any traction. So how's life in glamourous Hollywood?"

Some animals shouldn't have any rights. I shrugged. "It ain't all that."

"Oh, c'mon. Don't tell me you're bored already? I knew it." He took his reading glasses out and grabbed the menu. "I hate to say I told you so."

More like scared shitless. "Not exactly bored, but it's not turning out how I had hoped."

"It's only been a couple of weeks, right? Maybe just give it some time." He looked up at me from the menu. "You know, I hate to say this, but you do look a little . . . frazzled."

Just a few short days ago, 1,446 people thought I was sexy and hot. "Jet lag. Had to fly to Ecuador for a couple of days. Just got back last night."

"Ecuador? Damn, that's the last place I would expect to see *Keeping Up With the Kardashians*. Looks like they're out for worldwide domination."

"Well, the firm does represent them in New York, London, Moscow, we're even opening an office in . . . Beijing." Come to think of it, why open in those particular cities? Worldwide domination. Why didn't that phrase sound as innocent to me as Lloyd had meant it?

"Yep, they're hitting all the power centers. How come no office here in DC?"

The DC project that Kris mentioned in one of Spencer's videos. That must be what I was laying the groundwork for. I felt lightheaded. Had I unwittingly stumbled into some plot by the Kardashians? But I hadn't stumbled. Trina specifically hunted me down for this job. I was her perfect candidate. To do what? In the Alice in Wonderland universe that I had fallen into, I was a dupe for the lizard people who wanted to take over the world. "I think eventually they will."

"Makes sense." Lloyd looked back at the menu. "These Kardashians are way more popular than I thought. But I shouldn't be surprised. I mean, everyone wants to live like they do, right? No real jobs, just figure out where to have lunch every day. Live in a big fancy house. I think it's called universal appeal, no? People are just lulled into feeling like their life could be like that. Well, at least my wife does."

I nodded slowly. Universal appeal. Lulled. What was it that the creature had said to Spencer? Become compliant. Kim's touch made people compliant. Or did she make them feel like they could be lulled into being part of her pretty little life?

"After all, why should it just be us here in the US that get to burn brain cells watching this stuff. Make the planet dumb again!"

"Right." These Kardashian creatures were getting ready to take over the whole world. I was the only one who knew it, besides Spencer, wherever he was. Wasn't this the place in the movie where Bruce Willis grabs his gun and yells "Yippee-ki-yay, motherfucker"?

"Ready to order?" Lloyd motioned for the waiter.

"Sure." Was there something I could do? Maybe I should just file an FBI report and let them worry about it.

A waiter approached our table. "Would you like to know our specials?"

I handed over the menu. "No, that's okay. I'll just have the caesar salad and a sparkling water." The new game plan: quit and then contact the FBI. But I couldn't lose the awful nagging feeling that quitting wouldn't stop Miss Elsa from coming for me. Would it make Trina and her lizard people more suspicious of me?

I might never feel totally safe until that thing was dead.

"I'll have the crab cakes and a Guinness draught." Lloyd handed the menu to the waiter. "I don't think you should have any problem getting Kim in to see anybody. Well, anyone male over forty, anyway. Since I made those initial inquiries, there's been some buzz. Now I'm getting calls from these guys on the Hill asking to be "put on the list." I just tell them it's your baby."

"I have an odd question for you."

"What could be so odd in our world?"

"Kim has a fascination with . . . alien lifeforms. She was asking me if there was someone I could introduce her to that might be sympathetic to that fascination."

Lloyd frowned at me. "That is an odd question. Are you talking about somebody on the Hill? Even if I could track down someone like that, I don't think they would want it known, you know what I mean?"

"No, somebody whose job it is to know that kind of thing. I'm talking about the part of the government that would deal with Area 51 kind of stuff."

Lloyd stared at me, nodding his head for a few long seconds. I hoped he wouldn't start laughing at me.

"Let me see if I can dig someone up. I'm pretty sure some of the nerds at NASA wouldn't mind discussing alien lifeforms with Kim Kardashian."

15

Trina,

I am sorry to inform you that effective immediately I am terminating our agreement for the position of Public Relations Director, International and Do mestic Issues, for Kim Kardashian.

The position is not working out as I had hoped. I will return all bonus monies paid out minus expenses and pro rated salary for the time I have put in.

Good luck in your future endeavors.

Sincerely,

Maddy Ellis

I leaned back in my office chair at my condo and stared at the email on my screen. Instead of answering the dozens of emails I had waiting for me about the Serious kickoff, I had worked on composing this one email. I wrote it hours ago, but I could not bring myself to hit the send button.

The wording was fine. It said exactly what needed to be said and nothing more. I thought that the offer to return the money was fair. But the more I thought about sending it, the more I imagined how the lizard people would come after me.

"Miss? Excuse me, I'm done here."

The tech from the alarm company interrupted my thoughts.

I had totally forgotten he was even in my apartment. I had ordered an alarm system for the condo. Movement-sensitive, connected to my phone. Every window and door was now wired. If that little bitch came back to my door and even sneezed at it, I'd know right away.

I spent thirty minutes going over the instructions with the tech and then went back to the laptop.

I was pretty sure that Trina must be in on this whole thing. Clearly, she would read this and immediately know that I was onto something. Even if Trina was totally innocent, Kim and Kris would immediately know that something was up. Someone had sent Miss Elsa after me twice already. But why?

The headphones! Spencer said they could track them.

I saved my draft and closed my email. Sending it out might just raise their suspicions.

I couldn't get around this any longer. It all came down to the fact that the only thing that would make me feel safe was to kill the dog. The crazy old lady from the airport was right. I had to do it.

I needed a plan.

My advantage was that they didn't know what I knew. Right now they had no reason to think that I knew about Miss Elsa or the lizard tongues. They didn't know I knew how the magic headphones worked.

The only way to kill Miss Elsa was to fly back to LA and go into the office and shoot it.

Or maybe I could set a trap. She wanted the magic headphones, but I hadn't turned them on since Ecuador. I winced. If they could track them, then I may have led them right to Spencer.

I could leave the headphones out for her. Find a place where I could hide and wait for her to retrieve them.

I just needed to find the perfect place to leave them. It couldn't be here in my home. I needed to do some more thinking.

In the meantime, I would still go through the motions. I had to herd Kim through the meeting with her congressman tomorrow. No doubt Kris would be there as well. If anyone would be suspicious, it would be Kris. I had to act like everything was fine, that I was not secretly planning the murder of the owner of ME Communications.

16

I stood on the granite steps in front of the entrance to the imposing Rayburn House Office Building, waiting for the Kardashian circus to show up for their meet and greet with Congressman Royce. I had a filming permit in my hand, blue alligator Manolo Blahnik pumps on my feet, and a classic navy suit adorned with a simple string of pearls around my neck. I wanted this meet and greet to go smoothly, since this would be my last official act as Kim's PR rep.

The decision to go through with this meeting was purely self-preservation. I would still need my reputation to remain intact on the Hill after I quit ME. If I flaked out on this meeting, it would leave a bad impression on the congressman's staff. It would definitely raise Kim's suspicions, which could result in another visit from Elsa. I wanted this done quickly. In and out. I was here to protect my own name.

I still had to navigate a lot of different worlds this morning. There was the world of government, the stately regal offices of Congress, and all of the pomp and circumstance associated with being part of the oldest functioning democracy on earth. There was also the cartoonish reality world of the Kardashians, who were coming with a camera crew to film the meeting for an upcoming episode of their show. Then there was the secret world of lizard people.

We had five minutes until the scheduled meet time, with at least a fifteen-minute wait to get through security and another ten minutes to navigate the intricate maze of hallways to the congressman's office. There were only two security entrances, and the lines were getting longer. There was some kind of a hearing on public education this morning, and I had hoped that we could get in before the crowds began to show up for the hearing. I texted the congressman's office to let him know I was still waiting on the Kardashians. Congressmen were very busy people and usually scheduled their free time in increments of fifteen minutes. If Kim didn't show up immediately, there was a good chance we'd get bumped. I knew that the only reason the congressman had agreed to meet with Kim was because she was in his district. A courtesy to a famous constituent. He was looking for a photo op, not a meeting of the minds. His district was loaded with celebrities, so it wasn't as if he needed to meet with her; photo ops with celebrities could always be rescheduled.

His chief of staff responded, *"Please hurry!"*

I had been texting Kim, but she kept sending me the same message: *"Almost there! Any minute!"*

I couldn't help feeling a little panicked, trying to think of how to get Kim into the meeting on time. That was my sense of professionalism kicking in. But I still had a growing sense of dread, thinking about Spencer and the crazy old lady at the airport. I couldn't bring my gun with me into the capitol, that was the law. Could Miss Elsa just appear and tongue my leg? I reassured myself that it wasn't likely. This place was too public; the hall was already crowded with people trying to get into the building. Their conversations bounced all over the hall, which also provided enough cover to hide any of Kris's dentist office drill noises. Less chance for a headache.

I walked into the building and squeezed past the people lining up in front of the metal detectors. The building's lobby wasn't that huge. It was built way before the security concerns of the last century, and thus, squeezing all of the security apparatuses and a crowd of people in there was always a challenge.

I had been there before when there was some popular hearing going on, and the line had actually extended out the door and down the front steps.

The line was now doubled back and would soon be forced outside. I walked over to the guard's post at the end of the hallway. I recognized Officer Malone, chief of security, at his post. I had dealt with him in the past. The guy was older than dirt, had been here for at least four administrations, and was completely by the book. Bribes wouldn't work with him. I knew that there was a super-secret VIP entrance on the side of the building and thought I would see if I could get Kim in that way. Normally you had to have some level of top security clearance to get in that way, but I would give it my best shot.

He sat behind an imposing gray marble bureau, monitoring a series of security cameras built into the desk.

"Officer Malone? Maddy Ellis, ME Communications. I'm waiting for some VIPs to come in, and they're bringing a camera crew." I held up the filming permit. "Can we give them access to the VIP entrance? Otherwise, I can guarantee they will cause a major disruption simply by being here."

"Ellis? I think I remember you." Officer Malone took the permit from me and scrutinized it. "Who are your VIPs?"

Bribes wouldn't work, but would a little flirting work? Wasn't I hot and sexy now? I took a deep breath, fiddled with the top button of my blouse, and ran my hand through my hair. "Kim Kardashian."

He laughed to himself. "Kim Kardashian a VIP? I don't think so. She waits in line like everyone else. My crew can handle any disruptions."

I wanted to agree with him, that the Kardashians were hardly VIP level in DC, but they were still capable of throwing the lobby into chaos. I leaned in and smiled at him. "Maybe we can just get them to the head of the line quicker? They always bring a little bit of chaos with them—"

"Have a nice day." He cut me off, handed me back my filming permit, and returned his gaze to monitoring the security cameras.

Son of a bitch. Well, so much for hot and sexy.

A loud shriek bounced across the lobby. The general noise level rose as people in line pointed at the entrance and pulled out their phones.

They had arrived.

I saw her security crew enter first, headphones and all. They held open the doors and looked around suspiciously at everyone like security guards do.

The camera crew entered next, backing in through the brass-encased glass doors to film Kim and her entourage. I froze. She brought lizard girl. North clung to her mother's hand and looked through the crowd. She locked eyes with me. What was she doing here? This wasn't a goddamned family picnic. Would she bring that tongue out? No way. Not in full view of so many people. Not with a camera crew on them, I hoped.

Kris brought up the rear.

I did get a kick out of Kim's outfit. A form-fitting, somber black sweater dress and a Jackie O. pillbox hat. At least she was smart enough not to wear yoga pants today.

I hustled over to the crew and motioned for Kim to follow me. "We have to hurry, we're already late for the appointment and we still have to get through security. By the way, are your guards carrying?"

Kim nodded.

"Then they can't come in. It's illegal to have any type of weapon in this building. They could technically be arrested in the lobby right now."

There was a crowd forming around us, pointing and yelling

out to Kim. Kris leaned over to speak to me so I could hear her. "The guards have to come with Kim. She's had a lot of credible threats and I won't have her unprotected." She gave me one of her mean-girl faces just to make the point.

I no longer cared. I just wanted to get through this appointment and be done. Kris had no more leverage over me. "The guards do not come in. Period. We don't have any more time to waste."

There were a few seconds of silence. Kim finally spoke up, "We'll be fine, Mom." She turned to her guards. "Wait out front for us, okay?"

I won. I almost felt like doing an endzone dance. "By the way, why didn't you tell me you were bringing North? I didn't tell Congressman Royce that you were bringing your daughter. I don't want him to think that we were deliberately keeping that from him for any reason." Congress people did not like surprises. Even little ones. With lizard tongues.

"I thought it was important for her to see how government works," Kim declared. "I want my daughter to be woke."

North smiled up at me and rocked her head back and forth. "Woke."

Kris looked over the line snaking throughout the lobby and addressed me. "Where's the VIP entrance?"

"We don't qualify for VIP here." I ducked to get out of a camera shot.

Kris grabbed Kim and whispered into her ear as I texted the congressman's office that we were on our way with added guest North West.

He replied right away: *"Just a couple of minutes left to see Kim today."*

The line at the security entrance started to break up as more people began to recognize Kim.

A group of businessmen held out their cameras. "Hey, Kim! Give us a wave!"

Another young man shouted from the end of the line, "Where's Kanye?"

A cluster of women broke from the end of the second line, walking toward us, cell phones held high. "I can't believe she's here in the Rayburn Building! Is she coming to the hearing?"

Dozens of cell phones were held up high, trying to record her, voices calling out for selfies. People were crowding us, trying to get an autograph on their meeting agendas, or just any loose scraps of paper.

We were never going to get through this crowd and make it on time. I tried to think of a plan B if we couldn't get in to see Congressman Royce. Knocking on doors was the only thing I could think of. I'd seen protesters do it when they couldn't get a meeting scheduled. They'd traipse down the hallway, knocking on the doors of any Congress people, hoping to luck out. That would be hellish. Having Kris breathing down my neck about getting access with lizard girl in tow.

Kim turned from the crowd and marched to the security desk. The crowd and the camera crew followed behind. I pushed my way through the mass of people to catch up with her.

Kim smiled at Officer Malone and extended her hand. "Hi, I'm Kim."

Officer Malone shook her hand and nodded.

"I'm really late for this meeting with my congressman. It's, like, a big deal, you know? Can me and my crew get in any quicker?"

"Against procedures," he replied curtly.

Kim sighed and nodded. "Well, is it against procedures to take a selfie with me? You are, like, so cute."

Officer Malone cocked his head, like he wasn't sure what he had just heard. "What? Selfie?"

He tried to say something else, but Kim was behind the counter with her phone out and had wrapped her arm around his arm before he could object. "Okay, Mr. Malone, say 'serious'!"

He looked up into the camera and before he knew it, he was in a selfie with Kim.

Kim showed him the photo. "Wow, the camera really loves you, huh?"

Officer Malone looked at the photo and then took the phone from Kim as he continued to stare at his own image. "I guess it is a really nice picture. Can you send me a copy?"

"Of course, but I need your phone number. Don't worry, I promise not to stalk you or anything." Kim giggled.

The hall behind us that led back to the security entrances was now mobbed by bystanders. I saw people coming out of elevators with their cell phones in hand. Word must have gotten out among the staffers and they were now coming down from their offices to see the Kardashian spectacle for themselves. It would be impossible to find the line, let alone wait at the end of it.

Officer Malone looked over the crowd. "We'd better get you inside here quickly. C'mon, follow me." He guided us back to the entrance and unhooked a red velvet rope that kept the lines in order.

She got Officer Hard Ass to break his rules?

I remembered meeting with Kim at the Prada store weeks ago, being amused at her lighthearted powers of persuasion, her innate ability to get total strangers to do what she wanted, but now it seemed to me less lighthearted and more malevolent. She wasn't being persuasive; she was forcing people to become obedient. I remembered the video of Miss Elsa attacking Spencer. The android voice insisting that he become compliant.

Officer Malone made a clearing for us at the security checkpoint. The crew went first, covering their equipment, sending it through the X-ray machines, and walking through the metal detectors. I followed behind. North emptied her pockets and then stepped into the metal detector, setting off the device. I walked over to see if I needed to facilitate her entrance. Maybe her tongue was made out of metal.

Kim called out to Officer Malone, "She has a metal pin in her hip from an operation."

Officer Malone nodded and waved her through.

I was pretty sure that was total BS, but I was also pretty sure that Officer Malone had become compliant. She could have told him that North was wearing a vest full of explosives and he would have waved her through.

The alarm sounded again as Kim walked through. I wondered what the hell they were bringing in with them. Did she have a gun or something else hidden? It couldn't be weapons. No, that wasn't Kim's style. She was way too high-profile to march into a lawmaker's office with a gun. It was something else. Did it have something to do with this technology that made the buzzing noise and spoke through the headphones? Lloyd's innocent observation echoed in my mind: worldwide domination.

The guard took out her wand as Kim put her hands in the air. "This is so embarrassing. It's my bra. It's, you know . . . underwire. Heavy-duty because of . . . you know."

Officer Malone signaled to the guard. "She's fine, let her go."

I noticed that all activity had stopped at the other scanner as the rest of the guards grabbed their phones and took videos of the proceedings. Officer Malone must have been pretty deep under Kim's influence, because that was definitely against security rules.

Finally, it was Kris's turn. While she put her purse through the scanner, Kim was signing autographs and taking selfies with the other security guards.

The alarm went off again as Kris walked through. She stared at Officer Malone.

"Just let her through."

Kim had just finessed her whole family through a series of security alarms that guarded the nation's top lawmakers. I let that sink in. She did it effortlessly and with a Mona Lisa smile. In all of my panic to make sure I was doing my job, I didn't think about what might happen if Kim actually met with this congressman. Could she make him become compliant? Compliant to what?

I didn't know the answer. But now I assumed that whatever Kim was trying to accomplish couldn't be good. Was I becoming a lobbyist for the lizard people? Yes. This was who I was. As crazy as it sounded, Trina hired me for access, but really she just needed me to get them into the building. I remembered Kris's angry words: "Just get Kim in the room with them, she'll do the rest." The rest of what?

I began to rethink rushing to make her appointment. *Maybe I should make sure she misses it.* Easy to do in this building. If you didn't have a detailed map of the endless series of hallways, you might never find the right office.

"Which way?" Kris demanded, glaring at me.

I could hear the faint humming under the echo of the noise in the hall.

Why should I care if she missed an appointment? I had already decided that I was going to quit. Yes, I would slow-walk this bitch. "Follow me."

∞

We arrived at Congressman Royce's office thirty minutes late for our appointment. I smiled inwardly. I wasn't sure what I had just prevented from happening, but I was sure I had done the right thing.

As we pushed open the thick oak door, I could see that the young man at the reception desk was already shaking his head. I introduced myself and explained that we were held up by the crowds at the entry.

"I'm sorry, the congressman's schedule is really tight and he's already in another meeting." He pointed to the closed door just ten feet from his desk. "We'll have to reschedule."

"Damn." I turned to Kim. "I'll go ahead and reschedule, but maybe we can get you a private tour of the House, since you're here." The appointment could be rescheduled after I was gone from ME. They could find someone else to be their lizard lackey.

Kris leaned over the receptionist's desk. "Does he know that we're here waiting? Maybe if you told him Kim Kardashian is here, he'd be able to find some extra time."

Kris actually smiled. It was the first time I'd ever seen her do that, and I think it was even more frightening than her regular angry face. It was a mechanical smile, like she had been reading up on which muscles to move and forgot the part about acting like you were happy.

"I'm sorry, I can't interrupt the congressman."

I was pretty sure this guy wasn't just a receptionist hired to make appointments, he was a really polite combination pit bull and bouncer. To be this close to a lawmaker, you had to be a true believer. A staffer who believed in the congressman and the causes. They guarded their bosses like they were gold at Fort Knox. I knew we probably wouldn't get near the congressman today, but I thought I would make it look like I tried. "How about a walk-along? Is he going into the chamber today? We could accompany him down there."

He shook his head. "He's got a CNN interview scheduled for his walk-along today. But listen, he really wants to meet with you, so let's just set up another time?"

I looked at Kris and shrugged my shoulders. "If only you'd been on time." *I have maybe two hours tops with you, and then I will never have to see you again.*

Her mechanical smile faded away.

The receptionist spotted North lurking behind Kim. "Who's this little cutie?"

She poked her head through Kim's arm. "I'm North."

"Well, North, I think I have something for you here." He grabbed a dish of candy from a shelf behind him and took a lollipop out of it. "I have to hide these from the congressman, but I'm sure he wouldn't mind giving one of his constituents a little treat."

Oh, God no! I pictured her long, snake tongue wrapping around the candy.

North reached her hand out to take it, but Kim stopped her. "No, sweetie." She pulled North's hand back. "I don't like her having all that sugar. C'mon, now, let's everyone take a selfie before we leave, okay?"

I froze. The selfie. That's where Kim took control. I didn't know how to stop it without looking like a madwoman. I couldn't just scream "Don't!" I watched helplessly as Kim, Kris, and North stood behind the reception desk. I saw Kim put her arm around his shoulder and extend her cell phone in front of them.

Minutes later, the receptionist was marveling at his improved likeness, and it only took a few more minutes before he was interrupting his boss's meeting to introduce the Kardashians.

The Kardashians filed into the congressman's office, followed by their camera crew.

I was watching something happen, something bad, and I

wasn't sure what it was. I knew I should stop it, but what was it I was going to stop? I tried to reason out what actions I could take. Run into the office and grab her phone? In front of their cameras? I needed to get in there right now and see what they wanted the congressman to do.

From the open doorway to the congressman's office, I heard Kim ask, "Where's Maddy? North, go tell her to come in here."

North peeked out of the congressman's office at me. Her eyes were fixed on mine. She slowly produced a smile and walked a few steps out of the doorway toward me.

I wouldn't miss lizard girl when I quit.

She opened her mouth and wiggled the tip of her tongue.

I could now hear the humming. It was full dentist drill. I had to cover my ears. I considered just walking out. Running out of the building, going home, and hitting the send button on my resignation.

Her tongue rolled out of her mouth, it moved slowly across the office toward me. I felt moisture gathering under my shirt, across my forehead. Was she going to do to me what Miss Elsa did to Spencer? Right here in broad daylight? I backed away from her and bumped into a chair. Spencer had said how quickly Miss Elsa's tongue had shot out of her mouth. Could North do that? I was afraid to make a sudden move.

Her tongue continued to roll out, longer than I'd seen before, reaching at least five feet, and then it stopped at the desk. There was saliva dripping off the tip, onto the ink blotter, splattering into a dark black stain. I tried to yell for help, but the words slid out of my mouth like a whisper; my throat had gone into shock. Who would help me anyway? No one here. I began shaking uncontrollably.

Is that how it was for Spencer? He said he had stomped on Miss Elsa's tongue to get away. What could I do? I saw a letter opener on the desk. Could I reach it in time? I moved my hand slightly to make a grab for the opener, but I was shaking too much and I was too slow. That tongue would be all over me before I could get near it.

Her tongue slowly dipped into the candy dish that the receptionist had left on his desk and pulled a lollipop out. North held her hand out as her tongue recoiled back into her mouth, pausing to drop the lollipop into her waiting fingers.

"Mommy says you should come in here." North put the lollipop into her pocket and went back into the office.

If she had decided to come after me, there was nothing I could have done. If I had my gun with me, would I have shot her? And if I did, what would I have killed?

17

I put my shopping bags down in the hallway outside the door to my apartment, turned off my alarm, and took my gun out of my purse. I slowly opened the door. The lights were on just as I had left them. I did a thorough check of the place before bringing my bags inside and turning the alarm back on.

I had made my decision. Miss Elsa had to die.

After seeing lizard girl's tongue roll out at me yesterday, I knew I was well on my way to becoming Spencer. Afraid of being anywhere the dog could jump out and attack me. I couldn't live like that. But what about the lizard girl? Or the other kid with the tongue? Maybe they all needed to die, but Miss Elsa was the only one who had shown up uninvited at my door. Wherever that door was. So for now, I would start with Miss Elsa.

I needed to try on my killing outfit. I still had time to exchange anything if I needed to.

The black work pants were the hardest to find. I had to go out to an Army Navy store in the suburbs to find them. I wanted something thick, like what construction workers wear, that wouldn't rip in case Elsa tried to claw her way to my leg. I threw on the black T-shirt and then the heavy black leather biker's jacket. So far so good.

Industrial black work boots as well. Good for resisting bites and slimy tongues, and heavy enough to stomp a little dog's head. A far cry from my Jimmy Choos.

I wasn't sure about the black gloves. Although they could protect my hands from Miss Elsa's teeth, they also padded my trigger finger a little too much. Maybe just a glove for the other hand.

I was still up in the air about the black ski mask. I wasn't sure if that was over the top. However, the less exposed skin for Miss Elsa's tongue to grab, the better. I'd wear it.

I wished I could do this somewhere in broad daylight. Somewhere I could feel safe, surrounded by people. But I knew that shooting a gun anywhere in public would bring out a SWAT team before I could reload my magazine. It had to be done in the dead of night, someplace deserted. I couldn't get around that.

I had spent all morning on the laptop doing research and finally found Canal Park. A small park near the waterfront. The park closed at ten p.m., and the area would be deserted at night. There was absolutely no security presence after closing—years of budget cuts to DC Parks had seen to that—so all I had to do was hop a fence and I would be in. The park had a small amphitheater that would be the perfect place to off her. If she took the bait and went inside the band shell, she'd be trapped inside with no way to escape, giving me a perfect shot from the benches above.

I had one magazine loaded in the gun. Sixteen shots. I'd bring along two extra magazines just in case. I also had a hunting knife with a serrated blade and a Taser. A plastic garbage bag for disposal. Since the park was so close to the Potomac, it would be easy to just bag it and throw it in the river. This bitch was going down, one way or another.

The plan was to leave the headphones on the stage of the amphitheater, turn them on, and just wait.

I checked my emails before going out.

A thank-you from Anthony Royce's office for the introduction.

He had agreed to a seat on the Board of Directors of The Serious Foundation before I could get into the office and do anything. By that time, I was too shaken up anyway. I wasn't sure what other plans they had for him, but I wasn't going to be part of those plans any longer.

An email from Kim asking for a status meeting when she returned to LA. I could ignore that.

Finally, an email from Lloyd:

Maddy,

Looks like there's a lot more of these people out there than I thought. I have three contacts and I think they should be able to handle Kim and her curiosity. I've listed them by order of relevance:

Alden Hastings - NASA scientist, retired last year, wrote a dozen books on the likelihood of life outside of our planet. Has done a lot of consultant work in Hollywood. Advises production teams on what an alien would most likely look like or how it would function in a given location or situation. Think this guy is your best bet.

Natasha Woronov - Contractor for JPL. Has worked on the Space Station. Considered an expert in possibility of lifeforms outside our solar system. Usually gets called in as an expert for NASA when they are trying to convince Congress to fund a deep space mission. Not as user friendly as Alden but knows her shit.

Chris Palover - This is the guy at the FBI who checks out alien sightings and reports. Just in case Kim has seen an alien she wants to report. Nice guy, but I think the other two would probably be more fun for Kim.

Chris Palover was exactly who I needed to talk to. What would I tell him? "I would like to report a sighting of the lizard people?"

He'd probably heard worse.

I called his number and got his voicemail.

"Hi, Chris, my name is Maddy Ellis. Lloyd Anderson gave me your number. I'd like to talk to you about something really odd I saw. I'm not talking about a bright light in the sky, but something that happened in front of me. And I'm not a crazy person. Honest. This is not the type of call I would ever make, but this . . . thing I saw is . . . crazy. Also, can I assume this is confidential? Please call me back as soon as possible. Thanks."

I hung up the phone. Time to kick some lizard ass.

∞

At ten-thirty p.m. I climbed over the fencing around Canal Park and made my way to the amphitheater. All of the security lighting was focused on the stage and the band shell that covered it. There was a cement orchestra pit with about a four-foot drop from the stage, and then about fifty feet beyond the stage the cement seating was laid out in steps. The seating area was pretty dark, and there was a small wall, about two feet high, that separated the seating from the orchestra pit. I could use that as my cover.

I went to the edge of the stage, left the headphones on the floor, and turned them on. I ran behind the wall that divided the orchestra pit from the seating section. Fifty feet? Yeah, I could easily get an accurate shot off from here. I pulled the ski mask over my face, crouched down, and waited.

Would she just walk in like a normal dog? There was a two-foot cement ledge that divided the walkway from the seating on each side of the aisles, and I was pretty certain that she was too small to see over them. The only way she would spot me beforehand would be if she came down the center aisle from the back where the refreshment stand was. I could still react quickly if she came in that way.

How did she get around? Maybe she could just beam herself to places like they did on Star Trek. I started to perspire. I was scaring myself. There were so many unknowns. If this was some kind of alien being, it could have all kinds of powers I couldn't even imagine. What if there was more than one? Stop. I had to stop scaring myself.

At twelve forty-five I wondered if I should leave. Go home, get a good night's rest, and rethink the plan. Maybe it would make more sense to do this in broad daylight in the ME office. I was no longer sure if Miss Elsa would take the bait here in the park, whereas in the office, I knew she would be there and I could get a close-range shot. I doubted she would roll out the tongue in the office for everyone to see. Would she? I could be arrested for shooting a gun in an office, but at this point I didn't care.

I was about to call it a night when I heard the humming. Then, the scratching of claws on concrete.

I crouched down in the shadows below the concrete divider. The area around me was pitch black, so I felt safe to take a peek. Miss Elsa walked up the steps of the stage and then over to the headphones. I removed the glove from my trigger hand and brought the gun up to my eye to aim.

She sniffed around the area and then sniffed the headphones. She was moving too much for me to get a clear shot.

She sniffed some more around the stage and walked toward the edge, where I had jumped off. Fuck. She was following my scent.

She looked into the audience seating. Her cold black eyes met mine. Better do this now.

In an instant the tongue unrolled from her mouth like a

speeding bullet. It wrapped around my bare shooting hand and pulled. I managed to pull the trigger, but the shot went off to the side and the gun dropped from my grip.

The tongue wrapped around my hand tighter. It felt like a million tiny wet suction cups against my skin. My hand was burning. I tried pulling my hand away, but the more I pulled, the more heat her tongue generated.

I couldn't get out of her grip. I reached for the gun with my free hand.

I had the feeling that Miss Elsa's thoughts were being transmitted into my body through the tongue, into my nervous system, my mind. She wanted me to know that she was my friend, an ally. She wanted to bring me happiness, help me get things that would make me happy.

I had visions of shopping trips with Kim. We were laughing and trying on clothes, having lunch at an outdoor bistro. Shoes, pictures of gorgeous shoes appeared in my mind. My foot fitting perfectly in a set of heels that matched my outfit.

I had to concentrate on resisting her. *I don't want your goddamned shoes!*

But I did. Oh God, I really did.

I concentrated harder on getting away. Spencer. I remembered him. He was sitting with me in Ecuador, recounting what he had done to fight her off. He did something to her, but I couldn't remember exactly what he had said. And then he was gone from my memory.

I was now the backseat driver in my own brain. She was controlling the levers.

"No!" I willed myself to fight her, but I was losing. My mind flashed on Kim's huge, beautiful kitchen, where the French doors opened by themselves to the patio where Kim sat on a lounger, smiling at me.

"Do you want to take a selfie?"

I would get so many likes. More and more people would look at me and think I was sexy and hot.

Miss Elsa was now moving toward me. I could hear the humming getting louder, drilling into me.

I also felt the heat in my head, climbing throughout my body, trying to take control of every part of me. My voice, what I thought of as me, was disappearing. She was inside my brain, manipulating me. I felt like pretty soon I would no longer exist.

The gun dropped from my other hand. I swallowed hard. Her total takeover of my being seemed inevitable.

Become compliant.

I heard those words clearly from her. But there was a danger associated with becoming compliant. Those words triggered an old memory. I was in a bar in Ecuador again. I was watching a video of Miss Elsa terrorizing someone.

I started to cry. I had to do something.

A memory of an old lady banging against a car window, her crazy eyes, her powdered face, and bright pink lipstick. *"You know what to do!"*

The space in my brain where I could think my own thoughts was shrinking.

A crazy-looking old lady kept screaming at me, *"You know what to do!"*

This was the only thought I could process.

I reached into my jacket pocket and pulled out the hunting knife.

"Do it now."

I plunged the knife into her tongue.

The heat stopped. Miss Elsa screamed a high-pitched dog scream that jolted me from my trance. The tongue loosened its grip on my hand. Miss Elsa was about ten feet from me. Her teeth were bared, and there was foam coming from her mouth. She crouched down. It looked like she was getting ready to jump.

"You know what to do!"

I picked up my gun, took aim, and pulled the trigger.

Another scream. She was down but still squirming. The tongue still laid out in front of her, wiggling.

Kill it. Kill this thing dead. As I slowly walked closer to her, my legs felt like jelly, like they could give out from under me at any second. My hand shook as I squeezed the trigger and pumped shot after shot into her body, until she fell over and stopped moving.

I loaded another magazine into my gun and fired more shots, then stopped. I was completely drained, like I could easily lie down on the cement and go to sleep. I took deep breaths until I could think clearly again.

Part of me wanted to just sit down and rest, try to process what I'd just experienced. I felt like I'd been in an accident and was waiting for the trauma to take hold. But my survival instinct said, *No, do not rest. Not yet. Dispose of the body.* I kept my gun aimed at her head and kicked her a few times. Dead. There was dark liquid all over the place. It didn't look like blood, but some kind of dark ink. Some of it had splashed onto my clothes. Still a little dazed, for a second, I wondered if I could wash it out, and then my brain started functioning again. *Throw these clothes out when you get home. Burn them.*

I pulled out the plastic garbage bag from my jacket pocket. I didn't want to pick her up. I'd seen too many science fiction movies where the dead alien comes back to life at the last second. I used my foot to push the body into the bag.

The tongue. It was still lying unraveled. I tried to bend over and grab the tongue, but I could not make myself touch it. It was like knowingly trying to touch a hot burner on a stove. Even though I had my gloves on, I didn't feel safe. I didn't know what this thing was capable of. Maybe it could still try to do something to me, even if its owner was dead.

I took aim again and fired another three shots until the tongue was separated from her throat. Screw the tongue, just leave it there. I sealed the plastic bag and held it out in front of me. Dump it in the river. A good ten-minute walk from here. I shuddered. I wanted to get away from here as soon as possible. My mind couldn't focus on what I had originally planned to do. I needed to get away from this thing as soon as possible.

There was a dumpster by a refreshment stand at the back of the seating area. I ran over to the dumpster, threw Elsa in, and slammed the dumpster closed. I waited a few minutes to see if something would happen, like the dog coming back to life in the dumpster or the tongue moving on its own, but nothing happened. I took another deep breath and ran out of the park.

I jumped into my car and started shaking and crying. I couldn't control myself. I had to tell myself over and over again that I was safe. My stomach gurgled, and then the gurgling moved up to my chest. I opened the car door and leaned out into the street to vomit on the pavement.

When I was sure that my stomach was empty, I sat back up behind the wheel and took more deep breaths until I was calmer. I didn't know how much time passed before I felt ready to drive home.

Inside my condo, I turned on the shower and stood under the hot water. When I reached for the soap, I noticed that my hand looked like it had been sitting in the sun for a couple of days. I had to cleanse this whole night off of me. The memory of Elsa, the Kardashians, of that tongue still lying on the pavement in the park.

I climbed out of the shower, exhausted, but I wasn't ready to sleep. I rummaged around the kitchen and found a bottle of vodka I had received from a client about a year ago. I poured some orange juice into a glass and made myself a drink.

I'm safe. It's over. It's done.

I turned on my laptop and opened up my email drafts folder. I found the resignation letter to Trina and hit send.

Hasta la vista, lizard bitch.

18

I was sitting in the passenger seat of Kim's car. She was driving us somewhere, but I wasn't sure where we were going. It didn't really matter because we were having a good time driving around. She was telling me stories about her family and gossiping about people on other reality shows. I didn't know any of the people she was talking about, but it was good to hear her chitchat. I was a little high on this new experience of having a girlfriend confide in me. I thought I was doing fine as a loner, but now with Kim by my side, I was on top of the world, indestructible.

We pulled up to a store and I saw that there were thousands of people standing around waiting for us on the sidewalk. They were standing on either side of a red carpet that led into the store, holding up their phones, ready to record us. They weren't talking, either. In fact, they weren't making any noise, just watching us.

"C'mon, let's go!" Kim put the car in park and jumped out.

I sat in the car, threatened by the crowd. I knew that they wanted to be with Kim, they wanted to be some part of her world.

Would she go to them and forget about me?

Kim pulled my door open. "Let's go shopping."

I stepped out of the car onto the sidewalk. Kim was waiting for me a few steps ahead. She held out her hand to me. "It's okay, it's safe here. I won't let anything bad happen. These people are just fans. They're the ones who like our pictures. They can't be my friend like you are."

Their silence scared me. "Why are they so quiet?"

Kim put her finger to her lips. "They're asleep."

"But their eyes are wide open!"

Kim giggled. "I know! It doesn't make any sense, does it?"

I didn't know why, but I thought this was the funniest thing I'd ever heard and started laughing along with Kim. I took a deep breath and reached out to her waiting hand. Of course nothing bad would happen! She pulled me into the store, and we raced down a long aisle like two schoolgirls headed out of class to recess.

We stopped in front of a massive, glowing white wall. It had endless white cubby holes containing beautiful new shoes, purses, jewelry, and perfume. I was in awe. The selection was infinite, and I wondered how we would get through everything in time to choose what we wanted and leave the store before it closed. I looked at Kim. "I want everything. All of it. Is this a dream?"

Kim sat down and patted a chair next to her. "It's better than a dream. I'm really good at this. Let me show you how."

Shoes and purses appeared on the floor right in front of us. They showed up faster than I could keep track of. I started trying on shoes, but they were wet and sticky. I felt a gooey liquid on the bottoms of my feet. I pushed the sticky shoes aside and grabbed some of the purses surrounding us, but they were also wet with the goo.

"Kim, these things are all wet, we can't shop here."

Kim laughed. "It's fine. I told you I won't let anything bad happen." She pointed off to the side where her daughter North was grabbing items out of the cubby holes with her tongue, dripping with saliva, and laying them at our feet. She was so quick

I hadn't even noticed.

I stood up. "We have to go!" The bottoms of my feet were still sticky. I tried to wipe the clear, bubbly goo off of me, but the residue from North's tongue had seeped into the carpet as well. "It's not safe here! I'm wet!"

∞

I was lounging on a recliner in front of Kim's pool. Kim lay beside me in another lounger. The sun was beating down on us, but I was still wet. I looked into the pool and saw North splashing us. "We're getting wet again!" I yelled out. I suddenly noticed I was wearing a bikini and I had huge boobs. Kim-sized boobs. I could barely sit up straight because I wasn't used to the new weight on my chest. They were so big that I couldn't fit my hand around them. But they felt so real, so soft.

"What do I do with these?"

Kim giggled and gave me a light slap on my right boob. "They're fun, huh? You'll get used to them after a while. They look really good on TV, too. You must be very thirsty, no?"

Kim was right, I was so thirsty that it was painful to talk. "Are you really my friend?"

Kim nodded. "There's nothing better than friendship."

Kris walked over to us with a tray of drinks and food. She was smiling and laughing, like we had known each other forever. I was filled with pride that I had finally won over her friendship, that she finally trusted me.

I took a drink off the tray and downed it quickly. It was a thick drink, like a milkshake, but with liquor. It filled my stomach quickly and made me feel queasy and bloated.

"Can I have one, too?" A man's voice.

That voice sounded familiar to me. I lifted my chin over my huge chest and looked past my boobs into the pool. Spencer stood wading in the shallow end. "Spencer! It's you!" He looked tan and healthy. The sun's glare bounced off of his bright white smile. His face was clean-shaven, showing off deeply carved dimples. "Oh my God, have you seen my boobs?"

"I know him," Kim told me. "Drink."

I tried to gulp more of the milkshake, but I felt like my stomach was expanding and I felt bubbles rising in my chest. Something was wrong. I was having some kind of reaction.

∞

I bolted up in my bed. I was drenched in perspiration and my stomach was heaving. I heard my belly grumble, felt pressure building in my throat and pushing up to my chest. I was going to be sick. I ran to the bathroom and threw up.

After a few minutes, I sat on the bathroom floor with my back against the wall, catching my breath. I glanced down at my hand. My fingers were white and the rest of my hand was a deep red sunburned color. *I really did kill Elsa last night.* I remembered the tongue tightening around my palm, not being able to control my thoughts. That slimy suction cup feeling on my hand.

"I am your friend." That phrase had been fed into my brain over and over again. It was still back there, rattling around my mind like a broken record.

A Miss Elsa hangover. My dream felt like the residue in my mind from Miss Elsa's attack. But the most disturbing part of the dream was that I had truly enjoyed my time with Kim. Last night, while she was rooting around my mind, Miss Elsa had found this place, this hidden, deep, dark, bottomless longing for connection. A longing to stop always being on guard and let people into my life. She ripped open this lonely, cold, empty hole and filled it with Kim. I thought I had hidden those feelings so well from everyone, even from myself.

But that deep, dark place was the reason I took the job in the first place, wasn't it? I was tired of being a lone wolf. No friends, just contacts. Miss Elsa was able to exploit that, make me yearn for Kim's friendship and acceptance.

I still couldn't shake the odd feeling of being connected to Kim. That she cared about me, and that I could trust her. Was that really a dream, or some aftereffect from Miss Elsa's tongue?

And why did Spencer appear in my dream? He looked vibrant, happy. I felt a strange connection to him as well. The thought of him running away, maybe for the rest of his life, made me sad. I needed to let him know that Miss Elsa was dead. She could no longer harm anyone. There had to be a way to locate him.

I had to get past this neediness. It wasn't me. It wasn't natural. Miss Elsa was stone-cold dead and could no longer harm anyone. End of story. I stood and washed my face off with cold water. This bullshit was done. Over. I would put the Kardashians in my rearview mirror and move on.

I went into my bedroom and saw the pile of black clothes I had worn last night lying on the floor. I instinctively grabbed my hand and rubbed it. I remembered the blood spattering all over my clothes, the high-pitched scream coming from her mouth after I shot her.

It was over. She was dead. Dead, dead, dead.

I saw the gun on my nightstand. I wanted it with me, just in case. Just in case of what? I didn't know, but just in case. I grabbed the gun and walked into the kitchen.

The bottle of vodka I had opened last night was still on my kitchen counter. Maybe a drink to ease my nerves? No, not yet. I still needed to get Miss Elsa out of my brain. I wasn't sure how liquor would affect that.

I made some tea and I turned on the TV. I needed to see the normal, boring world. I hoped the banality of everyday life would soothe me, make me feel like I was achieving re-entry into the real world again. Whatever the real world was.

I sipped my tea and watched a morning talk show. The hosts were debating about some upcoming trial, but I was so out of the loop on current events that I had no idea what they were talking about. Life was going on, just as before, without any lizard people taking over. Nice.

A commercial for the ASPCA. Nothing but dogs that looked like Miss Elsa.

Could I ever look at another dog again without being triggered? Would I wonder if every dog I saw was a secret alien being?

Was I really safe? Was this world safe?

I covered my sunburned hand. Miss Elsa was still stuck inside my brain, like broken shards of glass. Any movement, any thought, could set off a painful memory.

Stop thinking. I changed the channel to HGTV. Nothing calmed my nerves more than watching couples tour houses for sale and trade benign banter on the home's features.

I settled back on my sofa as a couple from Atlanta argued about the color of the granite countertops in the home they were looking at.

The same granite as in Kim's kitchen. The granite that covered her massive island, where I first saw Kris Jenner. That's where my whole nightmare began. Kris's glare, her shapeshifting face. Was she the brains behind this whole thing? She had given Miss Elsa to Trina, so she must have known about the dog.

Did she sic Miss Elsa on Trina, make her compliant? Maybe she had unleashed Miss Elsa on Kim as well.

If Miss Elsa had succeeded with me, what would have happened? I guessed I would have become compliant. No longer able to think for myself. I thought about the list of lawmakers that Kris had given me. That was the plan, wasn't it? They wanted me to help them get to the most powerful people in the country and mess with their brains.

Was Kris actually using her daughter to accomplish this plan? I just didn't see Kim as the type of person who had that kind of ambition. Sure, she wanted fame, she wanted followers, money, but power? I could smell ambition for power a mile away, and Kim just didn't have that smell. That seemed to be Kris's thing.

When I thought about my interactions with Kim, they were all pretty innocent. She liked to shop, she liked to look good. Maybe she wasn't the sharpest tool in the shed, but she had a good heart. She loved her lizard children.

How did that happen? Did she mate with Miss Elsa? I shuddered. What had Kris put her through? Kim had to have been a victim, unless I was missing some signals.

Maybe there was something in her manner or her speech that fooled me. I grabbed the TV remote and did a search for her show. Last season's episodes were available to watch. I hit play.

A typical episode. Kim faced the camera, makeup and hair perfectly in place. She was wondering about returning to Paris. Her sisters were practicing for an upcoming poker tournament. In between Kardashian musings were shots of the sisters lounging by their beautiful Southern California pools, the green hills in the background. They were living through all of their internal drama, but in an ethereal, picturesque landscape. Kim and her sister were having an argument in the gazebo by the pool. Her sister walked off. I wasn't sure what the argument was about, but it didn't matter. Kim faced the camera seconds later. "I can't believe that Khloé just walked away. How could she not know that I would never hurt her? I would never, ever hurt my family, no matter what. That's not who I am."

I believed her. Kim didn't have it inside of her to hurt another person the way I sensed her mother did.

Her show was so oddly calming to me. Maybe I was already getting better. Kim didn't trigger me.

My phone rang and I froze. I grabbed my gun. What if Trina called? Or Kim? My phone screen read "FBI." That guy I had called yesterday.

"Hello?"

"Maddy Ellis? This is Chris Palover, FBI special investigations, returning your call."

How would I explain this to him? How could I not sound like I'd lost my mind? "I have something to report."

"Go ahead."

I breathed into the phone for a few seconds and tried to organize my thoughts, but they were still jumbled. Collateral damage? "I guess the first thing is that I had an encounter with something. I also want you to know I am not a crazy person. But this is difficult."

"Okay, Ms. Ellis, I understand. First, let me reassure you, this is what I do for a living. I've done this for a while, and I have heard a lot of things that might sound crazy, so don't worry about that. Secondly, I know that Lloyd Anderson referred you. I know Lloyd pretty well, and if he trusts you, then there's a good chance you're not a crazy person, okay?"

I exhaled. "Okay."

"So, before we begin, let me reassure you we take these kinds of reports seriously. I want you to feel confident about that. If there's a way we can check out your information, we will do that, okay?"

His voice soothed me. I was sure he must be very well-trained to calm down crazy people, but it worked. "Okay, I'll just . . . blurt it all out. Last night I killed something. It looked like a dog, but it wasn't a dog. It had a thick, slimy, snakelike tongue that could stretch for fifty feet at least. It tried to . . . hurt me with this tongue. Jesus Christ, that sounds insane, doesn't it? But I saw it. I felt it. That slimy tongue wrapped itself around my hand, and I have burn marks from it." It felt good to say it to somebody. I rubbed my hand.

"Where did you see this dog?"

"At Canal Park, down by the waterfront."

"And you say you killed it? Can you tell me how that happened?"

"I shot it. I can't remember how many times." The memory of the tongue lying on the pavement, shot off, kept flashing in my brain.

"Were you just walking at the park and you happened to see it?"

"No." I took a second to collect my thoughts, to try and lay out what happened. "I lured it to the park. Please, just bear with me. I knew this dog, and I knew that this dog was not normal. I had an acquaintance who was attacked by its tongue, so I set up a trap, and when it showed up I killed it." I heard him typing through the phone.

"How did you lure it into the park?"

"I had something it wanted. A headphone, actually. The headphone has a tracking device in it, and I knew the dog would come looking for it."

"How did you know?"

Oh God, maybe I should hang up. The more I said it aloud, the more insane this sounded. "This acquaintance had told me. Oh, I have this friend's video of the dog coming for the headphones."

"Can you send me the video?"

"Sure."

"What time did this all happen?"

I looked at the clock. "Maybe nine hours ago. I put the body in a bag and put the bag in a dumpster. I shot off the tongue and left it out in the amphitheater there. Oh shit, I just remembered, the headphones are still out there, too." Should I explain about lizard people taking over the world? No, not yet, that might be a bit much.

"This friend who took the video, where is he?"

"I don't know. He was so scared by what he experienced that he completely freaked out and left the country. I saw him in Ecuador last week. He told me what happened to him." I wondered if they could help me find him. "If he knew that this thing was dead, he would come back, but I don't know how to find him. Maybe the FBI could help?"

"Maybe. Are there any other circumstances surrounding this dog that would help us? For instance, did the dog belong to anyone?"

"To my boss, Trina Altman. She's the CEO of ME Communications." Would I have to explain the whole Kardashian world to him right now?

"Really, what do you do for ME?"

"I am—or was, I just quit—the PR director for Kim Kardashian's political foundation."

"Did you say Kardashian?"

"Yes. Why?"

"Can I put you on hold for a minute?"

"Okay." Did he already know about the lizard people?

"Ms. Ellis?"

"I'm still here."

"We're going to go check out your sighting. Are you positive about the location?"

"Yes."

"Okay, I'll alert the local authorities to close up that section of the park. We'll do a complete search and look for this body. Is it possible for you to get down there?"

I sat up straight and gripped the phone with both hands. The cavalry was here! "Yes, of course."

"Great. The local police should be there in a few minutes, but I'd like you to meet me there. I'll be down there in about an hour, and I'd like you to walk me through what happened."

"I can do that, I think. Let me ask you, Chris. Have you had this kind of . . . report from anyone else? You seemed to react quickly when I said 'Kardashian.'"

I heard him draw a breath. "All I can tell you is that we are taking this report very seriously. I think we can talk more about this after we meet at the park, though. I'll meet you in front of the refreshment stand in an hour."

"Thank you. Thank you so much. I can't tell you how much better and . . . safer I feel."

My body relaxed. I went back to my bedroom and put my black killer outfit in a trash bag. I felt better, less jumpy.

A flash of memory: Kim's smile, her hand brushing across my knee while she drove me around and gossiped. That wasn't my memory, that was only a dream. I rubbed my hand where Elsa had grabbed me, trying to push the memory of the dream away.

I needed to focus on something to take back control of my thoughts. I opened my closet and forced myself to think about what I was going to wear. Jeans? No, a suit. I wanted to look businesslike, respected, not a crazy person who believed in UFOs. Shoes? Flats today. Nothing fancy. High heels seemed too frilly for a meeting with the FBI.

∞

Thirty minutes later I was dressed and ready to go.

My phone rang and I jumped. God, I was still scared that Trina or Kim would call, but it was the FBI.

"Ms. Ellis? Chris again. Can you confirm the location of the body one more time?"

"Sure, the dumpster next to the refreshment stand in the back of the amphitheater."

"Okay, and you're sure it was Canal Park?"

"Positive, why?" Something was wrong.

"The police are telling me that there wasn't a body in the dumpster. No tongue or headphones found, either. However, they did find about a dozen bullet casings."

My heart started beating faster. Could it have risen from the dead? I wasn't safe. Miss Elsa could still be out there. She would come after me again. "I'm telling you the truth, this was what happened last night."

"I believe you, I do. I just needed to double-check. Listen, I'm on my way down there. You can walk me through it when we meet, okay?"

"The blood!" I remembered Elsa's blood on the cement. "There was a lot of blood on the cement, in the orchestra pit!"

"Okay, I'll alert our team to look for the blood."

"I'll see you soon."

If Miss Elsa was still alive, that meant she could be anywhere. Or had somebody taken the body? I ran back into the bedroom and grabbed my gun. I needed to be ready to fight her again.

I summoned the elevator and went down to the parking garage. As I approached my parking spot, my heart stopped. I heard dog paws clicking on pavement. It couldn't be. But I did hear them, it wasn't a mindfuck. The clicking grew louder, closer to me. I remembered Miss Elsa's cold eyes staring at me from the stage and started rubbing my hand again. I couldn't let her back in my mind. I ducked behind a car and pulled out my gun. How many times would I have to kill this thing? Maybe there were more of them? I felt sweat drip down my face, my gun was shaking. I didn't know if I could take another showdown with the tongue.

I peeked over the hood of the car and swallowed hard. My finger traced the trigger of my gun, ready to pull. A few seconds later, I saw a neighbor and her dog walking to the elevator. She glanced over at me and gasped.

I was more screwed up than I had realized. "I'm sorry!" I stood up and put the gun back in my purse. "I thought you were a . . . stalker. I've had some problems . . ." The best I could come up with.

The neighbor ran to the stairs with her dog.

My hands were still shaking. I had to calm myself down.

I waited a few seconds until the shaking stopped and the sensation of the tongue around my hand faded away. Take control. That was nothing but a mind game, and like all mind games, it would stop with time.

I heard the humming noise again. The dull drone of electricity that probably occurred in most enclosed spaces in the world now filled me with dread.

Could be the fluorescent lighting in the garage. I knew those lights made a buzzing noise.

The noise grew louder, and I wasn't able to tell if it was nearby or just inside my head. Maybe, out of fear, I was just imagining the high pitch. *Ignore it and keep moving*. Still, as I approached my car, I put my hand in my purse, gripped the handle of my gun, and walked slower. I looked up at my car and started shaking again. I was perspiring from every crevice in my body.

North West sat on the hood of my car.

She waved a finger at me. "You did a really bad thing."

She was about three cars away from me. I ducked behind the

car in front of me and aimed my gun. Could I shoot a child? No, but she was no child. She was a monster.

She stood on her toes. "I know where you are!"

Just die, bitch. I pulled the trigger.

The sound of gunfire crashed the silence. In a split second her tongue whipped out from her mouth and swatted the bullet away. I heard the bullet bouncing to the ground and her devious giggle echo throughout the garage.

Good God. That tongue pushed a bullet away. But was it fast enough to swat a round of bullets? I fired four more shots and ran back to the elevator without looking back.

I stopped in my tracks. North's younger sister, Saint, was standing in front of the door to the elevator lobby. "Want to be our aunty?"

I heard the sound of four bullets dropping onto the pavement and North laughing behind me. I aimed my gun at Saint, but her tongue unraveled faster than I could press the trigger and wrapped around my hand. The heat! No, not the fucking heat again. It burned my hand and traveled up my arm. The gun dropped to the pavement.

Saint's tongue was different from North's. Thin, like a ribbon, more like Miss Elsa's. A child's delicate tongue.

But these were not children. They were little wild animals, and I had to fight back like an animal.

I swung my free hand out and dug my nails deep into the tongue, pressing into the slimy surface as hard as I could. I wanted to puncture it, rip it, tear it to shreds.

I felt the grip loosen, but I couldn't reach my gun. I had to do something. Become an animal! I leaned forward, opened my mouth, and bit down into her tongue as hard as I could. For a second the greasy taste of her saliva filled my mouth and poured into my throat. I began to choke as the gooey liquid slithered down my windpipe and dripped onto my face. My lips were burning from the goo, but this was my only defense. I bit down harder.

"Ow!" Saint screamed.

I unclenched my teeth and her tongue retracted into her mouth.

My hands and mouth were burning now, like I had come too close to a campfire, and my face was numb. The heat was also inside me; I could feel it racing through my veins to my brain. I bent down and grabbed the gun off the pavement. I felt a thick tongue wrap around my ankle. I tried to kick at it, but it wouldn't budge. It was North. She stood a few feet away from me, waving her finger and shaking her head.

The humming was drowning out my own thinking, like I had a dentist drill inside of my head. I wanted to cover my ears, but I had to fight back. I grabbed the gun with both hands, held on tightly, and aimed at North.

Chicago West, the youngest sister, ran out from behind a car. "That's not nice, Aunty!" Her tongue unspooled from her throat and wrapped around both of my hands, cradling the gun between them like a prayer.

"Be our aunty. We can all have fun together!"

Were they saying this out loud? I wasn't sure, but I could hear their voices clearly. Clearer than my own thoughts. I felt the suction and the sticky liquid from her tongue drip over my fingers.

I heard footsteps. Heels. A woman was approaching. Maybe a neighbor again? I couldn't see anyone. I yelled out, or at least I wanted to yell out, "Help, get help." I could barely hear my own words over the humming.

Kim stood in front of me, smiling. "I can help."

I had one clear shot at Kim, but I was weakening. Saint's tongue pulled at my hands, but my fingers were still free. I could still pull the trigger.

Tears trickled from my eyes. Who was I anymore? I visualized myself, a strong woman, a survivor. I could not let these . . . things win. I was a fortress. A stone castle, impenetrable. No one and nothing would get through.

It was now or never.

Kim held her hand out to me. "Don't worry, it's safe here. I won't let anything bad happen to you."

That was part of my dream. We were shopping. Two girlfriends having a mindless afternoon, gossiping and shopping. The dream where I was part of her family.

"It's better than a dream."

Did she just say that? Or was that from my dream? She was trying to break my strength. I valued that strength, didn't I? It had gotten me so far.

My whole head felt like it was dipped in fire, the heat coming out of my eyes, my nose, my mouth. I felt like I could exhale flames.

"Be our friend, be our aunty."

Stop! I was a fortress!

But I wanted to change, to be vulnerable. I wanted to let people in. Kim accepted me. She shared her world with me.

I couldn't think clearly any longer. Was Kim evil? Or was I just confused? "Are you really my friend?"

Kim nodded. "There's nothing better than friendship."

She was right. There really was nothing better or stronger than friendship. I didn't know why I had avoided this my whole life. I wasn't a fortress, I was weak. With friendship, I could become stronger than I'd ever thought.

I let the gun drop from my fingers.

"You okay?" Kim was leaning toward my face. She looked concerned for my health.

My tears were dripping on the ground. Flats? Ugh! Where were my pumps? These flats were so dull, too.

She stepped beside me and put her arm around me. "Feeling okay?"

"I think so. I feel good, but a little odd." At last, the humming noise faded away and I could think clearly again.

Kim massaged my neck and my muscles relaxed. I suddenly realized that I felt safer than I had ever felt in my whole life. All of my doubt vanished with her touch. God, she was so good at this.

"Better?"

I nodded. "Excellent." The girls' tongues retracted like window shades, snapping back into their housing. Jesus, that was funny-looking, like a Bugs Bunny cartoon!

"Want to go to lunch with us?" Kim held her hand out for her children.

North jumped up and down. "Come with us, Aunty Maddy!"

"I would love to!" But I had something else to do, didn't I? I took out my phone. "I just have to cancel a meeting, okay?"

Kim gathered Saint in her arms. "Are you sure?"

"Yeah, it's not that important." I looked down again at my shoes and felt embarrassed. They were so plain. They needed some bling.

I definitely needed some bling in my life.

EPILOGUE – FEBRUARY 2020

"Lloyd Anderson is here for your lunch appointment." The receptionist's cheerful voice coming from my intercom interrupted my train of thought. I finished up the email I was working on.

"Great! Send him into my office." It would be nice to see Lloyd again. It had been about a year since I had last spoken with him. When I was going through my dark time. Thank God that was over. No more darkness. 2020 was looking to be a banner year!

Lloyd pushed open the glass door to my office and his eyes immediately went to the view behind me. "Wow! Perfect view of the Washington Monument from here, huh? These are some nice digs." He walked past my conference table, straight to the window.

"It is pretty fabulous; you can see just about all of DC from here. That's why we did the offices all in glass. That, and of course, since we're a non-profit, so transparency!" I walked over to him and opened my arms. "No hug?" *Damn, I forgot Lloyd's swag bag!*

He turned to face me, shook his head, and leaned in to hug me. "You really surprise me."

"How's that?" I walked back to my desk and grabbed my purse.

He raised his arms. "This! The whole shebang. I mean, you really stuck with it. It looks like you're enjoying it, right?"

"Loving it!" I pressed the buzzer on my intercom. "Hey, mind bringing a swag bag to my office?"

"And you look . . . great." Lloyd walked toward me and scrutinized my face. "This work must really agree with you, because you look years younger. Really."

I smiled. Lloyd finally noticed how I looked. "Sweet of you to say. But honestly, I have had a few . . . minor patch jobs here and there. When in Rome, right? Or maybe when working for the Romans."

"I guess so. I mean, you're even wearing yoga pants." He laughed.

I glanced down at my legs. All these years I had turned my nose up at yoga pants, but I had no idea how comfortable they felt. And they didn't look bad with Jimmy Choos. "These are official Serious Foundation yoga pants." The white-on-gray block letter Serious logo that ran up the side of the leg gave them a little panache. I had to do battle with Kim to keep the logo off the ass; this was definitely a lot classier.

The glass door to my office opened again. Spencer came in and handed the bag to Lloyd. "Here you go. All of the latest Serious products for the wife."

"Lloyd?" I turned to Spencer. "This is Spencer Golden, head of PR for The Serious Foundation. He is an absolute master at publicity."

Spencer blushed. "Shucks."

"I was really lucky to find him. I couldn't imagine getting everything I need done without him here." I grinned. "I'm so glad that he finally decided to join the family."

"Great to meet you." Spencer shook his hand and turned to me. "You heading out?"

"Yeah, we're off to lunch to get caught up. God, I can't remember the last time I saw you, Lloyd. It must have been . . . before I opened the Serious office, right?"

Lloyd nodded. "Yeah, I think so. It was definitely before you got Kim that visit to the Oval Office for that prisoner pardon thing." He nodded at the life-sized selfie of Kim and the president that hung on my wall.

"And Kanye," I added, and pointed to the framed photo of Kanye in the Oval Office, surrounded by the president and dozens of journalists.

"That was you?" Lloyd smiled.

"Just the beginning. Trust me. Kim is a force to be reckoned with."

Lloyd looked around and lowered his voice. "Is the scuttlebutt I'm hearing really true?"

I raised my eyebrows. "What scuttlebutt?"

"Kanye is running for President? First lady Kim?"

I smiled. Technically he wasn't my client, so I never have any kind of dialogue with him on his plans, as if anyone could have a dialogue with him on his plans. I shrugged my shoulders, signaling to Lloyd that I can't say anything. Besides, Kanye was becoming increasing out of compliance. Sooner or later Kim would have to do something about that. Everyone in the head office was worried about some out-of-compliance incident in China, but I think this is more serious. I took a small vial of SERIOUS by Kim out of my purse and gave myself a spritz. "Ready?"

"Sure. This is your treat, right? And no Denny's?"

"Definitely no Denny's."

Lloyd held the door open for me. "You know, this office is beautiful, but you need to speak to someone about that annoying buzzing noise."

ACKNOWLEDGEMENT

"I believe friendship is the most genuinely human relationship of which we are capable. To be understood and appreciated for oneself is a vital experience."

- Daisaku Ikeda

Thanks to the following people, who in the course of writing this book, helped me to becoming closer to becoming a genuine human because of their friendship. And their patience. A whole lot of patience.

John Rechy – A great, great writer and the best (and fabulously entertaining) teacher. Thank you for seeing potential before I could see it myself.

John and Natalie Bates – Amazingly talented writers but more importantly wonderful humans and the best friends you could ever wish for.

Adam and Michele Dreiblatt – My very patient, loving and supportive family.

Jimmy Ng, Patty Griffith, Bridget Llanes and Julian Bustamente – More great writers and great friends who patiently waded through the various drafts and were willing to give me the feedback I needed to hear. Whether I *wanted* to hear it is another issue.

Jeff Ourvan – For his hard work, vision and support.

Shinji Ishibashi – For his unwavering friendship and guidance.

The SGI – For everything, especially the profound friendships.

ABOUT THE AUTHOR

Ross Dreiblatt

Ross Dreiblatt grew up in New York. His father was a truck driver, and his mom was a retail manager. Ross attended Hofstra University and moved to Los Angeles where he attended Cal State Northridge. While in LA, he studied under John Rechy's master writing workshop at UCLA.

He has worked in the corporate offices of major retailers in Los Angeles, San Francisco, New York City and Florida, toiling on spreadsheets by day and the imaginary lives of celebrity monsters by night. Ross loves to travel and will get on a plane going anywhere, as long as it eventually lands safely. Despite the dour photo he is kind of a happy guy.

He currently resides in South Florida. For more information about Ross and his works visit www.rossdreiblatt.com.

Made in the USA
Las Vegas, NV
12 April 2023